PRAISE FOR THE ALASTAIR STONE

"The magic is believable, the characters could be people you know, and the twists, turns and mysteries to be solved glue your eyes to the page. You will never forget these characters or their world."
—*Jacqueline Lichtenberg, Hugo-nominated author of the Sime~Gen series and* Star Trek Lives!

"Alastair Stone is like Harry Potter meets Harry Dresden with a bit of Indiana Jones!"
—*Randler, Amazon reviewer*

"Somewhat reminiscent of the Dresden Files but with its own distinct style."
—*John W. Ranken, Amazon reviewer*

"I am reminded of Jim Butcher here...Darker than most Urban Fantasy, not quite horror, but with a touch of Lovecraftian."
—*Wulfstan, Amazon Top 500 reviewer*

"An absolute delight for 'urban fantasy' fans! Smart, witty and compelling!"
—*gbc, Bookbub reviewer*

"In Alastair Stone, author R.L. King has a major winner on her hands."
—*Mark Earls, Amazon reviewer*

"Once you enter the world of Alastair Stone, you won't want to leave."
—*Awesome Indies*

"You will fall in love with this series!"
—*Amazon reviewer*

"It's getting hard to come up with something better than great to describe how good this book was."
—*Ted Camer, Amazon reviewer*

"You cannot go wrong with this series!"
—*Jim, Amazon reviewer*

"Warning—don't start reading this book if you have other things to do."
—*ARobertson, Amazon reviewer*

"Once you start, you need to get comfortable because you will stop reading all of a sudden and discover many hours have gone by."
—*John Scott, Amazon reviewer*

"R. L. King has my purchasing dollars with fun-to-read, suspenseful, character-driven stories…Damn fun reads."
—*Amazon reviewer*

"I have been hooked on this series from the first book."
—*Jim P. Ziller, Amazon reviewer*

"Awesome and exciting. Love this series."
—*Cynthia Morrison, Amazon reviewer*

"Amazing series. The characters are deep and identifiable. The magic is only a small part of what makes these books great. I can't wait for the next one!!"
—*Amazon reviewer*

ALSO BY R. L. KING

The Alastair Stone Chronicles

Stone and a Hard Place
The Forgotten
The Threshold
The Source
Core of Stone
Blood and Stone
Heart of Stone
Flesh and Stone
The Infernal Heart
The Other Side
Path of Stone
Necessary Sacrifices
Game of Stone
Steel and Stone
Stone and Claw
The Seventh Stone
Gathering Storm
House of Stone
Circle of Stone

The Madness Below
Boys' Night (Way) Out (novella)
An Unexpected Truth (novella)
Death's Door
Blood Brothers
Homecoming
Mortal Imperative
Balance of Power
Rite of Passage
Winds of Change
Awakening
Blood Ties
Vicious Circle
The Lost Scion
Demon Blade
Shadows and Stone (novella)
Turn to Stone (novella)
Devil's Bargain (standalone novel)
Stone for the Holidays (short stories)

Happenstance and Bron

The Soul Engine
Chariots of Wrath
By Demons Driven

Calanar

Hard Way
The Mechanic
House of Cards

Shadowrun (published by Catalyst Game Labs)

Shadowrun: Borrowed Time
Shadowrun: Wolf and Buffalo (novella)
Shadowrun: Big Dreams (novella)
Shadowrun: Veiled Extraction

STRANGE BEDFELLOWS

ALASTAIR STONE CHRONICLES: BOOK THIRTY-THREE

R. L. KING

MAGESPACE
PRESS

Strange Bedfellows: Alastair Stone Chronicles Book Thirty-Three
First Edition: May 2023
First Paperback Edition: May 2023
Magespace Press
Edited by John Helfers
Cover Art and Design by G&S Cover Design Studio

ISBN: 978-1-953063-17-5

CHAPTER ONE

ALASTAIR STONE had dined in many fine restaurants throughout his life—everything from a tiny, exclusive eatery in Prague where you had to know the right people, *be* the right people, and grease the right palms to even find out about its existence, to the hottest see-and-be-seen spots in New York, London, and Paris. He'd been raised in luxury since childhood and it had never intimidated him; in fact, he held more contempt than admiration for the sort of people who vied with each other to see who could be photographed in the best locations with the most beautiful and influential companions, and he readily admitted he was much more comfortable in a grotty old pub or an unassuming, family-run Mexican restaurant in the company of good friends.

Still, even he had to acknowledge that Thalassa Nera's choice of venue for their discussion impressed him.

He didn't even know where it was, since she'd used her draconic ability to bring a scion along on her ley-line journey, and when he'd discreetly checked his phone's GPS once they arrived, he'd found no signal.

Not that that had surprised him.

When her prim, efficient associate (another one who looked like she moonlighted as a librarian) had arrived on Stone's doorstep with the invitation, exactly one month had passed following their previous discussion at her penthouse apartment in New York City. That didn't surprise him either. That was how long she'd given him to think over her astonishing proposal, and lack of punctuality had never been in her nature.

In truth, he hadn't spent that much time thinking about her proposal. He would never tell anyone (especially not her), but while she *had* occupied a significant portion of his thoughts over the previous few weeks, those thoughts had centered more around what had happened the last few minutes before he'd left her apartment than anything that might occur in the future.

He also wouldn't admit it to anyone, but those few minutes had been a large part of why he'd accepted the invitation.

"So," he said, doing his best to keep his voice casual, "you still want me to father your child, then."

The restaurant was at the top of a dizzyingly tall building—Stone was beginning to suspect Thalassa, despite her name, preferred the air to the water—and surrounded on all four sides by glass so clean and clear that it was nearly impossible to detect its presence. The effect was both profoundly beautiful and highly disconcerting, as if they were seated on a platform thousands of feet above the ground with nothing to keep them from tumbling over the edge. The waitstaff was efficient and unobtrusive, the food and wine magnificent, and the view breathtaking. There were other customers, but the combination of the dim light, the arrangement of the tables, and a faint ripple in the air made it impossible to see them as anything but shadowy figures.

Thalassa offered him a cool smile. "Right to the point, Dr. Stone. I like that about you." She wore a shimmering blue dress that fit her as if she had been poured into it; like the one she'd worn at the penthouse, this one also had a high neckline but bared her pale shoulders. This time, she'd accented it with a simple necklace, the gems glowing with an inner fire that had to be magical. Her ash-blond hair was done in a deceptively simple, upswept style that probably would have taken a human woman at least a full day in a high-end salon to achieve, and her makeup was understated but perfect.

"And you're right on time." Stone sipped his wine, his gaze locked on her glittering green eyes. She had beautiful eyes. He'd never paid that much attention to them before, because every other time he'd been in her presence, he'd been half-afraid she might toss him off a balcony or swallow him whole, but now they watched him with measured appraisal and he found himself getting lost in them.

"I gave you a month to consider my offer. Tonight marks the end of the month. Do you have an answer for me?"

He'd done as she'd requested, and not discussed anything about her with any of his friends or any of the other dragons. How could he? It wasn't the sort of thing he could just drop into casual conversation: "So, this ancient, terrifying female dragon has decided she wants her very own scion, and she's picked me as the lucky father. Pass the butter, please." He was fairly sure a couple of the more knowledgeable of his acquaintances—namely his son Ian and Gabriel—had suspected *something* was up, but neither of them had asked.

He took another sip of his wine and broke the gaze to look around the restaurant. No one was paying them any attention; this wasn't the first time he'd wondered if this whole place was an illusion. He'd seen precedent, after all—Gabriel had conjured an entire illusionary Japanese restaurant for their first meeting. He supposed it didn't matter, though. Thalassa's power level was so much higher than his that he was completely at her mercy, and there was no point in disputing it. Might as well sit back and enjoy the ride—and the excellent meal.

And the very compelling company.

At least he didn't feel underdressed tonight. Despite his preference for comfortable jeans, black T-shirts featuring pub or obscure-band logos, and his ever-present black wool overcoat—they'd become almost a uniform for him over the years, a sort of trade-mark look—he still knew his way around formalwear and didn't feel awkward in it as many men did. He even had his own tailor back in London, a cranky mage older than Aubrey with the skill of a master and the patience of a saint. Tonight, he'd gone for simple but formal, wearing a severe black tuxedo with no embellishments beyond black onyx shirt studs and cufflinks, and a higher-end version of his preferred overcoat. Thalassa must have approved of his choice, because aside from looking him over from top to toe when he first arrived, she hadn't commented on it. With that particular dragon, no news was usually good news.

"So," he said, "About my answer."

Her eyes narrowed. "Yes?"

A little shiver ran down Stone's spine, but he didn't show any reaction. He was glad his aura control was good, though he doubted it was good enough to fool a dragon. To put it out of his mind, he pressed on. "First, I want to make sure I understand the terms of your proposal."

Faint disapproval flashed. "I should think it would be simple, Dr. Stone."

"Alastair."

A sculpted eyebrow crept up. Stone hadn't met too many women who could do the classic single-eyebrow raise, but she had it down cold.

He shrugged. "If we're going to be talking about producing a child together, don't you think you should start calling me by my given name?"

Her lips crept up in a sly smile. "Does that mean you intend to accept my offer…Alastair?"

"Now, hold on. Let's not get ahead of ourselves." He drained the last of his wine, set the glass down, and leaned back in his chair. He was probably pushing things, but at the bottom of it this whole process was absurd, so why not enjoy it? "You want me, as one of the only two scions currently unaffiliated with another dragon, to assist you in producing your own scion by agreeing to father the child."

Her chin dipped in a barely perceptible nod, and something in her eyes changed a little. "Yes..."

He pretended to ignore the change, despite being acutely aware of it. The one thing he couldn't afford to do tonight was let himself get complacent and miss anything important. "Please don't take any of my questions at this point as implying agreement. I'm simply gathering information."

She didn't answer, but that meant she didn't tell him to stop, either.

"You said a ritual was involved, and preparations would have to be made."

"Yes."

"What sort of ritual?" He considered his words with care before continuing. "Please forgive me for being a bit crude, but...how is this process accomplished? Can it be done...remotely? Or would the two of us need to...?"

Her lip twitched, and he got the impression of amusement. "The process must be completed naturally. It is an important part of the ritual in question."

Another little tingle went up Stone's spine—a slightly different kind this time, and originating a bit lower than the previous one. "Right, then." He forced casualness into his voice, but knew he wasn't fooling anybody. "Let's talk about responsibility, shall we? Legalities. You're asking me to father a child. I take that obligation rather seriously."

Her smile grew, but it didn't reach her eyes. "Come now, Alastair. Please don't insult me by trying to make me believe you want to be involved in the child's life—at least before she is sufficiently mature to provide intelligent company. Do you truly wish to convince me you want to change diapers, sit on the floor and play children's games, or any of the other trappings of modern-day fatherhood?"

He met her gaze head-on. "No, honestly." He wasn't proud of that aspect of himself, but he'd never gotten anywhere in life by trying to deny the truth. It wasn't the sort of thing he'd tell anyone, but a small part of him was secretly glad he hadn't met Ian until his son had grown out of things like diapers, tantrums, and early-teenage rebellion.

But on the other hand, his recent interactions with Jason and Amber's four-year-old daughter Alice had literally been the first time he'd ever spent any time with a young child in his life—at least since he'd been one himself—and he'd survived unscathed. So far, at least. Some of it had even been—dare he say it?—pleasant. "But suppose I *did* want to be involved in her life, at least to some extent? What would you say to that?" He replayed his words and tilted his head at her in suspicion. "Hang on…you said 'her'. How do you know it won't be a boy?"

"Because, unlike you humans, we have control over such things. The child will be female." Her tone suggested clearly that this was not up for discussion.

"Fair enough. I won't presume to think I would have any influence over the choice, even if I wanted to." He thought about pouring another glass of wine, and decided against it. "But what obligations and responsibilities would you expect of me with regard to the child?"

"None."

Stone snapped his head up. "None? So, you're saying you simply want me to do the deed and then wash my hands of the whole matter?"

"Does that bother you?" She narrowed her eyes and fixed him with an odd, contemplative gaze. "I expect nothing of you, aside from the obvious. You will have no financial, moral, or parental obligations, responsibilities, or privileges. I believe you humans have a similar concept."

"You only want me for my genetic material. A bloody sperm donor." Stone didn't know whether to be amused or annoyed. At least she was honest about it.

The smile was back, tiny and mocking. "I am a dragon, Alastair. I have no intention of...co-parenting with a human, even if he is an uncommonly powerful scion. When the child arrives, I will raise her as I see fit."

"And I get no input. Do I even get to meet her?"

"Do you want to?"

He glared. "She'll be my *daughter,* Thalassa." He slipped into using her given name without changing tone to draw attention to it. "You're right, I'm hardly the horsey-rides and tea-parties sort of father, but I'd like to...I don't know...at least have some idea what she looks like."

"We can discuss that at a later date. It might be possible to arrange for you to visit her, on occasion. But she must not know who you are."

"Why not? You aren't going to be able to hide her from the other dragons, are you? Won't they know who her father is as soon as she's born?"

"No."

"No?" That surprised him. "I thought dragons could detect scions—even ones that aren't their own."

"We can." Her smooth brow furrowed ever so slightly, and Stone got the impression of growing impatience. "But it does not occur automatically—we must make a specific effort. And it does not reveal the child's parentage, but only that she is a scion."

Stone filed that away. Slowly, ever so slowly, these little bits of disparate information he was amassing from various draconic sources were contributing to a collection of data about them. "And you're banking on the fact that, since you've never shown any interest in creating scions in the past, none of your fellow dragons will expect you to do it now."

She inclined her head. "As I said before, the new circumstances regarding yourself and Mr. Harrison have presented opportunities unlike any that have ever occurred since we arrived in this world. But, as you might expect, our ability to take advantage of them is limited."

He almost asked what she meant, but then he got it. "Because Harrison and I are currently the only game in town and we're both men, so only female dragons are eligible for this particular prize."

"Yes."

"How many female dragons *are* there?" Stone knew he was letting his curiosity get the better of him, but he could no more help it than he could look away from Thalassa's very distracting presence. "I know about Madame Huan and Nana, of course—are there others?"

She paused, and it was clear she was deciding whether to answer. Finally, she said, "Of those of us currently residing on this dimension, there is one other of whom you are not aware. She is highly reclusive, and the oldest among us."

"And you don't think she'd have any interest in shagging Harrison or me in the hopes of starting her own little dynasty?"

"I do not." There was no doubt about it—she was definitely starting to look impatient now, her green eyes flashing. "We are wasting time. Perhaps you have forgotten that the original oath you swore to me, regarding The Unspeakable's artifact, is still in effect? I have offered you this alternative in an effort to provide both of us with a more agreeable outcome, but my patience is not infinite."

Stone drew a slow breath and let it out just as slowly. He'd been hoping she wouldn't bring that up for a while. He'd actually been enjoying the dinner and their verbal sparring. He still couldn't truthfully say he *liked* Thalassa, but it was certainly possible to find someone compelling without liking them as a person, and she qualified more than anyone he'd ever known.

But now she was calling in her marker, and he didn't think she'd let him get away with stalling any longer. He either had to accept the terms of the original oath, and allow her to inflict increasing amounts of pain on him until he somehow found a way to secure the artifact and deliver it to her—not bloody likely, given that other dragons had it and he had no idea where it was—or agree to this new offer she was making.

To become the father to a child he would have no control over, who would be raised and trained without any input from him, and who, despite Thalassa's words, he might not ever even get to meet.

He did pour another glass of wine then. He waved the bottle at her in offer, but she shook her head. Her steady, unblinking green gaze was fixed on him now. He'd momentarily allowed himself to forget how dangerous she was, but he wasn't getting out of here tonight without giving her an answer.

He looked at her again. Damn, but she was beautiful. Not drop-dead, supernaturally stunning like Dierdre Lanier had been, but enticing in the smart, mockingly-amused-at-the-world way that had always flipped his switches. Had she been that beautiful all along, or had she made subtle changes to her appearance to attract him? He couldn't be sure, because he'd never looked at her all that closely prior to their current interactions. Before, he'd been more concerned about what she might do to him if he put a toe out of line.

Without conscious effort, his thoughts returned to the night he'd come to her to ask for help in locating The Unspeakable's artifact knife and dealing with its demonic entities. He remembered how he'd felt, standing before her in nothing but his shorts, shivering in the chilly air as she examined the wounds the demon creatures had inflicted on him. It should have been profoundly uncomfortable—and it had been—but it wasn't until well after he'd left her presence that it had consciously occurred to him it had also been strangely, irresistibly sexy. The idea of being so symbolically vulnerable in front of a being of such unimaginable power had been almost unbearably sensual. Those had been thoughts that had made it difficult to sleep for a while, and when he had slept, his dreams had been…shall he say, *interesting*. The threat of The Unspeakable had overshadowed the whole thing when it had been active, but afterward…

He shook his head sharply, clearing the thoughts. The last thing he needed right now was to let something other than his brain make the decision for him. "If I'm to agree to this," he said firmly, meeting her gaze head-on, "I have three conditions."

If she were anyone else, she might sigh, or roll her eyes. She did neither, but she gave the impression of both. "We already discussed this. You are stalling."

"No. These three are different, and they're not negotiable. If you don't agree, then I guess I'll just have to see how I deal with the consequences of the original oath."

"You will not deal well with them," she said. "You sealed the oath, and failed to comply with its terms. I will not be merciful."

"No, of course not. I don't think you've got that in you. But at least hear my conditions." When she didn't respond, he forged ahead. "First—I expect your word that, during the entire course of this process, you won't lie to me in any way—up to and including altering your appearance to make yourself more alluring or appealing to me, or making any changes, magical or otherwise, to my mental state. If we do this, it's with you as you are, and with me as *I* am."

"Agreed," she said instantly, as if it weren't even a consideration. "I never had any such intention."

He blinked. Well—*that* had been easier than he'd expected. "All right, then. Good. The second is that, regardless of how much you let me become involved in the child's life—or not—you'll never use or influence her in any way against me, my friends, family, or interests."

Her impatience grew. "Alastair, you flatter yourself. Very little of this is about you. When our business is concluded, we will both go on our separate ways."

"Still, you can't begrudge me a bit of protection."

She sighed. "Done. I give you my word."

So she meant it, then—she probably didn't intend to let him have any involvement with the child. He wasn't sure whether to be relieved or disappointed, but all he said was, "Brilliant."

"And the third?"

He tilted his head and offered her a smile. "I guess you might call me an old-fashioned bloke, Thalassa. While I have been known on occasion to spend a no-strings-attached evening with an attractive and willing young lady—"

"You have a reputation for such...*occasions*...that has carried even to the dragons," she said dryly.

"Well...yes, all right. But when we're talking about something as serious as having a child together, even if I might never even get to meet her, my standards are a bit different."

"What does that mean?"

"I want to get to know you better before we go through with this."

Now it was her turn to look confused. "I do not follow."

He chuckled. "If I'm to father your child, it's not going to be as a nearly-anonymous sperm donor. You dragons are never shy about mentioning that you play the long game, so...another three months won't make a difference, will it?"

"Three...months?" Her expression went cold again. "Alastair, I have already given you a month to consider the matter. If you expect me to give you three more—"

"No, no." He waved her off. "Nothing like that. Not exactly, anyway. All I'm saying is that if we're to have a child together, I want to know you. I want to take you out to dinner, to shows, on holidays. Long walks on the beach, as the cliché goes—though frankly I don't fancy the beach and I hate getting sand in inconvenient places. The point is, I want the chance to know the *real* Thalassa Nera, not the terrifying dragon who once tried to have me pitched off a seventieth-floor balcony."

Her eyes narrowed, showing challenge. "How can you be so certain that is *not* the real Thalassa Nera?"

"Who knows? Maybe it is. I don't know that it will make a difference, honestly." He thought back to the night at her penthouse, when the two of them had kissed with an intensity that had left them both tasting blood. He wanted to do it again, right now—to lunge across the table, pull her into his arms, and have his way with her. From the look of her, she had the same thing on her mind. "But now *you're* stalling. What do you say, Thalassa? You've said you don't like me, and I don't particularly like you. Maybe we can change that. And if not, at least we've got…other things to keep us occupied."

She didn't answer for a while, but now she was looking at him differently. Her gaze, still sharp, now carried a certain searching quality, as if she were trying to determine his ulterior motives. Finally, she drummed her long-nailed fingers on the table with contemplative precision. "If I were not certain you knew better, Alastair, I would think you might be trying to initiate some sort of…romantic relationship with me. Surely you know that is impossible. I am a dragon, and you, while your status as a scion elevates you above the rest of your kind, are still a mere mortal human. Your lifespan is but an instant to my people."

Stone kept his sly smile to himself this time. *A lot* you *know.* The funniest part of the whole thing was he was fairly sure she didn't mean her words as a deliberate insult. Her face didn't show any contempt or distaste. She was simply stating a fact, in the same way Stone himself might state something similar to an ant or a mouse.

Instead, he chuckled. "I hate to break it to you, Thalassa, but you look fairly human to me at present." He ran his gaze up and down her body, or at least the part of it he could currently see, in a deliberate imitation of the blatant way she'd done the same thing to him more than once. "I don't know how long you lot have been on Earth, but it's my understanding that it's been at least several hundred years—probably a good bit longer. You've been existing in a human body for more time than a lot of our nations have been around. Do you mean to tell me that, in all that time, you haven't become at least a little bit acclimated to the idea?"

She didn't answer.

He spread his arms. "You told me before—grudgingly, true, but still—that you found me..." He made a show of rubbing his chin, pondering, "'not unattractive, for a human.'"

Still, she didn't respond, but her gaze was locked on him.

He leaned closer, flashing a challenging smile. "Not only that, but you chose a form that you must know humans would find pleasing. Why would you do that, if you didn't care about such petty things as physical attraction? *And,*" he finished, smile widening, "there's no way in hell you're going to convince me that you didn't feel something the night I came to your place in New York. Even *you're* not that good a liar. Well—your mouth might be, but your body damned well isn't."

Almost unconsciously, she leaned closer as well.

With deliberate, amused calm, he leaned back. "In answer to your question—no, I'm not trying to initiate a romantic relationship. You're beautiful, you're bloody sexy, and I won't lie—I'm half-tempted to pick you up, rip that gorgeous dress off you, and have my way with you across this table, without even clearing it off first—especially considering I'm fairly sure you want that as much as I do." Without giving her a chance to answer, he smiled. "But a relationship? No. Because that would require me to like you as a person, and I don't. You're cold, you're arrogant, and you think you're better than everyone else around you."

"And you, Alastair," she said calmly, "are as arrogant as I am. As well as irreverent, uncouth, ill-mannered, and not nearly as impressive as you think you are."

Damn, but she was sexy.

She picked up her wineglass between two fingers and contemplated it. "I have a persona I use—a socialite in New York City, owner of a series of high-end art galleries along the Atlantic coast. I will insist you cultivate a similar persona when we are seen in public."

Something fluttered along his spine. "Ah...I see. You'll allow me to squire you around, raising eyebrows and providing fodder for stuffy society columns, as long as nobody knows it's *us.*"

She didn't say *take it or leave it,* but it was right there on her face.

In truth, it could solve a couple of potentially messy problems. "What about the other dragons?"

"What about them? We do not, as you humans say, keep tabs on each other, especially if we remain discreet in our activities. It is considered an unforgivable breach of protocol to do so. As long as we do not break our agreements, we are free to do as we will." She set her glass down. "I agree to your suggestion, Alastair. Three months. But afterward—"

Stone wondered if he hadn't moved too fast, caught up in their give-and-take verbal sparring. If he agreed to this, he would be agreeing to father a child with a *dragon.* That wasn't something to be taken lightly.

That was what the month had been for, he reminded himself.

And, while he didn't want to acknowledge it even to himself, the idea did intrigue him.

"Afterward," he said firmly.

"Then I have your agreement? You have accepted my offered alternative manner in which to discharge your oath?" Now she was watching him with such intensity that he wasn't entirely sure she wasn't reading his mind.

But when he responded, his voice was firm and steady. "Gods help me for what I might be getting myself into, but yes. You've got yourself a deal."

She nodded once, as if to say, *all right, then,* and stood. "Excellent. That concludes our business for this evening, then."

He didn't rise. "Just like that?"

"Is there something else? We have finished our meals, and the wine, and now we have completed our discussion."

"All right. If that's the way you want to do it." He made a show of standing in a languid manner, tossing his napkin on his plate. He kept his outward demeanor calm, but inside his nerves were jangling. "Is the number you gave me before still the best way to contact you?"

"I will contact you." She was still watching him.

He took a step closer, mindful of the shadowy figures around them in the restaurant. So far, none of them seemed to be paying the slightest bit of attention to him and Thalassa—almost as if they weren't truly there at all. "As I mentioned before, I'm an old-fashioned bloke. I like to do the asking."

Her eyes glittered, and the sharklike smile was back. "We do not always get what we want in this life, Alastair. I am very busy, and I am not one of your…conquests, waiting breathlessly for your call. I will contact you when I have available time." She, too, took a step closer to him. They were less than three feet apart now, and neither of them had broken the gaze.

"You are a difficult woman…or whatever, Thalassa Nera," he murmured. "Most men might find you intimidating." Another step.

"And you do not?" She remained where she was, but her body subtly leaned toward him.

"I should, if I had any sense. You could eat me alive. Literally." Smaller step, bringing her into his bubble of personal space. He thought he could almost feel the energy crackling around her, but perhaps that was just his own body—or wishful thinking.

"I could." Her voice took on a purring tone that suggested she might be considering it, as once again her eyes moved from his face downward, then back up.

He kept his fixed on her eyes. "I can think of worse fates…" His jangling nerves surged, and he gave up trying to hold control. What was the point?

He took the last step, but she made the first move. Her steel-strong arms snaked around him, pulling him into a crushing embrace.

His back thrumming with muddled pain and pleasure, he leaned in and pressed his lips to hers. At this point, he didn't care if the people in the restaurant were real, illusions, or space aliens. No one but Thalassa existed for him.

She held the kiss for several seconds, hard and brutal and utterly exquisite. She raised one hand from his back and sank her fingers into his hair like a spider, making it impossible for him to pull back even if he wanted to.

He didn't want to. He tightened his arms around her, his hands moving around her bare back. Her skin was hotter than a human's. He didn't dig his fingers in as she had done with him, but pressed forward against the kiss until he once again tasted their shared blood mingling with the wine they'd drunk.

Then, as quickly as she had struck, she pulled back. She ran one red-nailed finger around her lips, then, still smiling challengingly as if defying him to stop her, she dragged it down the spotless white front of his tuxedo shirt, leaving a bloody trail.

"Good night, Alastair," she said, a hint of a throaty rasp in her voice.

And then she was gone—and so was the scene around him.

For a moment, he didn't even notice. He stood there, panting, eyes closed, trying to hold on to the feeling for as long as he could before opening them.

He stood in a windowless, mostly-empty room, with only a single table and chairs in front of him. The "waiter" had whisked away their plates a while ago, but even the wineglasses were gone.

It didn't occur to him to consider he had no idea where he was. That didn't even seem relevant at the moment. He took several deep breaths, swallowed, and waited until his heart's thudding—and other physical responses—settled to a reasonable level.

So, it was going to be like that, then.

It shouldn't have been a surprise, that she could be such a tease. Despite his flippant demeanor, he had never forgotten that she held almost all the cards in this game. Especially now that he'd agreed to her terms.

He smiled, then chuckled, as he realized he didn't mind.

He glanced down at the blood on his shirt and pulled his phone from his pocket.

To his lack of surprise, the GPS worked now. He was somewhere in Brooklyn. She certainly seemed to like New York City.

It didn't occur to him to consider that the location wasn't on a ley line. Nearly without conscious thought, he formed the pattern in his mind and released the energy, appearing a moment later in the living room of his Encantada house.

Raider, seated on the back of the sofa, leaped onto the coffee table and rose, putting his paws on Stone's chest and leaning in to sniff the blood. He made a questioning *mrrrow?*

Stone scratched him behind the ears, shifting to magical sight so he could see the cat's larger, pantherlike Changeling form. "Don't worry, mate. She's dangerous, but that's what makes her interesting. And now, if you'll excuse me, I'm off to take a long, cold shower."

CHAPTER TWO

ALDWYN THOUGHT he'd arrived in the wrong place.

The first thing he noticed as he shimmered into existence, even before his vision cleared, was the heat and the oppressive, arid wind. He narrowed his eyes against the gritty dust that swirled around him.

Damn these weak human bodies, anyway. Even after all the years since his exile, he'd never grown accustomed to existing in one. They were so soft, so frail and vulnerable compared to his true form that was nothing but a distant memory now. Of course he could compensate for a lot of that with magic, and his draconic nature meant even this fragile form was significantly tougher, stronger, and more resilient than any native resident of Earth. But that didn't mean he had ever learned to like this puny, two-legged shell he was forced to inhabit.

He pulled up an invisible shield to keep the dust away and took stock of his surroundings.

Had he arrived in the wrong place? Had he somehow made a mistake in his calculations, traveling to some unknown world on some unknown dimension?

That was absurd, though. He didn't *make* mistakes. Not in something like this, anyway. He'd spent several weeks sequestered in his Bavarian Alps lair, carefully examining the data he'd gathered from his two former scions, tracing the unexpected source of their powerful magic. Even now, he still smarted from the indignity of losing his scions, but they had never been the most important thing to him.

Not when compared to this wellspring of energy he had used them to track.

It was an unfortunate fact that the dragons' innate powers weren't nearly as potent when stuck in human bodies, but Aldwyn and the other exiles still had access to abilities humans could never hope to match. For one thing, their sensitivity to magic was much stronger, even when they weren't actively looking for it. Dragons didn't have the concept of "magical sight," because they maintained a low-level version of it at all times even in human form. If need be, they could augment it significantly. The interplay of magic with the world—ley lines, illusions, spells, even the inherent arcane energy that existed almost everywhere—was as much a part of a dragon's worldview as the ground beneath their feet, the sky above them, or the beings who shared space with them.

Now, as Aldwyn looked around him, he saw magic *everywhere.* It swirled in the air and crept across the ground. Sparks and shafts of it appeared and disappeared in every direction, crackling around rocks, energizing the stunted plants, floating languidly across a far-off body of water like low-lying fog.

The magic was almost *alive* here. Even through his shield, Aldwyn's skin tingled with it.

He smiled thinly. He could do so much here, he was sure. Stone and Harrison had kept this power source to themselves, but no more. He had given his word to them that he wouldn't interfere with them or their interests, but there was no need to be concerned about that. There was enough magic here for all of them.

He turned in place, looking around. As far as he could see, there was no sign of any sort of city or settlement. No far-off buildings, no roads, not even ruins. The ground was dry, cracked, covered in scrubby, near-dead vegetation and jagged rocks. Had his ex-scions discovered the place by accident—a dimension brimming with magical energy, but otherwise uninhabited? Perhaps the opposite of the one they had lured him to, where magic was almost nonexistent?

The similarity didn't extend to one aspect, he was sure. The low-magic plane had been a true pocket dimension, tiny and self-contained. This one, he could clearly see as he turned slowly in place and looked around in all directions, was much larger. He supposed it would have to be, to contain this level of magic.

Aldwyn considered his options. Now that he'd discovered the place, he could return here whenever he liked. He couldn't do it instantaneously—even dragons couldn't pop between dimensions in the blink of an eye—but only a simple ritual requiring less than an hour was necessary to establish the connection. After that, a few minutes' preparation was all he would need. As long as he was here, he might as well look around a bit, and do a few experiments.

He focused on a pointed rock in front of him. It stuck out of the ground and sparked with arcane energy. The magic around him felt comfortable, like a heavy, reassuring blanket settling over his shoulders. It *begged* to be used, mastered, harnessed.

Aldwyn smiled. He pointed his hand at the rock, gathered the willing energy from around him, and released it.

The rock exploded into tiny shards that flew in all directions as if he had dropped a bomb on it.

His smile widened. He stood far enough away from the explosion that none of the shards reached him, but his shield would easily have blocked them if they had.

Not that he even spared that a thought. He was too busy reveling at the power singing through his body. Of course, he could have produced a similar explosion back on Earth, but it would have required a small amount of effort. This—this was *effortless*. Almost literally.

He thought of Stone and Harrison, and the power they had wielded against him in the place they'd taken him. If this place was the source of their magic, and they had managed to access it even from a place where magic shouldn't have been possible, that meant *he* should be able to do that too. And if—*when*—he figured out how to do it, that would change a lot of things. As a dragon, his own power level was orders of magnitude above even the most powerful normal human mage's. Even Stone and Harrison, two of the strongest human talents he'd ever encountered, had been forced to result to subterfuge and careful planning to catch him unawares. But with *this* power—even the other dragons wouldn't be able to stand against him.

Never mind Stone and Harrison. He'd made his agreement with them, and he'd keep it—but they were inconsequential. Having this power at his command would open up many more interesting possibilities than dominating a pair of humans who would, by his standards, be dead in the blink of an eye.

But all of that was for later. He had time to wait. For now, the priority was to study this place, to learn its secrets. That meant he would need to—

He didn't notice the silent shadow plummeting down from above until it was nearly upon him.

Big and black, it filled his vision with a wide maw full of sharp teeth, beating wings, and red, burning eyes. At the last second before it hit, it opened its mouth even wider and let out a harsh, ululating shriek.

Stark, unnatural terror flooded Aldwyn. Everything in him cried out to flee—or to cower. He couldn't fight this thing. There was no hope.

Like hell.

With an effort of will and rage, he threw off the fear-effect before he pitched himself forward.

His action caught the creature off guard. Clearly, it had meant to swoop down and scoop him up in its massive mouth, but his drop to the ground had thrown off its aim. Instead, it raked its lower jaw across his back. Its massive, black wings beat against the ground, flinging up billowing clouds of gritty dust as it swept by and struggled to regain its altitude.

Pain ripped Aldwyn, joining with the disorienting dust to disrupt his thought processes. What had that thing *been*? Obviously, this dimension wasn't completely uninhabited. It had been too fast for him to get a good look at it, beyond that it was black, it had wings, and it intended to make him its prey.

That was *not* going to happen. Aldwyn was *nothing's* prey.

He flung himself over on his back, ignoring the pain as much as possible. It didn't matter—his natural regeneration processes would take care of it, probably faster here than they would on Earth. Right now, it was more important that he get himself into a position he could fight from. He couldn't attack it if he couldn't see it, and he was certain it wouldn't give up after a single attempt. From the look of things, prey wasn't plentiful out here—wherever *here* was—so no predator would let such a tasty morsel get away so easily.

The dust was settling. Between that and Aldwyn's natural magical affinity, he immediately spotted the creature. It was higher now, wheeling around for another pass at him.

Aldwyn raised his shield, rose to his feet, and took a moment to stare at the thing in astonishment. It was as black as the night sky, with massive wings, a long, sinuous body ending in a snakelike tail, and two clawed front legs. It was difficult to gauge size from this perspective, but he guessed its head alone was at least as big as his body, making the whole creature massive indeed.

Was it possible—?

But no, the thing wasn't a dragon. Even after all this time, the memory of their true forms remained clear in Aldwyn's head: huge, graceful, with four legs, long tails, and wings far more impressive than this creature's. This thing was an animal, nothing more. Large and physically imposing, yes, but that was all.

Aldwyn kept his gaze locked on the creature as it circled for another pass. It had definitely injured him; his breath came in deep, grating rasps, and he could feel blood trickling down his back, joining with the perspiration from the hot, dry air. The wounds wouldn't kill him, but he couldn't heal them until he dealt with this more imminent threat.

He widened his stance and raised both hands, pointing them at the beast as it fixed on him and pulled out of its lazy, circling course into another dive. When it reached a point low enough that its black form began to obscure the sky above him, Aldwyn gathered energy around him and let loose with bright shaft as big around as a man's leg. He bared his teeth in a fierce, predatory grin as once again the magic sang through him like he was born to wield it. The ecstasy joined with the pain in his bleeding back to produce a sensation he couldn't even find a word for.

The shaft hit the creature just below its neck. The spell seemed to hesitate a moment, as if encountering resistance, but then continued on, boring a hole through the creature with the precision of a drill bit and extending through to the other side. Aldwyn wasn't close enough to smell the singed flesh, but there was no mistaking the creature's shriek of surprised agony. This time, though, there was no fear component to it, except perhaps its own.

It took a few seconds for the thing's nervous system to realize it was dead. It beat its vast wings, its clean, precise dive turning into a desperate attempt to pull up and put distance between itself and this deceptively small and dangerous thing it had thought was prey. When the spark of life left it, twenty feet above the ground and almost directly above Aldwyn, its wings stopped flapping and sagged, its momentum carrying it forward and past him. It crashed to the ground with a bone-jarring impact, twitched a few times, and lay still.

Aldwyn paused, still breathing hard. He scanned the skies in every direction to make sure no more of these things were waiting for their chance to ambush him. Apparently, they either weren't pack hunters or this one was a rare lone predator, because he saw neither physical nor magical signs of anything else in the sky. Satisfied that nothing else nearby was foolish enough to try attacking him, he approached the dead beast.

On the ground, it was easier to discern its size. It was big—at least thirty feet long from the tip of its snout to the end of its tail. It looked like a winged black snake, thicker through the "chest" area where the wings attached and tapering to a thinner tail. Its single pair of legs, almost vestigial, ended in clawed paws. Overlapping, armored scales covered its body.

Aldwyn circled to its head, which now looked far less threatening as it lay on the ground, mouth half-open, its long tongue extended. The fearsome red lights were gone from its staring eyes, and the last shreds of both magic and life energy had already all but drained away from it. Up close, the stench of rotting meat, especially around its mouth, was overpowering. Was it normally a scavenger, preying on carrion? Had his unexpected arrival in its territory offered it a rare chance at live meat?

Aldwyn looked around again at that thought. If this thing *was* a carrion feeder, he'd just created what was probably the biggest piece of carrion this blighted land had seen in a long time. If others—not just these things, but different creatures—were sensitive to presence of death, they would be coming soon. Best if he wasn't here when they arrived.

Besides, he wasn't here to study the wildlife.

He raised a spell around himself to keep living things from noticing him, then trudged away from the downed creature. He picked the direction that would take him toward the body of water he'd seen before; his intent was mostly to get away from the corpse before anything else came sniffing around it, but if anything else was alive around here, it might be near the water. He wasn't worried about approaching potential dangers in an injured state, since his natural draconic regeneration would take care of the slashes on his back long before he reached his destination.

As he continued walking, it didn't take him long to realize two things.

First, the body of water was farther away than he'd anticipated. It didn't seem to be getting any closer, no matter how long he continued. It glimmered in the distance almost like a mirage, the weird, unfamiliar magic dancing around its edges.

Second, his draconic regeneration was *not* taking care of his injuries—at least not nearly as quickly as it should be.

That took him a little longer to catch on to. During his time stranded on Earth in human form, it had always been a given that there was no need to concern himself with even the sorts of injuries that would kill a human being, because even on Earth he and his fellow dragons retained useful abilities left over from their draconic heritage. Functional immortality, for one: they didn't get ill, they didn't age, and anything short of catastrophic mundane injury wouldn't kill them. None of them were eager to test that belief, of course, but over the centuries the dragons had been exiled, some of them had experienced harm severe enough to convince them that, short of complete disintegration or powerful forces, their innate connection to magic would bring them back from the brink.

But as he continued to walk, still not getting any closer to the water, it began to occur to him that his back not only still hurt from the slash wounds, but a vague sense of physical unease was beginning to surface. Dragons, even in human form, were naturally warmer than humans, but now his body was feeling uncomfortably hot. Not because the air around him was hot, but more like he was suffering from a fever.

He'd never actually *had* a fever, of course, since dragons didn't get ill, but he'd read about the phenomena in humans. And this one seemed to be coming on a lot faster than the type from Earth.

Had there been something on the creature's teeth? Something strong enough to overcome his body's ability to handle it?

This was ridiculous. Something as simple as a relatively minor injury wasn't going to take his focus off his purpose here. He looked ahead, noting that the body of water—it looked like a small lake from here—still wasn't any closer. Magic danced around it, arcing between the water, the plants, and more jagged, multicolored crystalline rocks arrayed around it. Was it some kind of oasis in the middle of this arid wasteland—or was it a trap, a mirage luring him closer to something hidden and waiting for prey to approach?

Normally, Aldwyn wouldn't consider that a problem. As the undisputed apex predators on Earth, the dragons didn't worry about anything threatening them. With the possible exception of something like a nuclear bomb, the humans didn't possess anything they couldn't deal with when properly prepared. And since the humans didn't even suspect their existence, that had never been an issue.

Aldwyn stopped, his breath still coming in short, sharp bursts. His back was on fire now, sweat dripped from his forehead and soaked what was left of his fine suit, and an unfamiliar weakness was beginning to grip his body. He could keep going, he was sure—even here, he doubted much was stronger than his will if he applied it with enough effort.

But should he?

With a last glance toward the magical oasis-lake and a quick look around to make sure nothing was preparing to ambush him from above, he drew in a deep breath and focused his magic inward. His regeneration would take care of the problem on its own even if he did nothing to aid it, but suddenly he didn't want to be at anything less than his strongest in this unfamiliar land that might be hiding more than he'd originally suspected.

Without warning, the world changed.

Around him, the dry, scrubby plants and dusty ground shifted sickeningly, replaced by discordant, flashing colors. The faint, swirling wind picked up speed, spinning into a series of sparking whirlwinds surrounding him.

And *things* were shimmering into being all around him, stepping out of the whirlwinds and advancing on him from all sides. Despite his best efforts, he couldn't make out their forms, which seemed to shift in and out of phase and skate away from his consciousness every time he tried to get a good look at them. Every single one of them crackled with unfamiliar magic, their auras flaming with colors human eyes had never seen.

As if coordinating their efforts, three of the entities crept closer, seeping across ground that was no longer dusty and dry. They reached out long arms—several each—alight with magical energy, reaching toward him, grasping at him as if drawn by his life force.

For the first time since he'd arrived on Earth all those centuries ago—and probably considerably longer ago than that—Aldwyn felt actual fear.

Worse than that, as he struggled to look away from the strange colors, he felt his mind begin to slip sideways as the strange, unworldly colors began to creep past his defenses and into his brain. Even though somewhere deep in his mind he knew he couldn't let those grasping tentacles touch him, his thoughts refused to obey him.

Closer…closer…

They didn't seem to be in a hurry, as if they knew their prey wasn't getting away from them.

One of them lashed out, its energy-tentacle slipping past Aldwyn's shield and settling across his arm.

He screamed.

There was no way his brain could put words to the sensation the tentacle sent through his body, his mind, his *soul*. It was as if everything he was had been flung into a combine, spun and tumbled until nothing made sense. There was no reality, no magic, no illusion—and there were all of them at once, with no way to differentiate between them. It wasn't pain, but yet it was—the kind of pain so profound that it reached past physical sensation and into the psyche, summoning the kind of primal, terrifying concepts that even dragons refused to contemplate.

Another tentacle reached for Aldwyn...

When he acted, it was purely from instinct. There was nothing left within him capable of conscious thought or motivation as long as that vile tentacle grasped his arm. The only idea that made it through—hacked and fragmented nearly beyond recognition, but barely coherent—was that if he didn't do something *now* to get away from whatever this was, he was lost.

Everything was lost.

What kind of gods-forsaken place had his scions led him to?

He screamed again, but this time it wasn't with fear but with rage. He drew on muscle memory, mental and physical, that hadn't seen use in centuries, millennia—but that didn't matter. It was the core of his being, something baked into him and his kind so deeply that it would never be forgotten.

He changed.

His body morphed, rippling and growing, throwing off the tentacles. Powerful legs drove him from the ground, massive leathery wings unfurling to launch him past the tentacles and the things and the whirlwinds and into the sky. When he opened his mouth to roar again, it stretched wide, pointed teeth bristling, the sound of his rage shaking the very air around him.

And then he was aloft, his wings powering him up and up until the last of the fear and the confusion and the disorientation dropped away. Even though he hadn't done anything like this in countless human generations, the practice came easily to him—as easily as if his body had been waiting for it all this time.

He wheeled around, angling his wings to bank first to the left, then to the right. His eyes, sharp enough to spot a mouse on the ground even without his magic, scanned the space below.

Up here, he was high enough to get a bigger picture. The blasted landscape stretched out as far as he could see, all dusty ground and stunted plants and jagged rocks. His more expansive view revealed something else, too: he'd been right about the place being alive with magic, but what he hadn't realized was how *wrong* the magic was. Something had gone seriously awry in this strange land, sending the normal, ordered magical structure into a mad tailspin of confusion and disorientation. Even Aldwyn, with all his thousands of years of experience with magic, had never seen anything like this.

He barely noticed that most of his pain had faded as his larger, hardier draconic form threw off the comparatively minor injuries from the black creature's teeth. What he felt now, looking down at the magical miasma spread out below him, was a different kind of rage. This was an *affront*. Magic was beautiful and orderly, a force that could be both understood on an intellectual level and experienced on a far deeper and more instinctual one—something he could manipulate to his needs, but always something to respect. Even as strong as the dragons were, magic was stronger. Dragons were *made* of magic. The *universe* was made of magic.

So to see this, the primal stuff that infused all living beings, from the smallest insect to the biggest dragon, *corrupted* like this—

It was...*sacrilege.*

Who had done this? How were his scions accessing this twisted magic without becoming twisted themselves?

Had they somehow been *responsible* for twisting it?

He beat his wings harder, propelling him forward faster. Even considering his sense of bone-deep insult at what had been done to the magic here, he couldn't deny the sheer joy suffusing him at finally, after all this time, existing in the form he was meant to inhabit. He reveled in the sensations, his mouth stretched in a toothy grin, and it was all he could do not to send a triumphant roar to the heavens.

Instead, he kept going. He knew he couldn't do it forever—one of the downsides of having such a massive body was that it took a lot of fuel to sustain it, and he thought it highly unwise to eat anything he might find among the sickened magic of this place. He did notice, however, that most of the corruption didn't seem to extend this high above the ground. As he soared on the air currents, his head swiveling on its long, sinuous neck, he spotted patches of swirling, eerie magic in the sky, some of them quite large, but with his acute arcane senses it was easy to avoid them. He looked for more of the winged black creatures, but didn't see any.

He was, at least for the moment, alone up here.

He remained vigilant, noticing that some of the swirling patches moved faster than others, and once he had to bank sharply to avoid catching the leading edge of one of them. As he flew, he glanced occasionally down with pride at his powerful forelegs, at the overlapping, deep-red scales covering them, at his long, sharp claws, at the rippling muscles beneath his skin. Fortunately for him, dragons didn't live by food alone—magic was every bit as necessary to keep them going in this form as calories—but if he planned to remain this way for long, he'd need to land and find something safe to eat. He hoped that, whatever this corruption was, it was confined to a small area.

He didn't know how long he had flown, but it must have been at least an hour by Earth reckoning before a different kind of glow appeared in the far distance ahead of him.

To conserve energy, he'd been using his wings to glide as much as possible, taking advantage of the air currents to soar. Since he had no idea which direction he wanted to go, he let the currents carry him where they would, exerting energy only when another of the swirling patches of corrupt magic appeared near him. He remained more vigilant than he wanted to—what he truly wanted was to continue reveling in the sensation of flight after all this time, to claim his position as ultimate predator for whom nothing else in the world presented even the hint of a threat. But as much as he wanted that, he couldn't allow himself to do it. This strange, unfamiliar plane had already proven it could hurt him, and he didn't plan to give it another chance to do it.

Not until he understood what made it tick, anyway.

CHAPTER THREE

E VERY TIME HE CAME BACK TO IT after taking a break, Alastair Stone remembered how much he loved teaching.

Life, for the first time in a long while, had actually calmed down for him, reminding him of something else—how easily bored he got when nothing was going on. When Beatrice Martinez had called him two weeks ago to ask if he'd be willing to conduct an impromptu seminar on seventeenth-century British occult practices, he'd accepted without even pretending to need time to think about it.

It wasn't as if he had much else to do. Between their children and their work at the agency, Jason and Amber had been so busy they'd been regretfully declining Stone's invitations to lunch or drinks, assuring him that things would be calming down "soon." Verity was deep into her alchemy study with Hezzie and Marie-Thérèse Broussard, while also co-managing both branches of Sybil's Apothecary. Stone had met Ian and Gabriel for drinks a few times in various places around the world, but Gabriel was still caught up with whatever most of the other dragons had been dealing with, and Ian would be departing with some of his old mage friends for a mountain-climbing trip to China while he was busy. Stone had even called the Obsidian a couple times, but Nakamura had told him Trevor Harrison was away and had only returned once, for a single day, a few weeks ago.

As for Eddie and Ward, they were always up for pints at the Dragon, but there were only so many nights you could go out drinking before even the allure of that began to wear off. Stone had quickly found himself settling back into his old solitary habits: magical research, taking long runs around Encantada and the surrounding areas, starting to plan out the portal he wanted to build on the Bermuda Triangle island (he'd need to name the place at some point, since Bret Fontaine hadn't bothered to christen it with anything beyond its number designation), and spending time with Raider. Fortunately for him, the cat hadn't seemed to alter his personality at all when he'd become a Changeling. If Stone didn't use magical sight, he could easily believe his old friend was the same rangy, housecat-sized tabby he'd always been. He still did look at him that way sometimes anyway, though, because the sight of Raider's larger, fairy-creature-beautiful form always gave him joy.

And then there was the elephant—or the dragon—in the room.

He hadn't heard anything from Thalassa Nera since their evening at the illusionary restaurant. It had already been a little more than a month, and he couldn't help wondering if she was avoiding him on purpose. He quickly and angrily put those thoughts aside, though. There was no way in hell he was going to reduce himself to acting like a pathetic wallflower waiting for someone to phone him for a date. Sure, a few thoughts of a more...*physical*...nature had intruded on him at inopportune times, not to mention several dreams of the type he hadn't had often since his days with Deirdre Lanier, but those were beside the point. He certainly wasn't going to chase Thalassa Nera. If she wanted him, she could call. And if she didn't call, it was probably for the best anyway.

The woman—the dragon—was infuriating.

He wasn't a teenager, and there was no way he was going to allow her to take up that much space in his head.

Maybe she'd changed her mind about the whole scion thing, and didn't want to tell him. That might be for the best too.

The seminar had been a welcome insertion of normal life into the whirlwind of oddness that normally surrounded him. He stalked back and forth in front of the tiered rows of seats, reveling in the feeling of keeping a roomful of jaded graduate students enthralled with his lecture. It was one of the things he'd almost forgotten about the old days, and he realized he missed it.

Maybe he *would* meet with Martinez about taking on a regular class. He could probably handle one, assuming life didn't heat up again.

That was never a good assumption these days, unfortunately.

He was winding down the lecture and preparing to call for questions when his phone buzzed in his pocket. He didn't answer it, of course—that would be bad form and break the spell he'd been weaving over the room—but he did still wonder who might be calling him this time of day.

The students had a *lot* of questions. By the time he answered most of them and managed to duck out through the door behind the lectern, it was after four p.m. He pulled the phone out and glanced at it.

Voicemail – Renata Huxley.

That couldn't be good. Ren never called him for social reasons.

He felt a little guilty that he hadn't made any serious effort to track any of the eleven demons The Unspeakable's artifact knife had summoned into the world, aside from asking Gina to keep an eye out for any mentions of strange crimes or events that could possibly be supernatural—but she already did that on her own anyway. So far, as far has he knew, the demons hadn't caused any major trouble. Maybe it took them a while to settle into the world, or maybe they were keeping a low profile while they gained power and attempted to grow their bases of operation. Some of them might even have decided they didn't like it here and returned to their home planes as soon as they were free of The Unspeakable's influence. Stone had already accepted the fact that there might not *be* a way to get rid of some of them, unless the dragons wanted to get involved.

Which it didn't seem they did lately.

In any case, Ren's call might be related to something completely different. Demons weren't the only supernatural threats her agency dealt with, not by a long way. Perhaps something new had popped up and she needed a consult.

He waited until he got back to his car, which he'd had to park a considerable distance from the lecture hall, before calling her back.

She answered right away. "Huxley."

"Sitting next to the phone waiting for my call, Agent?" He put a bit of mocking amusement in his voice, and tried not to dwell on his earlier thoughts about Thalassa Nera.

"You wish." There was fondness in her tone, though—she might find him exasperating sometimes, but there was no doubt he'd pulled her bacon out of the fire on more than one occasion. That had to be worth at least a little bit of respect.

"What can I do for you today?" He tapped the speaker icon, slipped the phone into the holder on the BMW's dashboard, and pulled out of the parking lot.

"I hate to keep calling you." The fondness was gone now, replaced by a combination of businesslike briskness and an odd reluctance.

"I enjoy your calls. They always make my days more interesting—if also usually more painful."

"Well, I hope this isn't one of those, but I'm afraid it might be."

"What's going on? I'm driving now—where are you? Did you want to meet somewhere?"

"Can't, I'm actually out of the country right now, working on another case." She paused, then let out a long, meandering sigh. "I've got a pair of agents missing, Stone."

"Missing? Where?"

"The Detroit area. We got a lead a couple of weeks ago about someone—or some*thing*—moving to take over one of the street gangs up there. We couldn't get much, except that nobody can give a clear description of this person or whatever, or even if it's just one or a group. Everybody who's seen them describes them differently."

"That's not so odd," Stone said. "Especially if it *is* someone with supernatural talent. A middling mage could employ illusions that could fool all but the most perceptive mundane. Or it could just be a group of mundanes."

"I know that. I get it. And you might not be wrong. But my gut tells me this is supernatural, and that there's more to it than just a mage using illusions. I sent my people up there to investigate. They're both mages, nowhere even close to your level talent-wise but experienced agents. They were supposed to nose around, talk to people, and see what they could find out. The plan was, once we had a little more intel, to try sending somebody in undercover."

"Seems reasonable." Stone exited the rear of the campus and turned onto the road that would take him back to the Encantada house.

"Yeah. Except a week ago both of them stopped reporting in," she said grimly. "Nothing. We can't reach them at all, and they've missed every scheduled contact since they disappeared."

"Hmm." That wasn't good. "What have you done to try to locate them?"

"We had another of our mages go to the area and do a tracking spell. Obviously, we keep samples on all our agents for just that reason. But she didn't find anything."

"Dead?" Stone tried to keep his tone gentle, but that was the usual reason for failed tracking spells.

"No clear way to know. And before you ask, she's experienced with tracking spells, so she knows how to interpret what she gets back."

Stone pondered. "What do you mean, 'no clear way to know'? If she can't find them, they're either dead, out of range of the spell, or hidden under magical cover."

"Right." Ren sounded impatient, probably to emphasize that she already knew all of that. "All she says is that she doesn't get a clear indication that they're dead. She thinks they either are or somebody's shielding them. Or both. But regardless, she can't find them."

"So, what do you want me to do? If your agent is good with tracking spells, it's unlikely I'll find anything she didn't find."

"I know." Her tone wasn't impatient anymore, but tired. "And I know you're busy. But I've known these two for a long time, and they're not just agents—they're friends. At the risk of stroking your already overdeveloped ego, I don't want to give up on this until I've had the best in to take a look."

Stone didn't chuckle as he normally would have, or make a flippant remark. When Ren had said the agents were friends of hers, a little twinge had gone off somewhere inside him. He thought about how he might feel if Jason and Verity had disappeared without a trace, and remembered that Ren had, not that long ago, lost her longtime partner during a case.

"Fine," he said. "I'll take a look. Send me whatever you've got, including tether objects for a tracking spell if you've got more. That also includes anything about what they were supposed to be looking into."

"You'll have it. I can send you the online files as soon as I get off the phone. As for the tether objects, our agent is still in Detroit. If you can get there in the next day or two, she can give you what she has. I know there's a portal in Chicago…and I'm also pretty sure you don't care. Are you ever going to tell me what's going on with that?"

"No."

"Fine. I'll stop asking, then. I guess if I want you to help me, I've got to let you keep your secrets."

"A wise idea, Agent—not that it will make the slightest bit of difference regardless of what you do. Send me the information and I'll let you know what I come up with."

"Thanks, Stone."

It had been a while since he'd heard her sound so exhausted—mentally and physically. "I'll sort it out," he said gently. "One way or another, I'll get you an answer."

"Yeah. I'm just really afraid I'm not going to like the answer you get me." The line went dead with a soft *click*.

The emailed information arrived within a few minutes. Stone spent the next half-hour poring over it, gently pushing Raider out of the way as the tabby tried to cuddle up with his laptop keyboard.

On the surface, there was very little indication of supernatural involvement in the case. Stone didn't know much about Detroit, aside from the fact that it was—or at least used to be—the place where most American cars were built, and that there was a lot of crime there. Ren's information was concerned with the latter.

Apparently, one of the numerous, vicious, and frighteningly well-armed gangs that controlled the most dangerous areas of the city had begun expanding its territory recently. The odd part, Ren noted on the files she'd sent, was that such things, when they occurred at all, were usually slow and steady. The expanding gang gathered forces, pushed boundaries, and held the new territory against their opposition long enough to lay claim to it. The smaller gangs had already been swallowed up or destroyed by the larger ones, leaving the city's crime divided among several powerful gangs and the Mafia. Skirmishes were expected, of course, especially along the borders of various organizations' territories, but for the most part the city's crime factions stayed out of each other's way and conducted their own business.

All of that had changed over the past few weeks. Rumors had begun to bubble up regarding one or more new players in town—players who operated at an entirely different level than even the strongest of the current crop. Several high-ranking gang members and even a couple of the mobsters had turned up messily and publicly dead, but without any accompanying message regarding why. No one had claimed responsibility.

Nobody knows what's going on, Ren's comments said. *Most of this stuff is taking place in parts of town the police don't even go into after dark. So far, it's confined to the gangs themselves, and hasn't spilled over into civilian casualties. But everyone's worried it will.*

Stone kept reading, a little impatiently. So far, he still hadn't seen anything to indicate this was more than simple mundane crime. Unfortunate, certainly, but not something he needed to get involved in. Especially not when it was halfway across the country in a town he'd never visited and didn't particularly want to.

The notes continued, written in the familiar, just-the-facts style popular with law enforcement. The case had caught the attention of Ren's agency for two reasons: the first was that literally nobody could give a description of any of the newcomers instigating the violence. The police had consulted informants, rounded up and questioned street-level members of numerous gangs, and even arranged meetings with some of their higher-ranking operatives. The mere fact that these people had agreed to the meetings at all indicated how scared they were, even though they'd die before they admitted it.

The second reason was the sheer, primal brutality of the crimes. The shadowy newcomers' goal seemed to be to end up on the top of the city's crime heap, taking over the territories and operations of the other gangs. At least so far, they seemed to be succeeding by mounting a campaign of terror designed to frighten the others into rolling over. That wasn't easy when dealing with brutal, hardcore gang members who didn't flinch at guns, knives, bombs, or other conventional weapons, and weren't squeamish about the kinds of wounds more common on a battlefield than a city street. But when high-ranking members of several of the gangs—the types it shouldn't have been possible to even reach through their cadres of bodyguards and hangers-on—had turned up with their heads literally ripped from their necks, hanging from the sides of buildings with their guts strewn around below them, or with their skin removed from their bodies, it was impossible for both the gangs and the cops not to take notice.

Ren had sent two of her organization's agents—a pair of longtime partners named Jack Groszek and Isabel "Izzy" Freeman—into Detroit two weeks ago. They had interfaced with the local police unit heading up the investigation, gathered as much data as they could, and then headed out to see what they could find on their own. Only a day later, before they'd had a chance to report any useful information back, they'd lost contact.

Stone returned to the file and clicked on the data sheets for the two agents. Groszek was a fifteen-year law-enforcement veteran, formerly of the FBI after a brief stint in the military. His photo showed a grim, athletic white man with short-cut dark hair and a nose that had been broken more than once, glaring at the camera like he wanted to punch its lights out. He looked like he'd be more comfortable in a T-shirt and jeans than the suit he was wearing. Stone flicked his gaze to the section on the man's magical talent; he was classified a C+, which meant his abilities weren't anything to write home about but he had solid training in how to use them. He specialized in combat, defensive, and concealment magic.

Izzy Freeman was a trim, plain-looking black woman with short dreadlocks. Unlike her partner, she faced the camera with a dazzling smile, and her eyes glittered with intelligence and good humor. She'd only been with Ren's organization for four years; Ren had recruited her personally from the Chicago police department after she'd showed signs of magical talent. She too was a C+. Stone wasn't surprised; Ren had told him it was hard for them to recruit more powerful mages, but no doubt they had the resources to give them enough training to help them survive against low-level supernatural threats. Freeman's magical specialty was surveillance: tracking, long-range vision and eavesdropping, and disregarding spells.

Stone minimized the two personnel files and pulled up the one describing their mission. The gang the newcomers seemed to be focusing on was called the NorthSide SickBoyz, formerly a medium-sized collection of ex-cons and other nasty individuals who claimed territory south of 8 Mile Road near interstate 10. None of this meant much to Stone, of course—his real-life knowledge of street gangs was limited to the Evil-affiliated Dead Men Walking, which had disappeared years ago, and the map Ren had included that showed the locations of other local gangs was more confusing than enlightening.

The notes continued that the SickBoyz had, up until a few weeks ago, mostly kept to themselves. They hadn't shown much inclination to expand their territory, and though they were willing and able to defend their own space, they were content to do that. One surprising note indicated one arm of the SickBoyz had begun recruiting Changeling members a couple of years ago, making them one of the few multi-racial operations in the city. Stone had no idea if that was relevant, but he filed the information away. Maybe the people trying to take over the gang were bigger, badder Changelings.

He wondered if his limited experience with the DMW had relevance here. They, too, had been a small-time gang elevated to higher-tier status when bigger fish—in their case, the Evil and Gordon Lucas's organization—had muscled into their power structure.

Regardless, he was fairly sure Ren was right: there *was* super-natural involvement here somewhere. Mundanes rarely made changes this big and this fast, since they didn't have the firepower to back them up. Supernaturals, especially strong ones, could do it with ease.

Hell, *he* could probably do it if he was so inclined. Lack of knowledge didn't preclude brute-force intimidation tactics.

One thing he knew for sure, though: if he was going to take this case on, and he'd already told Ren he would, he was going to need help. He grabbed his phone from under Raider's paw and tapped out a few texts.

CHAPTER FOUR

S TONE MET JASON, Amber, Verity, and Gina in Thayer Investigations' conference room later on the same day Ren had contacted him, after the agency closed and Derik the receptionist had gone home. All of them had responded to his text quickly, saying they were interested in helping with the case. Ian had begged off because he was in Guangzhou with some friends and nowhere near a portal, but promised to drop everything and come home if he was needed.

"So, Detroit," Jason said. He'd ordered dinner in for the meeting, and spoke as he dished up chow mein and broccoli chicken from the cartons in the middle of the conference table. "That's not exactly in your jurisdiction."

"No, but Ren is convinced there might be significant supernatural involvement." Stone had already forwarded the files the agent had sent him, and he'd spent the last ten minutes catching them up on the latest.

"So she wants you to find her two friends, or find out what happened to them?" Gina asked. "That could be tough, even *with* magic. The bad parts of Detroit aren't the kind of place you want to just wander into." She indicated her open laptop. "I've been doing some research, based on what you sent us. There are some very nasty people around that area. It's possible the agents pissed off the wrong folks and somebody made 'em disappear. It happens, even to mages."

"I'm well aware." Stone hadn't taken any food yet, but had accepted a cup of steaming tea. "Ren says these two have significant experience, but I don't think their magical abilities are strong enough for them to depend on against anything but low-level supernatural threats."

"What are you proposing we do?" Verity asked. "Do you want to go there and look around yourself? Do you want us to come along with you?"

"Not at first. Ren said the agent who did the tracking spell will be in town for another day or so, and if I can meet up with her, she'll give me more information about what she found and provide me with tether objects so I can try my own spell. I'm leaving tomorrow morning. Once I've got more definitive information, we'll see where we can go from there."

"What do you expect to find?" Amber was looking grim. "I hate to say it, but from everything you've told us so far, it sounds like they're probably dead."

"You're likely right," Stone said. "But if there's a way to know for sure, I want to explore it. I'm sure this agent is very talented with tracking spells—possibly more than I am—but I guarantee she doesn't have my range and sensitivity. I'm hoping she might have missed something."

"What will you do if you find them?" Jason frowned. "Gina's right, Al—I know you're damned tough these days, but you're going to stand out like a sore thumb walking around the bad ends of Detroit."

Stone flashed a wry look around at his friends. "I'm hardly the only one, I think. But that's a question we'll answer when we have more facts. The first thing I should ask is if you *can* accompany me. I know you've all got your own things going on, and Jason and Amber have their children to look after." He smiled at Gina. "And you—I know you don't do fieldwork, so I'm not even going to ask."

"I don't like you going by yourself," Jason said. "Unfortunately, though, we've got a hot case that's going to take at least a couple more days to round up, and it's not something we can just drop. I'd send Luther, but he's off visiting his family somewhere in Montana for the next two weeks. So it's just Amber and me."

"That's quite all right." Stone rose from his chair and paced, holding his tea. "I'm reasonably certain Mr. Groszek and Ms. Freeman are either dead—in which case a few more days won't matter—or else they're deep undercover and don't want to risk communication, so they aren't in danger at all." He sighed. "I just wish I had more information about what might be behind this. Ren didn't give me much to go on. It's powerful, nobody knows what it looks like, and they aren't even sure whether we're dealing with one entity or multiples."

"And it's willing to commit some pretty horrible murders," Gina said. "I mean, street gangs don't exactly have slap fights when they're pissed at each other, but they're a lot more likely to do drive-bys, stab each other, or maybe use some low-level explosives. I've never heard of gangbangers ripping each other's heads off, or disemboweling each other and hanging the bodies from the sides of buildings. That's hardcore even by gang standards."

"Do you have any suspicions?" Verity asked Stone. "Have you ever seen anything like this before?"

He shrugged. "Not much, at this point. It could be a number of things." He indicated the files, then looked at Gina. "Ren said this 'SickBoyz' gang our target is trying to take over is a Changeling gang, and the only one of its size in town that's racially integrated."

She nodded. "Changelings don't give a damn what race you are, for the most part. If you look like a humanoid cat or an ogre or something, whether you're black or brown or white is kind of a secondary consideration." Her expression sobered. "It makes sense, too—there definitely *are* Changeling types—ogres, for one—that are strong enough and mean enough to pull somebody's head off or rip their guts out if they piss them off. I don't want to perpetuate any stereotypes, but a lot of ogres *do* tend to have anger-management issues. It has something to do with the changes that occur in the psyche when the Change hits."

"Anger management is one thing," Amber said, "but pulling people's *heads* off? You'd have to piss someone off pretty thoroughly to get them to do that."

"Or else they want to make a really big statement," Jason said. "Think about it—if you don't have any moral objections to doing stuff like that, you can't deny it will go a long way toward scaring the shit out of the street-level gang types, especially the younger ones. A lot of those guys aren't hardcore gangbangers yet—they're just street kids who get hooked into running with the gangs because they don't have too many other options."

Stone had resumed his seat, thinking as Jason spoke. "One thing that doesn't make sense about that, though," he mused.

"What's that?"

"Well…if this gang is made up of Changelings…why would they *want* to take over other gangs? It seems like it might be more trouble for them than the benefit would warrant."

"What do you mean?" Verity asked.

But Gina was following along. "You're right. I mean, Changelings are people so you can't lump them all together under one umbrella, but it doesn't make sense that a Changeling gang would go after non-Changelings."

"Not even if they're just after their slice of the pie, crime-wise?" Jason asked. "I'm guessing the SickBoyz didn't form a gang so they could go to cultural events and hold mixers." He nodded toward Stone's file. "They're hip-deep into all sorts of bad stuff—drugs, prostitution, extortion—same as the other gangs and the Mob. Maybe greed is a bigger deal than Changeling solidarity."

"Possible," Gina said. "Especially if somebody new came in to take over and change their focus. Changelings can be as power-hungry as any other person, and if they're strong enough to get everybody else to go along with their plan, it could happen. Doc, I think your best bet is to try to figure out what happened to the two agents, and see what you can find out about the leadership of the SickBoyz. I'm not having much luck yet, but that's because all I've had time for is internet stuff. Give me till tomorrow—I'll put the word out discreetly to some of my Changeling friends and see if I can get you some more intel on who's running the SickBoyz's show."

"Thank you, Gina." Stone wondered how he'd ever managed to find anything without Gina's impressive online skills. "Just send me the information when you get it. If I'm still in Detroit, it might help me do a bit more investigation."

Jason shook his head. "Al, I would *strongly* advise you not to go poking around the bad ends of Detroit by yourself. You can't keep your shield up twenty-four-seven, and all it takes is one guy to plug you in the back from somewhere you'll never even see. Even if they can't kill you, it's not gonna be pleasant if they toss your body in a river or something."

"Noted." Stone kept his voice light, but he knew his friend was correct. Magic was a big advantage, but even the dragons weren't immune to injury if they didn't see it coming and take proper precautions. "I'll let you know what I find out from Ren's friend, and we'll go from there."

As it turned out, a ley line ran through one of the safest areas of Detroit. Stone selected a small bar and grill on the waterfront and near the ley line, then texted Ren's contact and arranged to meet her there for lunch.

Gina had sent him some data on the city, including that the most tourist-friendly places were near the Downtown area and along the river.

"Just to tell you how dangerous it is to wander into the wrong parts of town," she'd told him, "they've actually got an app you can use to check out crime in real time. They've got some nice touristy areas, but you want to stay there as much as possible."

Stone wasn't that worried—with his magic he had the ability to remain unnoticed, and he could deal with anyone trying to hassle him—but still, there was no point in taking unnecessary risks or drawing unwanted attention.

Yet, anyway. He strongly suspected that, whatever he ended up having to do, it wasn't going to be in the safe part of town.

The bar and grill was called Delancey's, and it had a nice view of the river. It also had an outdoor patio, but the weather was cold and drizzly enough that nobody was using it. He pushed open the door and looked around.

Ren's contact had told him she would be wearing a gray Lions hoodie. He had no trouble spotting her, seated at a table near the window with a glass of beer in front of her. She was looking out the window, watching a freighter floating down the river.

He slipped past a knot of chattering tourists and dropped into the chair across from her. "Lovely weather we're having," he said dryly.

She didn't jerk. Her aura didn't even budge, making Stone wonder if she'd been unobtrusively observing him since he entered. "Yeah, if you're a mushroom, I guess." She looked him over. "You don't look anything like I pictured you from our friend's description."

Stone had chosen the illusionary disguise of a young man with dark brown hair and medium brown skin, wearing a light rain jacket and jeans. "Yes, well, I didn't know what I was getting into, so I thought it best not to look like myself."

"Smart. Anyway, nice to meet you. You can call me Heidi. You want a beer? They have some good ones here." She was of medium height and stocky build, with short, dark hair, brown eyes, and a pale pink scar on her left cheek.

Stone wondered if "Heidi" was her real name. "No, thanks. Bit early for me. It's barely nine a.m. in California. I shouldn't even be awake yet."

"Oh, you're one of *those*. I've been up for hours." Her smile faded, leaving her looking tired. "Hope you don't mind if I get some food while we're here. Haven't eaten since yesterday afternoon."

Heidi waited for the server to arrive and take their orders—a burger and fries for her and an iced tea for Stone—then leaned in closer to him. "Do you have a way to make sure nobody overhears us?"

"Yes. Hold on a moment." He quickly cast his 'cone of silence' spell—that thing was turning out to be one of his most useful bits of magic—then looked around. "Bit overcautious, aren't you? Are you expecting to be overheard in the middle of a crowded tourist restaurant?"

"Never know, and it's always a good idea to be careful. Especially when I haven't got a clue about what's going on."

"Fair point. So, I understand you're a dab hand with tracking spells."

"One of the best in our organization." Her no-nonsense voice held no particular pride. "But from what Ren's told me, I'm guessing you make me look like an amateur."

Stone caught something in her gaze and her tone, and a quick glance at her aura verified it—a faint defensiveness, as if she was used to people questioning her skills. "I doubt it, actually. My tracking spell is good, but it's not the focus of most of what I do. My guess is I've probably got a considerably longer range and more sensitivity, but as I'm sure you know, that's only part of the process.

I'm hoping we can work together to make use of our respective strengths to get the job done."

She relaxed a little. "Yeah. I hope so. Because I haven't been able to find a damn trace of Izzy and Jack, and that's bugging me a lot."

"Tell me everything. Ren said you weren't sure how to interpret the information you got from the spell."

She nodded without looking at him. "Yeah. That's what's bothering me the most." Her gaze came up, and her expression hardened. "I'm good at what I do. I've been doing it for years, and I've located a hell of a lot of people over that time. My success rate's the highest we have. I know how to tell the difference between when somebody's dead, out of tracking range, or under some kind of magical or natural cover. That's why this isn't making any sense."

The server returned with Heidi's meal and Stone's iced tea. He considered her words as he watched her dig in. "Okay. We'll sort this out, one way or another. Tell me what you found that's confusing you."

She scarfed down a few fries and a bite of burger before she answered. "It's hard to explain. I've never gotten this kind of result before. I'm sure Ren told you, we keep tether objects on all our people, usually in the form of hair or fingernail clippings. If we're going to send somebody out on a job we know is dangerous, we take a blood sample and use a preservation spell on it."

Stone nodded approval. Blood was by far the best way to trace someone, and depending on how good their preservation spell was, they could potentially keep it viable for as long as a month. "I assume you had blood samples on both of the missing agents."

"Oh, yeah." She snorted. "When you're dealing with a situation where people are getting their heads ripped off their bodies, that definitely qualifies as 'dangerous.'" She took another bite and indicated her oversized basket of fries. "Want some? Even this hungry, there's no way I'm gonna eat all those."

"No, thank you. So, when they didn't report in as expected, how long did you wait before trying the ritual?"

"A day. One missed report isn't that big a deal, especially for undercover agents. Sometimes, it's just not possible to call in without compromising themselves. But after they missed their second check-in, Ren got worried and brought me in."

"You're not local to this area, correct?"

"Nah, I'm based out of Chicago."

"How long did it take you to get here? Did you use the portals, or fly?"

"Flew." She shot him a quick grin. "That's one nice thing—we can get planes pretty fast, so depending on where the portals are, it can often be faster to fly direct than mess around with magic. Especially since there aren't any portals that we know of in Detroit. I got here two days ago, and set up the ritual in a warehouse near their last reported location."

"What's your range?"

"Fifteen miles…maybe twenty under optimal conditions. Long enough to pick up most of the metro Detroit area."

Stone made a noncommittal noise. His own range was as large as a hundred and fifty miles. Verity's and Ian's were around seventy-five, and even Eddie and Ward could manage fifty on a good day. He forgot sometimes that he spent most of his time associating with mages significantly above average, skill-wise, to the point where he tended to look at his and his friends' levels as typical.

But still, as Heidi had pointed out, her range was easily far enough to reach the vast majority of the Detroit area, especially if she performed the ritual near the center part of town.

"Okay," he said. "Did you perform one ritual combining the blood from both subjects, or two separate ones?"

"Two." She cut him a glance as if trying to determine if he was testing her. "As I'm sure you know," she said with careful emphasis, "combining multiple subjects' tether objects *might* increase the ritual's sensitivity if they're together and both alive, but otherwise can introduce anomalies."

"I'm not trying to tell you how to do your job, Heidi," Stone said, raising a placating hand. "I'm just trying to get all the facts about how you conducted the ritual. I don't want to make assumptions about anything."

She let her breath out. "Yeah, sorry. I don't mean to be defensive. I'm just worried about Jack and Izzy, and pissed because this is supposed to be what I'm an expert at and I still can't fucking *find* them." She bent to rummage in a bag next to her chair and pulled out a leather portfolio folder. "Here," she said, opening it to a page and shoving it across the table at him. "There are all the notes about the ritual parameters. Tether used, circle construction and composition, and results. Take a look and then ask whatever you want."

Stone perused the file while Heidi finished her burger. As far as he could tell, she'd done everything correctly. The ritual diagram was a well-tested design; he'd seen and used more complex examples himself, but this one was easily good enough to get the job done. The components used were solid as well, and the actual ritual was a textbook version with a few clever personalizing nuances. Nothing wrong with any of it.

He skipped down to the "Results" section of the notes. Heidi had documented the process painstakingly, but when she got to the part about what she'd found, the language became less precise. As she'd told him, she'd found "something," but aside from being sure the targets weren't dead, out of range, or behind standard magical or natural cover, she couldn't explain why she got the strong impression they were still alive.

Heidi swallowed a bite of fry and washed it down with a slug of beer. "I've got a video if you want to see it. I always video my rituals, even though obviously none of the magical components show up on the recording. You can see if you notice anything wrong."

Stone waved her off. "Perhaps later. From what I see in your report, it doesn't look like you did anything wrong, so I'm going to assume for now that you didn't. Especially since you said you've been doing these for years. You could probably instruct *me* in a few aspects of this ritual."

A brief look of pride flashed across her face, but then she was all business again. She shoved her plate aside. "Okay, then—what *do* you want to do? You just want me to send you copies of all this stuff? Or do you want to re-create the ritual and see if you get different results?"

"You've still got some of the blood left?"

"Yeah. I only used about a third of what we had for each of them. And don't worry about offending me by checking my work. I *want* you to check my work, if you're willing. Even if you can't find them either, maybe you'll recognize the results better than I did."

"Actually," Stone said, "what I'd like is for *both* of us to re-create the ritual."

She frowned. "Both? You mean one after the other? That seems inefficient, doesn't it? Especially since we've only got two more samples and that would use them both."

"Not one after the other. Together."

Her frown deepened, and she tilted her head as if he'd said something crazy. "Together? Uh...you know you can't combine tracking rituals, right?"

Normally, she would have been correct. Until recently, classical magical teachings had instructed that tracking rituals were a single-person working, and adding more than one practitioner to the process wouldn't get any useful results. But a while back Stone, Eddie, and Ward had worked out a way to add more members to the ritual, allowing the participants to combine their expertise.

"Yes, well…that's not exactly true anymore."

"What are you talking about?" She leaned forward, her lunch forgotten, her face alight with professional interest.

"My friends and I have worked out a way to do a multi-person tracking ritual. Things get a bit tricky when doing it with more than two, but with your level of expertise, we should have no trouble."

She stared at him. "You're kidding, right?" But she didn't bother to wait for an answer. "Why haven't I heard about this?"

He rubbed the back of his neck ruefully. He'd been meaning to write up the process and make it available at Caventhorne and the London Library, but life had intervened and he hadn't gotten around to it. Eddie and Ward had done most of the work on it, using some obscure reference material from the Library, but it had been at Stone's behest so they'd probably figured it was up to him whether he wanted to make it public. "We…haven't exactly publicized it yet. I should get 'round to that, so thanks for the reminder. But if you've got access to a ritual space and materials, we can give it a go."

She was still looking at him, in that dumbfounded way that clearly said, *You just* invented *a revolutionary new magical technique and didn't bother to document it?* She let her breath out slowly, as if counting to ten before speaking.

"Okay," she finally said. "Yes. If you know a way we can combine a tracking ritual, that might be just the thing we need to figure out what's up." She narrowed her eyes. "But you *are* going to make this available, right? That's something our organization could get a lot of use out of."

"I'll talk to my friends about it, and we'll do it—as soon as I get the time. I promise."

"Right…" she muttered, probably softly enough so she didn't think he'd heard her.

The ritual space was an abandoned warehouse a couple miles from the restaurant.

They took Heidi's car, leaving Stone to take in the sights out the passenger window. This place didn't look nearly as tourist-friendly as the restaurant near the river; on their way to their destination, he saw three different small groups of hard-looking men loitering on street corners, giving the car the side-eye as it passed.

"Is this town as dangerous as I've heard?" he asked, pointedly not making eye contact with any of the men. Sure, he could handle them easily if they tried anything, but often the best way to deal with trouble was to avoid it in the first place.

"Parts of it are probably *more* dangerous than you've heard." Heidi was paying subtle attention to their surroundings as she drove. "I bet you didn't know they actually have an entire zip code in the northeast part of the city, 48205, that you're not supposed to go into if you're smart. The locals call it '4820-die' because of the crazy-high crime rate there. But don't worry, the place we're going is pretty safe. It's on the edge of a gang's territory, but they won't bother it. Not in the middle of the day, anyway." She turned left onto a street lined with grim-looking two- and three-story build-ings. "Still, if you've got a good disregarding spell, this might be a nice time to use it."

Stone glanced around with magical sight, checking for lurking auras. He spotted a couple of men walking down the street at the other end of the block, but they were heading away from the car. He quickly summoned the spell around them. "There."

"Good. Mine's okay, but it's hard for me to maintain it very long, especially when I'm driving." She slowed in front of one of the buildings and tapped a button on a fob in her pocket. A roll-up door ground its way high enough to let her drive in, then back down again. A few banks of overhead fluorescent lights flickered on.

The space looked like it might have long ago housed some kind of light manufacturing or industrial operation, like HVAC or metal fabrication. Most of the useful bits and fixtures had been cleared away by this point, leaving a large open space with an oil-stained floor and a pair of heavy workbenches built into one wall. Heidi pulled the car off to the other side, got out, and popped the trunk.

"I hope you don't need anything too exotic," she said as she pulled a large, green canvas duffel bag out. "I've got everything here for standard rituals, including a couple of reference texts and some notes. Grab the samples from my bag on the seat, will you?"

The samples were in a series of small glass tubes stored in a black leather snap case. There were four in all, each one with a label sticker on the side that included a number and the agents' initials—two each for Izzy Freeman and Jack Groszek. Magical sight revealed a faint arcane glow around the tubes, probably from the preservation spell.

Stone brought them over to the bench, where Heidi had already opened the duffel and was laying out gear. "Nothing special. The difference is in the execution and the ritual preparation, not the materials."

She looked skeptical, but willing to go along with him. "Okay, then," she said, indicating the items. "I guess this part is all you, then."

"I'm afraid so." He was acutely aware of her discomfort—as the agency's expert on tracking magic, she obviously wasn't keen to stand on the sidelines while the hotshot newcomer took over the show. To soften the blow a bit, he said with wry humor, "In my other life I'm a university professor, and I've been told by more than one person that I love the sound of my own voice. Suppose I narrate my process here, and you can take notes. That will give you a head start on learning the ritual yourself, and perhaps you'll discover some way to refine it further."

"Not a bad idea." She pulled out her phone. "How do you feel about video recording?"

"I'd rather you didn't, honestly. And besides, the act of taking physical notes sometimes helps to cement the knowledge more effectively."

"Got it. You're camera shy." She flashed him a quick grin, retrieved her notebook, and hopped onto the workbench. "Okay, go."

Creating the circle took Stone nearly an hour. Part of that was because the multi-person circle was more intricate than the single-participant version, part was because he was working without reference materials and wanted to make doubly sure he got it right, and part was because he slowed down to narrate every step of the process to Heidi as he implemented it, complete with side comments detailing the reasons behind what he was doing.

Heidi remained silent and sharply attentive, scribbling away as fast as she could. By the time Stone finished and stepped back from the circle to examine his work, she had a small stack of sheets next to her. She jumped down and paced the circle.

"That *is* complex," she said. "But it makes sense. Now that I see it, I can see what you guys did—how you extended the basics to leave room for another participant. This is pretty elegant stuff."

"Thank you. I'll pass your praise on to my friends back in England. They did most of the research—I just put my two cents in for the implementation."

"Okay, so how do we do this?"

He explained the last part to her, how they would both sit inside the circle on either side of the chosen sample, and he would bring her in once he'd established contact with the tether. "At that point, we continue as in a single-person ritual, combining our range and sensitivity and hopefully finding something we can use."

She still appeared doubtful it would work, but hopeful he was correct. She pulled one of the tubes of blood from the case. "Let's start with Izzy. I got the impression last time that they weren't far apart, but not directly together, either."

As they settled into their places in the circle, Stone gave Heidi a few last-minute instructions on how the ritual was likely to progress. "I don't know what we'll get, but it's doubly important that, whatever we find, we remain as calm and focused as possible until we end the ritual. Any problems with one person are amplified with two—it's the main reason why it's much more difficult to do with larger groups."

"Got it. Don't worry—I've done hundreds of these things. You just worry about figuring out where Izzy is, and I'll do my best to support you."

Stone glanced toward the closed door to make sure no one was trying to enter the space. Then he put all thoughts of the outside world aside as he pulled in a few cleansing breaths and dropped into the deep, meditative version of magical senses he used for rituals. He lit the candles around the circle, then fed power into it until the familiar, ordered lines of energy sprang into being around them, enclosing the two of them in a dome of interlocking, brightly-colored magic.

He focused on both Heidi sitting across from him and the blood, which he'd already poured into the small vessel in the circle's center.

"All right," he murmured, reaching his hands out. "We should be ready now. Take my hands, and concentrate on the sample. Whatever you know about Izzy, picture it in your mind. I'll take the lead to start with, but if you notice anything, squeeze my hands and I'll back off and let you take over."

"Got it," she whispered back.

Together, the two of them stared down at the blood sample. Stone's hands began to tingle, then glow softly as the magic grew around them. He obviously had never met Izzy Freeman, so he centered his thoughts on the photo Ren had shown him, trying to connect it with the blood.

Across from him, Heidi leaned slightly forward, her eyes closed and her lips moving as she spoke soundless words. She gripped his hands firmly but not tightly.

Stone switched his attention back to the swirling energy in the brazier. He watched it as it formed into the familiar tendril, gathered itself, and shot up through the high ceiling. So far, everything had progressed exactly the way he'd expected.

It didn't take long, however, for him to see that things wouldn't proceed as they would in a normal tracking ritual. He followed the tendril up through the roof, feeling Heidi's presence alongside him, and traced it as it cast around, looking for the missing agent.

If Izzy was dead, he would know it right away. That was actually the easiest and most definitive of the possible results. Even if a target was well out of the ritual's range, the tether retained some attachment as long as the target remained alive. That was especially true for blood, which was the best possible tether object.

But if the target was dead, the trace would wink out almost immediately—and that didn't happen. That was encouraging news, at least.

Sort of encouraging, anyway. Just because they now knew Izzy was still among the living didn't mean they were any closer to finding her. Stone reached out with his consciousness, moving closer to the tendril and trying to pick up any subtle nuances from it as it stretched out first in one direction, then in another. The faint tingle in his hands grew stronger and began radiating up his arms and into his core. A vague, undifferentiated unease settled over his body.

He felt Heidi across from him, feeding him power through their bond and reaching out to do her own inspection. It was difficult and unadvisable to talk during a ritual, but sometimes it was necessary. "Are you getting anything?" he murmured through gritted teeth. His stomach roiled, making him glad he hadn't taken Heidi up on her offer of food. The tingling intensified, bringing with it a burning sensation centering around his chest. Not a pain, exactly, but not pleasant. He wanted to rub it, but he dared not let go of Heidi's hands.

"Still think she's alive," she grated. Her face was dotted with sweat. "I can't *find* her, though." She gripped his hands tighter, spasmodically.

Stone ignored the odd sensations and focused harder, trying to will the tendril to pick a direction. It was getting harder to do it, though—the rising nausea joined with the pain in his chest, and now he was sweating too.

Something was resisting them, or at least trying to throw them off the scent.

The ritual was working as intended—Heidi's power joined with his was the only thing making this possible at all. Even with his power and sensitivity, Stone didn't think he'd have gotten as far as they had on his own. There was no way Heidi could have. Experience was important, but in cases like this, sheer power was what mattered most.

What was blocking them? The gang Ren suspected was composed of Changelings—while he'd heard of a few who had quasi-magical abilities, none could extend them this far. Changelings, by their very definition, weren't mages. If they had any magic at all, it was innate and related to their true form. How could that stop two trained mages from tracking another one?

Could she be blocking us on her own?

It made sense. Mages could prevent other mages from tracking them, though level of talent still affected their success. A weak or middling mage couldn't hide from someone with Stone's power, but they could make it more difficult to find them.

But why would Izzy be actively trying to prevent her own people from finding her? If she didn't want that to be possible, she could have refused to provide the blood sample.

"Dr. Stone—?" Heidi's voice sounded strained.

Stone wrenched himself from his speculations. The tendril was still there, pointing vaguely to the east, but it still hadn't chosen a definitive direction. He got the impression it was trying hard, but something was impeding its progress.

Heidi's hands tightened harder on his. At first, he thought she might be signaling that she wanted to take over the ritual, but her palms were bathed in sweat, and her grasp was more a desperate jerk than a confident hold.

He swallowed hard, trying to stave off the nausea. "Heidi?" He squeezed back, trying to convey that he was there and ready to help, but she didn't even seem to notice him anymore. Her eyes were shut, her teeth gritted, and her face pale and blotchy. Sweat poured down from her forehead and dripped off her nose.

Stone didn't want to stop the ritual, but something was clearly wrong. "Heidi!" he called, louder this time, and squeezed her hands three times. "We've got to stop this. Something's—"

She moaned, her body going rigid and arcing backward, her neck jerking so her face was pointed toward the ceiling. The only thing that stopped her from going over all the way and crashing into the circle's boundary was Stone's hold on her hands.

"Heidi!" Lightning-fast, he considered options. If he broke their grip without making proper preparations, it would create a jolt of psychic feedback that would probably give them both headaches for hours. But, joined as he was with Heidi in the ritual, he could sense her body's rhythms—her heartbeat, the rise and fall of her lungs, even the flow of blood through her veins—and something was definitely wrong. Her system was rebelling against whatever was happening with the tendril. It was as if the ritual was fighting back now—

—or as if something on the other end had caught on to what they were doing, and was tracing it back to them.

But that shouldn't be possible!

That was what the circle was for—to keep them safe and prevent anything from doing just that.

All chance for more speculation departed, though, as two things happened: Heidi screamed, her heartbeat spiking up and up further until it seemed as if her heart might explode, and Stone's chest lit up like someone had just lashed him with a burning whip. His hands closed around hers in an involuntary death grip as his head exploded with white-hot agony.

If he screamed too, he didn't remember it.

CHAPTER FIVE

THE GLOW AHEAD came in conjunction with a cooling of the air, and the wind. It had been subtle at first; Aldwyn had been so focused on watching for the patches of bad magic he hadn't noticed the gradual lowering of the temperature. But there was no mistaking the fact that the currents had changed, the air around him becoming less like a blast furnace and more like a pleasant, slightly chilly breeze.

Ahead, still several miles away, his sharp eyes picked out the rough edges of a coastline. Beyond it, a gray body of water stretched as far as he could make out on both sides before fog obscured it. Strong, choppy waves pounded the coast. Probably a sea—with as much as he could view from this height, it would have to be a truly massive lake if he couldn't find the other side.

It took him a moment to notice that the strange magical fluctuations in the air had faded. He could still spot traces of them when he wheeled around to look behind him, but the closer he flew to the coast, the weaker they grew.

Interesting.

Large bodies of moving water had always had a cleansing effect on magic—nothing a skilled practitioner couldn't overcome, and certainly nothing to even slightly inconvenience a dragon, but perhaps there was some stronger correlation between the dangerous, chaotic magic on this plane and the water.

He swung around to head back toward the coast, still luxuriating in the strength of his body, the power in his widespread wings, and the magic that coursed through him like the blood that kept him alive. He couldn't put into words how *good* it felt to be back in his proper form again. It would be hard to return to Earth now—like folding himself up to stuff himself back into a tiny, confining prison. He'd have to do it eventually, but it didn't have to be soon. Even if there weren't any other sentient beings here, nothing prevented him from stretching his wings, as it were, for as long as he liked.

Well, except that he'd need to eat soon. His body was already reminding him again that he couldn't remain in this form much longer without finding something to sustain him. He yearned to sink his teeth into some herd creature, feeling the hot blood spurting into his mouth, swallowing massive chunks of flesh and muscle, bringing strength back to his body.

But there didn't seem to be any herd animals around here, which meant if he was to remain, he'd have to switch forms soon. He had never studied this aspect of the magic he and the rest of the dragons employed, but they all knew how it worked: human forms required human-sized amounts of food, while dragon forms needed much, much more.

He had begun gliding back and forth, trying to spot something that might make a good meal, when something else caught his eye. Far in the distance to his left as he faced the sea, a collection of structures appeared that looked far too regular to be more jagged rocks.

Could that be a settlement of some kind? Was this godsforsaken place inhabited after all?

Instinctively, he summoned magic to fade him to invisibility. If someone *was* out there, he wanted to get a look at them before he revealed himself. He doubted any other dragons called this blighted land home, and he didn't want to be the first one the residents saw.

Banking, he beat his wings a couple times to get altitude, then glided silently toward the structures. It didn't take long before they came into better view, and he was pleased to see he'd been right: they *were* made by sentient beings. From the look of things, the settlement was quite large, sprawling along the coast. Aldwyn circled a couple of times, taking in the area. For a moment, he thought it odd that the outer edges of the settlement, closest to the interior part of the continent, looked to be in far worse shape than the parts nearest the sea—in fact, magical sight revealed them to be almost abandoned, with only a few telltale, flickering glows of auras moving furtively around them. From this high up he couldn't make out the inhabitants' forms, but their auras looked similar to those of the humans back on Earth.

A bit of thought suggested a hypothesis, though: whatever existed in the central part of the continent—the black-winged creatures, the strange magical fluctuations, and the chaotic magic—would be deadly to these smaller beings. Perhaps the ruins surrounding the city were a sort of buffer zone, where the residents had withdrawn closer to the sea to guard themselves as much as possible against the encroaching danger. That would be doubly true if the people here didn't have magic. Some of what Aldwyn had found had threatened *him,* and in his true form. Human-like creatures without magic wouldn't have a chance against them.

He decided he'd best investigate this place before he returned to Earth, even if it *did* mean shifting back to a human form. The idea repulsed him, but he couldn't very well swoop down there in his natural body.

Not until he figured out what was going on, anyway. If the residents were primitive enough, perhaps they might serve him as snacks until he found something larger to eat.

He had angled himself downward and was preparing to land on the outskirts of the town when something unexpected twinged at the edge of his senses.

Magic.

Strong magic—but not twisted or chaotic this time.

He tensed, whipping his gaze back and forth. Had something spotted him, and was coming out to investigate? Had he missed something invisible approaching him?

He didn't see it until he happened to glance up while searching for the black-winged creatures from before. What he saw nearly stopped him in midair.

A winged creature as large as a dragon shouldn't be able to hover, but dragons did not fly by wing-power alone. A bolt of tense excitement rocketed through Aldwyn's body, and without thought he summoned the magic to hold him steady in the air while he took a closer look at what he'd seen.

It was a city.

A floating city.

It drifted serenely above the town, nearly lost in the thick clouds perhaps a mile up. It was no wonder Aldwyn hadn't seen it right away; if he'd been looking only with normal vision, the clouds would have effectively obscured it.

But the level of magic it was putting out was impossible to miss.

Aldwyn continued to stare at it, fascinated. It was much smaller than the city below it, concentrated into a series of tall, soaring towers. He couldn't make out any detail because of the clouds, but it appeared as if the towers extended upward from an almost equally large base below—as if a giant had uprooted the whole thing from the ground below and cast it up into the sky.

What was going on here? *Why* was this place here? Did it have some connection to the city on the ground? It seemed impossible that it didn't, since the two were clearly in close proximity to each other. Did the people below know about it? Did they travel back and forth between the two? Were there more of them around?

So many questions, and he wasn't going to get any answers without closer investigation.

His stomach rumbled again, deep and urgent. Regardless of what he decided to do, he couldn't stay up here much longer. Normally, a good feeding lasted a dragon much longer than the same relative amount of food sustained a human, but it had been centuries since his draconic stomach had been filled.

His only choice was whether to start with the floating city or the ground one. The floating city's tantalizing magic and mysterious towers held far more temptation, but Aldwyn had never been one to give in to temptation over intellect. The ground city, comparatively dull as it might be, probably held more and safer answers. It was *unlikely* that anyone or anything here could challenge a dragon's power, but best not to take chances until he had more data.

Invisibility spell still active, he circled down and landed just outside the edge of the ruins. With a wrench of reluctance, he paused to savor a last moment in his rightful form. A flick of magic was all it took to shrink him back to his accustomed human guise, slamming down a gate over a significant part of his senses. After all these years, he'd forgotten what it felt like to change from dragon to human—it was as if someone had thrown a thick bag over his head that he could barely see, hear, or smell through. How did humans manage to get anything *done* with such limited senses?

Curling his lip in disgust, he switched from true invisibility to a lesser version that would allow others to see him but ignore him as unimportant. That would serve him until he could see what the creatures here looked like, then he could craft a better disguise.

At least he wasn't hungry anymore.

He set off walking toward the main part of the city, moving with a quick, confident stride. He could have remained invisible and floated through, but he wanted to see this place as its residents did. The more information he had, the more effectively he could use it.

The buildings here were almost all ruined, few intact even to a single story. They were made of wood and stone, with little metal or other advanced building materials in evidence. The road Aldwyn followed looked as if it might have been cobblestone at one point, but now potholes, chunks of rock, and overgrown vegetation obscured most of it. The air smelled of smoke, the sea, and the faint whiff of far-off dead things.

He kept walking, swiveling his head to look for any signs of auras. He spotted a few—small animals, mostly—but they quickly ducked away as if they'd noticed him watching them. He supposed it made sense for anything that lived around here to be wary, if it wanted to survive long.

The closer he got to the main town, the better overall condition the buildings were in. Still nothing above a single story, though, and it was obvious the residents had long since scavenged anything valuable or useful. To his surprise, though, he did begin occasionally to notice what were clearly the rusted remains of vehicles.

He frowned, pausing to examine one more closely. Everything but the twisted frame had been taken—tires, doors, seats, even the steering wheel off its primitive-looking column—but the thing had unmistakably been a pickup truck at some point in the distant past. From the overall shape, he judged it to be the rough equivalent of 1950s technology back on Earth. In the years since he'd awakened from his two-hundred-year sleep beneath Stone's Surrey house, he'd amassed a collection of rare and valuable specimens of such vehicles, ranging from the early days of their invention through around the 1970s, so the structure wasn't unfamiliar to him.

So he was wrong, then—these people did have quasi-modern technology by Earth standards. Were there more such vehicles in the city proper? Were they powered by magic? He certainly didn't get any sense of magic out here, beyond a faint, lingering feeling of unease. He thought he was probably right about this area being a buffer zone.

He moved away from the old pickup truck and continued forward, following the blasted street. He estimated he was perhaps another half-mile from the town, so he increased his speed a bit.

"Hey, friend!" called a voice from somewhere to his right.

He stopped, catching himself before he spun to attack, and waited.

Someone appeared around the corner of one of the ruined buildings—a man, from the look of his build and clothes—and raised his hand in greeting as he approached.

Aldwyn's innate magic, which allowed him to speak and understand any mundane language by picking up intent and mental impressions from the speaker, automatically translated the man's words. He was of medium height, stocky, with an unkempt beard and shaggy brown hair under a wide-brimmed hat. He had a large, heavy cloth bag slung over one shoulder. Aside from his clothing, which was of a style Aldwyn had never seen before but clearly meant for manual work, he could have been plucked bodily from Earth and placed here.

Odd, indeed.

Behind the man, Aldwyn picked out the forms of another man and a woman, still half-concealed behind the ruins and obviously more cautious than their friend. He didn't answer, but waited for the first man to come closer.

"Hello, friend," the man said. "I don't think I've seen you out here before." He wasn't nervous, exactly, but his aura sparked to indicate wariness. It made sense—strangers around here could be dangerous.

Aldwyn nodded, projecting harmlessness. "I am…new to this area."

The man didn't seem to think that was unusual. "Not much to scavenge here, I'm afraid." he said ruefully, removing his hat to swipe his brow and then replacing it. He indicated the bag. "I found a few metal scraps, but I think we'll need to go out further to find anything good." He looked around behind Aldwyn. "You out here on your own?"

Aldwyn studied him a moment, but there was no ill intent in the man's words, as if he might be planning to take advantage of a lone stranger. "For the moment, yes."

The man frowned. "If you're new to this, take some advice—don't go out too much farther by yourself. There's been an abomination spotted in the area, couple days ago. Prob'ly gone by now, but never worth takin' chances."

Abomination? Aldwyn didn't ask him what he meant, since he didn't want to appear ignorant. He wondered if the black-winged creature he'd encountered previously counted as an "abomination." The word certainly applied.

"Thank you," he said. "I will be careful."

The man eyed him a moment longer, almost as if he sensed something unusual about him, and then waved again. "Be safe, friend. Good scavenging." He hurried off, rejoining his two companions behind the ruin before Aldwyn could reply.

Aldwyn watched them go, waiting until their auras disappeared behind more ruins before resuming his path toward the city proper. He'd considered questioning the man further—perhaps to gain more knowledge about the town he was approaching, such as its name, or its relationship with the magical structure floating in the clouds above it—but there had been no point in drawing further attention to himself. He had time.

It wasn't as if anything here could threaten him, after all. If anyone grew suspicious, it would be easy enough to make them disappear without a trace.

Moving at a steady, confident pace, it took him another twenty minutes to reach what was obviously the edge of the main town. The delineation was evident: a low rock wall separated the blighted area beyond from the relatively more prosperous one on the other side. The wall looked old and weathered, made of scavenged chunks, but obviously purpose-built to mark a boundary. Beyond it, he immediately spotted more auras of various colors moving around.

He climbed over the wall and paused a moment, taking in the town. "Prosperous" was a highly relative term: even on this side, the place still looked as if it had been cobbled together without much organization or plan. The buildings were of better construction, made of wood, stone, and even some metal, but it seemed as if whoever had constructed them had done so without much regard for what was around them. The cobblestone roads were in far better repair than the ones outside the wall, but they still meandered without much aim, crossing each other and snaking away around more buildings.

Clearly, this town didn't have anything resembling a planning commission. Aldwyn wondered if they even had a government.

He'd adjusted his illusionary disguise after the three scavengers had left his sight, so he now wore clothing similar to the bearded man's. He'd skipped the hat, and his beard was neatly trimmed instead of wild, but he figured he could pass as an anonymous workman long enough to enter the town and see if he could make sense of where he was.

He kept walking, heading toward where he imagined the center of town to be, looking around as he went without being too obvious about it. He didn't want to mark himself as a tourist or a stranger until he knew how such people would be received. Maybe there *weren't* any tourists or strangers. He didn't think this place was the only settlement on the continent, but best not to make assumptions.

The town was attractive, in its rough way. Most of the buildings, none over three stories so far, were constructed of dark wood, and abundant trees lined the winding, cobblestone streets. The air beneath a cloud-choked gray sky was damp and drizzly, and the sea-smell was strong.

There weren't sidewalks, *per se,* but most of the buildings had wooden walkways alongside them. Aldwyn mounted one of these and pressed his back against a wall, pausing to observe for a moment before moving on.

Here, closer to the center of the town, the bustle of activity had increased significantly. People—mostly men and women, with a few children, hurried past, most of them ignoring Aldwyn but a few nodding polite greetings as they passed. All were dressed similarly to the scavenger man and Aldwyn's disguise, in rough, simple clothes that showed signs of frequent repair, and sturdy jackets. Even most of the women wore trousers; he only spotted a couple in long skirts made of heavy cloth. Despite the light rain that had begun to fall, nobody had an umbrella, though more than half wore wide-brimmed hats. The styles were different from those on Earth, but Aldwyn placed the general era, once again, at around the middle part of the twentieth century there—the clothes of a working-class population from between the 1930s and the 1950s.

This was all fascinating—as someone who had lived on Earth for many human generations, Aldwyn had developed a scholarly interest in their history and the evolution of things like clothing styles, transportation, and industrial development—but it wasn't getting him the answers he desired. He didn't care about who these people were; he wanted to know *why* they were here, what connection they had with the strange city floating overhead, and what was going on with the blighted area beyond the wall.

He supposed he could simply grab one of the town's citizens, take him somewhere private, and question him until he revealed the information—and he might still do that. He probably *would* still do that. Since he could get back and forth between Earth and wherever this was with ease now, there was no urgency to his need.

It wasn't as if Stone and Harrison had any idea he was here, and even if they did, what could they do about it? What would they *want* to do about it? He wasn't violating the agreement he'd made with them. Just because they pulled their magical energy from this place didn't mean they had ever been here personally, nor knew anything about its denizens. And even if by some insane possibility they did, they still couldn't claim an entire dimension as their legitimate area of interest.

In the street below the walkway, a wagon filled with boxes of fish, drawn by an odd-looking, ox-like animal, rounded a corner and trundled past. A bored-looking man guided the creature with a light touch of his whip, and the boy sitting next to him on the wagon's bench looked sullen, like he'd rather be anywhere else. Behind the wagon, a battered flatbed truck with a large wooden box strapped to it patiently rolled along.

Aldwyn watched with interest. The two vehicles, which would be from wildly different time periods if they were on Earth, seemed to co-exist peacefully with each other here. The truck's driver wasn't honking angrily for the wagon to pull out of its path, and seemed content to wait as long as necessary to continue on his way. Both vehicles looked old and well-used; the truck showed only a few flashes of dull color on a body that was otherwise rust and primer, its tires mismatched and bald. As it passed Aldwyn, its tailpipe emitted a blatting, echoing backfire. Everyone ignored it, even the animal pulling the wagon.

After a moment, the wagon turned a corner and the truck continued past. Aldwyn noticed it didn't increase its speed. Perhaps its slow progress wasn't due to the wagon blocking it, but rather because the driver was afraid to put much load on the elderly tires.

He pushed off the building and joined the stream of people heading closer to the town's center. Without much actual knowledge he got the impression that many of the taller buildings were apartments, while the single- and two-story structures were businesses, perhaps allowing their proprietors to live and work in the same place.

There were a lot of such businesses here. To his surprise, Aldwyn noticed immediately that almost none of the signs outside them bore obvious writing, but rather identified themselves with pictographs; directly ahead of him, he spotted one with the image of something that looked like an odd cow, another with a pair of fish, and a third with a tankard that unmistakably identified it as a bar. How convenient, given that his innate mental translation abilities didn't extend to written communication. Apparently, the population of the town didn't value literacy highly.

Above, the sky flashed as a bolt of lightning lit up the clouds, followed a few seconds later by a rolling peal of thunder. The drizzle in the air changed to a cold, steady rain.

Aldwyn could easily have used a magical shield to keep the rain off, but it would have looked suspicious for him to be strolling down the street, dry and comfortable, when all around him people were pulling up their coat collars, settling their hats lower on their heads, and ducking under overhangs before continuing on their way.

Perhaps this might be a good time to stop sightseeing and finally get some information. One thing he'd learned a long time ago from the humans: one of the best places to do that was a bar.

CHAPTER SIX

S TONE'S HEAD WAS STILL POUNDING.

He stirred, momentarily without any idea where he was, why he was there, or why his body hurt so much.

The surface under him was hard, cold, and unforgiving. The air smelled like oil and diesel and…blood?

His eyes flew open, then he immediately clamped them shut again as the harsh glare of the overhead fluorescents assaulted them. More carefully this time, he turned his head away from the lights and tried again.

The first thing he saw were the blasted remains of crystals, along with twisted, melted candles.

Something inside his head stirred, bringing with it another wave of pain.

Right. The ritual.

Something had gone wrong.

He jerked his head up, which was a big mistake, but he ignored the thudding pain.

Heidi.

What had happened to—

Oh, dear gods.

The agent lay splayed on the other side of the circle, half-in and half-out. She was face-up, her wide-open eyes staring up at nothing, her arms flung wide where she'd obviously fallen over backward and knocked over the candles and crystals nearest where she'd sat.

Drying blood ran from her nostrils, her ears, and her mouth, pooling beneath her neck and soaking her dark hair.

No, no, no…

Heedless of the debris he was knocking aside, Stone scrambled across the floor to Heidi's still body. It was obvious even without magical sight that she was dead, but he checked anyway. There was no sign of an aura. He didn't know how long he'd been unconscious, but at this point there was nothing he could do.

Nothing anybody could do.

He pulled his phone from his pocket and checked the time. They'd started the ritual at a little after one p.m., and it was almost two now. He'd been out about half an hour.

For a moment, he could do nothing but sit there on his knees, looking down at Heidi. His body still hurt, his head still felt like someone was performing a drum solo on it, and the dampness on his upper lip told him he'd probably had a nosebleed, but he barely noticed any of those things. His mind whirled, unable to settle on a thought save one.

She's dead. She's dead. She's dead. The words repeated on the same beat as the thumping in his head.

How could she be dead?

Tracking rituals didn't kill people.

If one went terribly wrong it might knock someone out for a while, but they didn't kill people.

His chest twinged again—a hard, sharp little pain, not strong but definitely there.

He frowned. That was odd. The headache made sense. The body aches from lying on the cold concrete floor for half an hour and the nosebleed from magical overload made sense. But why would his chest be twinging? It almost felt like—

With a shaking hand and a growing sense of dread, he lifted his T-shirt and looked down at his chest.

The slash there, the one that ran from the lower right side of his abdomen to the upper left side of his chest, had healed by now, leaving a thin, pale scar that was only noticeable if someone stood close to him. Now, though, a faint, angry red outlined it from top to bottom. It appeared already to be fading, but it was definitely there.

"Oh, gods..." Stone murmured, reaching up to touch it with one trembling finger.

That scar had been inflicted by an ancient and incredibly powerful magical artifact—a knife that had contained the spirit of a demon from the dawn of time. Madame Huan had told him the scar might contain some residual demonic energy, and when he had shown it to Grace Diaz, she'd told him she wouldn't heal it—not because she couldn't, but because she believed she *shouldn't*.

The twinge was already fading, unlike the rest of his pain.

Was it possible...? If the scar was hurting now, was it trying to tell him—

He let the front of his shirt fall back into place, his shoulders slumping.

He should have known. It made sense now. It had to happen—it was inevitable.

There were eleven demons out there, left over from the abortive summoning of the one called The Unspeakable. If everything had gone according to plan, they, along with the twelfth one whose summoning Stone had prevented, would have been consumed in the ritual to bring The Unspeakable over into this world. That hadn't happened—thank the gods—but that meant the remaining eleven demons were still here. They had been quiet so far, so Stone hadn't expended much energy on trying to track any of them down, but they were out there.

And now, he was very much afraid at least one of them was finally making itself known.

He stared down at Heidi's lifeless form, and this time the twinge he felt wasn't pain, but regret. He'd known her for only a few hours, but he'd liked her. She was a good mage, a good agent, and her no-nonsense demeanor had been refreshing.

And now she was dead, and he knew what he had to do next, even though he'd rather do almost anything else.

He picked up his phone from where it had slipped out of his hand. It was one of his burners, the ones he used when he went places he wasn't supposed to be able to get to as fast as he did, so he hadn't entered any contacts into it. With a numb finger he tapped in a number he'd long ago memorized.

"Please answer..." he whispered. Even though he didn't want to have to give her the terrible news, it would be worse if he had to wait.

She picked up on the second ring. "Huxley." Same brisk voice as usual.

"It's...Stone." His tone came out colorless.

"Stone?" Something changed—grew sharper, more focused. "Where are you? You were going to meet Agent Royer in Detroit to try to track—"

"I'm in Detroit."

She must have picked something up in his voice. "Is something wrong?"

He looked at Heidi again. He should have closed her eyes; she was still staring up at the ceiling as if still following the tendril from the tracking spell. The blood pool under her head shone dark red and terrifyingly real in the overhead light. He tried to speak, but couldn't get the words to come out.

"Stone! Talk to me. What's going on?"

He took a deep, shuddering breath and forced himself to look away from Heidi's face. "She's...gone, Ren."

"Gone? What do you mean? Were you not able to meet up with her? Do I need to—"

"She's dead."

There was a long pause. When Ren spoke again, it was in a careful, precise tone. "Dead."

"Yes." He thought about getting up, but didn't think he could manage it. "I...need help, Ren. I need you to send someone."

Another pause, and breath. "Okay. Stone, I want you to tell me everything. Where are you now?"

He realized he didn't know. Heidi had been driving, and he hadn't been paying attention to street signs. "Some sort of...industrial building. It's where we were doing the ritual." It had been a long time since he'd felt this ineffectual. It was as if any sense of volition he normally possessed had died with Heidi. He couldn't let that continue, though. He needed Ren's people to come here and deal with the situation. "I'm sorry—I haven't got my normal phone, so I can't even check the GPS."

"Is Agent Royer's phone there? Check her bag." Ren had shifted to her efficient "agent" voice, probably because she was as shocked as Stone but somebody had to take charge and he wasn't doing it.

"Hold on..." Stone dragged himself painfully to his feet and staggered over to where Heidi had put her bag. He rummaged in it, acutely uncomfortable at the thought of digging through a dead woman's possessions, and finally located her phone. "I've got it," he said into the burner. "But I don't know her password."

"Stone, I need you to keep it together for me, okay?" A little more kindness now, of the firm variety a teacher uses on a stressed student. "Hold it up to her face."

Of course. *Pull yourself together, Stone.* Annoyed at himself for missing something so simple, he carried Heidi's phone over to her body and knelt next to it. His hand shook as he held the phone over her face, glad now that he hadn't closed her eyes.

He had to move it around a bit before it worked, but after a moment the screen—showing a smiling Heidi with her arm around a large German Shepherd—unlocked. He tapped the GPS to get their location, then snapped a photo of the map and texted it to

Ren, all the while trying not to think about the dead woman lying next to him.

"Okay," Ren said after a moment. "I know where you are. That's one of our regular locations in Detroit. You sit tight, Stone. I'll make some calls and get somebody over there. But can you tell me *anything* about what happened? How did she die? Did someone attack her? Are *you* all right? Is there anything dangerous I need to warn my people about?"

Stone closed his eyes, letting the barrage of questions buffet him, then replayed them and answered in a numb tone. "I'm fine. Nothing dangerous. The ritual…went wrong."

"Wrong? Does that mean you found out Izzy and Jack are dead?"

"We only got through the first one, looking for Izzy. She…might still be alive, but we don't know where she is." He took a deep breath. "Ren…I think at least one demon is involved."

"Demon?" Her voice rose, but then she lowered it again. "Demon?" she repeated. "You mean like those things you dealt with before, with the knife?"

"I think it's one of them, yes. There are still eleven of them around."

"Fuck," she whispered. "Yeah, I know that. So far, nothing's turned up about any of them. You think this is one of those, or a different one?"

"No way to tell." He touched his T-shirt where the scar was. "But I'm fairly sure I'm right." He glanced at Heidi again. Normally dead bodies didn't faze him, even gory ones, but he wasn't used to being around ones that had been alive and talking to him less than an hour ago. "Ren—listen—I need you to send someone. We can talk about this later, but…"

"Yeah," she said gently. "You're right. I'll get somebody over there as soon as I can."

He switched his gaze from the body to the remains of the circle. "Are they…in the know? Do I need to take care of anything before they get here?"

"No, it's fine. They're not part of my agency, but they know about the weird stuff we do. They won't ask any questions. Just stay out of the way and let them do their thing, and call me when you're away from there. Are you going to be okay, Stone?"

"I'll…be fine. This was just a bit of a shock. I've never seen someone die during a routine tracking ritual before."

"Okay. Hang in there. I'll try to make this quick."

It was nearly half an hour later before anyone showed up. Stone had spent it pacing the space, his mind wandering more aimlessly than he would have liked. He didn't want to call any of his friends from here, so there wasn't much else he could do. He'd considered covering Heidi's body with a tarp he found, but decided against it because he was afraid he might contaminate evidence, so after doing his best to wipe away the blood from his nosebleed, he'd settled for staying as far away from the ritual scene as he could manage.

When his burner phone rang, he was seated disconsolately atop the workbench, staring into space. He picked it up with none of his usual animation. "Yes?"

"Agent Huxley sent us, sir," a female voice said. "We're outside. Can you let us in?"

Stone trudged across the space and opened the smaller door next to the roll-up. Two people stood there: a stout white woman and a tall, thin black man, both wearing street clothes. He checked their auras; hers was yellow and his green, both tense but not agitated.

He stepped aside to let them in, and didn't say, "It's about time you got here," even though he wanted to.

The woman flashed a badge and ID in a leather wallet. "We're Agents Sampson and Brawley, from the Detroit branch of the FBI." She looked Stone up and down. "We sometimes work with Huxley's agency, though we don't have much idea about what they do."

Stone nodded. "Yes, well, I'll stay out of your way, then. Let me know if you've got questions." He returned to his spot on the workbench.

He'd have thought the crime scene would be a lot busier, based on the other deaths he'd been involved with. He'd expected a coroner, at least, and perhaps a couple of crime-scene investigators. Instead, Sampson and Brawley drove an unmarked white van in through the roll-up door and parked it behind Heidi's car. After taking many photographs of the scene from all angles, they zipped Heidi's body into a black bag and stowed it in the back of the van. Then they gathered the spent ritual components and the rest of the gear and took them as well. They didn't do anything about the bloodstain on the floor, which seemed odd to Stone but he didn't ask.

They worked efficiently, finishing in less than an hour. While Agent Sampson closed up the van and checked Heidi's car, Agent Brawley walked over to Stone. "Do you need a ride anywhere?"

Stone noticed they hadn't asked him any questions—in fact, they hadn't even asked his name. That seemed odd too. He wondered what branch of the FBI this was, and what kind of agreements and understandings they had with Ren's organization. *I'm going to have to ask her at some point what the bloody thing's called,* he reminded himself. *If it's even got a proper name at all.*

"Er...yes, I suppose I do. I left my car back at the restaurant where we had lunch today." He didn't remember the address, but at least he could give them the name. There was no car, of course, but that was where the ley line was.

"Okay. Sampson will take the van, and I'll drive you back to the restaurant in Agent Royer's car." Brawley tilted his head at him, getting a good look for the first time. "Are you going to be okay, sir? Do you need any help?"

The words barely registered on Stone. "What? Er—no. I'll be all right. Thank you."

He avoided looking at the bloodstain on the floor as he climbed into the passenger seat of Heidi's car. He also tried to avoid remembering their brief interaction at the restaurant and on the way over here. He knew there was no way he could feel guilty about this one—Heidi was as much an expert on tracking rituals as he was, and they'd both done everything right—but regret was another thing. There was nothing he could do about that.

Brawley drove him back to the restaurant and let him out near the entrance. After asking again if Stone needed any help and telling him Ren would be in touch, he drove off. Stone stood there and watched as the taillights receded, then trudged the short distance to the ley line. There wasn't anything else he could do here to be useful, and right now all he wanted was to be back in familiar surroundings as soon as possible. He wasn't looking forward to the conversation with Ren, but at least he could have it with Raider in his lap.

Raider, as it happened, seemed worried about him. As soon as he sat down on his living-room sofa and prepared to call Ren with his proper phone, the cat jumped into his lap. He craned his head forward, sniffed at Stone's T-shirt, and made a soft little growl in the back of his throat.

Stone stroked his head. Could he know? Was he picking up on some tiny amount of residual demonic energy from the ritual? He shifted to magical sight, and Raider instantly morphed into his Changeling form, the size of a large dog. His eyes, normally green, glowed a faint purple-blue as he continued to nuzzle at Stone's chest.

"Come on, mate," Stone said with a weak chuckle. "Everything's fine." He was fairly certain that wasn't the case at all, but Raider's presence *was* calming him. Something about his deep, rumbling purr did the trick every time.

Ren answered on the first ring this time, as if she'd been awaiting his call. "Hey, Stone. You okay?"

Everybody kept asking him that, but he supposed it made sense. Even powerful mages weren't immune to watching their allies die right in front of them—not if they still retained any humanity, anyway. "I'm…getting there," he said, suddenly tired. "I'm sorry, Ren. I don't think there was anything I could have done to stop that, but—"

"Enough of that," she said briskly. "I know it wasn't your fault. Royer was a good agent and she knew what she was doing. It sucks, but this isn't exactly a safe job. Let's just make sure her death wasn't in vain, okay? Tell me everything you remember."

He leaned back against the cushions, letting Raider drape himself across him, and described everything he remembered from the initial meeting at the restaurant to when he'd awakened and found Heidi dead.

"You two did a tracking ritual together? I didn't think that was possible."

"It is, but it's not well known. Some friends and I worked out a way to do it. Your people will probably find some notes among Agent Royer's effects—I showed her how to do it."

There was a long pause. When she spoke again, it was with more care. "I hate to ask this, but do you think something went wrong with that? Like, maybe she didn't know enough about how to do it?"

"No," Stone said instantly. "That wasn't it, I'm certain of it. The ritual was going fine—well, not fine, because it still wasn't giving us a definitive result. But nothing that should have been dangerous."

"Do you have any idea what *did* happen, then? You said you thought one or more of those demons might be involved."

"I'm certain of it. I don't know exactly what happened, but if I had to make an educated guess, it would be that the demon figured out we were trying to find Izzy, and sent something nasty back through the connection."

Another silence crackled on the line. "Why do you think it killed Royer, but not you?"

There are a lot of answers to that question, he thought, but all he said was, "Again, this is a guess, but either the demon targeted her specifically because it might have recognized her from her previous ritual, or else my natural shields are just stronger than hers. I'm not sure we'll ever know, at least not until we find the demon and deal with it."

"We. Does that mean you're still going to help us out with this? You said you thought Izzy might still be alive. Is that thing holding her and Jack prisoner somewhere?"

"It's possible. It might be trying to drain magical energy from them. Mages are...well...*tastier* in that regard than mundanes."

"So we might be able to find them?"

"Possibly. You said you knew where these—what was that Changeling gang called again?" It was something stupid, but he couldn't remember it.

"The SickBoyz."

He was right: something stupid. "Yes, them. You said you know where their territory is, right?"

"Yeah."

"Well, odds are good that's where we'll find our demon, then."

"Stone—" Her voice took on a warning tone. "You're not pro-posing to just—what—*walk* into the middle of a gang hot zone and say, 'Pardon me, good sirs, but I think you've got a demon here, and I'd like to have a spot of tea and a chat with it,' are you?" She affected a plummy British accent for the quote.

Stone was too tired to be offended. Instead, he sighed. "Not in so many words. But if there's a chance your agent's there—that *both* of them are there—we've got to do something. But before I do that, I'm going to have a chat—no tea, probably something stronger—with a few friends. If I do go in, I don't want it to be without the best intelligence I can get. And not alone."

"Well, at least you've got some sense, so thank God for small favors. I'll send you everything I've got about the SickBoyz, but it's not much."

"Have you hired any Changeling agents since we last spoke about it?"

"Unfortunately not. We've got some feelers out, but most Changelings don't trust authority too much."

"Right, then. I'll consult Gina. There's no way I'll get her out of her chair and into the field, but she's better utilized behind her computer screen. I'll ask her to give you a call so you two can compare notes. But for now, if you'll excuse me, it's been quite a bad day. I know we've got to get on with this as soon as possible, but I've got to have a shower, a stiff drink, and a bit of time to decompress."

"Go," she said, back to her tough-love motherly tone. "I'll call you if anything else comes up. But please—don't take too long. If Izzy and Jack are still alive, I want them back."

"I get it," he said softly. "Believe me, I do. And please give my condolences to Agent Royer's family."

"I would, if she had one. Far as I know, it was just her and her big goofy dog."

Stone hung up, suddenly and inexplicably sad at the thought of Heidi's dog waiting patiently for her, not knowing she'd never be coming home.

CHAPTER SEVEN

A FTER HIS LONG SHOWER, Stone discovered he didn't need to rest after all. In fact, he didn't think it would be *possible* for him to rest. Instead of a stiff drink, he settled for a Guinness and half a sandwich, and then he called Jason's agency.

"Hey, Al," Jason said. "Are you back from Detroit already? Did you find anything?"

"That's…not an easy answer. How's your case going?"

"Oh—yeah. Believe it or not, things actually went our way this time. We were hunting for a guy who'd skipped out on a business deal with a couple hundred thousand in company funds. I thought we'd have to send Amber to sniff him out, but Gina tracked his digital trail and we nailed him at the airport, getting ready to take a plane to Mexico. We even recovered the money before he was able to transfer it somewhere nobody would ever see it again. So, case closed, at least a day before I expected."

"Brilliant. You really should give Gina a raise, you know."

"Already did, just a couple months ago. But she'll get a bonus for this. The client was thrilled."

"Glad to hear it. Do you mind if I come by? Is Amber there?"

"Nah, she's home with the kids right now."

Stone glanced at his watch. It was already after three. "Do you think you could both come by my place for dinner tonight? I've got some things I want to discuss with you two and Verity."

"This is about the Detroit case?"

"Yes."

There was a pause. "I can't speak for Amber, but I'll give her a call and see if she can get Sarah to come over and watch the kids." He chuckled. "You know, life would be a lot easier if you could build one of those dedicated portals between our place and Amber's family's place in Tahoe. You know, like V has at her shop. That way, if we need to take off in a hurry, we could just take the kids there in a few minutes. Between her three brothers, their wives, and their kids, they practically fight over who gets to have them visit."

Stone rubbed his chin. "You know, that's not a half-bad idea. Those are a lot easier—and less expensive—to build than normal portals. I'll have a chat with Ian and Gabriel about it when they turn up—or maybe Harrison. For now, though, I suppose I could come to your place if you prefer."

"It might be easier," he admitted. "Especially if you want both of us there."

"Right, then. I'll contact Verity and ask her to come too."

"Al, is everything okay? Did you go to Detroit today?"

"I did. And no, everything isn't okay. I'll give you the details when I get there."

Verity wasn't busy that evening, so she immediately agreed to attend the meeting. She took the private portal to the Sunnyvale shop, where Stone met her in his car so they could drive together.

They made it a few miles up Highway 17 in silence, except for the muted sounds of Pink Floyd through the speakers, before Verity glanced over toward Stone. "You okay?"

"Not really." He kept his gaze fixed on the road ahead.

"Something went wrong in Detroit, didn't it?"

"It did." As hard as he tried, he couldn't erase the vision of Heidi lying there in the pool of blood, her wide-open eyes staring unseeingly up at the ceiling.

She gripped his arm gently. "Do you want to talk about it?"

"I do, but only once. Let's wait until we get there so I don't have to repeat myself." He shot a quick look at her and with effort dragged his thoughts away from the events of the morning. "I haven't seen you in a while," he said with obviously false briskness. "What have you been up to?"

"Crazy busy." She went along with his change of topic even though she obviously didn't want to. "Running the shops takes a lot of work even with Hezzie and Bianca there, plus Hez and I have been working with that little magical hospital in San Francisco where we took you after the demon attacked you." Her voice took on a little more animation. "They've given Sybil's Apothecary a standing contract to produce various alchemical concoctions they use in their treatments. It's turning out to be pretty lucrative for us."

"Brilliant." His smile this time was genuine. He never ceased to be proud of how successful his former apprentice had become. "Are you still working with Scuro?"

"Yes, but not as often anymore. I just don't have the *time.* He calls me in for the really big jobs like yours, but I found him another healer for the smaller ones now."

Stone's hands tightened almost unconsciously on the steering wheel at the thought of his tattoo—now his *former* tattoo. He realized he'd never told Verity, or anybody else, about what had happened to it when the same artifact blade that had given him the scar on his chest had cut through the tattoo and essentially burned it out. The magical pigments had drained from it, leaving him with another, even fainter scar. Only a few people knew about it, as far as he was aware: Gabriel, who'd seen it when he was injured, and Grace Diaz and Jason during the quick visit to Mexico to return the broken pieces of Grace's sword. Stone thought Jason would have mentioned it to Verity, but apparently he hadn't.

Verity, as usual, was perceptive. "Something wrong?"

"Talking about Scuro reminded me of something. I take it Jason didn't mention what happened to my tattoo."

"What? No. Did something happen to it?"

"It's gone."

"Gone?" Shock filled her voice, and when he glanced sideways at her again, it was mirrored on her face. "What do you mean, gone?"

"I can't explain it all. Let's just say when somebody sliced through it with The Unspeakable's knife, aside from leaving a scar, it…drained the ink and the power out of the tattoo. All that's left now is a tiny trace you can barely see."

There was a long silence from the other side of the car. "Wow. And Jason knew about this?"

"I thought he might, but it's been years since he's seen it and I usually kept it hidden, so maybe he forgot. Grace wanted to look at the knife wound, so if he did remember, there wasn't any way he could have missed it." He tried for the forced briskness again. "It doesn't matter, I suppose. It's not like I need it anymore."

"Still…"

Yes…still. A sudden memory returned of how she used to enjoy playing with it when they were together. To his surprise, the thought didn't bring the usual twinge of almost-regret, the second-guessing about whether the two of them had done the right thing by ending their relationship all those years ago. All he felt now was his usual warm affection for her, but it was affection for a dear friend, not a lover.

That thought brought back the image of Thalassa Nera, and he shivered. He had no idea when—or even if—she was going to contact him, but now he hoped it wouldn't be any time soon. Mixing that kind of relationship with whatever he'd have to do to deal with the demon in Detroit was probably a very bad idea.

Fortunately, they were getting close to Jason and Amber's place now, so he didn't have to continue this increasingly uncomfortable conversation. He turned onto the smaller road that wound up toward the house and fell silent, hoping she'd get the hint.

She did, though in his peripheral vision he still caught her shooting him a couple of searching looks. He ignored them and pulled up in front of the house.

Amber opened the door before they'd made it halfway up the walk. "Hey. Thanks for coming all the way out here. It really does make things easier." Jaden, her and Jason's two-year-old son, stood behind her, peering at them around her legs.

"Not a problem. Hello, Jaden." Stone shifted to magical sight, causing Jaden's chubby toddler form to morph into something that looked halfway between a shaggy gray bipedal wolf and a dog. The boy's Changeling manifestation brought Heidi back to mind as he wondered again what would happen to her dog. He shifted back quickly, hoping to dispel the thought, and instead cast a significant look first at Jaden, then at Amber. He hoped he got his wordless point across: *this isn't going to be a discussion for little ears.*

She was as perceptive as ever. "Don't worry—the kids have already eaten, and we're putting them to bed. They just wanted to say hello to you two before they went."

"Unca Alicer!" shrieked a voice from behind Amber. A small, fast form rocketed down the hall and flung her arms around Stone's legs, nearly knocking him over. "Auntie Verity!"

Verity grinned, putting a hand out to steady Stone. "Hi, kiddo."

As quickly as she'd glommed onto Stone, four-year-old Alice pulled free and repeated the gesture with Verity. "Hi! You gotta see! Fletcher gots a friend now! Her name is Agatha and she's a *stegosaurus!*" She wore pink and green footie pajamas with dinosaurs on them, and looked like she was fresh from her bath.

"Come on, Alice." Jason appeared behind them, looking stern but amused. "I told you you could say hello to Uncle Alastair and Auntie Verity, but that's all. They're not here to play tonight."

"I wanna *story!*" she protested as her father pried her loose from Verity and picked her up. "Unca Alicer tells the best stories!"

"Not tonight," Amber said in a no-nonsense, mama-bear voice. "Come on, you two. Off to bed. Now." She bent to swing Jaden into her arms, then shot a look over her shoulder at Stone and Verity. "Go ahead and sit down at the table. Everything's ready to go. We'll be back in a few minutes."

It was considerably longer than a few minutes before they returned. Stone and Verity sat at the table, exchanging amused looks as various protesting shrieks and wails came from down the hall. Stone thought about Thalassa again, and wondered what kind of mother she would be. Knowing her cold, imperious ways, she'd probably be more likely to farm the child off on nannies and tutors than Stone would.

"Okay," Jason said, swiping a hand across his forehead as he and Amber came in. Both of them looked a bit frazzled, but also energized. It was obvious to anyone with an ounce of perceptiveness that they loved being parents. "Gremlins have been corralled, and dinner's served."

Amber had put together some kind of tasty, spiced meat stew that smelled delicious. After they all had bowls and glasses of the red wine Stone had brought, Jason said, "Okay, Al. What's going on? You said something went wrong in Detroit."

Stone's mouthful of stew suddenly turned to a cold lump. He swallowed hard. "Yes. The tracking ritual went…unexpectedly. The agent I was doing it with…was killed." He looked away, unable to face Jason's clear gaze.

"Killed?" Verity asked in shock. "Wait a minute. You don't die from tracking rituals."

"You do when demons are involved."

Three pairs of wide, fearful eyes locked on him.

"Demons?" Jason asked. "You don't mean—"

"I mean at least one of the eleven that were summoned as part of the Unspeakable's ritual, yes." Speaking quickly and forcing himself to keep the emotion out of his voice, he told them the rest of what had happened earlier in the day.

They listened in silence, their astonishment growing. When he finished, they all looked at each other. Nobody had taken a bite of stew during the entire story.

"So..." Verity said carefully, "You're saying you think the demon traced you two back through the spell and...killed Heidi?"

"That's my best guess, yes. I don't know why it hit her so much harder than me, but I've got a couple of theories. Either my shields are a lot stronger than hers were—which is almost certainly true—or else it recognized her from her previous attempt and was waiting for her to try again."

"Do you think it knows about *you* now?" Jason asked.

Stone shrugged. "Not a clue. But I *am* planning to go back there and see if I can track it down. Especially since I think at least one of the agents we were looking for is still alive."

Amber frowned. "Do you think she's *still* alive, even after you two found her? Why wouldn't the demon just kill her? Obviously it has no problems with killing people."

"That's true," Stone said. "But that's not *all* they do. Demons need life energy—soul energy, in their reckoning—to power themselves on this plane. If they want to stay here permanently, they need enough soul energy so they don't have to maintain a pool of power on their own home dimensions." A sudden thought occurred to him. "This lot might need the soul energy more than usual."

"Why is that?" Jason resumed eating; even horrific news like this didn't often affect his appetite for long.

"Because they were brought here by The Unspeakable to use as sacrifices for the ritual to bring it over. They didn't come voluntarily, and they were never meant to be around long. All demons maintain a connection to their home plane unless they gain enough power to sever it—or somebody else severs it—but if they were brought here against their will, they probably didn't have time to fill it with much power."

"So you're saying that these demons need to gather a lot of soul energy in order to power themselves," Verity said, looking grim. "That's probably why they haven't been doing much in the past couple months—because they're busy gathering power."

Stone pointed at her with a *right* gesture. "Yes. I mean, obviously they got here with some power, since they were able to create those beasties that attacked me, and Crazy Charlie was causing quite a bit of havoc in Denver. But that won't last unless they supplement it."

"Okay," Amber said. "So that's why you think the woman you two located with your ritual might still be alive. And the man too?"

"No idea. Possibly. It doesn't make sense for the demon to kill them before he's drained enough power out of them, and mages are a lot more desirable for that sort of thing than mundanes. Think of soul energy as human life energy, and magical power as…" He pointed at his half-eaten bowl of stew. "Tasty spices. Mages don't have more life energy than mundane humans, but they do have much more *interesting* energy. Sort of like the difference between a slab of raw meat and a gourmet-prepared steak."

"I don't know whether I've just been insulted," Jason growled, but he obviously wasn't serious.

Stone was barely listening, because another thought had just occurred to him. "I wonder… There are eleven of these demons on Earth, assuming none of them have decided to pop home. They're of varying strength and intelligence levels, but all of them are seeking the same kind of power. I wonder if they're not playing a sort of game with each other."

"Game?" Verity narrowed her eyes. "What kind of game?"

"Chicken, in a way. This is just speculation, and I need to ask my knowledgeable sources about it, but I'm told demons don't usually get on well with each other. That means they've probably all staked out their own individual territories and are busy consolidating power, and I'm wondering if they're all trying to do that as long as possible before making a move."

"I think I see what you mean," Amber said. "The first one that starts making obvious moves might gain some advantage in the short term, but it will lose some too, because the others will end up with more power."

Again, Stone shrugged. "It's just a thought—but it makes sense. It also means that our demon in Detroit is almost certainly one of the weaker ones."

"Why do you say that?" Jason finished his bowl of stew and swiped his roll across the bottom to gather the last of it before dishing up another.

"Because the weak ones have lousy impulse control," Verity said. "Right? You said before that the first two or three probably weren't much more than demon thugs—strong and nasty and hard to take down, but no magic power to speak of."

"Exactly." Stone was pleased he didn't have to explain everything.

"And what does that mean?" Amber asked. "You're going back to Detroit to…what? Try to track it down?"

"It shouldn't be that hard, now that we know what we're looking for. If it's taken over a Changeling gang that could make things a bit more problematic, but it's not like we're dealing with heavy-duty magic."

"I'm in," Jason said immediately. "I can call Gina and have her do some more investigation, and you can find out any last-minute stuff from Ren."

"I'm in too," Amber said. "You'll have to give me time to take the kids to Tahoe, though. I can do it in less than a day."

"Me too, of course," Verity added. "I assume you're not going to try another tracking ritual, since you don't want to risk alerting the demon."

As always, Stone was touched by their loyalty. They all knew how dangerous these demons could be, even the weaker ones, but yet they instantly volunteered to go along. "I wish I could," he admitted. "We've still got two more blood samples on each of the agents. But I think our best bet will be to find out as much as possible about these…SickBoyz." He couldn't help it, he felt stupid even uttering such an insipid name. "If we know how and where they operate, we might have a chance of working out where they might be keeping the agents. We—"

His phone buzzed in his pocket. He held up a "hold on" finger and pulled it out. When he saw the name on the display, he tensed.

"It's Ren," he said, and then hit the button. "Stone."

"Hey, Stone." She sounded exhausted.

He gripped the phone tighter. "I'm here with Jason, Verity, and Amber. They're going to help with the Detroit situation. I've just finished telling them what happened today. Mind if I put you on speaker?"

"Fine." If anything, the despairing exhaustion worsened. She sounded as if she'd been awake for days.

Stone tapped the button and slid the phone to the middle of the table. "All right, we're all here. What's happened?"

"They found Jack."

From her tone, it was obvious the news wasn't good. "Dead?" he asked gently.

"Yeah."

"Where?"

"Now, that's an interesting question." Now there was bitterness, too. "His head was in the freezer at the restaurant you two were at today. His torso was in the place you did your tracking ritual. We haven't found the rest of him yet."

CHAPTER EIGHT

ALDWYN HADN'T VISITED too many different dimensions; before his and his fellow dragons' exile from their home, he'd been mostly content to remain there. Why wouldn't he? Everything he'd needed had been there: enough magic to power anything he wished to do, lush, beautiful and varied landscapes the likes of which he'd never seen anywhere else, an advanced, innovative civilization replete with beautiful art, literature, and music, and enough room for even the most contentious of his fellows to avoid each other as much as they liked.

But the one thing that had become a constant, at least in his limited view, was that a bar was a bar. Every civilization he'd ever visited had some form of intoxicating liquid (or gas, or solid), and every one had places designated for the citizens to get together and enjoy each other's company while indulging in it.

This place was no different. When Aldwyn opened the heavy, dark-wood door, some of the smells that wafted out weren't entirely familiar—the spicy aroma that was probably some kind of liquor was like nothing he'd ever experienced before, for example. But others, like sawdust, damp, unwashed bodies, and smoke—weren't unlike those he might find when entering a dive bar back on Earth. Not that he *did* enter dive bars—if he had to be limited to this tiny, confining form, he preferred his pleasures of a considerably higher class—but you couldn't live on Earth for centuries without picking up all sorts of useful experiences.

Nobody paid him much attention as he entered, partly because his disguise was good, and partly because he still maintained a spell that allowed him to blend into the background. It was probably too early for a crowd, but the place was still half-full, mostly of men dressed similarly to the others Aldwyn had seen.

He chose a table near the back and sat down to observe the place. It was small and intimate, with no windows, dark walls, and a long bar that looked as if it had been put together using various pieces of mismatched scrap wood. One, on the far side, had something painted on it that might have been an actual word rather than a pictograph; in a flash of intuition, Aldwyn wondered if perhaps the wood comprising the bar had come from one or more wrecked ships. The place certainly did seem to have a nautical theme, with nets and floats on the wall, painted murals of boats on rough seas and large, angry-looking fish, and a full-sized harpoon hanging on one wall.

He considered conjuring an illusion of a mug of ale to keep anyone from getting suspicious about why he was sitting here without ordering anything, but his time in dragon form without sustenance had depleted even his human resources enough that he was hungry. He approached the bar and watched long enough to see how these people handled transactions—the currency appeared to be small, metal coins of different colors—then caught the sturdy, wild-bearded bartender's attention and ordered "the special" in both food and drink.

It was a safe bet. Every bar had a "special."

He paid for it with illusionary coins that wouldn't fade until well after they'd been placed in the bar's lockbox, took his mug of ale and basket of something that looked like breaded fish, and carried it back to his table.

The ale wasn't bad. He'd been right—it had been responsible for the spicy aroma he'd noticed upon entering, and had a nice bite to it. The fish was good too, as befitted a town that probably based a good portion of its economy on the sea. He ate and drank slowly, directing his senses outward with a flick of magic so he could eavesdrop on the conversations around him without arousing suspicion.

To his annoyance, he didn't get the name of the town. He supposed it made sense, though—how often did people in a particular town refer to it by name? What he did pick up in the next half-hour, though, were a few other interesting bits of information.

As he'd guessed, many of the people here made their living in the fishing industry. One group of men was talking about their morning's catch, while another discussed working on the docks, and a third making deliveries to the various restaurants around the area. Everyone here was of working class, their conversations rough, earthy, and full of good humor. They mostly spoke of their jobs and their family life. There was little mention of leisure activities, but that made sense too—these people looked like they lived hard lives, and probably didn't have much time for frivolity beyond these trips to the bar.

It wasn't long before Aldwyn began to grow bored. He wasn't fond of most humans on Earth, and these people were similar enough in both appearance and interests that he found them equally uninteresting. What did he care about the dull lives of a bunch of drudges? Perhaps he'd need to find some other place to eavesdrop, or return to his original plan to grab someone and question them.

He was about to get up and leave when he caught an unfamiliar word: "Zaps."

He tilted his head, adjusting the directionality of his listening spell as he took another pull from his ale glass. The word had come from a group of three men, all dressed in the same style of work clothes as most of the other customers. They were leaning in closer to each other, speaking more quietly beneath the louder, raucous conversations of those at the tables close to them.

Almost as if they didn't want to be overheard.

Aldwyn smiled behind his glass. This was more like it. He settled in to listen.

"—Zap came to the warehouse a couple days ago," one of the men was saying, his voice full of disgust. "Poked around like they do, for at least an hour. Damn Zaps should mind their own business."

"Yeah," one of his friends agreed. "You'd think they'd figure out the work would get done better and faster if they didn't stick their high-and-mighty noses into things all the time. It's not like anybody wants 'em around."

The third, a smaller man with shaggy brown hair, glanced around nervously before speaking. "Like they care. Trust me, guys—it's not smart to talk about 'em, even here."

The first man snorted. "Even *they* don't have ears everywhere. Magic isn't that good."

Aldwyn's ears perked up at the mention of magic. He took a thoughtful bite of breaded fish and appeared to be studying the mural on the wall opposite him. Perhaps things would get more interesting here after all.

"You don't know *anything*," the shaggy-haired man said, his voice rising a little with either fear or anger. "They can have *spies* everywhere. Just last week, a couple of 'em came into Bara's packing plant. They said they'd heard Tular had insulted one of 'em at the Full Sail the night before. Not even one they knew, just some random Zap. Tular tried to tell 'em he hadn't—he practically got down on 'is knees and begged 'em to leave 'im alone—but they weren't havin' none of it." He shuddered. "They hit 'im with some spell that had 'im rollin' around on the floor, screamin'…I'm still havin' nightmares about those screams. When they were done, they left 'im there for us to deal with."

The second man swallowed hard. "Dead?"

The third one didn't answer, but the look on his face and the red flares in his aura told the story. "I ain't gonna talk about the Zaps, here or anywhere else. If you're gonna do it, I'm leavin'."

"Okay, okay." The first man didn't sound completely convinced, but he took a big slug of his ale and swiped the back of his hand across his mouth. He leaned back in his chair, resuming his more relaxed posture, and began discussing crew position openings on his fishing boat.

Aldwyn finished his ale and set the glass down, disappointed the men didn't continue talking about the "Zaps." It sounded as if that was their insulting nickname for people who had magical ability. It also sounded like at least some of those people didn't have much regard for their nonmagical counterparts, and that the working people didn't have much respect for them—at least when they weren't around to retaliate.

He glanced around the bar, paying closer attention to auras. Dragons could tell a lot from looking at auras, even when stuck in human form—but they weren't any better than human mages at using them to identify magical power. Even so, he didn't even suspect any of the auras here as belonging to mages; almost all of them were relatively faint and close to their owners' bodies, shot through with various red and dark patches indicating chronic illness, substance abuse, and general depression. Clearly, these people didn't have pleasant lives.

If he wanted to get any useful information without wasting more time in this dreary place, he'd have to be more proactive. He kept his attention focused on the man who'd originally spoken of the "Zaps"—at the rate he was downing ale, he'd have to head to the bathroom soon. Aldwyn planned to intercept him there and ask him a few pointed questions.

However, the man seemed to have a superhuman bladder. Nearly an hour passed, during which time he drank two more ales—he and his two friends, now joined by two more, were taking turns buying rounds for the group—and showed no sign of needing to get up. Neither did any of the others.

Aldwyn sighed softly. He had never been patient, particularly with humans, and he didn't plan to start now. If the man didn't move soon, he would have to come up with a way to *make* him move.

The door opened and three more people entered—two men and a woman, all dressed in similar work clothes to the existing customers. Aldwyn wouldn't have paid them any attention if not for the fact that all three of their auras flared fever-bright with terror.

All around the bar, the others had noticed as well. It was almost as if they possessed some kind of sixth sense, because every one of them, including the bartender, turned to face the newcomers. Everyone ceased their conversations, the whole place seeming to hold its breath.

One of the newcomers closed the door and made sure it was closed before a second, the woman, spoke loudly enough to carry through the room.

"Zaps!" she called, her voice strong but shaking with fear. "Two of them. They're next door now, at the Drubo's Rest. They're looking for somebody. They've already killed Kala and Mord. We slipped out the back before they spotted us."

Behind her, her two companions were scanning the area—one in front of him, one behind. They had the look of men who expected threats to come oozing out of the walls.

Her words had a galvanizing effect on the bar's patrons. Immediately, a buzz of urgent conversation rose as chairs were shoved backward and people headed for the back door, their bodies crushing into each other as they all tried to enter the hallway at once.

The three newcomers, their message discharged, didn't wait around to see what effect it would cause. They opened the front door and disappeared through it before Aldwyn could stop them.

Aldwyn was the only one who hadn't moved. *Hmm. Interesting.* He rose calmly, watching the customers shoving and jostling until they all managed to fit themselves into the hallway. Even the two servers had made themselves scarce.

After a moment, the only two people remaining in the bar were Aldwyn and the bearded bartender. The man eyed his last customer with a mixture of confusion and suspicion. "Ain't you gonna leave?"

Aldwyn wondered why the bartender didn't immediately think he was one of these "Zap spies" the other man had been speaking of, but didn't spare much care about it. "I will leave by the front door, as I entered."

The man's eyes narrowed. "I don't know you, and you talk funny. Get on out. I need to close up."

A little vestigial anger rose at the bartender's disrespect, but Aldwyn let it go. He had more important people to find. He left the bar without reply, closing the door firmly behind him.

"*The Drubo's Rest, next door,*" the woman had called the place. Aldwyn stood in the street for a moment, looking back and forth between the buildings on either side of the place he'd just vacated. He didn't know exactly what a "drubo" was, but his magical translation spell rendered it as some type of herd animal. The translation hadn't been necessary, though, because on the bar's right side stood a two-story building, its lower floor dark and faint light coming from the second. The image in the window identified it as a bakery, obviously closed.

On the left side, however, beyond a dirt lot with a few battered vehicles parked in it, was another structure. The large, brightly-painted sign out front had a stocky, shaggy horned creature on it.

Aldwyn started toward it at a leisurely pace. The street, he noticed, was utterly deserted, with no sign of even a lurking aura behind any of the vehicles.

Word of these "Zaps" got out fast, apparently.

The door to the Drubo's Rest was closed. He paused a moment outside it, then pulled it open and entered, wondering what he would see. Perhaps the Zaps had found what they were looking for and already moved on.

He immediately knew that wasn't the case, though.

The Drubo's Rest was larger than the other bar, and more crowded—but also utterly and completely silent. As Aldwyn stood in the doorway, sweeping his gaze around to take in the scene, it wasn't simply a lack of conversation. No feet shuffled, no music played, no one coughed—he couldn't even hear the sound of breathing.

The middle of the room had been cleared. All the customers—around thirty at a quick glance—stood huddled together, their backs pressed against the walls. All their eyes were on Aldwyn, and their auras billowed bright red with terror.

To his shocked surprise, he realized part of the terror was aimed at him—not *of* him, but *for* him.

It was then that he noticed the two figures that *didn't* have auras. A man and a woman, they lay on the floor in the middle of the room, slumped over each other like a pair of discarded dolls, obviously dead though they didn't have a mark on them.

"Well, well," said a sly voice from the rear doorway. "What have we here? Another little pig who's come join the fun?"

CHAPTER NINE

STONE, VERITY, JASON, AND AMBER made their preparations to return to Detroit the following day.

There hadn't been much else Ren could tell them beyond the shocking news about the discovery of Jack Groszek. They'd managed to keep a lid on the find at the restaurant, mostly because the owner was the one who'd found it before closing, and he had no more interest in the news of a severed head in his freezer getting out to the public than the agency did. The FBI agents had found Jack's torso at the ritual site when they'd gone back to arrange cleanup for the bloodstain.

"Odd that nobody bothered them when they showed up," Ren had said. "Needless to say, they got pretty spooked when they found it—it was right there on the floor next to the bloodstain, still dressed in a T-shirt with Jack's cover's ID tossed on the top. Obviously, whoever put it there wanted us to find it."

"Bloody hell," Stone murmured.

"Yeah." She sighed. "Stone, I don't know what to do. I mean, we can send some people to lean on the SickBoyz and see if they'll give up the demon, but without any proof, it'll be hard to get authorization. Whoever did this was smart enough not to leave any trace evidence behind. And that's not even taking into account how dangerous it will be for our mundane agents. Our mages are all deployed on other cases right now, and it wouldn't be easy to recall them."

"I'll look into it," he told her. "That's why the others are here. They're going to help me. We can go back to Detroit tomorrow, after Amber takes care of having her and Jason's children looked after. We'll have to take the portal, though, so if you could arrange a flight for us, that could speed things up."

"No problem. Just let me know when you'll be there. We can have a driver meet you at the portal and take you to the airport."

The dinner had broken up fairly soon after that, so Stone and Verity could head home to prepare. As they drove back over Highway 17 toward Sunnyvale, Verity leaned against the passenger window and stared moodily out into the darkness.

"All right over there?" Stone asked.

"Just thinking. I've never really dealt with demons before. The only ones I've heard about, you pretty much handled on your own, or with Grace's help." She made a bitter little chuckle. "I guess I hadn't quite internalized how bad they are. I mean—*demons.* Of course they're bad. But to cut somebody up and leave parts of him for his friends to find..." She trailed off.

"I know." He kept his eyes on the twisty road, since deer had been known to dart out in front of traffic here. "It's making a statement, that's certain. First Heidi, and now Jack. It wants us to leave it alone."

"Do you think Izzy's dead too?"

"No idea. I think there's a chance she isn't, but not a great one."

"Why do you say that?"

"On the one hand, she's likely the only mage it's got easy access to, unless it's gone out hunting on its own. I don't know whether Changelings have the same appeal as mages, but I'd guess probably not since they're essentially somewhere between a mundane and wild talent. But on the other, we're clearly dealing with one of the lower demons in the hierarchy that's here, and I'm guessing its impulse control isn't good. Especially since it now knows we're on to it. It might not be aware we know it's a demon, but it's certain to know we've got a line on it now."

"So you think it will up its terror game in hopes of scaring us off."

"It's what I'd do, if I were it."

"Have you got a plan? You said you didn't want to do another tracking ritual. Are you sure? I mean, I'm a lot stronger mage than Heidi probably was, and you did teach Ian and me the trick for augmenting our shields against demons."

"That's true, but I'd still rather not take the chance. I think we've got a better chance of seeing if we can talk to one of these SickBoyz. I'm guessing not all of them are chuffed about having their operation taken over by something big and nasty they can't hope to fight."

"You should talk to Gina. I know she was looking into the Changeling scene in Detroit. Maybe she's found something, or she can focus her concentration." She chuckled. "Give her a call when you get home, actually. I'm pretty sure she doesn't go to bed before three a.m."

Stone took the ley line down to San Jose the following morning to chat with Gina, who'd agreed to drag herself out of bed and get to the agency to meet with him. He, Verity, Jason, and Amber couldn't leave until Amber returned from her early-morning flight to Reno, where the oldest of her three brothers and his wife would meet her and pick up Alice and Jaden, so Stone figured he might as well get something done in the meantime.

He knew the best way to Gina's heart was through her stomach, so he showed up bearing a box of gourmet donuts, along with a steaming mocha for her and a black coffee for him.

She grinned when she spotted them. "I knew there was a reason I liked you, Doc. That, and you probably hated getting up this early as much as I did."

Derik didn't arrive for another hour, and even Jason wasn't here yet, so Gina led Stone back to her cluttered office. By the time she settled in her oversized "command chair" behind her array of monitors and machines, her expression had sobered. "I'm sorry to hear about those agents."

"Yes, so am I. That's why I want to get this taken care of, so we don't lose any others."

She nodded, already tapping away at her computer. "Okay. Sorry I didn't get back to you sooner, but I had to wait for a couple of feelers I put out to come back. The good news is, I think I've got some stuff that will really help you."

Stone leaned forward, hoping she was right. "Brilliant. Go." He sipped his coffee while he listened.

"I don't have any personal friends among the Detroit Changelings, but it turns out I *do* know a guy who knows a guy there. That's who I was waiting to hear back from."

"I suppose it's too much to hope for that he's a member of the SickBoyz."

"Well...yeah. Especially since I'm guessing they're not much in the mood to talk right now, especially to strangers." She finished a donut and grabbed another, then nodded toward the box. "Aren't you having any? Oh, that's right—I keep forgetting you're one of those heathens who doesn't do donuts. That just ain't right, Doc. Everybody loves donuts." She took a breath, dragging herself back on topic. "Anyway, my friend's friend finally got back to me late last night. He doesn't want his normie name revealed, but he's a goblin Changeling who goes by Fingers."

Stone nodded. He hadn't done as much research on Changelings as he probably should, but he'd learned a lot from listening to Gina, who had been a major Changeling advocate since the phenomenon's earliest days. One thing he'd learned was that, while every Changeling was different, some types were more common than others. The "goblin" form was one of these. Goblins were usually small, smart, and perceptive, but tended to be sloppy and a bit lazy in their personal habits. As Gina had once put it, "they're built for comfort, not speed, and they don't give a damn what anybody thinks of them."

Another thing he'd learned was that many Changelings adopted a different name when relating to other Changelings or others in the know, to separate them from any dealings they needed to have with the "normies." These names were either chosen by themselves, or preferably given to them by their friends. "Is this Fingers bloke willing to talk to me?"

"He's scared, and I don't blame him. Something big and nasty is going down in Detroit, and the SickBoyz are right in the middle of it." She frowned, looking thoughtful. "The interesting thing is, though, that Fingers isn't sure they want to be."

"What's that mean?"

"He said his ex-girlfriend was dating one of them, two or three months ago. One night, he showed up at her house, really nervous, and told her he had to leave."

"Leave?"

"Like, leave town. He asked her to go with him, but they hadn't been dating that long and she couldn't afford to just up and leave her job, so she told him no. He told her to be careful and to stay well away from anybody connected with the SickBoyz."

Stone set his coffee aside. "Did he tell her why?"

"Not in so many words. But from what Fingers told me, she got the impression that somebody bad had shown up, muscled in on the gang, and was scaring the crap out the members. Pushing them to do stuff they didn't want to do. That kind of thing."

"She told Fingers this?"

"Yeah. They broke up, but it wasn't nasty. She needed some-body to talk to after her boyfriend left, so she called him."

"What happened to the boyfriend? Did the SickBoyz track him down?"

"Surprisingly, no. But this was really early on, when whatever happened was just starting out. Fingers thinks the guy was able to slip away before the big bad knew about him, and the other Sick-Boyz weren't gonna rat him out. He says they were probably glad at least one of them made it out before the shit hit the fan."

Stone pondered. "Did anyone say exactly what this new arrival wanted the SickBoyz to do that made them uncomfortable?"

"Yeah. That part was more obvious. You have to understand, the SickBoyz are small potatoes as far as Detroit gangs go. They used to be bigger, but when the Changelings started joining up, a lot of the normie members moved on. You know how strange some Changelings can be, even to people who can't see their real forms. Anyway, after that they mostly evolved into providing a safe space for young Changelings to hang with each other. They're not choir-boys, I get that—they're into all kinds of bad stuff like extortion, gambling, theft, drugs, prostitution—but compared to some of the bigger fish, they mostly keep to themselves and defend their own turf. Up until now, most of the other gangs left them alone."

"Why is that? I'll admit I don't know that much about street gangs, but I always thought they were all about trying to expand their territories. Isn't that why they're always getting into fights with each other, and gunning each other down to make statements?"

"Well, yeah. That's true. But remember who we're dealing with here. Changelings aren't mages, but we do have a lot of advantages normies don't have. Especially when the normies don't have a clue what they're dealing with."

"Ah, of course." Stone was annoyed with himself for not catch-ing on, but then again, it *was* at least two hours before he was usually awake and the coffee hadn't kicked in yet. "The Changelings have ways to protect themselves that probably spook the other gangs."

"Exactamundo. If the SickBoyz were trying to expand, the others would probably send more firepower after them. But since they're not, everybody's content to just leave 'em alone. Especially since their territory isn't in a particularly desirable area." She glanced at something on her screen, then looked grimly back at Stone. "But now, they *are* trying to expand. Big-time."

"Because of this newcomer."

"Yeah. Or newcomer*s*. Like Ren said, nobody's ever seen them."

"How can somebody run a gang and terrorize the members if nobody's seen them?"

"Actually, it's more like nobody's seen the same one. Whoever it is looks different every time anybody meets with them. So nobody knows for sure if it's one guy using an illusion, or a bunch of guys, or…something else. And anytime anyone gets in their way or tries to argue with them—whether it's one of the SickBoyz or somebody in one of the gangs they're trying to take over—bad stuff happens. That's where the ripped-off heads and the dangling guts come from. At this point, the SickBoyz with any sense have learned to keep their heads down and their mouths shut, and the other gangs are a lot more nervous about messing with them than they should be."

Stone let his breath out and took another sip of his coffee, which was cooling off now. "That does sound like a demon's MO—especially one that's more brawn than subtlety. Have the SickBoyz made any progress taking over more territory?"

"Yeah. In fact, I just got some new information last night, that Ren will probably tell you when you talk to her. There's another gang that shares a border with them, called the North Side Hustlers. Another small-time organization, mostly drug dealers, maybe like twenty guys with a small turf. Their leader, a dude named Hardass, turned up dead. They found him with his arms pulled off, buck naked, buried in a pile of garbage in a vacant lot with only his ass sticking out." She shook her head, looking at the computer screen instead of Stone. "Word is there was a flag in the SickBoyz' colors poking out of—"

"Yes, yes, I get it. Bloody hell."

"Yeah."

Stone leaned back in his chair, finished his coffee, and levitated the empty cup to the edge of Gina's desk. "Okay. Let's switch gears here for a moment. What can you tell me about the SickBoyz? How many of them are there, what happened to their previous leader, where exactly their territory is, anything you think might be helpful."

Gina consulted her screen. "I've got a file here that I'll send you so you can look it over in detail. Short answer: There are about thirty of them, plus a few hangers-on who aren't full members yet. They're basically the only gang in Detroit who not only doesn't care what race you are, but they take women as full members, too. For Changelings, it doesn't really matter what your normie form looks like. If you're one of them, you're one of them."

"How noble," Stone said dryly.

"Yeah, but like I said, they're not exactly fluffy bunnies. They're as bad as the rest of the gangs as far as what they do, so don't underestimate them if you end up talking to them."

Stone remembered a time before his three-year sleep, when he and Verity had ended up in the middle of a street disturbance between a group of young Changelings and some mundanes. One of them had used some kind of psychoactive saliva to send him on a bad trip, and only Verity's quick thinking had extricated him from the situation. "Trust me, I won't."

"Their leader was a guy named Truck. He's an ogre."

"Was. I take it the demon made short work of him?"

"No, he's actually still around. He was smart—when the new guy showed up and started throwing his weight around, Truck saw which way the wind was blowing and took a demotion. From what I heard from Fingers, he's kind of a liaison between the top guy and the rest of the gang now. He does his best to provide a buffer between his guys and whatever this thing is."

"So he might be the one we need to talk to," Stone mused.

"Hold off on that. I'm working on getting you a meet with one of the other members, but I've got to be careful about it. I don't want to end up getting anybody killed—you *or* them. Even though these guys are basically scum, Changelings or not, I still figure this whole mess isn't really their fault."

"No. I'm not, nor do I want to be, any kind of law enforcement. The police or Ren's agency or whoever else wants to do it can deal with the gang. All I care about it taking down the demon. And getting Izzy back, if she's still alive."

"Working on finding out what I can about that, too, but I have to be even *more* careful so it might take a little longer. Once you guys leave for Detroit, I'll text you anything else I get."

"Thank you, Gina. Your information might end up making the difference."

She beamed. "Aw, shucks, boss. Just doin' my job."

Stone was about to say something else when a door closed out in the front office, and a familiar voice called, "Jason? Gina?"

Gina winced. "Great, the one day Derik decides to show up early. You'd better get out of here, Doc, before he spots you. You know how he likes to gossip."

CHAPTER TEN

STONE, VERITY, JASON, AND AMBER met at Sybil's Apothecary early that afternoon.

"Are the children sorted?" Stone asked Amber as they stood in the portal room preparing to leave for Chicago.

"Yeah. The trip couldn't have been smoother. Jonah and Heather were happy to have them as always, and their kids are excited." She smiled wryly. "They keep trying to convince Jason and me to move our whole operation over to the compound so the kids can all hang out together full-time."

"I'm tryin' to get Al to build a dedicated portal between here and there," Jason said.

Amber narrowed her eyes, her interest obvious. "Is that right? Can you do that, Alastair? It would be expensive, right?"

"I can, and it is—but not as much as you might think. It's on my list. But I warn you, it's fairly far down at this point, so don't hold your breath. Let's get this demon situation handled first."

That sobered everyone. Stone had filled them all in on what Gina had told him, and spent the time while waiting for Amber to return reading over the files she'd given him. He swept his gaze over his friends. "You know I've got to say this, so I don't want to hear anything about it. What we're doing is going to be dangerous. From what Gina tells me, the area where we'll be is bad even when we're only talking about mundane standards. Add in a load of Changelings and this demon, and things get exponentially worse. I won't fault any of you if you decide to take a pass on this, but now's the time to say so if you do."

Jason rolled his eyes. "You done?"

"Yes, yes," Stone said with a sigh. It wasn't as if he'd expected anyone to take him up on his offer to sit this one out, but he felt he still had to make it anyway.

He looked them over. All, including him, wore functional street clothes: jeans, T-shirts, and heavy boots. Jason, Amber, and Verity wore leather jackets, while he'd opted for his usual long black over-coat since he'd built some magical protections into it. Jason and Amber both carried black backpacks, which Stone knew contained tactical gear including Kevlar vests, radios, and their personal pis-tols. Stone had checked with Ren when he'd made the arrangements for the flight to Detroit, and she'd assured him it was a private plane and the weapons wouldn't be a problem.

He reached into his coat pocket and withdrew several small pendants on chains, which he offered to his friends. "You'll proba-bly need these. I still haven't worked out how to adjust them so you can change them yourself, but you can turn them off and on so that's something."

Verity grinned, taking one. "Haven't seen these for a while."

"Well, sadly we don't often work together these days."

"Illusion generators?" Jason asked, slipping his over his head. At Stone's nod, his expression went serious. "This takes me back. They'll always remind me of Vegas, and the first time we met Harrison. Remember?"

"A little hard to forget, mate. I wish he was here now, honest-ly—he'd go a long way toward evening the odds against the demon, if we find it." He nodded toward the pendants. "Anyway, for now just put them on. We'll sort out what we need to look like when we get there. Ren is meeting us in Chicago for a briefing before we head to Detroit."

The trip through the portal was as uneventful as it usually was. They stepped out into the basement of the familiar Chicago bar, and a disregarding spell got them up the stairs and out through the front door without anyone noticing them.

A gray van was double-parked out front, as oblivious to the honks and middle fingers other drivers were flashing as a whale in a sea of tiny fish. When Stone and the others appeared on the street, the back door slid open. They quickly piled in and the van nosed back into the flow of traffic.

The driver didn't turn or acknowledge them in any way, but Ren Huxley was in the passenger seat. She twisted around to regard them as they belted themselves in. "Thanks for coming, all of you," she said. "Losing Royer was bad enough, but Jack too—"

"I'm sorry for your loss," Stone said.

"Yeah. Thanks. I know what I said before, that this is a dangerous job—but this is above and beyond. Our people get shot. Sometimes they get zapped by magic, or even occasionally get eaten by things most people don't even want to see in their nightmares. But this—" Her professional mask slipped for a moment, and she turned roughly away before the others saw anything. When she turned back, it was in place again.

"We understand," Verity said gently.

"I'm surprised you came in person," Stone said, trying to get the discussion back on track. It wasn't only because he wanted to get on with what they'd come here to do, but also because he thought focusing on the task at hand might help Ren deal with her grief.

"I was in the area, and this is our most important case right now, so I figured I might as well at least brief you in person." Her gaze cut away. "I feel like I ought to be going with you."

Stone managed not to look alarmed. He'd mostly gotten over his worry about bringing his non-mage friends along on missions like this—Amber wasn't really a mundane, and with his adrenaline-based magical strength and resilience, Jason was a lot harder to hurt these days than a normal human, even a trained one in good physical condition—but Ren had no such enhancements.

Verity, ever the diplomat, spoke into the silence. "Your job is to run the operation, not do field work."

"Yeah, yeah, I know." She sounded tired. "But when I start losing people like this, it's a little harder to just sit my ass down in a chair somewhere safe and watch from the sidelines."

"I understand," Stone said. "But Verity's right. That's why you asked us to deal with this situation. You said you had something for us?"

It was hard to tell if she was pleased or annoyed that they kept trying to change the subject. She eyed them for a moment, then sighed. "Yeah. The SickBoyz have been up to trouble again. Last night around four a.m., a group of them killed two of the North Side Hustlers. Just showed up at one their crash pads and took them down in their beds. The local police questioned a couple of the other Hustlers, but nobody saw the SickBoyz go in or out. And now the SickBoyz are saying the Hustlers better clear out or they'll kill one or two more every night until they're all gone."

"Brilliant," Stone muttered. "Gina said there were about twenty Hustlers. Is that right?"

"Eighteen now, give or take. But yeah. And if they're smart, they won't stick around too much longer. The SickBoyz are getting a rep for being ghosts—extremely violent ghosts. Even the hardcore gangbangers and the local Mob are starting to take notice. And I never want to say this, but even the cops are nervous."

She spent the rest of the trip to the private airfield on the edge of town updating them on the latest developments around the other nearby gangs. "I'm fairly sure, given their previous actions, that the SickBoyz aren't going to stop with the Hustlers," she said grimly. "We have to assume they'll try to range out even further once the Hustlers are off the board."

"But how are they going to hold that kind of territory?" Jason asked. "Gina has some Changeling contacts, and she told us the SickBoyz only have around thirty people themselves. Even with Changeling abilities, that's going to be stretched thin before long."

"Not if the demon's doing most of the work," Stone said. "I don't know much about this demon, but I've got a few educated guesses based on the summoning hierarchy. I'd bet a lot of money that this is the first or second one summoned. That means, while it's nothing impressive magically, it's tough, strong, and essentially impervious to both magical and mundane damage."

"I thought mundane damage was one of the few things that *could* hurt demons," Verity said.

"It can—but unless you sever their tie to their home plane—if it's even got one anymore—their regenerative abilities are terrifying. If you don't take them down in one go, they just pop right back up, undamaged and ready to play."

"So what does that mean?" Amber asked. "What do we have to do to take it down? I assume guns aren't going to do the job."

"Not ones like you've got," Stone said. "Possibly something big, like a machine gun—but even then it's not a sure thing."

"That's good," Ren said dryly. "The agency's fresh out of machine guns."

"Okay," Jason said as if she hadn't spoken, "So…what *do* we do?"

"Right now, the first priority is to get Izzy back, if she's alive. The demon probably has her stashed somewhere, which means if we can figure out where that is, we might be able to sneak in and grab her while the demon's not around."

"So you don't think it's guarding her?" Verity asked.

"Demons don't need to feed constantly. In fact, if it's keeping her around to draw energy from, there's an advantage to letting her recharge a bit between feedings. So it's probably got some of the SickBoyz guarding her. The good news is, if I'm right and this demon isn't a magical type, that likely means she's not behind wards or other arcane protections."

"But that still means we'll have to go through the SickBoyz to get to her," Jason said.

Stone glanced at Ren. He wasn't sure how she felt about what they might have to do.

"Damn straight," she said, her expression hard. "Do what you need to do. This demon's got to be stopped, and if that means taking down its people—officially, I have to tell you to do your best to minimize casualties. Unofficially—do what you have to do to stay alive and take those bastards down."

"We might not have to," Verity said. "Remember what Gina said about thinking a lot of the gang are just going along with this because they're scared? Maybe if we show them we can stand up to it, they might back off."

"No point in speculating," Stone said. "We can't make any decisions until we know what we're dealing with. So I'm formally clarifying, Ren: do we have your agency's blessing to take care of this in any way we deem necessary?"

"I wouldn't exactly call it a 'blessing.' But yeah. As long as you do everything possible to keep civilians out of it."

"We will," Amber said firmly.

Stone nodded. Despite his earlier wish for Harrison to join the party, he supposed it was probably for the best that he didn't. He was a lot more of a 'by any means necessary' kind of guy than they needed for this operation. "We'll do our best."

They left from a small, private airfield on the outskirts of Chicago. Ren stood next to the van, which the driver had pulled up alongside a functional-looking, no-frills transport plane.

"Keep me updated when you can," she said. "I don't want the story getting back to me from the eleven o'clock news."

Stone didn't answer, because he couldn't promise they'd do that. Once they got to Detroit, the situation could change in any number of ways they couldn't predict.

The plane's interior was small and cramped, with none of the amenities of a commercial flight. As soon as they were inside with their gear, the pilot closed the door and a few minutes later they were airborne. Stone had just settled back in his seat, planning to do a little mediation during the short flight, when his phone buzzed.

It was Gina. "Hey, Doc. Where are you?"

"In the air, somewhere between Chicago and Detroit."

"Good thing I caught you. I've got some good news for you."

"Brilliant. We could use some right now." He leaned forward in his seat, aware that the others were watching him with avid interest.

"Remember Fingers, the goblin whose ex-girlfriend had a boy-friend who ran away from the SickBoyz?"

"Yes, of course."

"Well, I managed to convince him to talk to her again, and she's found you somebody connected with the SickBoyz who's willing to talk to you."

Stone sat up straighter. "That *is* brilliant, Gina. Good job."

"Yeah, well, don't say anything yet. This guy isn't a member—he's the younger brother of one, and he's scared shitless his broth-er's gonna end up dead. He says if there's any chance you can help, he'll talk, but he's also scared—understandably—of being caught. If you want to talk, he says it's only if he gets to pick the location and only one of you can be there."

"Sounds like it could be a setup."

"Maybe, but I don't think so. This guy really is worried. His brother's the only family he has left."

"Is he a Changeling?"

"No. That's why he's not a member. That used to bother him, but now he's glad he's not in the middle of this mess."

"Okay. Well, go ahead and set it up. I'll meet with him. Find out where and when. We can have the others in the area as backup."

"On it. I'll text you back with the details. It's probably not going to be until after dark, so be careful."

Stone had barely put the phone away before Jason said, "Was that Gina?"

"Yes. She's got me a meeting with the brother of one of the SickBoyz members. She said he's afraid for his brother and willing to take a risk if there's a chance we can help."

"What do you mean, she's got *you* a meeting?" Verity narrowed her eyes. "You're not going alone, Alastair."

"I've got to—he won't meet with more than one person." Before she and the others could protest, he held up a hand. "But that doesn't mean I don't want you to be nearby. I'm confident all of you have ways to conceal yourselves. If anything goes wrong, you'll be right there."

"Yeah, okay," Amber said. "When's this meeting going down?"

"Not sure yet—she has to set it up. She said it won't be until after dark, though."

"Good," Jason said. "We'll talk to some contacts and see if there's somewhere we can pick up some gear here in town in the meantime."

"We should stay together," Verity said.

"Agreed," Stone said. "I don't think it will be wise for anyone to be wandering about by themselves until we get this handled."

Ren had arranged for rooms and a vehicle for them. The vehicle was waiting at the airfield when they landed—another nondescript gray van with tinted windows. They stowed their gear in the back and headed off, with Jason driving and Stone in the shotgun seat. All four kept a close watch on their surroundings; normally that would have been overly paranoid, but with demons involved it was never smart to get complacent.

Their rooms were in a small motel not far from the downtown district. "It's not quite as safe as the tourist hotels," Ren had told Stone, "but it's a lot less likely any toys you bring along will get noticed." None of them cared much, since they didn't expect to be using the rooms for long if everything went well.

Jason made a couple of calls to his contacts, and got the name of a shop that specialized in surveillance gear. "Apparently," he told the others on their way over, "they also have a side business selling less legal stuff, but you have to know the right people to get in."

"What kind of 'less legal stuff' are you talking about?" Stone asked.

"Stun grenades, flash-bangs, stuff like that," Amber said. "Along with tasers, various riot gear, tear gas, the works. The kind of stuff you technically need to be law enforcement to buy."

"You're planning to take all *that* into this?" Verity looked shocked. "I thought the whole point was to *avoid* a riot."

"Nah," Jason said. "That's just what they have, not what we're buying. Mostly we want some high-tech comm and surveillance gear so we can stay in contact. But a few stun and flash-bang grenades probably wouldn't be a bad idea, especially if we're tryin' not to kill anybody."

Stone waved them off. "You do whatever it is you do, and leave me out of it."

He expected the shop to be in a sketchy neighborhood, with heavy bars on the windows and questionable-looking characters lurking outside. To his surprise, it ended up in a strip mall next to an escape room and a flower shop.

"Maybe you and V should wait here," Jason said. "We won't be long."

Stone had no objection to that. He watched them go in, then twisted in his seat to face Verity, who was looking pensive.

"I wish we could do another ritual," she said. "I'd like to know if there's a chance Izzy is still alive."

"So would I, but I don't think it's wise to alert the demon to our presence. It might kill her out of spite."

"Is that what you think it did to Jack?"

"I wouldn't be surprised." He shook his head. "You've got to understand, Verity—demons make the Evil look pleasant by comparison. Most of the Evil only did what they did because they needed to feed. Demons need soul energy to feed, but they don't have to tear people apart to get it. That's nothing but *true* evil."

She shivered a little. "That's what's got me concerned. Plus, the Evil were limited by the bodies they possessed. Most of them were just normal people, so it wasn't hard to handle them."

"That's the difficult part, yes. I honestly don't have too many ideas yet about how to deal with this demon if we find it." He pointed at the shop. "I don't imagine they sell real bombs in there— and even if they did, it would probably take one capable of blowing up a building to even make a dent in the demon. We can't risk that kind of collateral damage."

"So, what do we do if we find it? You didn't answer that before."

"That's because I don't know. I'm still working on it."

"What about asking Gabriel or Kolinsky or somebody? Would they know?"

He thought about Thalassa Nera, and wished the dragons were a bit more hands-on about the demon problem. Once again, it seemed as if their concern was confined to threats so far above

Stone's pay grade that he couldn't even contemplate them—things that made The Unspeakable look like a second-class problem by comparison. A few demons lurking around threatening the humans in a few cities wouldn't even register on their radar.

That's why they keep you *around,* he thought, half amused, half exasperated.

To Verity, he said, "They probably wouldn't be much help, honestly. Most of what I already know about demons, I got from them in the first place. Trust me, they aren't going to drop what they're doing and help us with this."

She fell silent, looking out the window, and Stone turned back around so he could watch the shop door.

Fifteen minutes later, Jason and Amber emerged, each carrying a bulging gray tote bag with the shop's logo in black on the side.

"Looks like Christmas came early for you two," Verity said with a grin.

"Yeah. We even got presents for you two kids." Jason got back in the driver's seat and drove off.

Stone was about to give a smartass reply when his phone buzzed again, this time with a text from Gina. It included an address and a time: 11 p.m. *Don't be late,* she'd added. *In fact, you should probably be a little early, and be careful. The spot's not in gang territory, but it's not a good place for a tea party, either. Guy you're looking for will be in a gray hoodie, and the meet's in an abandoned house so don't be seen going in. Remember he's scared, so turn on the charm. If you spook him, he'll probably take off and I doubt I can get him to talk again. And bring some money, just in case.*

Got it. Thanks, he sent back, and put the phone in his pocket.

"So?" Verity asked. "I assume that was Gina."

"It was." He quickly filled them in on what she'd told him.

Amber had her phone out and was looking up the address. "That's on the north side, not too far from the SickBoyz' territory.

From the look of the satellite view, Gina's right—it's a house in a neighborhood that looks pretty janky."

"Let's drive by while it's still light out," Jason said. "I want to get a look at the area. Al or V, can you do whatever you do to make us blend in?"

"I got it," Verity said.

The neighborhood was every bit as blighted as Stone expected it to be. He watched soberly out the passenger window as they rolled past houses that were either abandoned, falling apart, or badly in need of repairs. A few wary children played in tiny, fenced-in yards, and small groups of teenagers and young adults loitered in vacant lots or near old cars. The spell worked, so nobody paid any particular attention to the van, but Stone had no trouble sensing their tense awareness even without magical sight. They looked like prey animals at a watering hole, on constant watch for threats.

The house where the meet would occur was on a corner. It had two stories, its windows were boarded up, and a few halfhearted attempts at graffiti decorated its lower walls.

"I don't think those are gang tags," Jason said. "I did a little checking on the area gangs before we left, and these don't look like any of the ones I remember. Gina's probably right that this area is near the SickBoyz' turf, but not part of it."

Amber was leaning forward, looking out through the windshield. "House next door is abandoned too—we can probably set up there. Alastair, we've got a radio you can take with you, so we can listen in and get over there fast if anything goes wrong. It's got a little earpiece so you can hear us, if you think it's safe to use it."

"I can hide it with an illusion," Stone said. "Not a problem."

"I'll sit on the roof with a disregarding spell up," Verity said. "That way, I can use magical sight to keep an eye out for anybody approaching."

"Sounds good to me. I'm not going to critique your plan. This is your department, not mine. Come on—let's get something to eat before we have to go."

They returned to the neighborhood half an hour before the scheduled meet, all of them on considerably higher alert than they'd been before.

The area looked even more ominous in the dark—definitely not the kind of place any of them would have wanted to be if they were mundane humans. The street had a single functional streetlight; it flickered and sputtered nowhere near their target house, so the only other sources of illumination were a moon barely visible behind drifting clouds and the occasional headlights of a passing car.

The children were all gone by now, of course. Even the loitering groups had vanished, making Stone think they hadn't been affiliated with any of the local gangs. The far-off sound of a siren warbled and faded.

They parked halfway up the street on the other side, still keeping the disregarding spell on the van. In the back, they all donned their illusion-generator pendants, and Stone made them all look unassuming in dark-colored hoodies, jeans, and athletic shoes.

"Okay," Jason said, stashing items from their bags in his pockets. "Can you two keep us invisible long enough to get to the house where we're going to set up, so nobody sees us leaving the van?"

"Yeah," Verity said. "If we walk fast."

He handed out the radios, and they all tested them to make sure they were working. After Stone and Verity settled invisibility spells over all four of them, they slipped out of the van, locked it, and hurried across the street. Once they were safely under cover alongside the next-door house, the spells faded.

Stone looked at his watch. They had twenty minutes before the meet. "All right," he said under his breath. "I'll go in a little early, and you lot can listen. Don't do anything unless there's imminent danger, though. We need to hear what this bloke has to say, assuming he's not trying to trick us. And remember, I can deal with most of what they can throw at me, unless the demon shows up itself."

"I'd feel better if we did a little recon," Amber said. "As long as we've got some time, I'm going to check out the immediate area."

Jason started to say something, then nodded. "Good idea. Just stay in contact so we know you're safe."

She gave him a thumbs-up and slipped off.

"Her tracking is amazing," Jason told them. "And her nose sometimes makes her even better at it than a mage. You can hide auras behind walls, but you can't hide smells from her."

Verity smiled, obviously amused at her brother's pride in his wife.

The time dragged on interminably, even though every couple of minutes Amber would update them with some variation of "all's well." When she returned, seven minutes remained until the meet time.

"I did a sweep of this whole end of the neighborhood," she told the group. "Didn't notice anything out of the ordinary—at least ordinary given where we are. If this is an ambush, they planned it well and the bad guys are waiting somewhere else. We'll keep an eye out. There's definitely somebody in that house, on the second floor. He smells scared."

"We'd better get in position," Jason said. "Al, you should get going too. The guy probably won't freak out if you're five minutes early."

Stone switched to magical sight and watched as Verity turned invisible again and drifted upward. A moment later, her voice came over the radio: *"In position on the roof. Don't see any auras."*

Jason and Amber slipped around the corner of the house, leaving Stone alone. He gave them thirty seconds, then set off walking toward their target, keeping his steps deliberate so as not to attract unwelcome attention. Counting on the disregarding spell to keep anyone from noticing him, he headed up the walk past a neglected, weed-choked yard. A set of rickety porch steps led to a doorway with no door. Someone had nailed boards to it, but most had been ripped free, leaving a hole large enough for Stone to weasel through. He kept magical sight up and checked for auras on the other side, but saw none.

Inside, a stairway led up on his left side, and a doorway to his right revealed a shadowy living room. It had no furniture, but debris and old boxes covered the moldering carpet. Amber had said the guy was on the second floor, so Stone carefully mounted the stairway, half-afraid it would break under his weight. He pulled out the small flashlight Jason had given him and examined the steps, nodding in satisfaction when he spotted recent footprints in the dust. That was a good sign.

He reached the top and directed the flashlight beam around, revealing four rooms. None of them had doors. He was about to move forward when a shaky male voice said, "Turn that light off!" It sounded young—late teens at the oldest.

Stone did as he was told, but kept magical sight up. "I'm here to talk to you," he said. "I'm not a threat. I just want information. Maybe I can help your brother."

There was a long pause, and Stone could almost picture the kid working up his nerve. "Okay," he said at last. "Come on. Not too close, though. Stay in the doorway." The glow of a flashlight appeared in the third doorway, then switched off again.

Stone walked slowly forward, trying to be as nonthreatening as possible. He'd deliberately chosen the illusionary disguise of a mild-looking man in his twenties. "All right," he called. "I'm coming."

"I got a gun, so no sudden moves." The voice was still shaking, though it was obvious its owner was trying vainly to quell it. Stone wondered if he really did have a gun.

As soon as he appeared in the doorway, the flashlight came to life again, bathing him in bright illumination and dazzling his eyes so he couldn't see more than a vague outline of the person holding it.

"That's far enough," the voice ordered.

Stone stopped, raising his invisible shield just in case the boy wasn't lying about the gun. He held up his hands to show he was unarmed. "I'm not here to hurt you," he said. "Let's talk. A friend of a friend said you might have some information about what's going on with the SickBoyz." Magical sight filtered out the flashlight to reveal a medium-yellow aura, shot through with red flashes indicating fear and agitation. He was as scared of Stone as he expected Stone to be of him.

"I might." Now the voice was guarded. "Who are you? What did you mean, you might be able to help my brother?"

"I don't know yet if I can." Stone remained calm, keeping his voice even and steady. "But I'll try. Let's hear what you've got to say first."

"What do you wanna know?"

"*Everything's fine out here,*" Verity murmured in his hidden earpiece.

"*Nobody approaching the house,*" Jason said. "*I think he's alone.*"

"*I can practically smell his fear even from over here,*" Amber said.

Stone took in the information but didn't make any movement indicating acknowledgement. "From what I understand, someone showed up recently, took over the gang by intimidation, and started forcing the members into doing things they didn't want to do. Is that correct?"

From the other side of the room came the sound of heavy breathing, and the red patches in the boy's aura flared brighter. Both hands were at his sides; if he had a gun, he wasn't pointing it at Stone. "Yeah. He's bad news. Or they. Nobody knows if it's one guy or more."

"Nobody knows? So no one's seen them?"

"I dunno, man. Fish ain't seen 'em."

"Fish?"

"That's my bro."

"Do you know where he is now?"

"Fish? He don't tell me much. I think he tryin' to keep me safe, y'know? But I'm scared this dude or whatever's gonna fuck him up."

Stone considered. He was probably right about that—demons weren't known for their patience, nor their tolerance for anyone disagreeing with them. Carefully, he asked, "Do you know about the SickBoyz? What they are?"

"What you mean?" Suspicion, and another aura flare.

He hated having to dance around this, but if the kid didn't know about Changelings, that could complicate the discussion. Still, he suspected from the flare that the kid at least knew *something*. "Did your brother ever tell you anything about why they're together?"

"The SickBoyz?" Feet shuffled. "I ain't s'posed to talk about it. He wasn't s'posed to tell me nothin'. But we tight, me an' Fish. Least, we used to be."

Stone didn't need magical senses to hear the doubt in his voice. "I'll help you if I can, I promise. But you've got to be honest with me."

Snort. "What can *you* do, man? You just some skinny dude don't know nothin' about nothin'. You ain't even from around here, not talkin' like that."

R. L. KING

"You're right—I'm not from around here. But you're wrong that I can't do anything. I can, but you've got to tell me what you know. I'm looking for someone."

"Who?"

"Did you hear anything about a man getting killed recently?" He purposely didn't say 'did you hear about the SickBoyz killing a man?'

"What man?" The aura flared again. He knew exactly what Stone was talking about, and it made his fear spike. Stone guessed Jack Groszek's gory death might have been what finally tipped this kid over the edge and made him agree to talk.

"I don't know what he called himself. But bits of him turned up in a restaurant and an abandoned building. They still haven't found the rest of him."

Sharp intake of breath, but no reply.

"Look," Stone said, trying to sound as persuasive as possible. "I'm not interested in bothering your brother, or any of the other SickBoyz. I'm not law enforcement. But the man they killed has another friend who was with him—a woman. She's the one I'm trying to find. I'm not even sure she's still alive, but if she is, I want to get her out of there before she suffers the same fate."

The kid remained silent for a long time, almost as if turning Stone's words over in his mind. "I don't know nothin' about no lady," he said at last. "And that's the truth. And if they do got her, I don't know where. Fish don't tell me SickBoyz biz. Says it's safer if I don't know."

That made sense. Stone began to get a picture of a man who wanted to keep his younger brother well away from the darker side of his life. "Do you have any idea at all? Maybe you overheard him talking to someone at some point? Think hard—it might be life or death for this woman, and possibly for your brother too."

Feet shuffled, and the flashlight beam dipped a little before steadying again. "Sorry, man, I wish I could tell you. But I don't *know*."

Stone sighed. "Listen—it sounds like you know as well as I do that your brother and his friends don't want to be doing this. Am I right?"

Another long pause. "They scared," he finally admitted. "This ain't their thing. You know—killin' people and tryin' to spread out. They just wanna be left alone, y'know? That's what Fish told me."

Stone wondered if "Fish" had gotten his nickname due to his particular Changeling type. "When was the last time you saw Fish?"

"Week or so ago. He ain't been home. Says he's busy, and he'll come home when he can."

"Are you on your own when he's not around?"

"Yeah, mostly. There's a few of us in our building—we help each other out."

"From what I understand, there aren't that many SickBoyz. Is it possible Fish might be one of the group guarding this woman, if she's alive?"

"I dunno. Maybe. Whoever took over the Boyz got them doin' all kindsa stuff. Fish told me that before he left."

"Okay." Stone paced back and forth in the doorway, thinking. He didn't want to keep this kid for long, since he was obviously scared. He didn't think there was any way the demon could find out about the meet, but best not to take chances. He'd thought per- haps he could convince the kid to give him something of Fish's and use it for a tracking spell, but that was dangerous. That had been what got Heidi killed—and probably Jack, too. "You have a phone, right?"

"Yeah..."

"You said Fish told you he was busy, but he hasn't been home. Did he call you?"

"Yeah." The voice had a 'duh' edge to it.

"Think hard—did you hear anything in the background that might have told you where he was?"

"Man, this is *stupid*. I gotta go. You ain't gonna help Fish. I—" He stopped, the flashlight beam dipped again, and the aura flared— but this time with excitement, not fear.

Stone stopped pacing. "What is it?"

"Wait a sec, I did hear somethin'! Last time he called, couple days ago, there was this rap song in the background. It was by this dude named GobDog. He used to be a SickBoy before he got drilled in a drive-by last year. Only one place I know plays his stuff any-more—Big Gee's. It's one o' their old hangouts. They mostly moved somewhere else Fish won't tell me about a few months back, but I remember that."

"*Already looking it up,*" came Amber's soft voice in Stone's ear.

"Thank you," Stone said, both to the kid and to Amber. It might not be where they were holding Izzy, but if other SickBoyz were hanging out there, they could lean on them for more information.

"You serious about helpin' my brother?" For a moment, he sounded less like a tough kid and more like a hopeful young boy.

"Very serious. I promise, we'll do everything we can." He considered, then made a decision. "I'm going to reach in my pocket now, so if you really do have a gun, don't shoot me, all right?"

"No guns." The hopeful boy was gone and the young tough was back.

"No guns." He'd stashed some loose cash in his coat pocket on Gina's advice, and now pulled out a hundred dollars in twenties, along with a card with his phone number on it. "Your help might save your brother's life. Until he comes back, though, take this to help you get by. I'm giving you my number, too—if you come up with anything you think could help, call me. Day or night." He laid the bills and the card on the ground in front of him. "I'm leaving now—please don't try to follow me."

"No problem, man. I ain't interested in where you goin'. But if you see Fish, tell 'im to get his ass home, okay?"

"I will absolutely do that."

Stone slipped out of the house and rejoined his friends on the far side of the neighboring house, hidden under a disregarding spell.

"I expected an ambush," Jason said.

"You and all the rest of us," Verity agreed.

"Well, if you're looking for an ambush, we might find one at this Big Gee's," Stone said. "Did you find where it's located?"

"Yeah." Amber held up her phone, which displayed a map. "It's not far from here. We're only a couple blocks from the SickBoyz' territory, and the bar's smack in the middle of it. We'll have to be careful unless you want to go in guns blazing."

"Not a good idea," Stone said. "I'm sure we can handle the gang—nonlethally, I hope. But if the demon's there, things will get more difficult."

"Plus they'll probably kill Izzy if they figure out they've been made," Jason said. "We need to do some recon."

"Do you want to do it now?" Verity asked.

"I think we need to." Stone motioned for her to join him in the invisibility spell, so they could get back to the van without being observed. Once they'd made it and were settling into their seats, he said, "If Izzy *is* still alive, I doubt she will be for long. I'm fairly sure demons can't continue draining their victims indefinitely."

"Let's do it, then." Amber's eyes held a feral glitter. Not only did she not look at all fearful or apprehensive, she seemed to be looking forward to the challenge.

CHAPTER ELEVEN

A LDWYN SNAPPED HIS HEAD UP to face the man who'd just entered the room.

At first glance, the only thing he had in common with the terrified customers was that he looked human. At that point, the resemblance ended. There was nothing huddled or frightened about the tall, slim figure who stood proudly straight, framed in the doorway like the star of a show pausing to drink in the adulation of the audience before taking the stage. He had shining blond, shoulder-length hair, a chiseled jaw, inhumanly handsome features, and bright blue eyes. Unlike the drab, functional clothing the bar's customers wore, every line of his own outfit was perfect, impeccably tailored, and spotlessly clean. Dominating his ensemble was a calf-length, deep-red coat with a high collar, its tail sweeping around his lower body as if artfully blown by its own tiny, personal fan. His full, sensual lips twisted into a nasty smile as his gaze settled on Aldwyn.

Aldwyn met the gaze straight on, himself expressionless. With his draconic senses, he saw what no one else in the bar could.

Everything about this man was an illusion, from his clothes to his uncanny beauty.

Almost everything. His imperious demeanor was all too genuine.

"What are you looking at, pig?" The man sneered. "Eyes down, unless you want to suffer the same fate as your...*friends* here." His lips curled around the word, as if he didn't think it possible such a wretched creature could *have* friends.

Aldwyn didn't lower his gaze. Who did this man think he was? He thought on occasion that he might overdo the superiority a bit when dealing with the humans, but this man made him look humble by comparison.

And for *what*? He certainly didn't have much to be conceited about. Beneath his lavish illusionary disguise, he was middle-aged, scrawny-chested, with patchy skin, a receding hairline, and a drooping left eye that gave his whole face the appearance of sagging.

Around them, the bar's patrons remained utterly silent, their eyes wide and their auras pumping out fear so strong it was almost visible in the air.

"These people are not my friends," Aldwyn said calmly. "I have never met any of them before."

The long-coated man tilted his head, then his smile returned. "Ah, so you are merely unlucky to choose this place to wander into for your nightly face-stuffing and intoxication. That's unfortunate for you."

"No, I think it is unfortunate for *you*." Aldwyn continued to watch him with a calm that was almost amused.

"What's going on, Loriar?" called another voice from the rear. A moment later another figure, this one a woman, appeared behind him.

"I've found a little pig who doesn't know his place," Loriar said without taking his gaze off Aldwyn.

"Oh, have you?" The woman stepped around Loriar. She was half a head shorter than him, with an impressive figure and shining, curly red tresses that tumbled down over the shoulders of a stylish, high-collared coat similar to her companion's. She narrowed her eyes at Aldwyn, but didn't address him.

Aldwyn took her in. Her breathtaking beauty was as illusionary as Loriar's—beneath it she had a lined face, pale, thinning hair, and rounded shoulders. Peripherally, he was aware of the bar customers shifting around. He wondered if some of them were assessing their chances of ducking out one of the doors while the two "Zaps" and the new stranger were otherwise occupied.

"You seem very brave, pig," Loriar said. He indicated the bar at large. "Or very foolish. The others here know their place, but you seem not to. Are you perhaps new in Nargul?"

Ah, so this conversation *did* have a purpose. He now knew the name of this town. "In fact, I am," he said smoothly. "I have many questions. And it seems as if you might be useful in answering them."

A soft gasp arose from somewhere in the crowd.

Loriar's eyes widened a little. His expression suggested he'd never been spoken to in such a manner before, and he wasn't certain how to react to it. Finally, he widened his smile. "You are drunk, little pig. But I am feeling magnanimous tonight, so I will give you another chance. Get over there with the rest of your dirty companions and remain quiet until we decide what to do with you."

Aldwyn didn't move. He knew the type: petty bullies strong enough to assert their will over weak people for no other reason than to stroke their pathetic egos. He himself had been accused on many occasions of using his power to intimidate lesser beings, but the difference was he almost always only punished those who actively defied him by their actions. He rarely cared about their words. How could words harm him?

"This is ridiculous!" the woman said from next to Loriar, her face darkening with anger. "Don't be soft, Loriar. We can't let him live after he has insulted us. It will set a bad example for the other pigs. You know how they babble among themselves." Without waiting for Loriar to respond, she pointed her hand at Aldwyn. A stream of crackling golden energy burst from it and streaked toward him.

Aldwyn remained still, his eyes cutting down with faint curiosity to where the gold energy fizzled and died without reaching his body. The woman's magic was middling in power level, certainly nowhere near potent enough to penetrate his invisible shield.

The crowd's fear billowed again, and a couple of them broke ranks and dashed for the door.

Neither Loriar nor the woman paid them any mind as they made their escape. Both of them were focused fully on Aldwyn, their eyes wide and their mouths open.

Aldwyn didn't give them a chance to regroup. "Was that supposed to be magic?" he asked in a conversational tone. "If so, it wasn't very impressive. Let me show you."

He didn't point his hand at them. He didn't make any gesture at all. But a second later, the woman's body simply came apart, the pieces curling into ash and drifting to the sawdust-strewn floor. She didn't even get time to scream.

"There," Aldwyn said with satisfaction, still not taking his attention from Loriar. "Is that what she meant to do to me?"

Loriar didn't answer. His eyes got bigger, and his quick glance down at the pile of ash that used to be his companion was obviously involuntary.

"P-please don't hurt us, sir," one of the customers begged. "Y-you don't look like one of the Talented, but we'll do whatever you say if you spare us."

Murmurs of agreement came from a few of the others.

Aldwyn had no further patience for any of them. His interest at this point was fully on Loriar. "Go," he said, waving a dismissive hand. "All of you, get out, and ensure no one else enters this place tonight."

For a moment, the air remained still and silent except for the panting breaths of the crowd—and of Loriar. Then, the customers' fear-induced paralysis broke and they all took off, pressing and jostling against each other as the people in the other bar had done as they all tried to get out the door at once.

Aldwyn waited in silence until they were all gone. Loriar opened his mouth to say something, but got a look at his captor's face and decided against it.

When the bar was empty except for the two of them and the door was shut tight, Aldwyn addressed the man again, still speaking as if having a conversation with a business associate. "The Talented," he said, rubbing his chin. "That is what they called you. What does it mean? In what way are you 'talented'?"

Loriar's expression changed again. Now, he looked like someone addressing a dangerous madman with a loaded gun. The wheels spun in his head as he clearly tried to come up with the right thing to say that wouldn't get him turned into ashes like his friend. "W-who are you?" he finally asked. His voice shook, but he made an effort to keep it respectful.

"You would not know my name, nor care. Answer my question."

Loriar took a breath. "We are...the Talented. It is who and what we are." The words had the tone of someone who was trying to explain a fact so obvious everyone should know it.

"Talented in magic?"

"Of course." He looked ever so slightly relieved. "How is it that you don't know that? Obviously, you possess the Talent as well."

"Obviously." Aldwyn let him hang for a long moment, crossing his arms and regarding him as he would a bug under a microscope.

Loriar squirmed obligingly. "What...do you *want* of me?" he finally asked. "Why did you kill Illindra?"

"She attacked me. As ineffectual as her efforts proved, I don't allow anyone to attack me without provocation. You should be thankful I made her death painless and quick."

Loriar didn't look very thankful. He licked his lips, swallowed, and shifted from one foot to the other. His boots, like the rest of his illusionary outfit, were utterly spotless.

"Let us begin by ridding you of that pretentious illusionary costume." Again, Aldwyn neither made a gesture nor spoke a word; while sometimes such things could be effective at impressing the lesser beings, they certainly weren't necessary for magic.

Loriar's illusionary disguise, which had been centered on a deep red pendant around his neck, dropped away like water, revealing him in all his droop-eyed, scraggly-haired glory. He still wore the high-collared coat, but now instead of rich, pristine red and exquisitely tailored for his false form, it appeared drab and simple, with a large stain on the left sleeve.

"There," Aldwyn said. "That is more like it." He backed up without taking his eyes off Loriar, and leaned against one of the tables. "You said before that this town is called Nargul. Is that correct?"

Once more, Loriar looked at him like he might not have all his mental faculties. "Of—of course."

"And you reside here?"

The man's innate snobbishness broke through his fear as a snort. "Here? No." He sounded as if the very idea was so disgusting as to be impossible to contemplate.

"Where, then?" Aldwyn thought he knew the answer, but he wanted to hear it from the man's own mouth. He watched Loriar's aura; his fear made it difficult to pick up anything else, but lies would be easy to spot.

Loriar apparently decided that playing along with the crazy man was his best chance of getting out of this horrific situation alive and intact. He jerked his chin toward the sky. "Prensyrrus, of course."

"Prensyrrus." Aldwyn savored the unfamiliar word. He still spoke with the cultured, British-accented baritone he'd cultivated over many years on Earth, not caring in the slightest if it sounded odd to residents of this world. "That is the city I observed, floating over this one?"

"Yes." Loriar didn't make any effort to move or sit down. His thin chest rose and fell with his harsh breathing, but he did try to calm himself. "Who...*are* you? How is it that you don't know about Prensyrrus, or even Nargul? Obviously you have the Talent, but yet you look like one of the...*pigs.*" His lips curled around the word, but then he froze, his aura flaring again. "Wait. I know what you are."

"Oh? Pray, enlighten me, then."

No answer. The man looked suddenly sullen, as if he regretted what he'd said.

Aldwyn didn't intend to kill him—not yet, anyway, since so far he was the most useful reference source he'd found—but he didn't need to let *him* know that. "I suggest you answer my questions...Loriar, was it? Answer me, Loriar, lest you end up decorating the floor like your unfortunate companion." He raised his hand, summoning red energy to dance around it like malignant flames. Sometimes, a little showy magic could get the job done, especially when dealing with human types.

Loriar jerked back. He appeared to be wrestling with something inside himself, but finally he let out his breath in a resigned sigh. "You're part of the resistance."

"That what?"

"The resistance." His tone still held a sullen edge, as if what he wanted to say was something more like, *you know full well what I'm talking about, so stop pretending you don't.*

Of course, though, Aldwyn genuinely *didn't* know what he was talking about. "What is this 'resistance'?"

Loriar shot a hopeful glance toward the door, clearly praying more of his "Talented" friends would come swarming in to rescue him from this powerful but insane man. When nothing of the sort happened, he sighed again and gave up. "Fine. I'll answer your odd questions if I have no choice, even though I can't believe you don't know these things. The resistance are traitors."

"Traitors? To whom?"

"To *us*," he snapped, once more regaining some of his old pride. He pointed toward the ceiling. "To our way of life. To every way in which we were raised."

"You aren't making sense." Aldwyn was beginning to wonder if getting the information he sought was going to take far longer than he wanted to devote to it. He'd found this place and its vast stores of magic, and he could access them now. He could even assume his true form here. Why did he need to know the details of how the people here lived? It wasn't as if they could cause him any trouble.

But still, he was here now, and he *was* curious. He could give it a little longer. He leveled a warning gaze at Loriar. "If you do not make sense, then you are not useful to me. And if you are not useful, I see no reason to keep you alive."

Loriar licked his lips and swallowed again. He glanced longingly at the bar, clearly thirsty enough to deign to drink the pigs' ale if it were offered to him. When Aldwyn failed to offer, he rubbed his forehead. "Fine—but don't punish me if I offend you by telling you things even the dullest Dim child knows."

Aldwyn didn't bother taking insult at his words. "Speak to me as if I am a stranger, unfamiliar with your ways here. As you suggest, instruct me as you would a child."

The man studied him a moment, as if trying to decide how much he could truly get away with, then drew a deep breath and spoke without looking at him. "This is Nargul," he said, gesturing around himself. "It is the home of the Dim—people who were not graced with the Talent."

"The Dim. The people you also referred to as 'pigs.'"

"Yes." There was the false pride again, but it didn't last long this time as Loriar locked it down. "They *are* pigs. They live in squalor, they care little for the finer things in life, and they possess neither the intelligence nor the Talent to better themselves. What *else* would you call them?"

Aldwyn didn't answer that. He was amused at how the man managed to speak the word "Talent" as if it were capitalized. Instead, he said, "And you—the so-called 'Talented'—live in the city floating above this one...this—" He paused a moment to recall the unfamiliar word. "...Prensyrrus."

"Yes."

"What are you doing here, then, if you have so little regard for squalor?"

Loriar's gaze cut to the ashes that used to be his female companion, then toward the bar. He seemed unwilling to look at Aldwyn directly. "We...some of us...visit Nargul sometimes."

"Why? It seems as if, by your own words, there is nothing here for you." Once again, Aldwyn knew exactly what was going on, but he wanted to hear it from the man himself.

Loriar's expression was half-defiant, half-miserable. "Sometimes, it is necessary to remind the Dim of their place," he muttered.

"I see. You come to their city to terrorize them." He said it with no judgment, simply as a statement of fact.

Loriar didn't reply.

That was all right, though. He didn't need to. Aldwyn's thoughts were already far away from this tedious discussion, on things like magically floating cities and large concentrations of mages. It seemed he would need to investigate this Prensyrrus, but he still had a few more questions for Loriar.

"How do you and your magical brethren travel between here and Prensyrrus?"

Loriar's gaze flashed back to him for a second, as if he still couldn't believe this man, with so much power, could be so ignorant. "We—use teleport pads, of course. We have our own complex in the center of Nargul, where the Dim are not permitted unless authorized."

Teleport pads. Interesting. So, aside from raw magic, they also had magical constructs. That suggested more questions, but Aldwyn let them go for now. He could probably learn those answers on his own, if he deemed them worthy of pursuing.

"You mentioned a 'resistance,' and that you thought I might be part of it. Tell me of this, and why you think so."

Loriar had clearly given up trying to figure out what this stranger was truly after. He answered in a dull monotone, all the fire gone from his demeanor. "I told you—the resistance are traitors. Talented who work together with the Dim. Who treat them as…equals." His lips curled around the word.

"Work together for what purpose?"

"Who truly knows?" Loriar shrugged. "To undermine the proper structure of society. They are too weak and cowardly to confront us directly, so they slink in the shadows like rats, sabotaging farms and factories, spreading their disgusting ideologies…sometimes even *coupling* with each other." The disgust on his face suggested he was struggling hard not to vomit at the thought.

"I see." Aldwyn pondered his words. Given the relative sizes of the floating city and this one on the ground, not to mention his firsthand knowledge of the relative frequency of magical talent in humans—at least on Earth—he was sure there were a lot more nonmagical "Dim" than magical "Talented." He certainly couldn't blame them for doing whatever they could to get themselves out from under the boots of their oppressors. Adding in the fact that not all the mages here could possibly be puffed-up buffoons like Loriar, and Aldwyn was beginning to form a picture. "And you believe I am part of the resistance because you cannot otherwise conceive of someone who possesses the Talent deigning to appear as one of the 'Dim.' Is that correct?"

"Yes!" Loriar spluttered, in the tone of *Finally, you're catching on!*

"Instead, I am to wear a ridiculous illusionary disguise as you and your friend did, to deceive the lesser beings into viewing you as something to admire."

Again, Loriar didn't answer. He continued to look sulky, though.

"All right." Aldwyn was truly tiring of the man's presence now, but he needed one more answer. "Tell me this, and then we will discuss your fate. When I arrived here, it was outside this town, in a blighted area full of chaotic magic. I—" He stopped when he got a look at Loriar, who was gaping at him, eyes wide with terror. "What is it?"

"Y-you were…in the *Wastes*?"

The Wastes. That was a good name for where he'd landed. "Apparently so. What are these 'Wastes'?"

Loriar's gaze skated away. "Now I know you're having sport with me. Everyone knows what the Wastes are—and no one in their right mind ever goes there."

Aldwyn frowned. "My patience grows ever thinner, Loriar. I suggest you confine yourself to the facts. I have no interest in your opinions."

"The *facts*," the man said, regaining some of his bravado, "are that nothing but abominations can survive in the Wastes. You used the word 'chaotic' to describe the magic there. That is accurate, but it isn't sufficient. The magic there is unpredictable, powerful, and deadly. Venturing into the Wastes to a point further than the Barrens is simply suicide." He snorted. "That is one of our primary means of punishing those who commit serious crimes—exile to the Wastes. No one ever returns. And you say you simply—*walked* here from there?"

Aldwyn couldn't help a thin smile. *No, you idiot, he thought. I flew here.* But Loriar's words still rang true—from what Aldwyn had seen of the magic in the Wastes, even formidable human mages would have a hard time surviving there for long. Even in his dragon form, he'd thought it wise to avoid the shifting clouds of malevolent arcane energy after one of them had disrupted his senses. "How large are these Wastes? How did they come to be?"

Loriar's shoulders slumped. "No one knows for certain how large they are anymore. They cover the entire interior part of the land, leaving only a thin strip along the coastlines safe for habitation. As for how they came to be—it was because of the War."

"War?"

"Many years ago—long before the memory of anyone alive now." He spread his hands. "It has always been so, as far as everyone, Talented and Dim alike, are concerned. The Wastes simply...*are,* and anyone who has any sense in their head avoids them."

Once again, Aldwyn began to form a picture. "The War," Loriar had said. But no conventional war could have caused the sort of potent arcane devastation that had lingered for at least a couple of generations.

For that, you needed magic—and a lot of it.

Had these people entered into some kind of magical war? Did that imply there were—or at least there used to be—many more of them? The power level necessary to cause this kind of lingering blight must have been immense.

That was something he *would* need to know more about if he planned to spend any significant time exploring and studying this odd world. But he certainly didn't need to get his information from this tiresome, stuffy little man.

Loriar appeared to sense that their conversation was drawing to an end. Several emotions flickered across his face: fear, hope, sly calculation. Each of them was mirrored so precisely in his aura that Aldwyn had no trouble reading him like a child's book:

Is he going to kill me?

Maybe I he'll let me go.

If he does let me go, what can I do to gain some advantage from this conversation?

Aldwyn didn't even pause to consider his next steps, since they had never been in doubt. "Thank you, Loriar," he said in his customarily formal way. "Your answers have been illuminating."

"Then you'll—"

He didn't get to finish his sentence. His aura didn't even flare with more fear, because Aldwyn neither changed position nor gave any other indication of intent.

Loriar's ashes fluttered down to join his female companion's on the floor.

Aldwyn turned without looking at them and left the bar. As he had ordered the fleeing crowd of bar customers, no sign of any living being appeared anywhere in the street or behind the windows of the nearby buildings.

CHAPTER TWELVE

EVEN WITH THE DISREGARDING SPELL at full strength, driving through the SickBoyz' territory at nearly midnight was an unnerving experience.

The place looked like a war zone. The few businesses, almost all of them closed or abandoned, had heavy bars covering their windows and doors, every vertical flat surface was covered with colorful, overlapping graffiti, and the ratio of burned- or shot-out streetlights to operational ones was about twenty to one. The figures slouching in doorways or on street corners looked a lot more menacing than the ordinary citizens from earlier that day.

"Their auras are alert," Verity said. She was doing the magical recon so Stone could maintain the disregarding spell. "I don't think anybody's noticed us yet, but I keep expecting them to. Changelings are different—sometimes the spell doesn't work as well on them because they use other senses besides sight. Everybody keep your voices down when you talk."

"What kind of Changelings are you seeing?" Stone asked.

"They're not all Changelings. About half of them are. See those two guys over there—the big one and the small one? The little guy's a goblin, and the big one is some kind of lizard."

Almost as if he'd heard them talking about him, the larger of the two figures, who looked to normal sight like a black man in an oversized hoodie, jerked his chin up and shot a suspicious glance toward the van. The goblin, a weaselly white man with stringy hair, did the same.

All four of the van's occupants remained silent and still as they rolled past, and after a moment the lizard and the goblin returned to their conversation.

Big Gee's was another block ahead on their left, set back from the street behind a dirt parking lot. A collection of around fifteen cars and motorcycles were parked with no apparent regard for order, and a few more people hung out around them, smoking and talking. The building itself had covered windows and a solid door so no light appeared from inside. Although the place's bright-orange neon sign was lit, there was nothing inviting about the bar. It had a distinct "keep out if you don't belong here" vibe.

"They're even more alert than the ones on the streets," Verity reported as they drove by. "They're checking out every vehicle that goes by. Looks like six of them, all Changelings."

"Six out of thirty," Jason said. "And probably more inside. Either they've added more guys to the gang, or they've pulled more of the existing ones in to keep an eye on something. And the kid said this wasn't their main hangout anymore."

"That all might be good news." Stone twisted in his seat to keep the parking lot in sight as long as he could, and didn't turn back until they'd rounded the corner at the end of the block.

"Why do you say that?" Verity asked.

"It might mean the demon itself isn't here. If Izzy *is* in there somewhere, it wouldn't need this many gang members to guard the place if it was here personally."

"If that's true," Amber said, "we need to get in there fast and get her out before it comes back. Probably safest to assume it *will* be coming back at some point."

"She has a point," Jason drove halfway up the block and parked in front of a shabby abandoned house. "Ideally, I'd like a little more time to prepare, but I'd rather get in and out before the demon shows up."

"We need to get closer," Stone said. "Verity, how's your clairvoyance spell?"

"Pretty good."

"Brilliant. Jason, drive around the back. I'll hold a stronger disregarding spell so they won't notice us. We've got a better chance of success if we know what we're in for."

Jason drove the van around the block behind the bar. It was another residential neighborhood lined with apartment buildings, so they didn't look out of place. He pulled to the side of the road, but left the engine running. "Go ahead and do it."

Stone took over the disregarding spell, pouring more power into it so it would be essentially impossible for anyone without either magic or highly enhanced sensory abilities like Amber's to identify them as anything but a clapped-out, empty van.

Verity settled back in her seat and closed her eyes. Everyone else waited tensely for several moments before she spoke in a clear but distracted voice. "Okay," she said. "It's a little hard to see because there isn't a lot of light in there, but it looks like the place has two entrances—the main one in the front and another one in the back. I can't tell what the back one leads to, though. Whatever it is, it's completely dark. There's a bar along the right side as you enter, some tables, booths along the left side, and a couple pool tables."

"How many in there?"

She paused. "Six, plus the bartender. Wish I could tell what kind of Changelings they are. They just look like a bunch of guys in their teens and twenties. One woman." Another pause. "The back has bathrooms and an office, and what looks like a stairway down."

"Basement?" Jason asked.

"Looks like it. Hold on…." Her brow furrowed, and her expression of concentration heightened. "It's harder to get a look down there. It's like everything's…hazy. It might be some kind of ward, but it's not completely preventing me from seeing."

"Is anybody down there?" Amber, sitting next to her, twisted in her seat. "Can you see Izzy?"

"Can't see Izzy, but that doesn't mean she's not there. There *are* people down there. Not sure how many, but it looks like three or four. Looks like one big room and a couple of smaller ones. Can't see into the smaller ones at all."

"That's got to be where we're headed," Stone said. "You said the stairway down is in the back?"

"Yeah, at the end of a hallway by the office, on the left side."

"Sounds like our best bet's to go in through that back door," Jason said. "It's probably a storage room or something."

Verity popped out of the spell with a loud exhalation. "Whoo, that spell isn't easy. Hold on." She dug in her bag and came up with a notepad and pen, which she used to sketch a crude floorplan. "That's the best I can do, unfortunately. The spell doesn't provide its own light."

"We've got to go," Stone said. "If Izzy's there and the demon decides to pay her a little visit for a top-off, I'd rather neither she nor we were anywhere in the vicinity."

Amber was already opening the bags they'd stashed in the back of the van. She handed gloves around to everyone, then passed something that looked like a skinny grenade to Jason along with a handgun, a box of bullets, and a radio with an earpiece, and took the same for herself. Two more radios went to Stone and Verity. "Alastair, can you shield us while we put on our vests? It's easier to do it outside."

Stone nodded grimly. It was starting to dawn on him now that this was real, that they were going into a gang's hideout to rescue someone, and likely they would be shot at—or worse.

Under cover of illusion, Jason and Verity exited the van and donned their ballistic vests. "We've got some for you and V too, if you want them," Jason said, nodding toward the bags.

"I'd rather not," Stone said.

"You should," Verity said, taking one. "Remember, Changelings can have abilities that can mess with magic. If they make you drop your shield, they could shoot you."

He'd forgotten about that. "Fine," he grumbled. "Let's get on with this."

Jason and Amber helped him and Verity strap into the vests like they did this every day. Stone rolled his shoulders, feeling uncomfortable and slow, but there was no helping it. Verity was right. At least the thing didn't make too much noise.

After testing their radios to make sure they were working properly, they used an invisibility spell to get them across the street and through an alley until they were crouched behind a dumpster in the vacant lot behind Big Gee's. From here, they could hear the faint, thumping beat of music coming from inside. It didn't appear that anyone else was in the vicinity.

Stone started to rise, but Amber pulled him back down. "Somebody's back here," she whispered. "I can smell him."

Stone shifted to magical sight. "I don't see any auras."

"Some Changelings are really good at concealment," Verity said. "A few of them can even hide their auras. Where, Amber?"

"Against the wall, about six feet to the right of the door."

"Right, then—two can play at this game," Stone said, re-casting the invisibility spell. He didn't want to do it again this soon, since the spell took a lot out of him, but there was no helping it. "Direct me, Amber. I'll take him out."

He crept across the parking lot, moving fast because he knew he didn't have long before he had to drop the spell. He felt exposed in spite of it, but Amber wasn't warning him of danger so he had to assume the Changeling hadn't noticed him.

He spotted the figure as he got closer, just a faint movement against the bar's grimy brick wall. It was some impressive concealment—even this close, if he hadn't known the Changeling was there, he wouldn't have noticed them.

The ganger didn't see the stunning spell coming. One moment he was blending in with the bricks, the next, a skinny young man in an oversized Lions jersey and baggy pants slumped to the ground next to the building.

Jason, Amber, and Verity hurried over. Amber and Verity kept watch while Jason pulled zip-ties from his pocket and bound the kid's arms and legs. "How long will he stay out?"

"Probably half an hour or so," Stone said. "If we're here that long, something's gone terribly awry."

"There's the door," Verity said, pointing.

They crept the rest of the way toward it, everyone keeping a close eye out for anyone coming around either side of the building. Stone snatched a quick glance at their auras; Jason's and Amber's were alert and on edge, while Verity looked more nervous. Stone wondered how often Jason and Amber did things like this in the course of Thayer Investigations' cases. One of the things they'd told him after he'd awakened from his three-year sleep was that Amber had taken the time to get her own PI license, so they were truly partners in the agency now.

"No cameras," Jason said. "Not surprised. These guys don't seem like a high-tech operation. Get the door, Al. We'll keep watch."

The lock on the door, substantial against mundanes, was laughably easy to pop with magic. They all stood back, Jason and Amber with their guns drawn and Verity with magic ready, as Stone used his own magic to swing it open.

Only darkness appeared beyond it. A quick look with magical sight revealed an empty room, so they all hurried through and closed the door before anyone outside could spot them.

Jason flipped his flashlight on, illuminating exactly what Verity had speculated was there: a storage room. Shelves lined three of its walls, stocked haphazardly with stacks of toilet paper, napkins, and a few boxes of beer. Whoever maintained the place obviously didn't prioritize neatness. On the floor, a couple of cockroaches skittered under one of the shelves.

"Nice place," Amber muttered, sniffing distastefully. "Trust me—don't eat anything here."

"Damn," Jason said. "I was hoping to pick up a burger or something on our way to busting out an undercover mage cop."

There was another closed door on the storeroom's other side. "Okay," Stone whispered. "According to Verity's map, this opens onto a hallway with the toilets, and the stairway down is at the other end. If we're lucky, we can get down there without having to face anyone upstairs."

"If we're lucky," Verity said. "Let's not count on that, okay?"

"I never do. Come on. Let me go first—I've got the best shield."

With the others behind him, he eased the door open. Outside, a wood-paneled hallway was covered in graffiti, stolen street signs, and posters of rappers on one side, with two restrooms on the other. The door to the men's room had been pulled off the hinges long ago, and the stench rolling out from the room made Amber recoil. Clearly, Big Gee didn't consider a regular cleaning staff to be a necessity to doing business.

At the end of the hall was another open doorway. Stone pointed toward it and began moving. He held his breath and glanced into the restroom as he walked past, but he didn't see anyone inside unless they were in the single stall. "Amber, can you tell?" he whispered into the mic.

"No. The stench is too strong to pick anything out."

"Hold on," Jason said. "I want to make sure."

The others waited in the hall while he drew his gun and sidled into the room. He glanced at them, then pushed the stall door open, then let it swing closed again. "Nobody."

He'd started to head back for them when Amber suddenly tensed. "Incoming!" she muttered.

That was all she got a chance to say when another, deeper voice yelled, "Hey, what the fuck?"

"Grab him!" Verity pushed past Jason, raising her hands at the same time Stone did.

They were too slow, though. The figure immediately disappeared through the doorway, back toward the front part of the bar.

"Bugger!" Stone snapped. "Now they're all going to be on to us."

Jason was already moving. He ran down the hall, pulling something from his pocket. When he reached the opening, he ducked behind it and flung the object into the room. A second later, a deafening *BANG* sounded, and a bright flash of light lit up the opening.

From the other side came yells, screams, and a series of thumps. Somebody shouted something, but it was too unintelligible to make out.

"Quick, what's the plan, Al?" Jason said over the comm. "We can't just all go down—they could burn us out."

Stone made a fast decision. "Verity, you and Amber stay up here and take care of this lot. Jason, you're with me."

Nobody argued. With magical shields up to protect them from stray gunfire, all four of them moved forward, Verity and Amber toward the open doorway, Stone and Jason to the stairs.

"Stay behind me," Stone told Jason. "I'm sure they know we're on our way."

Nobody appeared to be waiting at the foot of the stairs. Even magical sight didn't reveal anyone hiding.

"They're probably dug in, waiting for us to come down," Jason said. "Let's hurry, before they bring that demon back."

Stone was all for that. Shield still at full strength and back against one of the walls, he moved as fast as he dared down the rickety flight of stairs. More graffiti and posters lined the walls, and the whole place smelled like weed, beer, body odor, and the leftover stench from the upstairs bathroom.

He and Jason reached the bottom at the same time, but stopped before they entered the room. No light came from the area beyond. From upstairs, the sounds of yelling and loud objects thumping still came through clearly, but no gunshots so far. Stone pointed at himself, then pointed forward. *Let me go first.*

Jason nodded reluctantly.

Stone ducked low and, with magical sight up, pushed into the room.

He barely got the impression of a few auras hiding behind barriers before something large and heavy flew across the space and slammed into him, driving him backward.

Jason caught him and steadied him. "We need light!"

Stone caught his breath, regained his balance, and flung a bright ball of light into the center of the room. It illuminated a brick space around twenty-five by twenty feet, full of chairs, tables, and ratty old sofas. A couple of the tables had been turned on their sides to create barriers. One of the sofas had been the missile thrown at Stone; it lay on its side on the floor near the doorway. Two more doors at the far end of the room were both closed.

"Fuck!" called a voice. "What the hell are you?"

"Cops!" yelled another.

Stone didn't get a chance to reply, because a figure erupted from behind one of the barriers and charged toward him and Jason.

Without magical sight, it would have looked comical: a small, skinny guy in a hoodie, baseball cap, and baggy jeans, arms spread wide and mouth open in a rumbling roar of rage. To magical sight, though, it was a different matter. The skinny guy's true form was at least two feet taller, his chest and shoulders bulging with muscle, his head long-snouted and small-eyed. Horns poked from his head and light-brown hair covered his visible skin, making him look more like a bull than a human.

Before Stone could conjure a concussion spell to drive the guy backward, Jason acted. With a growl of his own, he surged forward and slammed the bull-man with a savage punch.

The bull twisted at the last second, taking the blow on his shoulder instead of his jaw. But its force still spun him around and drove him stumbling backward, where he fell over one of the over-turned tables.

"Bloody *hell*, Jason," Stone muttered, impressed. But there was no time for congratulations yet. The bull-man was already leaping to his feet, and two of the other three were coming up from behind their cover. To magical sight, one was a standard ogre, even bigger than the bull-man, and the other one had the same furry dog-wolf look as Jason's son Jaden—but a lot meaner.

"Get 'em!" the ogre yelled. He picked up one of the tables in a meaty hand and swung it at Stone like he was trying to hit a home run.

Stone threw himself to the side, but the table still hit the edge of his shield, sending a spike of feedback into his head. It wasn't bad, but they couldn't let this take too long. He wondered what Jason was thinking, watching two normal-sized guys hitting like trucks, but didn't have time to speculate about it.

"Fuck!" yelled the final guy, who was still crouched behind one of the barriers. "They're mages!" Unlike his two companions, he sounded scared.

"Don't matter!" the ogre yelled back. "Get out here, Fish, you little chickenshit!"

Jason, meanwhile, was wrestling with Bull-man. Now that his adrenaline-fueled strength, stamina, and resilience had kicked in, the two seemed evenly matched as they traded blows and slammed into walls hard enough to crack some of the brickwork.

Stone focused on the ogre and the dog. He couldn't let them get close to him—the ogre might be strong enough to take down his shield with a well-aimed punch, and the dog's teeth and speed both looked formidable. As they both hurried toward him, he raised his hands and created a wall of concussive energy between him and them, then pushed outward, sending them both stumbling.

"Listen!" he boomed. "I could kill the lot of you if I wanted to, but that's not why we're here. Give us your prisoner and we'll leave you in peace."

"Fuck that!" the ogre roared, lunging forward again. He slammed into the barrier and began pounding it with his fists, which to magical sight were as big as toasters.

Stone noticed something, though—in addition to his rage, his aura flared fear, too. So did the dog's. They were more scared of something—almost certainly the demon and what it would do to them if they lost Izzy—than they were of a powerful mage and a guy who could go toe to toe with them physically.

Stone shot a quick glance toward the other side of the room, where Jason was struggling with the bull-man. They didn't have time to waste. Jason was still holding his own at the moment, so he focused on the others. Fish still hid behind the barrier, only his head poking out. Stone could see now where he'd got his name: his whole bald head was covered in small, interlocking scales, and his features had a fishy quality to them. Was he hiding back there because he didn't have any Changeling powers that would be effective in a fight like this?

Stone had no idea if a stunning spell would work against these guys—they were a lot bigger than the chameleon they'd trussed up outside—but it was worth a try. Even though he had more lethal magic at his command if necessary, he didn't want to kill the Changelings if he had a choice.

Still, if it came down to getting out of here with Izzy before the demon arrived or going easy on the Changelings, he knew which way it had to be.

The ogre's pounding fists against the barrier were shooting more psychic feedback into his head. It still wasn't worse than a middling headache, but that wouldn't remain true for long. He raised his hands again, preparing to drop the barrier and hit the dog and the ogre with his stunning spell.

Before he could do that, Jason roared and flung the bull-man sideways, straight into the ogre, who stumbled.

Stone took his opportunity and dropped the shield. The ogre, who'd been leaning forward against it to hit it, lost his balance completely and fell forward, taking the bull with him. The dog danced out of the way, but not far enough.

With a yell of his own, Stone gathered Calanarian energy and formed it into a stunning ball of force, slamming it into the bull and the ogre as they struggled to get up. He didn't hold back—this might be a stun spell, but it was a potent one that would knock a normal human out for at least a few hours.

The ogre and the bull didn't even get a chance to yell. As the spell settled around them, crackling in the air, their eyes rolled back into their heads and they both dropped like someone had whacked them with a baseball bat. Oddly, the sounds they made when they hit were more like their human forms, rather than their massive Changeling ones.

The dog, eyes bulging, backed off. "Fuck, man!" His voice was high and shrieky. "You kill 'em? Don't kill me!"

"Nobody's dead." Stone pointed at Fish. "You. Get up from behind there. Keep your hands in sight."

Jason came up alongside him. He was puffing a bit, but looked energized, as if he'd enjoyed the fight. "We gotta get her and get out of here."

Casually, Stone hit the dog with the same stun spell as the other two, dropping him to the floor next to them. Then he turned to the last remaining ganger. "You're Fish, right?"

"How'd you know that?" He'd stood when ordered, but the overturned table still half-covered him. Despite his name, he had a humanoid body. He reminded Stone of the Deep Ones, from Lovecraft's horror stories—half fish, half human. To mundane sight, he looked like a dark-skinned guy in his early twenties.

"Bit obvious, isn't it?" He checked to make sure the three others were still fully unconscious, and lowered his voice. "I talked to your brother. He wants you out of here."

Fish's shock intensified. "You—talked to my *brother*?"

"He said you wanted out, too. Here's your chance."

Jason was already checking the two rooms. He slammed open the door to the one on the right, flashed his light around, then went to the left one. This time, he stopped. "Al, you're gonna want to see this."

"Gods, is she dead?" Dread crawling up his spine, he sidled to the door, keeping Fish in sight. "Watch him," he told Jason.

The room was small and as dingy as the rest of the place, barely big enough for the rough, metal-framed single bed that took up most of its space. A woman, skeletally thin and barely recognizable as the grinning Izzy Freeman from the photo Ren had shown Stone, lay on the bed. She had no cover and wore only a black sports bra and boyshorts, leaving her ribs and sunken abdomen visible. Her dark skin had an ashy, unhealthy pallor. For a moment Stone thought she was dead, but then her arm twitched, rattling a handcuff that held her chained to the bed's frame.

"Bloody hell…" he murmured. She looked like a concentration-camp inmate. Even if no one had been feeding her, she hadn't been missing long enough to have lost that much weight normally. It had to be a side effect of the demon's energy drain.

Trusting Jason to keep an eye on Fish and hoping Verity and Amber were faring as well upstairs, he dropped to his knees next to Izzy and used magic to pop the manacle free of her wrist. "Izzy? Can you hear me?" He spoke slowly and distinctly, trying to keep his voice calm.

She moaned, but didn't reply.

Stone made a quick decision. "Jason—pick her up, please. We're leaving."

"You can't!" Fish's voice was full of terror. "If you take her away, he'll kill us all!"

"That's not our problem, I'm afraid. If you're bright, you'll get the hell out of here *now,* go find your brother, and get as far away from Detroit as you can manage."

"We can't do that, man. We ain't got a car, or bus fare, or nothin'." All the fight had gone out of Fish now; his fear was already turning to resignation.

Stone glanced at Jason, who'd already gently picked Izzy up and wrapped her in his leather jacket. He pulled some cash from his pocket and offered it to Fish. "It's not much, but it should be enough to get you and your brother bus tickets out of here."

Fish looked like he couldn't believe what he was seeing. "You're—*helpin'* me?"

Stone didn't answer. He was already hurrying to catch up with Jason, who'd reached the door. "You're on your own now, Fish. It's up to you what you do with yourself. We're leaving." He slipped past Jason and raised his shield, and the two of them ascended the stairs with no idea what they'd find there.

They shouldn't have been concerned. Verity and Amber had the situation even better in hand than Stone and Jason had downstairs. Five Changelings—an ogre, a goblin, a rat, a female wolf, and a cat—were laid out on the dirty floor, unconscious along with the bartender. Some were bloody, some had no marks on them. The remaining one, a lizard, was currently stuck to the ceiling and watching the proceedings without malice, while Amber kept a close eye on him.

"And here I was worrying about you two," Stone said dryly. "Quite a fool, me."

Verity was barely listening. As soon as Jason had come into view carrying Izzy, her eyes widened and she hurried to intercept them. "Oh, God. She's in bad shape."

"We've got to get out of here, but can you do anything to help her once we're away?"

"I hope so. I can barely see her aura. If we don't do something soon, she doesn't have long."

"Don't take her," the lizard begged from the ceiling. "He'll kill us. He's gonna kill us all."

"Should have thought of that before you took her in the first place," Stone snapped. He didn't know why Verity and Amber had left him awake and unbound, but he trusted them enough not to ask. "I'll give you the same suggestion I gave Fish—get the hell out of here and maybe you'll have a chance. Better one than you gave this lady." He was having a hard time dredging up any sympathy for this group, even Fish, after seeing what they'd done to Izzy.

"Come on," Jason said, "Let's check outside and get out of here."

Neither Fish nor the lizard Changeling made any attempt to stop them as they headed out through the back door. Stone and Verity didn't see anyone lurking around when they checked with magical sight, so the four of them hurried through the vacant lot and piled into the van. They laid Izzy across the rear bench seat, using Verity's folded jacket as a pillow and covering her with Jason's. Verity crouched on the floor next to her, already beginning a healing spell.

Stone unlocked his phone, pulled up Ren's contact, and thrust it back at Amber. "Call Ren, tell her we've got Izzy and we need a place to bring her." Then he turned back around in his seat and focused on checking all around them with magical sight. Even though they were already a couple of blocks away from Big Gee's and moving as fast as Jason dared to drive, they weren't away safely yet. If the demon turned up soon, Stone didn't know how easily it could track them—or Izzy.

Amber had apparently reached Ren, because she put the conversation on speaker as soon as the agent answered. "We've got Izzy," she said. "She's in a bad way. She needs a hospital."

Ren didn't stop to ask questions. "Stand by," she snapped. A moment later, she rattled off an address. "That's a private hospital near Downtown. I'll meet you there."

"I suggest you summon any magical protections you can manage," Stone called without looking away from his scrutiny of the scenery around them. "I don't think anything's following us currently, but that could change."

"Understood. Let me go get things set up."

"How is she, Verity?" Stone asked.

"Can't talk now." Her voice was tight and strained.

Stone returned to his vigilance, hoping the young agent lasted long enough for them to get her to the hospital.

CHAPTER THIRTEEN

STONE WOULDN'T ALLOW HIMSELF to sleep, and neither would Jason and Amber.

The three of them had been pacing the area outside the emergency room at the small, private hospital for almost two hours, watching for threats and waiting for news.

Their last update had been shortly after they had brought Izzy in, but all they'd found out was that she was still alive—for the moment—and was being evaluated.

Ren had been there to meet them when they'd arrived, waiting at the emergency-room door with a full medical team and a gurney. They'd gently transferred Izzy from the backseat to the gurney and rushed off with her. Verity had gone with them, while Ren remained to get the update on what had gone down.

She wasn't with them now. As soon as they'd finished the briefing, she'd taken off to make some calls of her own and hadn't returned.

"I guess no news is good news, right?" Jason was on his third vending-machine coffee since they'd arrived, and hadn't sat down for more than a few minutes at a time before getting up to pace again. "I mean, if she'd died, V would come tell us."

"I presume so." Stone, too, had downed far too much coffee. The emergency-room waiting area was deserted except for them; he didn't know if that was because there were no other critical patients or because the other patients' visitors had been taken somewhere else. All he knew was that if they didn't get some news soon, he was going to barge in there and make them tell him something.

The door opened, and Verity emerged. She looked even more tired than they did, moving without her usual grace. Her eyes were sunken into deep circles.

The others immediately wheeled on her. "How is she?" Stone demanded.

"Is she alive?" Amber added.

"Is she awake?" Jason said.

Verity held up both hands to ward off the onslaught. "She's alive," she said wearily. "The doctors have done what they can physically, and another healer and I have done what we can magically. It's all up to Izzy now, and how much she wants to fight."

"What do you mean, how much she wants to fight?" Jason glared, but it clearly wasn't aimed at her. "She's an agent. She deals with stuff like this a lot. Of *course* she's gonna fight."

Stone recognized the vehemence in his friend's tone for what it truly was: a defiant plea to the universe, trying to make his words into reality by speaking them aloud. He sighed. "It's not so easy, Jason. She's had her life essence—her *soul*—drained by a demon. That doesn't just have physical ramifications. It's got mental ones, too. Psychic ones."

"What does that mean?" Amber asked, too carefully.

"It means she might not *want* to fight," Verity sounded even more tired than before, and reluctantly dropped into a nearby chair. "Alastair's right—having that kind of energy drained can leave you without much will to live. The doctors, both magical and mundane, can do everything they can to support her body, but not much to help her mind. The best we can hope is that she'll wake up and they can have some trained people talk to her."

"Any idea when that might happen?" Stone refused to acknowledge that it might not happen at all.

Verity spread her hands in a futile gesture. "Who knows? She's in bad shape physically—malnourished, dehydrated, just... *depleted*. They didn't hurt her physically, but it might have been better if they had."

Stone didn't want to ask, but before he formed the right words, Amber spoke in a soft, grim voice: "Did they...do anything else to her?"

"No." Verity stared at her hands in her lap. "I guess we can be thankful for that, at least."

"The demon probably didn't let any of that lot near her," Stone said. "It wanted her for itself, and that wasn't the sort of thing it was interested in."

Before anyone else could reply, the outer door opened and Ren entered. She still wore the same clothes she'd had on when they'd last seen her, but their usual crispness had wilted. "How is she?"

"Holding on," Verity said.

Ren let out a loud, ragged sigh and slumped into a chair near her. "That's all you've got? 'Holding on'?" But then she shook her head and waved it off. "Sorry. I'm a little frazzled right now. I'm sure you are too. I didn't get a chance to thank you for getting her out of there. I don't know how you did it, but I'm glad you did. At least she's got a shot now."

"Where have you been all this time?" Stone asked.

"Communicating with various people involved in the operation. Updating them, arranging for a few things. You have your job, and I've got mine."

"I hope one of those tasks is to make sure this place is well protected."

She glanced around, concerned. "Are you saying you think that thing might try to get in here and take her back?"

"Unlikely, given the shape she's in. I doubt it would want to risk being seen to get her back, since I doubt she would have lasted more than another day or so if we hadn't got her out of there. But it might try to send some of its people in, just out of spite. To be safe, I wouldn't allow any unknown Changelings anywhere near her."

"Don't worry. We've got both mundane and magical people, along with electronic surveillance, watching all the ways in and out. This isn't a public hospital, so we can restrict entry." She nodded toward the door to the emergency room. "I'll ask for the details on how you got her out of there later. Right now, give me an update on her condition."

Verity did that, while the others finally sat down. Stone was impressed at her crisp tone and the way she intermingled magical and medical terminology. Sometimes he still marveled at how far she'd come while he'd been "away" for three years, and still felt a little guilty about it, as if his presence had somehow been holding her back. Either way, though, it had definitely been for the best.

Ren listened, occasionally jotting something in her notebook. "Okay," she said when Verity finished. "You four should probably go get some sleep. It doesn't sound like she's going to be awake anytime soon."

Stone, Jason, Verity, and Amber all exchanged glances. "I don't think any of us fancy going anywhere," Stone said.

"Yeah," Jason agreed. "I don't want to be halfway across town if something goes down here."

"Is there someplace we can sleep here?" Amber asked. "A couple of empty rooms? Hell, I'll curl up on the floor if I have to."

Ren studied them, and apparently came to the conclusion that she wasn't going to change their minds. "I'll see what I can do." She turned to leave, then stopped and turned back. For a brief moment, her usual stern expression softened. "Seriously—thank you. If Izzy pulls through this, she'll have all of you to thank for it."

Nobody woke Stone and the others for the rest of the night. Stone hadn't thought he'd fall asleep at all, stretched out in his clothes across an uncomfortable bed in an unused room, but when he opened his eyes after thinking he'd dropped off for a few minutes, faint sunlight shone in through the cracks in the blinds. He sat up and ran a hand through his hair.

"Morning," Jason said from the doorway.

Stone jerked his head toward him. "How long have you been up? Where are Verity and Amber? How is Izzy?"

"Slow down. Haven't been up long. Amber's off getting cleaned up. They brought us toothbrushes and soap, but no shower facilities here. V was already gone when we checked on her. She probably went off to see what was going on with Izzy."

Stone grunted something unintelligible. His mouth tasted like old coffee.

Amber showed up while he was bent over tying his boots, and Verity arrived a few moments later.

"How is she?" the other three asked, practically in unison.

"Hard to say." She looked less exhausted than she had the previous night, and some of the dark circles under her eyes had faded, but still tired. "They got her stabilized, physically. They've got her on IV fluids, and her body's responding about as well as can be expected."

"Has she woken up yet?" Stone asked. "Or are they keeping her sedated?"

"She hasn't. They aren't sedating her, but so far she hasn't shown any sign of awareness beyond moving a little and making some sounds. Give her time, though. She's been through a lot."

"Nobody tried to mess with her, did they?" Jason was pacing the room again, as if all this inactivity was wearing on him.

"No, it was a quiet night." She looked at Stone. "Were you serious that you didn't think the demon would try to come after her?"

"I can't be sure, of course. I'm hardly an expert on demons, even after all this. But I don't think it would be in its best interest. Demons are tough, but they're not invincible, and I don't think this one is very subtle. If enough firepower were brought to bear against it, it could be taken down. My guess is it will look for other prey."

"What about the SickBoyz?" Amber asked. "Will it retaliate against them for letting Izzy get away?"

"The answer to that is yes," came another voice from the doorway. Ren Huxley stood there; unlike the others, she'd obviously managed to scare up a change of clothes and possibly even a shower.

A cold pit settled in Stone's stomach. "What do you mean?"

"We got a call about four a.m.," she said, looking grimmer than usual. "Big Gee's burned to the ground. By the time firefighters showed up, the blaze had engulfed the whole building. They're still picking through the wreckage, but so far they've found the remains of at least five people, burned beyond recognition. There might be more in the basement, but they haven't gotten that far yet."

"Bloody hell…" Stone whispered. He wondered if any of the Changelings he and the others had knocked out had managed to make it out alive. Had Fish taken his advice and gotten himself out of there to track down his brother before the demon returned?

Ren shook her head. "It wasn't your fault, Stone. You can't feel guilty about it."

"Yeah, we can," Jason grumbled. "Those kids might not have been upstanding citizens, but what they were doing lately wasn't their fault. That thing made them do it. And now they're dead."

"We had to get Izzy out of there, though," Stone said. "Honestly, I *don't* feel guilty this time. Do I wish it hadn't happened? Of course. But Izzy *didn't* do anything wrong, before or after this demon business. They grabbed her, and we had to get her back. We knew what we were up against. Demons don't play by the rules— it's sort of the essence of the job description."

"We're gonna have to take that bastard down," Jason said. "You know that, right? Otherwise, it's just gonna do the same thing all over again."

"I know." He was surprised Jason had come to that conclusion so quickly, but he himself had already reached it. Yes, there were still eleven demons knocking around, but so far the rest had kept their heads down. This one had no such subtlety.

"Now, wait a second," Ren protested. "You can't just go out gunning for a *demon.*"

"Not yet, we can't. But we've got to. Jason's right. It won't stop. It will probably escalate, since I doubt it's got many anger management skills. We've poked it in the arse, and it's going to poke back."

"How are you even going to *find* it?"

"Don't know yet. I'm hoping when Izzy wakes, she might be able to tell us something." He stood. "Until then, I need a shower and some hot coffee."

He didn't want to leave the hospital long enough for them to go back to their rooms for showers and changes of clothes, but if they had to risk it, it was better to stay together. Even so, they hurried as much as they could, returning in less than an hour after stopping at a drive-thru for coffee and a fast-food breakfast.

Stone half expected to see a blasted-out crater or the burning husk of the hospital, but to his relief nothing looked any different. When they got back inside, Ren assured them nobody had tried getting in.

"Maybe it has to rest," Amber suggested.

"Or maybe it's already given up on the SickBoyz and it's off looking for some other gang to take over," Verity said.

"I'm not sure speculation will do us any good. Let's just be grateful for now that we got a break. Any update on Izzy?" Stone asked Ren. "I'd very much like the chance to talk to her when she's awake."

"I don't think that's going to happen any time soon, unfortunately. She's got a long road ahead of her, and according to my last report, she's still not completely out of the woods."

"What's going to be done with her?" Jason asked. "Is she staying here?"

"She'll be here until she's stable enough to move. Then we're going to move her to Chicago. We've got a facility there where she'll be comfortable."

"You want to get her out of Detroit, don't you?" Stone paced back and forth in front of her. "I think that's a wise idea, actually."

"Do you think the demon will come after her if she's not here in town?" Jason asked.

"Not certain, but I'd bet not. As I said before, this one is almost certainly the weakest of the eleven, and it won't want to extend its reach too far. My guess is that it will try taking over another gang and resume its activities until somebody takes it out. It wants power, and it won't care where it gets it."

"Great," Ren said grimly. "Something else to look forward to."

"Any idea when you'll be moving Izzy?" Verity asked.

"Probably in the next few days. She's pretty fragile now." The agent looked like she had about nine different things on her mind and was trying to decide which one to settle on. Finally, she said, "Listen—there's no reason for you four to wait around, unless there's anything else you can do magically to help Izzy, Verity."

"I doubt it," she said reluctantly. "The other healers and I have done everything we can to stabilize her, and at this point the mundane medical people will have everything she needs. It really is mostly up to her at this point."

"What about the demon?" Jason asked. "Should we stay in case it shows up?"

"No," Ren said. "I can't expect you to stay here indefinitely. The hospital is on high alert, the area where we've got Izzy is warded, and we've got both mages and military personnel keeping the place under observation. More are on call and can get here in less than ten minutes if needed. I think we've got things under control for now." She swept her gaze around at all of them. "Go home, people. And thanks again. I haven't said that enough."

Stone waved her off. "We're not done yet. We'll head home for now, mostly because we haven't got a clue either where the demon is or how to deal with it if we find it. I've got to do a bit more research. But we'll be back." He leaned in and spoke in a softer voice. "If anything happens, call me immediately. I can get here faster than the others."

Ren didn't even bother asking about how, a testament to how frazzled this whole situation was making her. "Yeah. But I'm hoping the demon takes a few days off, at least. We can all use the rest."

They collected their gear from the van and the hotel rooms they hadn't even used, and took the agency's plane from Detroit to Chicago, where they returned via the portal to Sybil's Apothecary.

"You call us if anything comes up," Jason told Stone firmly as they stood in the portal room. "We're involved in this now, so don't leave us out."

"I won't," Stone assured him. "You lot were instrumental in dealing with that situation. I wouldn't think of doing this without you." It wasn't flattery—he'd been impressed at how all three of them had handled the fight at Big Gee's.

"Let us know when Izzy gets to Chicago," Amber said, addressing both Stone and Verity. "I'm still worried that thing will try to attack the transport on the way to the airport."

Stone was too, but they couldn't live their lives worrying about every potential eventuality. "You'll hear as soon as we do."

And then they left, Verity through the dedicated portal to the San Francisco shop, and Jason and Verity out to their car. Stone stood a moment, trying to quiet his thoughts, then re-entered the portal and stepped out at his Encantada house.

Raider was there to greet him, sitting primly a few feet away with his tail wrapped around his flank and his green eyes wide.

Stone smiled. "Hello, Raider. It's good to see you." He shifted to magical sight, his smile widening as the rangy tabby morphed into his larger, darker Changeling form.

Ever since Raider had undergone the Change, Stone had stopped keeping him out of the downstairs library/portal room and the upstairs workroom. The cat had become a lot more sensitive to magic, and a lot less likely to disturb anything. One indication of his new sensitivity was that he always seemed aware when someone was about to come through the portal. Stone wondered if the gateway generated some magical frequency Raider could hear or feel but he couldn't, or if some change in the area's magical ambient indicated portal activity. He supposed he might never know, though he'd mentioned it to Eddie and Ward and they were already doing some research on it. It had been slow going, though, because Raider was the only Changeling pet they knew and Stone wouldn't let them borrow him for even benign experimental purposes.

Raider leaned forward and sniffed delicately as Stone stepped away from the portal, then looked at his human questioningly.

"Yes, yes, I know, I need a shower. If you'll excuse me, I'm going to do just that. Then something to eat, and a cup of coffee."

Raider didn't reply, which was quite polite of him.

Stone paused to feed the cat before he headed upstairs. He had a magical feeder that provided all the kibble Raider wanted, but the canned stuff required human intervention.

He didn't wait for Raider to finish eating, but mounted the stairs to his bedroom, collected clean clothes, and soon was standing in his shower cubicle with searing hot needles of water bombarding his back. He let his shoulders slump, making no effort to wash yet. The water felt wonderful on his tired muscles. Around him, the steam rose and engulfed the bathroom.

He lost track of time, and was just about to consider that he should probably finish cleaning up and get out before the ceiling started dripping, when his phone rang.

He'd left it on the edge of the counter nearest the shower, not wanting to miss a call from Ren if something went wrong with Izzy. He swiped the condensation off the glass and leaned closer to peer at the screen.

Blocked.

"Bugger…" he muttered. He was really starting to hate blocked numbers, because they almost always meant trouble—or if not trouble, at least a disruption to his futile attempts at keeping order in his life.

He briefly considered leaning out of the cubicle and answering it. It could be Trevor Harrison, back on Earth and ready with an offer to get started teaching him Calanarian mechanomagical techniques.

Then again, it could be Aldwyn. Just because the old dragon couldn't hijack him anymore or force him to do anything he didn't want to do, that didn't mean he still couldn't call asking for favors—or making offers that would be hard to refuse.

"You can wait," he told the phone, and ducked his head under the stream of water. If it was something important, the caller would call back, or leave voicemail. And if it was a telemarketer trying to save his auto warranty's soul, he was better off without it.

The phone rang a couple more times, then went silent. Stone leaned out of the stream and watched for a moment to see if the caller had left voicemail, but they hadn't. Probably a telemarketer, then. He relaxed into the hot water, closing his eyes as it ran down over his face.

When he opened his eyes, a figure was standing in the bathroom doorway.

He jerked with a grunt of shocked surprise, nearly losing his balance on the wet floor. His back hit the cold wall tiles as he raised his hands, magic blooming around them.

The figure didn't move, but merely waited patiently in the doorway.

There was so much steam on the glass that all Stone could see was that it was humanoid. How had they gotten in past the wards? How hadn't Raider noticed?

An absurd, terrified thought struck him: had the demon from Detroit somehow tracked him all the way to California? Was it waiting to attack him?

But then he remembered how the scar on his chest from The Unspeakable's knife had twinged with pain when he'd touched the demon's energy during the ritual with Heidi Royer. He probed it with a finger now, but it neither flared red nor hurt in any way.

The figure still hadn't moved.

He reached out, his magical shield in place, and wiped away some of the condensation on the shower glass with his hand, enough to reveal the figure's face—

—and slumped back against the shower tiles again, half-relieved, half-annoyed.

"Seriously?" he demanded. "I don't answer her bloody call while I'm in the *shower,* so she sends one of her minions to find me in the *bathroom?*"

The figure, now revealed to be Thalassa Nera's familiar huffy-librarian messenger, merely watched him in silence.

Stone sighed loudly. Just when he thought his life couldn't get any more interesting, the universe seemed determined to prove him wrong. He pushed the door open and stepped out, making no effort to cover himself. He didn't want to give the messenger—or probably Thalassa watching through its eyes—the satisfaction of knowing she'd caught him off guard. With dignity, he grabbed his towel and wrapped it around his waist. "Okay, then—what do you want?"

The librarian watched with a tiny smile, her gaze moving up and down his body with oddly feline satisfaction. "Your company is requested this evening."

Stone grumbled something unintelligible. He was still soaking wet and was already starting to shiver, but he only had the one towel within easy reach. He could either pull it off and continue drying himself, or keep shivering. Either way, he was sure he was entertaining Thalassa.

He was also sure that "requested" was Thalassa-speak for "expected."

The dragon lady had great timing, he had to give her that.

Fine—if she wanted a show, he'd give her one. Why should he be uncomfortable, when her minion had intruded in one of the most private areas of his home? With a small, wicked smile and his gaze fixed challengingly on the librarian's face, he unhooked the towel, whipped it behind him, and began drying his back, all the while facing her head-on. "Where?"

The librarian pulled something from her pocket—another of the rolled scrolls Thalassa fancied—and set it on the other end of the counter, never taking her eyes off Stone. "Everything is included here. The reservation is at nine p.m., in Paris. Please do not be late."

He did a quick mental calculation. Paris was nine hours ahead of California, which meant he had around four hours before he'd have to leave. Good thing he hadn't eaten much for breakfast. "I wouldn't dream of it. Now, would you mind getting out of my bathroom? If you want a proper strip show, we'll talk tonight. Right now, I'm bloody freezing."

The librarian's impish, wicked smile mirrored his own, and he had no trouble seeing Thalassa's glittering green gaze behind her messenger's prim brown eyes. "The lady will look forward to it. Good day."

She vanished with a soft little *pop.*

Raider appeared in the doorway a few feet behind where she'd stood, tilting his head in curiosity.

"Lot of good *you* are as a watch-cat," Stone grumbled, but he was more amused than annoyed.

"Meow." Raider jumped onto the toilet seat and continued watching his human.

Stone finished drying off and got dressed before he touched the scroll. He carried it to the bedroom and sat on the edge of the bed, where Raider immediately leaped up and settled in his lap. "Okay. Let's see what you've got planned for us."

The scroll contained only two lines: a set of ley-line coordinates, followed by *Formal dress is requested.*

That wasn't much to go on. But then again, Thalassa always did like her surprises.

He let his breath out in a long exhalation and lowered himself back until he was lying on the bed. "Well, Raider—looks like I've got plans for tonight."

Already, his thoughts were going places his mind wasn't entirely comfortable with.

His body, on the other hand, was just fine with them.

CHAPTER FOURTEEN

No ONE APPROACHED ALDWYN on his way to the center of Nargul.

The streets remained empty for several blocks beyond the Drubo's Rest; apparently the nonmagical residents of the town had some kind of efficient grapevine they used to warn each other about the presence of the Talented in their midst. As he walked down the damp, darkened street, he noted every window was closed and shuttered, every light inside a structure extinguished, every vehicle either gone or parked and empty.

He strolled along, his pace steady and focused but not overly hurried. The air had the sharp, fresh tang of the sea, coupled with the fainter odor of garbage and a subtle fishy overlay. Above, the sky was cloud-choked, uniform in its darkness.

With one exception. When he tilted his head back as he walked, he spotted a small, shining point of light high overhead. It was too big to be a star and not round enough to be a moon, so that left only a single option: it had to be the same floating city he'd spotted before, lit up now in the black sky. Even from here, he could see the faint tinges of magic dancing around it.

So that was Prensyrrus, home of the so-called "Talented."

His next destination.

If he was to get the answers he sought, that was where he'd need to go. Clearly, the mages were more knowledgeable of the world at large than the drudges down here. If he could manage to put up with their insufferable egos long enough to question them without killing them, he might find out what he wanted to know.

He'd considered trying to travel there using the dragons' normal ley-line method, but when the unfortunate Loriar had told him of the teleport pads, he'd changed his mind. He was unfamiliar with the ley lines here and how they functioned, and, despite near-certainty that at least one had to intersect a magically floating city large enough to house thousands of people, he didn't yet want to waste his time hunting for a corresponding line here in this squalid, fish-smelling city. His draconic magical senses made ley lines as visible to his normal vision as other magic, but he hadn't spotted any in his immediate vicinity.

Another option would be to return to the edge of town, turn himself invisible, and change to his true form. Flying from the ground to the city above would be a barely-noticeable exertion, especially since he doubted any of the chaotic, unpredictable energy he'd experienced in the Wastes would exist between here and Prensyrrus. Loriar had told him the cities were located along the coastline because it was safe from such dangerous magic.

But no, he didn't want to do that, either. Part of why he'd chosen to remain here was because he wanted to learn more about this strange, magic-rich world and how he could use it to his advantage. As much as he valued magic, knowledge could often be just as important. Experiencing this world as its native mages did might provide useful information for the future.

So, the teleport pad would suffice for now. If, after exploring Prensyrrus and getting a few more answers, he decided he wanted to remain here for a while, he would make a study of the available ley lines. No doubt at least some subset of the mages in the city would be familiar with them.

It soon became apparent, however, that the city of Nargul was much larger than he had originally expected. He had envisioned a fairly small, compact scattering of buildings, but after he'd walked for half an hour and passed only more shabby businesses, apartment buildings, and other structures, he had to reassess his original hypothesis.

Fortunately, now that he was well away from the area around the Drubo's Rest, the grapevine warning the citizens of the "Zap" presence had begun to release its grip. More people appeared in the streets, either going about their nighttime work or returning home from their evening's drinking with friends. Vehicles were still rarer, mostly old rattletrap trucks or wagons pulled by animals, but no one gave Aldwyn a second look as he moved along in his workman's disguise, additionally shielded by his disregarding aura.

He stopped on a street corner after walking for another few minutes, considering his choices. If he wanted to find the town's center, he'd have to either levitate high enough to get a good view of the area, or simply ask one of the townspeople.

A truck rumbling up from behind and pulling off the road at the curb next to him made his decision. He watched as a man in a blue shirt and heavy pants alighted from the vehicle, hurried around to the rear, and retrieved a pair of boxes from the others stored there. The man moved past Aldwyn without appearing to notice him, rapped twice on a door, and handed the packages over to the man who opened it.

When he turned to go back to his truck, Aldwyn was standing in front of him.

He started, grinning self-consciously, and swiped his forearm over his brow. "Oh!" he said in a cheerful voice. "Sorry, friend! Didn't see you there."

"I need a ride."

The man frowned, clearly conflicted. He looked Aldwyn up and down as if trying to determine whether he was dangerous. "Uh—I still got a few more deliveries to make tonight, but if you're heading the same way I am—"

"I am heading to the center of town."

"Hey, I'm sorry, but that's not the direction I'm going. Maybe you can—"

"I need a ride," Aldwyn repeated. "And you will supply it." Without waiting for the man to respond, he walked past him and climbed into the old truck's passenger seat.

The man glared. "Hey, now! You can't—"

But then he stopped when he got a good look at Aldwyn's expression. "Uh...okay. Yeah. I guess I can be neighborly. I'll be a little late with the deliveries, but that's okay."

"Thank you," Aldwyn said with dragonly dignity. He sat upright, his hands in his lap and his gaze straight ahead, as the shaking man got in and fired the vehicle up. Even in his peripheral vision, he could see the man's aura going wild.

The man missed a shift, bit off a swear word with a quick glance toward Aldwyn, then pulled the rattling, blatting truck back into the sparse traffic. He drove in silence for a short while, but apparently he was the talkative type and couldn't help trying to make conversation. Either that, or he was trying to ingratiate himself with this frightening stranger. "So...uh...you new in town?"

"Yes."

He swallowed. "That's...uh...good. How you liking it so far?"

"I do not wish to indulge in small talk. Take me to the center of town."

"Sorry. Just trying to be friendly." His expression warred between controlled anger and fear, and he tightened his hands around the steering wheel. He drove for a while longer, making a couple turns and heading in what Aldwyn knew to be the correct direction. As they turned another corner, he ventured, "What part of town do you want to go to? The center of town's a pretty big area. Don't know if you know it, bein' new to town and all, but Nargul's pretty spread out."

"I wish to go to the teleportation platforms."

The truck jerked violently as the man missed another shift. His aura, which had begun to calm a bit, billowed bright red again, and he swallowed harder than before. He got the truck back under control, slowed, and looked at Aldwyn. "The...teleport platforms?"

"That is what I said." Aldwyn continued gazing out through the cracked windshield, though he kept an eye on the driver with his peripheral vision.

The man opened his mouth a couple times as if about to speak, closed it again, and continued driving. Finally, he appeared to screw up his courage. "Uh...friend?"

"Yes?"

"Are you one of the Talented, in disguise? Because if you are, I'm...uh...honored that you chose me to drive you. But—"

"I am not one of the 'Talented' as you know them." Aldwyn put contemptuous emphasis on the word. "But it would be in your best interest, nonetheless, to deliver me to my destination with all due haste."

"Uh—" He snatched another sideways glance, clearly not wanting to contradict his enigmatic and unsettling passenger. "Okay," he said, subsiding. "I'm not gonna argue with you. You got your own business, and I'm happy to help."

Aldwyn was certain the man didn't believe him when he'd said he wasn't one of the Talented. His experience at the Drubo's Rest had already shown him that the nonmagical dared not put a toe out of line when dealing with the mages, which left this poor wretch with a dilemma—did he play along and treat Aldwyn like the common working man he appeared to be (but didn't sound like), or did he slyly (wink, wink, nudge, nudge) imply that he knew otherwise? Aldwyn would have pitied him, if he cared.

He didn't, though. At this point, all he wanted was to arrive at his destination. He turned pointedly away from the driver, looking out the side window in obvious dismissal.

The man had apparently decided that his best chance to survive the night was to remain silent. He kept his attention on the road, drove carefully so as not to jostle his passenger, and kept his opinions to himself.

A few minutes later the truck made another turn, revealing a central square in which the buildings were both of more attractive design and higher quality construction than most of the rest of the city Aldwyn had seen. The man pulled off the road and parked at the curb.

"Here we are," he said. "This is as far as I can take you. Only authorized vehicles are allowed near the Talented's complex."

Aldwyn turned toward him, giving him a patrician once-over and noting that he was visibly paler than before, with little beads of sweat on his forehead. This was probably when he thought his life was going to end.

Contrary to popular belief about him, however, Aldwyn wasn't indiscriminately cruel to lesser beings. Unlike the sadistic Talented, who flaunted their power because they could, Aldwyn usually saved his wrath for those who had offended or opposed him in some way. He opened the door and climbed out of the truck. "Thank you. You may go now."

"Uh—it was a pleasure, friend. Have a pleasant evening."

Because Aldwyn was Aldwyn, he didn't smile at how quickly the driver managed to get his rattling old truck out of the vicinity while doing his best to act casual about it. By the time the vehicle rounded a corner and disappeared, he'd already forgotten about it.

He stood a moment, pondering his next move. The streets here were nearly deserted, with no foot traffic and only a few vehicles moving by. Further in, toward the fine building, even the vehicles vanished. But his draconic sight revealed strong, solid magic surrounding the entire area.

Clearly, given the Talented's contempt for the "Dim," he wouldn't get very far in his current disguise. He concentrated a moment, recalling Loriar's long red coat and fine illusionary trappings, and had no trouble reproducing them. He didn't concern himself with any small deviations from an exact match—he'd have time to adjust them when he reached the building, where no doubt he'd find more of the Talented to use as templates. For his own appearance, he used a younger version of the human visage he used on Earth.

Odd that the people here so strongly resemble humans, he mused idly, but put the thought aside.

He set off walking with a confident stride. It wasn't an act, since he was certain he was more than a match for any of these people should it become necessary. He hoped it wouldn't, though. Right now, he was satisfied to remain in information-gathering mode. The more he could learn about this strange society, the better he could determine whether, and to what extent, he could exploit it.

It was obvious which part of Nargul's central area had been claimed by the Talented. Everything about it, from the quality of the streets and sidewalks to the materials used to construct the buildings, was of significantly higher quality than anything in the rest of the city. Even the *air* smelled better, as if unseen generators were pumping a light, pleasant scent around. The area crackled with magical energy.

The centerpiece was a three-story building made of some light-colored stone, with soaring windows dominating its façade. A wide walkway lined with low walls in the same colored stone led up to it, with a magically-lit fountain in front of a short flight of stone steps leading to a pair of wide double doors. Aldwyn didn't see anyone entering or leaving, but two figures, one male and one female, stood on either side of the doors. They wore similar long coats to Loriar, but theirs were darker red and looked more like uniforms.

Aldwyn strode up the walkway and mounted the stairs like he'd done this a thousand times before. The knowledge that he could turn anyone who opposed him to ash gave him the kind of confidence that was difficult to stand up to.

"Good evening," the male guard said, using magic to open the door on his side.

On the other side, the female guard gave a polite smile and did the same with hers.

Aldwyn favored them with a regal nod as he swept past, but didn't otherwise acknowledge them. He filed away the notion that apparently even among the Talented, there were varying levels of social status.

Inside, a magically-lit atrium reached all the way to the top of the building's three stories. Its airy beauty, even at night, provided a stark contrast to the far grimmer conditions outside. Everywhere Aldwyn looked, he spotted intricate wood- and stonework, magical illumination, and a number of touches that were obviously there either to show off the Talented's magical abilities, or to give them something beautiful to look at as they moved back and forth between the floating city above and the ground-based one. Everything in the space was spotlessly clean and pristine, showing no signs of wear or even use. Though definitely attractive, it also had an oddly sterile feeling, like a fine mansion staged by a real-estate agent to be as unoffensive as possible to the largest number of potential buyers.

This time of night, the place was only sparsely populated. Aldwyn wondered if the urge to bully the Dim was common among the Talented, or if only a few of them—perhaps younger ones like Loriar and his unfortunate female companion whose name he couldn't remember—bothered.

It wasn't hard to find the teleport pads, since they were the building's centerpiece. There were three of them; all were circular, but the first and second were around five feet in diameter, and the third, on the right side, was twice that. All three were ringed by brushed-metal railings at waist height. Two guards or attendants, dressed in the same style of dark-red uniform coat as the doormen, stood on either side of openings in each of the railings, looking bored. All six of them eyed Aldwyn with faint interest, as if hoping he would choose their pad to give them something to do.

He was about to ascend the three steps to the leftmost pad, watching the crackling magic dancing around the area as he moved, when the rightmost one—the largest—shimmered and five huddled figures appeared in its center.

To Aldwyn's surprise, the figures weren't red-coated Talented, but nervous-looking nonmagical people dressed in rough work clothes. As soon as they solidified, the two Talented guarding their platform turned to glare at them.

"Well? What are you waiting for? Get moving!" one guard ordered, looking at them as if they were something foul he'd found on the bottom of his spotless boot. "No dawdling!"

The five newcomers, two men and three women, looked uniformly terrified. They stumbled off the platform and took off at a near-run toward the front doors without any side looks at Aldwyn or the other guards, clumped together like a gaggle of wary herd animals. They made it across the open space in a few seconds and disappeared into the night, red tendrils of fear trailing behind them like banners.

One of the guards on the pad Aldwyn had been approaching shot him a contemptuous look, accompanied by a snort. "Dim. It's a shame we have to sully our spaces with their filth."

Aldwyn wondered why they *did* have to do that—wasn't there some other way to move them around?—but he didn't ask. He merely made a noncommittal noise that could have been agreement, noticing out of the corner of his eye that the two guards on the platform where the nonmagical group had just arrived were now making a show of casting some kind of cleansing spell over it.

"Sorry to keep you waiting," the other guard on Aldwyn's platform said. Both of them stood aside, obviously waiting for him to step up. "Go right ahead."

He realized that this was basically a magical public-transportation system, with very little difference from a standard elevator or subway car back on Earth. Nobody was going to make a big deal of him being here—people no doubt used these things to go back and forth throughout the day. They were probably wondering why he was hesitating.

He gave them the same perfunctory nod he'd given the doormen and stepped toward the platform.

"Sir." One of the attendants spoke up, sounding almost apologetic.

"Yes?"

The man nodded toward a small carved box that sat on a pedestal next to the railing, as if expecting Aldwyn to know what he meant.

Aldwyn hadn't seen the box before because the guard's body had been obscuring it, but now that he noticed it, he saw similar boxes next to the other two pads. He had no idea what the man wanted, but clearly he was supposed to do something. He met the guard's gaze and remained still, waiting.

"Er—" The guard looked at the other guard as if unsure of what he should do. "Your identification, sir." He looked down at Aldwyn's hand, then his brow furrowed. "You don't have your ring?"

Damn. Of course a society like this would want to control access to their floating magical city. "I lost it," he said firmly. He offered a sly smile. "It was a…busy evening."

The guards looked at each other again. The other four, with nothing else to do, tried not to appear interested in the conversation, but they still kept shooting glances in that direction.

The first man, the one who'd been talking to Aldwyn initially, looked as if he'd rather be just about anywhere else. "I'm sorry sir, but I'm afraid I'm not permitted to allow anyone into Prensyrrus without proper identification." He brightened. "But if you'll wait for just a moment, I can summon someone who can look up your citizenship record and you'll be on your way. I hope you understand."

Aldwyn had had quite enough of this, and didn't plan to wait around while this herd of petty bureaucrats got their act together. He jerked his head up with an "aha!" look and patted his pocket. "Just a moment." He fumbled around and pulled something free, holding it out in his palm for them to see. "Forgive me. I forgot I'd put it in my pocket."

Of course there was nothing in his hand, but as he suspected, this group wasn't high on the magical-power scale. The simple illusion, coupled with a mental suggestion that it was exactly what they were expecting to see, had the two nearby guards nodding in satisfaction.

One of them returned his sly smile. "We know how it is, of course, sir." He indicated the box. "If you'll just—"

It was more obvious now what he was expected to do, so Aldwyn pretended to slip the illusionary ring onto his finger, then waved his hand languidly in the direction of the box. This time, he didn't bother with an illusion, but simply planted suggestions in the guards' minds that they were seeing exactly what they were expecting to see.

The effort proved laughably easy here, with all the magical energy flying around.

It was good to be a dragon.

The two guards smiled, tension draining from their postures. "Thank you. Please proceed."

Head held high and radiating dignity, Aldwyn stepped onto the platform.

A wrenching, mildly uncomfortable jolt went through his body, and then the scene around him changed subtly.

He was still standing on a teleport platform, and it was still surrounded by a similar brushed-metal railing, but the space here was even larger than the one on the ground, with more soaring windows, lighter-colored walls, and more intricate, dancing magical lighting. He glanced sideways, noting that instead of three pads, there were nine, all smaller-sized ones. Either the nonmagical who traveled from here used the same ones as the Talented, or their larger ones were hidden away where their betters didn't have to look at them. Aldwyn suspected the latter.

He stepped off the platform, intent on crossing the nearly-empty atrium area and exiting through the series of doors on the other side.

"Please stay where you are," an authoritative voice said. "Do not move, and do not attempt to use any magic."

CHAPTER FIFTEEN

S TONE HALF-EXPECTED to get a call from Ren Huxley in the next few hours, telling him that the demon had attacked the hospital or managed to sneak someone in to kill Izzy. The heightened tension from those thoughts, combined with his not-entirely-voluntary ruminations about what might occur tonight with Thalassa, meant he got very little rest when he tried to lie down for a nap before getting ready to leave. Even the presence of a purring Raider stretched out and pressed against his side didn't help.

Finally, he decided the best option was to take the initiative. Before he started dressing for the evening, he called Ren directly.

To his surprise, she answered. "Stone? Is something wrong?"

"That's what I was calling to ask *you*. I assume no news is good news, but I'm going to be out of contact for a few hours so I wanted to make sure nothing needed my attention." He hoped it didn't, because he didn't want to contemplate what Thalassa might do if he stood her up.

"No, everything's fine. For the moment, at least." She still sounded tired, and like her attention was being pulled in several directions at once. "All's quiet at the hospital. Nobody's tried to get in, and the wards haven't pinged at all."

"Brilliant. How is Izzy? Any improvement?"

There was a pause. "Physically, she's doing better. Still fragile, but better. Obviously, she's seriously malnourished and dehydrated, but that's being addressed."

"What aren't you saying?"

Even longer pause. "She's not waking up. They took her off the sedatives since it doesn't seem she's in any pain, but she's still unconscious."

"What does that mean? Do they think it's something mental?"

"They don't know. Her mental activity is strong, but…agitated. Something's going on inside her head, but we don't know what it is. We're hoping she'll wake up soon so we can talk to her. They're probably going to move her to Chicago tomorrow afternoon if her physical condition continues to improve."

"Well, that's good." He wanted Izzy out of Detroit as soon as possible, before the demon got any ideas about trying to get her back. "I should be back in contact by then, so call me if you need anything."

"I will."

"And get some sleep, Agent. You're no good to anyone if you're exhausted."

"Yeah. I'll see about that."

Thalassa had specified "formal" for their evening but not black tie, so Stone wore one of his finest bespoke suits. Most people he knew, familiar with his preferred style of jeans and black band or pub T-shirts, would never have suspected he had a full wardrobe of custom-tailored clothes—suits, shirts, and coats, as well as handmade Italian shoes—and that he was as comfortable in them as he was in his daily wear. For this event, he selected a charcoal-gray suit and a deep blue silk tie, along with a fancier version of his usual black wool overcoat.

He smiled as he buttoned his crisp white shirt, remembering how she'd dragged her bloody finger down the front of the one he'd worn with his tuxedo during their previous encounter. He had no idea what she had planned for tonight, and decided the best thing to do was not try to speculate too much about it. He had some questions he wanted to ask her, but aside from that, he was open to possibilities.

His phone buzzed with a text as he was doing up his tie. He glanced at it, prepared to ignore it, but then saw Verity's name at the top.

Haven't heard anything, she said. *Any news?*

Stone glanced at his watch. He still had time before he had to leave, so he tapped out a reply, pacing the room so he didn't mess up the creases in his trousers. *Called Ren earlier. Izzy is improving, but hasn't awakened.*

The dots cycled. *There wasn't much wrong with her physically. Most of the damage was psychic, or auric. That can sometimes take longer.*

I'll check in again tomorrow. Can't talk now, though. I'll be out of communication for a while, so you won't be able to reach me. Ren already knows.

Working on a project?

He smiled, deciding what he wanted to tell her. He supposed at least some of it wasn't a secret. *I've got a date, actually.*

More dots. *A lunch date?*

No. It's in Paris. I've got to leave soon.

Paris? Dots. *Are you going out with Marie-Thérèse?*

No. He hadn't been out with Verity's alchemy teacher since he'd taken her to dinner and a show after she'd assisted with sorting out Madison McClain and the Evil's reappearance. She'd been charming company and he'd enjoyed their evening, but the business with the demons had taken over his life for a while, and then

Thalassa had happened. Right now, he couldn't even think about seeing anyone else.

He could tell Verity was dying to ask more—such as why he was going on a date less than a day after the whole Izzy situation and hadn't mentioned anything about it before—but that she didn't want to pry. Finally, all she replied was, *Well, whoever it is, that's great. I've been saying you need to get out more. Have a good time!*

A few years ago, he might have read some subtext into that message. Now, though, he'd observed Verity's aura enough times, and in enough situations, to be certain that she'd truly moved on. Any lingering romantic feelings she might have had for him, and he for her, had finally faded into a deep but platonic friendship. *I expect I'll have an* interesting *time, at least. Must go now. Talk later.*

Thalassa's coordinates took him to a genteel alley in an obviously upscale Paris business district. He barely had time to wonder if he'd somehow miscalculated and landed in the wrong place when a shining white Bentley with blacked-out windows rolled silently up next to him. No one got out, but the rear door opened to reveal Thalassa sitting serenely in the passenger compartment, holding the stem of a champagne glass between two long-nailed fingers. Her glittering green eyes settled on him and she offered a tiny, amused smile. "Good evening, Alastair."

Her smiles always looked like she was considering him as a tasty snack—however that might be interpreted. He climbed in and settled into the butter-soft, black-upholstered seat. Immediately, the door closed and the car rolled off again. A divider between the front and rear obscured the driver.

"I must admit I wasn't expecting a limo," he said. "I thought you'd send me directly to our destination."

"The restaurant is, unfortunately, not on a ley line, but the cuisine is sufficiently exquisite to permit a bit of…inconvenience." She raised her glass. "Champagne?"

"No, thank you." He chuckled. "Bit of a busy day, so I haven't had much to eat. Don't worry—you'll have plenty of opportunity to get me drunk if that's what you want." He jerked his chin toward the divider. "Also, please tell your sexy librarians or whatever the hell they are that I don't fancy being accosted in the shower."

"You didn't answer your phone."

"I don't always answer my phone right away. I was in the *shower*."

"I'm aware." Her smile was small and sly.

"You could have a bit of patience, you know."

"I could. But I do not." Tonight, she wore a snug-fitting, metallic-gold dress that glittered in the limo's faint light. This one stopped at her knees, unlike the long ones he'd seen her in before, with a single, wide strap over her left shoulder. A narrow diamond necklace encircled her neck, and a she wore a matching bracelet. Stone wasn't up on women's designer shoe styles, but he was certain her stiletto heels were every bit as high-end as the dress.

Either that, or they were all illusions. She was a dragon, after all. She could be wearing sweats and trainers and hiding them under magic.

Somehow, though, he couldn't picture Thalassa Nera in sweats.

"I was beginning to think I wouldn't hear from you," he said in an effort to steer the conversation to safer waters. The more difficult stuff could wait until they'd reached the restaurant. He didn't worry about the driver listening, since he would have bet a lot of money it was another of her hench-librarians. "I thought you might have changed your mind about the whole thing."

"I have not changed my mind. Like you, I have been…busy. Believe it or not, Alastair, you are not the only subject capturing my attention." The sly smile was back. "You have been thinking about our arrangement, then."

"Can hardly blame me, can you? It's not every day you get propositioned by a dragon."

Her eyebrow crept up. She took a delicate sip from her champagne as the car smoothly turned a corner, but didn't reply.

Stone was beginning to wish he'd accepted a glass of his own. At least it would give him something to do with his hands. The Bentley's backseat was spacious enough that they didn't have to sit with their legs touching, but he could still feel the heat radiating off her. A sudden thought rose, that he might have preferred to suggest skipping dinner entirely and getting to the next stage of the evening—perhaps right here where they were—but he suppressed it. They were here to talk. He'd been serious about wanting to get to know her before they produced a child together. He had a lot of questions.

They drove in silence for a few more minutes. Stone glanced at Thalassa a couple times, but she seemed content to look out the window.

The car pulled up in front of a building Stone didn't recognize. He'd dined at some of the better restaurants in Paris—usually with Ian and Gabriel, occasionally with a date—but he'd never seen this one. It had a weathered, unassuming façade, small windows, and understated lights flanking a weathered red door. A quick glance found no evidence of the place's name.

Still, he remembered his manners. As soon as the car stopped, he quickly exited and moved around to Thalassa's side. This time, the door didn't open automatically—perhaps the librarian was giving him a chance to be a gentleman—so he opened it and offered Thalassa his hand.

She took it, gracefully rising from her seat. The door closed behind her, and the Bentley rolled off.

Stone didn't see anyone else on the street, but he remembered what she'd said before. "I've got an illusion generator—"

"There is no need. No one will disturb us here. It is one of the reasons I chose this place."

He wondered if that was because the restaurant was exclusive and discreet enough that the clientele wouldn't be impressed by another wealthy couple out for a night on the town, because her magic was obscuring their appearances, or because this was another illusionary restaurant with no other living patrons. He decided he didn't care. He would have been content to have their chat in a mall food court if that was what she preferred. The conversation was the important part, not the ambiance.

Thalassa didn't even have to announce herself. As soon as they entered, a smiling host immediately strode forward and greeted both her and Stone with a slight bow.

Stone looked around as he and Thalassa followed the host to their table. The place had an old-world charm to it, and he recognized that it had been around for quite some time, rather than trying to feign age with faux antique décor. Light classical music played in the background, barely audible against the low murmur of conversations. There were quite a few diners, but the layout was such that some of the tables had their own private, dimly lit nooks, while others were located more centrally and within view of each other. It was a common tactic in high-end restaurants—accommodate those who wanted to see and be seen, as well as those who preferred a more intimate dining experience.

To Stone's utter lack of surprise, the host stopped in front of one of the latter tables, tucked discreetly away next to a window with a view of the street. No one had even looked their way as they'd passed.

Stone once again played the gentleman, pulling out Thalassa's chair for her and waiting until she was settled before seating himself. "I feel a bit like a kept man," he said, amused. "Normally when

I dine at a place like this with a lady, I'm the one who's done the inviting."

"Does that bother you?" She waited as an attentive waiter swooped in to fill their water glasses and place leather-bound menus in front of them, then eyed Stone with glittering, narrowed green eyes. "Having a woman taking charge of the evening?"

He chuckled. "Bloody hell, no. First of all, you're a dragon, not a woman. And second, I prefer strong women. Shrinking violets bore me."

"Indeed." She tilted her head, studying him. "Given what I know of you, I would assume you would not be comfortable unless you were in control of any given situation."

He shrugged. "I'm not bothered either way. I'm happy to take charge or not. If you want to buy me an expensive dinner, I'm certainly not going to turn it down. I'll warn you, though—I'm not a cheap date. I've got expensive tastes, especially in wine. But," he added, meeting her gaze with a challenging one of his own, "Don't expect all our little evenings are going to be this way. I insist you let me plan the next one—it's only fair. Especially since, from the look of both our schedules, there might only *be* one more before..." He let that trail off meaningfully.

She redirected her study from him to the menu, and didn't say anything else until the waiter returned to take their orders. Then she looked at him. "What do you suggest for the wine, Alastair?"

Stone didn't smile—at least not outwardly. He wasn't sure if she'd been trying to catch him unprepared, but it wasn't going to work. He'd already discreetly examined the wine list, and was ready with a choice that would complement both their menu selections. The list hadn't included prices, but he was familiar with most of the offered wines and deliberately picked one of the most expensive.

Thalassa didn't offer an opinion as the waiter left. Instead, she leaned back in her chair. "You seem as if you have something on your mind, other than our evening."

He looked up, surprised, though he probably shouldn't have been. Dragons were a lot more sensitive to auric fluctuations than even the most perceptive human mage. "I suppose I am. Your call wasn't at the most convenient time, to be honest."

"Oh? You could have rescheduled."

It was another trap, despite her even tone. "Could I, though? I was the one who proposed these little soirées. It wouldn't have been a good look for me to turn down your first invitation."

She acknowledged that with a slight nod.

Even though she hadn't inquired, he said, "Remember the demons? The ones The Unspeakable's knife summoned, and are still knocking about because the ritual didn't happen so they didn't get consumed?"

Her eyes came up. "Of course."

He wondered if she was still feeling salty because he'd failed to deliver the artifact to her, despite grudgingly acknowledging there hadn't been any reasonable way for him to do it. "Well, one of them is getting up to trouble in Detroit. My friends and I have been trying to deal with it, but it's quite good at keeping its head down. And several people are dead as a direct result."

The waiter returned with a bottle of wine. He expertly removed the cork and poured a bit in Stone's glass for him to taste.

Despite his enjoyment of good wine and his knowledge of vintages, Stone wasn't a "wine snob." He didn't bother doing the swirling-it-in-the-glass show, nor did he pause to pull in a deep sniff to savor the bouquet. He merely took a taste to verify it was as excellent as he'd expected. He nodded to the waiter, who then filled both their glasses, left the bottle, and departed again.

"So," he said brightly to Thalassa, "there isn't any chance you could give us a bit of assistance with the demon thing, could you? You were very helpful dealing with the big boss—any chance you might fancy helping to clear out the underlings as well?" It was a long shot, but it couldn't hurt to ask.

She sipped her wine. "No. There is not."

Well, then. "I thought dragons didn't like demons."

"We do not."

"Then, why—"

Her gaze hardened. "Because we do not concern ourselves with such insignificant problems. You humans must learn to deal with your own difficulties."

Stone raised his hands to ward her off. That stare was a bit terrifying, though he'd certainly never admit it to her. "Fine, fine. I get it. You lot are more concerned with things a bit more…cosmic in scope. That's fair, I suppose."

She subsided, apparently satisfied. "The demons will no doubt cause trouble—in some cases, probably a great deal of trouble. But they are by nature antisocial with each other, so it is unlikely they will join together. If that should happen, our involvement might be necessary. Until then, it is not a subject I wish to discuss. That is not why we are here tonight." She let her gaze roam over the other diners. "You suggested these evenings because you wanted to… 'get to know me better' before our ritual." Her tone implied she had no idea why he might want to do that.

"Well…yes." He let the demon subject go gracefully; he'd taken his shot and was content to move on. "You sound like that surprises you. I really know very little about you except that you collect art and artifacts, you're not very fond of me personally, and you're bloody sexy. That's not much to base fathering a child on."

"And yet human males do it every day."

"Not this one. I've never made any secret about the fact that I'm not a fan of small children and usually prefer not to be around them. That's why I'm so careful during my…encounters with women, so there aren't any surprises."

"Except your son."

He flashed a glare. "That's different. I was young and stupid and very, very drunk. And I don't regret it in the slightest. But I'm older now, and I hope at least a bit wiser. If I'm to be putting all that care aside and fathering a child on purpose, which I'll still admit makes me uncomfortable, I need a bit more to work with. Given I haven't got much choice in the matter, I at least want to know what kind of woman—dragon—I'm going to be doing it with."

"Ask your questions, then. I do not guarantee I will answer them, however. It was not part of our arrangement that I provide you with personal details about myself."

Stone still wasn't entirely sure why he found her so enticing. He believed her when she'd given her word she wasn't doing anything to cause it, which meant it was all him. Aside from Deirdre Lanier, a special case, he couldn't remember the last time he'd felt such a visceral attraction to a woman. If he was being completely honest with himself, that even included Verity and Imogen Desmond. Even sitting here at this table across from Thalassa, a part of his mind—one he'd carefully shut a door on for the moment—was visualizing scenarios that might take place following dinner. It was definitely distracting.

To redirect his thoughts, he forged ahead. "Fair enough. That's all I ask. I've got to admit, you dragons intrigue me for a lot of reasons. I can't even imagine what it must be like to be around for as long as you lot have been. The history you must have seen."

"I suppose." She didn't sound terribly interested. "Human history, at least with regard to those without magic, however, holds little fascination for me."

"What about before you got here? Do you remember it? Your life, wherever you originally came from?"

"Of course I do." Her eyes narrowed. "How could I forget my home?"

He sipped his wine. "This is probably one of those questions you won't answer, but—what was it like? Your home, I mean."

To his surprise, her expression softened just a little. Her gaze went unfocused, as if she were visualizing something in her mind's eye. "It was very beautiful. Far more magical than Earth, full of lush forests and high mountains and vast, shining seas."

"You sound like you miss it."

"Of course I do." The wistful expression vanished, replaced by her usual stern visage.

"Do you ever think about trying to return? I mean, it's been a long time, hasn't it? Perhaps things have changed there."

"No. Even if we could do so, it would not be wise."

"Why not? Didn't Madame Huan say you knew where it was?"

"She was not entirely accurate. We knew where it was when we were exiled, but as I believe you know, dimensions do not remain fixed relative to each other."

Their meals arrived, and they paused to let the waiter serve them before continuing. "That's true, but I also know you lot are a lot more advanced regarding dimensional science than I am. Couldn't you find it if you wanted to?"

"There is no point."

She bent to sample her meal, but Stone could tell she was avoiding his gaze. "Because of what the others might do to you if you returned?"

Her head snapped up. "This is not something I care to discuss. It has no relevance to our arrangement."

"Fine, fine." He raised his hand again. "Bloody hell, Thalassa, I feel like I'm walking on eggshells around you."

"It is for the best. As I told you before, I have no wish to form any sort of romantic relationship with you. Our arrangement is a business deal, nothing more."

Stone snorted. "I'm sorry, but having a child together isn't a *business deal.* Whether you like it or not, I'm going to be her father. Even if you spirit her away and raise her without ever letting me meet her, that isn't going to change. Unless you plan to keep her wrapped in cotton wool and never let her experience the world."

Thalassa didn't answer.

He sighed. "I know you don't want me in her life. I'm not happy about that, but I'm also realistic, given that I've agreed to your oath. I told you, I've come to terms with that. But if I'm not going to be involved, I want to get some idea of what kind of mother you're going to be to her. I know what Ian's childhood was like without me, and I won't knowingly subject another child of mine to that—not even if I have to break the oath and take the consequences." He fixed her with a hard, unyielding stare from across the table.

She held his gaze, but still didn't reply.

"It's a fair question, Thalassa. I can hardly see you enrolling her in preschool and taking her on playdates. So what kind of life will she have with you as her mother?"

"I do not have to tell you anything, you know. That was not part of our arrangement."

"I know. But if you don't, then we'll have to re-evaluate our arrangement." He braced for her ire at the suggestion.

She merely looked at him, considering. "It is that important to you."

"It is."

To his surprise, her expression changed again—this time to something close to approval. "I will not give you specifics. But I give you my word, she will be well cared for, deeply loved, and will want for nothing." She leaned in a little closer. "I have waited a very long time for this, Alastair. I did not believe the stars would ever align to give me such a chance."

He frowned. "Such a chance? To have a child, you mean."

"Yes."

He took a breath to give himself time to consider his words. "Forgive me if this question is out of line, but…wouldn't you rather have a *dragon* child? I might be a bit of a special case, but I'm still just a lowly human." He wondered if that was even true anymore, but for all intents and purposes, he supposed it might as well be. "Couldn't you make an arrangement with one of the other dragons? Morathi, maybe? He seems pleasant enough. I know you and Kolinsky don't get on, but surely there's *one* of them out there you can put up with. Don't any of the rest of them want offspring?"

Her glare smoldered, clearly warning him against proceeding further.

He ignored it, as a sudden insight struck him. "Hang on. You...*can't,* can you?" he said softly. When she didn't bite his head off—which would have been difficult for even her to hide under an illusion—he continued: "It just occurred to me that, as far as I know, none of the dragons on Earth have children—except the ones they already had before they got here, like Stefan and Gabriel, and Vic and Cassius. If there are any scaly little dragon babies bouncing around here, none of you have ever mentioned them."

"Stone..." Her tone held a dangerous growl.

Still, he didn't stop—partly because, despite her threatening posture, he sensed something beneath it. Something that wanted him to know this. He could be seeing things, but the worst she could do was kill him—or try, anyway.

"I'm not sure if it's because none of you want to do it here on Earth or because the magic level here isn't high enough for whatever you need to do to reproduce, but I'm not wrong, am I?" He held her gaze, refusing to be intimidated.

When she still didn't answer, he pressed on, the words tumbling out as they popped into his head. "Whatever it is, some of the male dragons have made up for it by producing scions with human mages, making the best of what they had to work with, but it was never the same. And you—and maybe Madame Huan and Nana and this other female dragon you told me about—didn't want to do it at all."

He thought about Ian. Before he'd met his son, he'd never wanted children. He'd always thought he was too busy to deal with them, and too self-absorbed to want another person entwined with him to that extent. But these days, he would have gladly given his life to save his son's, and couldn't imagine existing without him. He softened his voice. "An immortal being…unable to carry on their line. How…*lonely* that must be."

"Do not pity me, Stone," Thalassa growled.

That sounded like a genuine threat, and Stone decided he should probably back off. "Believe me, I never would," he said, returning to his usual sardonic tone. "I'm just trying to understand you a little better."

"You will never understand me, or any of us. You cannot. Your lifespans are to us as those of insects are to you." There was no chill in her tone now; she spoke as if she were merely stating a fact.

"But yet, you want to produce a child with one of those insects."

He paused to savor his boeuf bourguignon as he waited for her to answer. It truly was superb—he wished he knew the name of the restaurant, because he might wish to return here someday. To lighten the mood a bit, he nodded toward his plate. "Excellent choice, by the way."

She looked at him as if considering whether to smite him into a column of ashes right there in his chair. Then she relaxed, settling back. "I knew you were going to be…difficult…when I chose you. It should not surprise me that you are behaving according to your nature."

He chuckled. "It's not too late to change your mind, you know. You could still ask Harrison. You two would probably get along great, honestly."

Her gaze bored into his. "I do not want Mr. Harrison, Alastair. I have chosen you."

Her words hit him like a bullet aimed straight at his libido. Without warning, the wall he'd been building between his desire for her and his wish to get answers to his questions began to crumble, and with it his interest in finishing the magnificent meal. Hastily, he tried to reconstruct the wall before she caught on, but to his surprise she appeared similarly distracted as she continued to look at him as if he were dessert.

He snatched up his glass and drained the rest of the wine, then swallowed hard. "Thalassa—"

Her eyes never left him. "The car is waiting outside."

Stone was glad the hench-librarian was driving the Bentley, since he could count on her discretion regarding what was going on in the backseat.

The limo wasn't a large example of its type, but its rear compartment was big enough that he didn't feel like some desperate high-school student struggling in a too-small space. The car had barely moved back into traffic when Thalassa had slid closer and pulled him into a crushing embrace. Her breath was hot on his face as he leaned in to kiss her, slipping his arms around her. He kept his eyes open and so did she; the two of them stared at each other with the fierceness of a couple of jungle cats, their hands moving over each other and their bodies pressed so tightly together that it was almost painful.

The pain was part of the allure. It was another thing Stone hadn't often experienced with lovers—some, including Verity and Imogen, had enjoyed a little roughness, but nothing more than the occasional hard kiss or digging their fingernails into his back. Magic had made him a good lover, allowing him to read minute changes to his partner's aura and make adjustments based on desires she might not even realize she had until he'd acted upon them.

But never before had he experienced something like this. Thalassa might look like a small, delicately-built woman, but the muscles under her silky-smooth skin were hard as steel. He had no doubt she could crush him if she wanted to—the thought that she might, far from raising his fear, increased his desire to pull her in harder, to push back against her, to dominate her as much as she was dominating him.

He didn't waste any thought about where this was coming from. He didn't care. She'd given her word she wasn't influencing him, and he believed her. Therefore, it must be originating somewhere within *him*—and he'd never been shy about acting on his desires with willing women.

Thalassa was most definitely willing.

He had no idea where the car was going, and he didn't care about that, either. They continued to stare, almost *glare,* into each other's eyes, hands roving over backs and fingers digging into hair, each of them halting the crush of their grip past the point of pain but just shy of injury. Stone shifted to magical sight, watching Thalassa's blazing green-and-gold aura dancing like rippling, snapping flame around her body, tinged all the way around with the deep, primal red of desire.

She could be faking, of course—he doubted he could see through a dragon's attempt at altering her aura—but he didn't think she was.

He moved his hand up, intending to slide the single strap of her dress off her shoulder.

Immediately her aura flared, but her hand was almost gentle as it covered his and moved it away before he could finish the action.

"No?" he rasped, surprised. It was only then that he noticed she had made no move to remove any of his clothes—not even his tie.

In answer, she leaned forward with a hungry, forceful kiss, burying both her hands in his hair, and he forgot whatever else he was going to say.

R. L. KING

He didn't notice they'd reached their destination until the car stopped inside a dim underground parking garage. He hadn't seen the building it was beneath; if there had been a gate, he hadn't seen that either.

He pulled back from their kiss long enough to ask, "You've got a place in Paris?" before resuming. The taste of the magnificent wine joined with the faint hint of blood to form a sensual cocktail he couldn't get enough of.

She shook her head without breaking the kiss, one hand stroking the back of his neck with uncharacteristic gentleness while the fingers of the other probed much more urgently into his hair.

They *weren't* in Paris? He didn't think he'd lost track of time *that* much.

He was about to ask her where they were, then, when suddenly both of her hands dropped to a tight embrace around his back.

An instant later, they were…somewhere else.

That was almost—*almost*—enough to make him jerk back from her. He broke their gaze only long enough to shift his back and forth, taking in the high windows, the soft sofa they were seated on instead of the Bentley's rear seat, and the spectacular view of New York City, but then he relaxed into her again as he caught on to what she'd done.

Of course. Dragons had the ability to bring "passengers" along on their ley-line journeys—but only if the passenger was a scion.

He had to admire the smoothness with which she'd done it. He hadn't felt the shift at all, and barely noticed the change.

"Thalassa…" he whispered. His body was hot against hers, his desire for this haughty, prickly, impossibly sexy woman rising until he wasn't sure he could contain it any longer. She'd brought him back home with her. Surely, that must mean something.

He crushed her against him. He wanted to rip her dress off, carry her into her bedroom, and accept the challenge of trying to satisfy a dragon. Could he manage it? Would she want things from him that he wasn't capable of providing? How did dragons even *do* this?

He moved his hand up to her dress's strap again, and once again she shifted sideways and pushed him away. All the while, though, she continued to kiss him, and her other hand continued exploring his back.

Confusion wasn't an emotion he was used to feeling during this particular act, but she was definitely giving him mixed signals. He pulled back, reluctantly, savoring the last bit of the blood-wine taste as he broke the contact. "Is something...wrong?"

"No..." Her voice was raspy, strangled, as she leaned back toward him, clearly wanting to resume the kiss.

It took all his willpower not to do it. Everything about her, from her body-hugging, gold-metallic dress, to the way wisps of her hair escaped her elegant style, to the intoxicating mixed aromas of her perfume, his cologne, and their shared wine compelled him to take what he wanted from her—or let her take it from him.

It couldn't be possible that she was teasing him. She might be a dragon, but he was uncommonly good at reading auras during times like this, and he would have bet everything he owned that she wanted this as much as he did.

So why was she holding back?

"Thalassa..." he whispered. "Tell me what you want."

She leaned forward again, but this time something in her eyes changed. She released her grip on him and pulled back. Not far—her knees still touched his—but far enough to break the embrace. Her gaze dropped away from his.

Stone had no idea what was going on. It was obvious something was on her mind, but what could it be? She'd been giving as good as she got, her desire for him burning every bit as strong as his for her. To magical sight, her green-gold aura still displayed the snapping red flags of desire—but something else was there, too. He realized with astonishment that she was making no effort to hide her aura from him.

Was she—could she possibly be—*hesitant?*

But why? It certainly wasn't possible she could be afraid of him. She could squash him like a bug if he made the wrong move. She held all the cards, and he had no illusions about that. It was a big part of what made her so damned sexy. But—

Her expression hardened, though her aura didn't. "I... have never..."

He almost asked her to explain—but then he got it. His initial astonishment faded almost immediately, though.

Of course she hadn't. She'd all but told him that before, but in the heat of the moment he hadn't picked up on it.

Still—

"Never?" he asked softly. "In all the time you've been here?"

"No." She wasn't meeting his eyes now, and some of her white-hot ardor had died down.

He considered her words, and his own. He'd have to be careful. This was still Thalassa Nera he was talking to, and despite their almost inexplicable physical attraction for each other, that didn't change everything else. "What about...the other dragons? Have you—"

Her eyes crackled with warning. "That is none of your concern." But then she looked into her lap again. "It is different. This is...confusing. Dragons..."

He waited.

"For us, it is only to produce offspring. There is no particular pleasure in the act. These...sensations..." She shivered. "They are..."

"Confusing," he said, keeping his voice gentle. "I get it. They're confusing for us, too, at first." He chuckled. "You should have seen me as a teenager. I didn't have a bloody *clue* what I was doing. I took a lot of cold showers." He turned serious. "But you're telling me you've never…experienced these feelings before, in all the time you've been here on Earth? Even if you didn't act on them?" Damn, but this was a strange conversation. In the back of his mind, he pictured how his discussion with Verity might go the following day:

Verity: How was your date?

Him: Oh, it was fine. We had a lovely dinner at one of the best restaurants in Paris—or at least half of one, because we couldn't keep our hands off each other. But then my date—who's a dragon, by the way, forgot to mention that—admitted she was a virgin in her human form and had no idea how to cope with human sexual desire.

Thalassa looked as if she'd rather be doing just about anything other than having this conversation. For a moment, he thought she might disappear, or grab him and zap him back to his own home. But then she sighed.

"I…have." Her voice held none of its usual imperious confidence. "Rarely. Perhaps a handful of times over the span during which I have been exiled here."

"But you never did anything about it."

Her eyes hardened, and her expressive lips curled. "They were…*human.* Attractive, yes, as you might see the beauty in a cat or a horse. But only so."

He almost said, *But I don't feel that kind of attraction for a cat or a horse,* but then he remembered who he was talking to. Instead, he maintained the same calm, even tone. "But you *are* human, Thalassa. For all intents and purposes. Physically, at least. With everything that implies. There's no shame in it."

"I never said anything about *shame,*" she snapped, but it had the feel of a rote response.

He refused to let her intimidate him. "Okay, then. But I stand by what I said: you're human. If it's possible for your lot to mate with humans, even if there has to be magic involved to actually produce offspring, that means you're as close to us as it's possible to be. And one of the best things about being human *is*—" He gestured between the two of them. "—this. I know you said you don't care much about our history, but surely you haven't missed that we humans do all sorts of things, good and quite horrible, to get it. It's one of our strongest drives."

She shifted next to him, her eyes still fixed on his, but still didn't reply.

"Look," he said. "You aren't fooling me—your body wants this, even if your mind is still in dragon mode. If you want me to follow through on helping you create a scion, there's no way around it. You said that, too: it's got to be done the 'natural' way." He remembered something she'd said the night he'd agreed to help her—the way she'd slyly suggested they could 'practice.' Apparently, that had been nothing more than a bluff, since she'd known he wouldn't take her up on the offer.

What would she have done if he had?

He shifted back, putting a few inches between them, and took her hand. "Thalassa...you've got all the control here. Even if you're an ancient, massively powerful creature that could turn me into a pile of ash where I sit, to me right now you're a human woman—and a very desirable one. Do I want this tonight? Desperately. But not unless you do too. If you've got misgivings, we can stop."

He'd never seen her—or any dragon—looking so conflicted. Usually, they hid any emotions they might be feeling behind a mask of illusion. "Thalassa...?"

Her hand squeezed his, hard enough to hurt, but it was trembling too. "I—my body—does not wish to stop. But these sensations...so...*animal.* How...do you cope with them?"

Stone chuckled. "Sometimes it's not so easy. It's one of those things we humans are stuck with. Most of us, anyway." He sobered and stood, his hand still in hers. "It's all right. I've enjoyed our evening, but I don't entirely understand this bit either, to be honest. You're a bloody *dragon.* You're terrifying. I don't want a romantic relationship with you any more than you do with me. But—" His voice dropped lower, with the edge of a rasp. "Gods, I want you, Thalassa. Something about you makes me want to—" He let the words trail off, certain she'd have no trouble picking up his intent from his aura.

Her breath came faster, and her hand tightened. Her fingernails dug into his skin, not hard enough to break it but hard enough to hurt. "Alastair—"

He leaned in and brushed a light kiss against her lips. "Next time. I'll plan the next evening, if you tell me when you're available. You're not ready yet, and no one has ever accused me of taking advantage of a woman. Not even if she's a dragon." He offered her a wicked smile. "Or…you know…just give me a ring when you *are* ready. If I'm not neck-deep in demons, you won't keep me away."

He took a deep breath and swallowed hard. That hadn't been easy. His mind might be on board, but his body was screaming at him to press forward. He honestly didn't think it would take much to tip her over the edge tonight, since her body so obviously wanted this as much as his did.

But her mind had to want it too.

She released his hand and looked into his eyes, then inclined her head. "It is…for the best, I think. I had thought I had come to terms with all that will be necessary, but…apparently, I was mistaken. A… bit more time to prepare, then. I will…contact you when I am ready."

"I won't lie—I'll be counting the days. And probably having a few dreams about you that I haven't had in a good long time." He stepped back and held her gaze for a few seconds. "Good night, Thalassa."

Her eyes remained on him while he formed the pattern in his mind and faded from view. Her expression as he disappeared hovered somewhere between hunger, confusion, and regret.

R. L. KING

He reappeared in the living room of the Encantada house, letting out his breath in a loud *whoosh.*

Bloody *hell,* that had been intense. His body still thrummed with unresolved desire, and Thalassa's image still dominated his thoughts as Raider padded up to him.

"Meow?" the cat said, looking up with luminous green eyes.

"Don't ask, mate," he muttered. He shrugged out of his overcoat, tossed it over the back of the sofa, and headed for the stairs, his mind in turmoil.

Halfway up, he remembered he'd switched off his phone so nobody would bother him while he was in Paris. He pulled it on his pocket and turned it back on.

Instantly, quick tones indicated he'd received several texts from Verity. All of them were variations on *Call me back as soon as you get this.*

He stopped on the stairs, thoughts of Thalassa fleeing as his tension grew. Had something happened while he was away and out of communication? Here in California, it was only a little after one p.m. Despite the surreal quality of his time with Thalassa, less than two hours had passed since he'd last communicated via text with Verity.

He decided to skip responding to the texts and go straight to calling Verity. He tapped her number and listened while it rang. After three rings, her voicemail picked up.

"Bugger," he muttered. What was going on? At the tone, he said, "Verity, it's me. You've been trying to reach me. Is something wrong? Call me back."

Unwilling to wait for her to get the message and return his call, he hung up and called Jason.

Unlike Verity, her brother answered promptly. "Hey, Al. V's been trying to reach you." His voice held an urgent edge.

"Yes, I've noticed. Is something wrong?"

"Yeah. She called Ren a while ago to get an update, and while they were on the line, Ren got another call. Izzy started having some kind of weird seizure on the way to Chicago from Detroit. They got her stabilized, but they can't figure out what's wrong. V's already gone back to Chicago through the portal to see if she can help."

CHAPTER SIXTEEN

STONE DIDN'T BOTHER changing out of his suit. By the time he dashed through the portal and popped out in the beer-scented basement of the Irish pub near downtown Chicago, less than five minutes had passed. His phone rang again as he was on his way up toward the ground floor. Verity's name appeared on the screen.

"Damn, I'm glad to hear your voice, Alastair." She sounded breathless and stressed. "Sorry if I interrupted your date."

"No, no, it's fine. It—didn't quite go as planned."

"I'm sorry about that."

"Don't be. Everything's fine. What's going on?"

"Are you still in Paris?"

"No, I just came through the Chicago portal. Tell me what's going on. Jason said something about Izzy taking a bad turn."

"Yeah, she did. We're at a private hospital right now. She's stable at the moment, but she's having some kind of weird seizures. The doctors can't figure out what's causing them."

"Have you examined her magically?"

"Not yet. I just got here a few minutes ago, and they're still working on her. How fast can you get here?" She gave him the address.

Once again, he made a vow to either throw more money at whoever was working on the ley-line map digitization project, or find himself a pocket ley-line guide. "How far is that from the portal?"

"About a twenty-minute cab ride, depending on traffic. Hang on." The line went silent for a moment, then she came back on and her voice dropped to a whisper. "There's a ley line here."

"Brilliant. I'll be there in a moment, then." He hung up, looked around, and then hurried into the men's room and closed himself in a stall. If anybody wondered later how the lock got engaged with nobody inside, they'd just have to be mystified.

Stone reappeared, under an invisibility spell, on the far side of the hospital's parking lot. He checked to make sure nobody was around, then shimmered back to view and took off at a jog toward the building. His thin-soled dress shoes weren't built for running, but he was more concerned with getting to Verity and Izzy as quickly as possible.

The nurse at the front desk gave him an odd look as he swept in, puffing, and inquired about Izzy. Keeping a suspicious eye on him the whole time, she called someone. She listened to the other party, looked him up and down, and said, "Yes, that's him."

Their response seemed to surprise her, but her expression changed from suspicious to efficiently helpful as she hung up. "Dr. Stone?"

"That's me, yes."

"Sorry for the delay—we're not supposed to let anyone unauthorized in. Agent Freeman is in the intensive-care unit. You can't see her now, but your friend and some of her associates are waiting for you in conference room 1019. Just through the doors, at the end of the hall before the turn."

"Thank you." Stone was already moving, his heart beating faster. They hadn't gone through all that effort to rescue Izzy only to lose her now.

Verity looked up from a discussion with a white-coated female doctor as Stone entered the conference room. Her attention settled for just a second on his fine suit, but just as quickly she returned to business mode.

"Thanks for getting here so fast. Though I'm not sure there's much you'll be able to do." She nodded toward the doctor. "This is Dr. Palmer. She's in charge of Izzy's case. Dr. Palmer, this is Dr. Alastair Stone."

"Pleasure to meet you, Doctor." Addressing both of them, Stone said, "What's going on?"

Verity spoke first. She looked stressed and frustrated. "They put Izzy on a plane about two and a half hours ago. Nothing bothered the transport to the airport, and the plane took off without any problems. About twenty minutes into the flight, though, Izzy started experiencing a seizure. She had a doctor and two senior nurses attending her, along with high-tech equipment. They were able to get her stabilized for most of the rest of the flight, but as they started their descent, it happened again."

"And they've got no idea what caused it? Any physical problems?"

"No," Dr. Palmer said. "That's the odd thing—physically, Agent Freeman is in reasonably good shape. Aside from the malnutrition and dehydration, which are already being addressed, the doctors in Detroit found no other injuries or physical problems."

"And I assume you've ruled out the malnutrition or dehydration as the cause?" He gave her a wry smile. "Verity might have introduced me as 'doctor,' but I'm a university professor, not a physician. So please forgive any stupid questions."

"It's not a stupid question," Dr. Palmer said. "Both malnutrition and dehydration can cause chemical imbalances that can lead to seizures—but not in this case. Agent Freeman hadn't been held captive long enough for such things to be enough of an issue to worry about. Especially since her treatments have improved her condition significantly." She shook her head, looking frustrated. "The truth is, we haven't got a clue what's causing this yet, and that bothers me."

Stone looked for a delicate way to phrase his next question. "Are you…aware of Agent Freeman's…peculiarities?"

"If you're asking if I know she's a mage, yes. I'm not one myself, but I'm very familiar with the magical community, and I've studied some of your unique challenges. And Agent Huxley explained some of the details of the case earlier." She narrowed her eyes. "Are you saying you think whatever she's suffering from might be magical in nature?"

"Given what she was subjected to, I'd be surprised if it wasn't. I suggest you let Verity take a look at her as soon as possible. She's an accomplished healer, and quite sensitive to this sort of thing."

Dr. Palmer looked back and forth between Stone and Verity. "I can't see how it would hurt. We've got some more tests we plan to run, but we've got Agent Freeman stabilized again. Ms. Thayer, if you'd like to—"

"I would. But I'd like Dr. Stone to come with me."

The doctor hesitated.

"He sells himself short," Verity said firmly. "Sure, he's, as he says, 'rubbish as a healer,' but he's also my teacher and a lot stronger mage than I am. He might spot something I miss."

"All right. I can give you both a few minutes with her. We'll be nearby if anything goes wrong. Follow me."

"Nice suit," Verity said with a faint twinkle in her eye as the two of them followed Dr. Palmer from the conference room and down another hallway.

"Yes, well, my date has expensive tastes."

The intensive-care unit was through a pair of double doors. Dr. Palmer led them to a room with solid walls on three sides and a sliding glass door on the fourth, facing a central area where nurses could monitor the patients. "I'll be outside if you need me. Please try not to agitate her too much. I'm worried about what might be going on in her brain, especially if she has more of those seizures."

Stone and Verity entered the small room. Izzy Freeman looked even smaller than before in the high-tech hospital bed, surrounded by monitoring equipment, cables, and beeping screens. Her eyes were closed, her body still, and her face still had the sunken, ashy quality they'd seen back at Big Gee's. The only visible improvement was that she didn't look quite as skeletal as she had before.

"Look at her eyes," Verity said, leaning in close to examine her.

Stone did the same from the other side of the bed. It was easy to spot: Izzy's eyes were moving behind her closed lids, darting back and forth as if she were having a vivid dream. "She's definitely in there," he murmured. Then, louder, "Izzy, can you hear me? If you can, give us some sort of sign."

They both watched closely for several seconds, but aside from her twitching eyes, nothing changed.

"What do you know about demons draining someone's soul?" Verity asked without taking her focus off Izzy. "Have you ever seen anything like this before?"

"No, unfortunately. The only people I know who have are Bron Broome and Nicholas Happenstance down in Los Angeles, but I doubt they'd be much help. Their situation wasn't similar to this. All I know is that if the victim can be kept alive long enough, the magical energy does replenish itself. But that doesn't mean there can't be complications—both mental and physical. It depends on the individual case, and probably the individual demon involved."

She watched Izzy a while longer, then looked at him. "I'm going to see if I can do a deeper scan. Will you keep an eye on me in case anything goes wrong?"

"Of course. I'll be right here."

She shot him a tired, grateful glance, pulled in a few slow, deep breaths, then settled three fingers on Izzy's forehead and closed her eyes.

Stone maintained mundane sight long enough to determine Izzy hadn't reacted to Verity's touch, then shifted to magical senses so he could monitor the auras. Verity's a strong, pulsing emerald green, blazed around her, especially bright around the point where she touched Izzy.

The whole process took nearly ten minutes, which seemed an eternity while expecting something to go wrong with either the agent or Verity—or both—any second. When Verity finally pulled back and released her breath in a long, tired rush, Stone had to use all his willpower not to pounce on her.

He waited for her to slump into the chair and gave her a moment to gather herself before asking softly, "Anything?" He used magic to pour water into a clean glass from a pitcher on the side table, and levitated it over to her.

She plucked it from the air gratefully and took a long swallow. When she looked at him, though, her expression was troubled. "I wish I could give you an answer. All I can tell is that she's definitely in there somewhere. Her mental activity is strong. If I had to say what I think it is, it's almost like she's dreaming—or more likely having a nightmare. Constantly. I tried to calm her down, but nothing I tried helped. I couldn't reach her, Alastair."

The despair in her voice tore at Stone. He moved around the bed and put a gentle hand on her shoulder. "Don't blame yourself.

You haven't got a lot of experience with demons. They can do things none of us expect."

She nodded, but with no conviction. "I guess all we can do is keep taking care of her physical body and hope as she heals, her mind will have a better chance of fighting off whatever's messing with her."

"I suppose." He pulled back a little, staring down at Izzy's unmoving form. Impulsively, he reached out and put his hand over hers, giving it a gentle squeeze. "Hold on, Izzy," he murmured. "We're going to—"

He stopped, as a faint flash of pain rose in his chest. It wasn't strong, no worse than a paper cut, but it was definitely there, extending from his shoulder down toward his side.

"Alastair?" Verity turned away from Izzy and faced him with concern. "Is something wrong?"

Without replying or even acknowledging her, he touched his chest with the hand that wasn't touching Izzy. The pain was still mild, but it was steady.

On a hunch, he broke his contact with Izzy.

The pain vanished instantly.

"Bloody hell…" he murmured.

"What is it?" Verity gripped his arm, more insistent now.

Now, he did turn his haunted gaze on her. "I think it's still in there. Or at least part of it is."

"*What?* What are you talking about?" Then she got it, and dropped her voice to a whisper. "The demon?"

"Not the actual demon. But perhaps some small remnant of it."

"How do you know that?"

He glanced at Izzy, who still hadn't moved. "When I touched her, I got a little pain in my chest. In the scar from The Unspeakable's knife. I think it somehow…reacts to the presence of demonic energy. The pain faded as soon as I let her go."

She drew a deep breath and let it out slowly. "What…does that mean? If you're right, what can we do about it? Do we need to get a priest in here to do an exorcism? Could it lead the demon to her?"

That was a frightening thought. Stone looked around the room, focusing on the glass door to their small cubicle, but everything beyond looked fine. The nurses still moved around tending to their patients or sat at desks tapping at computers, clearly not bothered by any lurking demonic presence. But Verity's question was a good one: if Izzy Freeman *did* have a scrap of the demon inside her, how were they going to get it out? He didn't think the exorcism idea had a chance of working unless the priest was magically talented, and the only people he knew who were even close to magical clergy— Reverend Edwin Blodgett and Grace Diaz—were too far away or too problematic to bring here.

Frustrated, he paced around the bed. If only there were a way to reach Izzy's mind, to see what she was seeing, perhaps they could—

"Wait!" he said triumphantly, spinning around.

"What?"

"Verity, I think this might be good news!" His words tumbled out as he struggled to organize his thoughts.

"What are you talking about? How can it be good news that she's got part of a demon inside her? Especially since it's obviously hurting her."

"Because if it's in there, that means we can get to it. We can get it out. Or, even better, if we're very lucky we can possibly even use it to track back to the real one."

She frowned. "Usually I'm pretty quick on the uptake, but I must be tired because I'm not following you at all. How are we going to—"

He grabbed her by the shoulders, forcing himself to be gentle despite his excitement. "Remember Jeremy Weldon? Back at the parking garage in Minneapolis? The portal?"

For a second, her expression remained confused. But then the light dawned and her eyes widened. "You want me to—go into her mind?"

"I want *us* to go into her mind. Maybe we can find the thing and do something about it. Have you still got any of that vile-tasting alchemical elixir you had me drink so I can tag along?"

Verity was obviously having trouble keeping up with his careening train of thought. "Uh—yes, I think I have some back at the shop. We even improved it a little since you've been gone. But—"

"How did you improve it? And how quickly can you get it here?"

Her expression firmed. "Alastair, *stop.*"

He didn't want to stop, but her sharp word startled him into backing off. "What?"

"This could be dangerous for Izzy. We don't know what we're going to find in there. She's already having seizures. If we set off another one—"

Stone shook his head impatiently. "We've got to risk it, Verity. Don't you see—there's no other option. If I'm right, and I'm certain I am, that demon fragment isn't going anywhere. It's going to stay in there and fester until one of two things happens: either she keeps having seizures until they kill her or destroy her mind to the point where she'd be better off if she *did* die, or else the demon will finally get 'round to using it to trace her here. I promise, it won't care about the sort of collateral damage it causes if it decides it wants her back."

Verity cast a nervous look out past the glass door. "We're going to have to talk to Dr. Palmer. I won't do it without her permission."

"Well, let's get on with it, then. I don't think Izzy's got a lot of time left." As they headed for the door, he said, "You said you improved the elixir. How?"

"It's been a while. We did it shortly after the business with Jeremy, but we haven't tested it. We don't get a lot of call for that kind of thing. Well, *any,* really, since I don't know any other mages who can even do the technique. But remember how before you could only talk to me, and you couldn't affect anything? It was almost like you were hitchhiking with me, just along for the ride?"

"Yes…"

"Well, Marie-Thérèse had some ideas for how to improve it. That woman has got plants I've never seen anywhere else before. Anyway, if it works the way we hope, you'll still have to hitchhike and you won't be able to do anything without me, but at least you'll be able to talk to anybody else we find in there."

"That's brilliant."

"Well, yes, but I don't know much about fighting demons. You won't be able to do any of the fighting, if there is any."

Stone waved her off. "Neither of us will be doing any fighting, if I'm correct about what we'll find in there. Whatever's inside her isn't actually a demon—it's just a tiny piece of one. *Izzy* is the only one who can fight it off and kick it out of her brain. But she hasn't got a clue what's going on. We have to go in there, contact her, and explain it to her. After that, it will be all up to her whether she can manage it on her own."

"And…if she can't?" Verity looked down at Izzy grimly.

Stone didn't reply. He didn't need to—she knew the answer as well as he did.

They had to do some fancy explaining to get Dr. Palmer to go along with what they suggested.

"You're telling me…she's got a piece of a *demon* inside her mind, and you two are going to—what, exactly?"

"It's a magical technique," Verity said. "We get past her mental defenses, figure out what the problem is, and hopefully help her deal with it."

"We've done it before," Stone said quickly. "Verity's brilliant at it, and between the two of us, I'm confident we can reach Izzy and make her understand."

"Understand *what*, though? I know you mages can do things we mundane medical types can't hope to match, but the fact still remains that Agent Freeman is having dangerous seizures. Forgive me for wording it this way, but if you two do—whatever it is you're planning to do—and you agitate her to the point where it sets off another seizure, it could kill her, or damage her brain so severely that she'll never recover."

"We're aware of that," Verity said with a sober glance at Stone. "But Alastair knows more about demons than I do, and he says it's the only way. We've got to get in there and help her kick it out of her head, or she isn't going to get any better."

"Please, Dr. Palmer," Stone said. "I know this sounds mad, but this isn't a medical problem. It's a magical one. And I wouldn't trust anyone more than I trust Verity to deal with it, if it can be dealt with it all."

The doctor shifted her gaze between the two of them, her medical judgment obviously conflicted with her understanding that there were aspects of this situation she couldn't do anything about. Finally, reluctantly, she said, "You're telling me that no matter what we do to stabilize Agent Freeman using mundane means—or even standard magical healing—it isn't going to help?"

"I'm telling you that you might be able to keep her body alive," Stone said. "But without dealing with the source, which is something you can't do, it ultimately won't make any difference. Think of it this way—she's got a deep wound with something inside it that's causing an infection. No matter how much you treat the wound, unless you get that object out of there, it's just going to keep infecting her. Magically speaking, that's what's happening."

Dr. Palmer hesitated again.

"You can be right there," Verity said. "You can bring in your team to monitor her while we're doing it, in case anything goes wrong physically."

"But you've got to understand," Stone said, "you can't intervene unless it's a life-or-death situation. It's likely some of what we'll be doing will cause some nasty physiological effects, but that's just the way this sort of thing works—especially in a case as bad as this one. If you agree to let us try, it's got to be on our terms. Otherwise, we're just subjecting Izzy to unnecessary discomfort."

"Does she have any family?" Verity asked. "Is there anyone who needs to be contacted for consent?"

Palmer shook her head. "No. It's just her. The agency is her life. She's given her medical power of attorney to Agent Huxley, so she'll have to be contacted."

"Do it," Stone said. "We've got to go fetch some things we'll need for the technique. Do you think you can get hold of her and have an answer in half an hour?"

"I—" She sighed. "Yes, fine. I don't like this at all, but I'm fresh out of other ideas. You do what you need to do, and I'll talk to Agent Huxley."

Stone ended up going after the elixir himself, since it would have taken too long for Verity to drive to the Chicago portal. He reappeared in the alley next to the San Francisco branch of Sybil's Apothecary and strode inside.

Hezzie, Verity's business partner and fellow alchemist, looked up from where she was helping an older woman behind the counter. Her eyes narrowed when she spotted Stone. "What are you all dressed up for?"

He'd forgotten about the suit. "Don't mind me," he said, sweeping past. "I'm retrieving something for Verity."

Hezzie shot him a sour look, and for a moment he thought she might object. But "Don't make a mess back there," was all she said, and turned her attention back to her customer.

"Good to see you too." He shoved through the beaded curtain that separated the main storeroom from the shop, then walked straight through the back wall into the illusion-hidden smaller room that no potential thief would be able to find even if they had magical talent. Stone himself had helped Verity with this illusion, and he was confident that, short of dragons or perhaps Trevor Harrison, the place was undetectable.

This was where Verity and Hezzie kept the "good stuff"—exotic ingredients and components, potions that were either expensive or dangerous, and other items they didn't get much call for from their regular customers. The aroma in the tiny room was an overwhelming combination of sour, sweet, acrid, and a faint tang of blood that always made Stone a little light-headed.

He turned in place, scanning the shelves full of vials, jars, sheaves of dried plants, and a few old books until he spotted the small bottle Verity had described to him. There was only one of its type, sitting next to a large jar of what looked like green mayonnaise. It wasn't labeled. He levitated it down from its perch and examined it more closely, verifying it was the right one, then stuffed it in his pocket and strode back out.

The older woman had left now, leaving Hezzie alone and leaning on the counter. "Find what you were looking for?" she asked in a tone that suggested she didn't particularly care.

Stone wondered if the young witch would *ever* warm to him. He knew her history and why she was edgy around men so he didn't hold her surly attitude against her, but it had been years since they'd met. "I did, thanks. I'm off again. Verity and I have got to see a woman about a demon."

He didn't give her a chance to ask, even if she'd been inclined to. He swept out of the shop without another word, hurried around the corner, and after a few moments to visualize the ley-line pattern, vanished.

When he returned, he found Verity pacing around outside Izzy's room in the ICU.

"Did you get it?" she demanded. "Any trouble finding it?" Clearly, now that they had arrived at a plan, she was as anxious to get on with it as he was.

He pulled the little bottle from his pocket and held it up for her perusal. "Did Dr. Palmer get Ren's permission?"

"Yes. Neither of them are too thrilled about the whole thing—especially since Ren won't be able to get here in time to observe—but they agree there's nothing else we can do." She nodded toward Izzy's room, where two nurses and an orderly were working around her bed. "They're getting her prepared. They want to do it in one of the procedure rooms that's better equipped if anything goes wrong."

"No more seizures?"

"Not yet. She's been quiet. I hate thinking about what she must be going through inside her head. We need to help her, Alastair. If this goes on too much longer, I'm worried about her sanity, never mind her physical condition."

Stone concurred. He had no idea what kind of psychological damage a demon fragment inside someone's head might cause, but judging by Izzy's constant agitation, it couldn't be good.

The orderly opened the sliding glass door, then turned back to help one of the nurses wheel Izzy's bed out of the small space. The other nurse followed, keeping a close eye on the patient.

As they moved by and out of the ICU, Dr. Palmer came in. "Oh, good, you're back," she said when she saw Stone. "Are you two ready for this?"

"I'm not sure it's entirely possible to be *ready*," Stone said. "But we're about as prepared as we're likely to get."

"Let's go, then. My gut is still telling me this is a bad idea, so I'd like to get started before I change my mind."

They followed her out of the room and down a couple of hallways until they reached a room labeled *PROCEDURE 2*. She held the door open and waved them through.

Stone wasn't sure what he'd been expecting—perhaps a full-fledged operating theater—but Procedure 2 turned out to be a spacious room lined with cabinets and shelves along two walls, with a series of monitoring equipment arranged around the central space where Izzy's bed had already been rolled. A shaded window dominated a third wall.

"You're not going to make us change into scrubs, are you?" Stone asked.

Palmer shook her head. "This isn't a surgical procedure. Honestly, I don't know *what* the hell it is. You two just do what you need to do, and let us know if you need anything. We'll stay out of your way unless things go wrong."

"Brilliant." He slipped out of his coat and suit jacket and laid them over a nearby counter, then loosened his tie.

Verity had pulled up two chairs next to Izzy's bed, one on each side. "Can you lower the lights, please?" she asked the room at large.

The overhead lights dimmed, plunging the room into a peaceful twilight.

"Okay," she said to Stone after he'd seated himself across from her. "Do you remember how this works?"

"We both drink your concoction, and then each of us takes one of Izzy's hands and each other's, to form a circle."

"Right." She looked around at the onlookers. "And remember, everyone, this *is* a real circle, so it would be bad to break it. So all of you need to stay back and just watch, no matter what you see. I can't stress that enough. Unless Izzy's going to die, don't intervene."

Stone pulled the bottle from his pocket and poured a capful. "If I recall correctly, I said this stuff tasted like 'carbonated arse' the last time I took it. I do hope you've added the minty-fresh flavor by now."

"Butterscotch, actually."

He had no idea if she was kidding, but either way he had to drink the stuff. He tipped the capful into his mouth and wrinkled his nose. "Well. You were serious. Now it tastes like carbonated *butterscotch* arse."

"Everybody's a critic." She took the bottle from him and poured her own capful, which she swallowed without making a face.

Stone supposed alchemists were used to drinking all sorts of things that tasted terrible. Too bad there weren't any alchemical mixtures that tasted like Guinness. *Enough faffing about,* he told himself, reaching out to grip Verity's hand in one of his, and Izzy's in the other.

Verity's hand was warm as it tightened around his, but Izzy's was as chilly as death, limp in his grasp. Whatever was going on in her brain wasn't translating to her body.

As soon as the connection was closed, though, Stone felt two things: the familiar tingle that told him the circle was functioning properly, and the faint, paper-cut pain in the scar on his chest.

The demon, or fragment of it, was definitely still there inside Izzy.

He shifted to magical sight. Verity's jade-green aura was strong and steady as always, as was his own purple, gold and silver one. Izzy's blue, however, flickered faintly, barely bright enough to show against the white of her bedsheet. As he continued to watch, small red flashes rose and subsided around various parts of her body.

"Okay," Verity murmured. "Are you ready, Alastair?"

By now, he'd forgotten there was anyone else in the room. His focus was one hundred percent on Verity and Izzy. "Let's do this."

The circle's tingle increased gradually, as if someone were turning up an electrical connection. The energy moved smoothly along the circle between the three of them.

"Here goes," came Verity's distant voice.

Around them, the world shifted.

CHAPTER SEVENTEEN

ALDWYN FROZE.

There were five guards covering the nine platforms. All of them were looking at him, as well as more red-coated figures who had shimmered into being in front of him. Their expressions were all grim, their auras stressed like cops who weren't sure they had enough firepower to deal with a potential threat.

Remaining utterly calm, Aldwyn flicked his gaze around to take in a couple seconds' view of his new surroundings. He noted glass-fronted rooms lining the walls at several levels high above. Administrative offices, perhaps? He wasn't sure and didn't particularly care. More magical lights, this time in the shapes of colorful birds, danced in the open, empty space, and soft music in an unfamiliar but not unpleasant style played.

"What is this about?" he asked in an even tone that allowed only a hint of impatience.

The guards and newcomers were spread around him in a semi-circle now, looking more than ever like wary police officers. The only thing that was missing were the guns. This group wasn't pointing anything at Aldwyn—not wands or magical apparatus or even their hands, but their eyes were hard and unyielding.

"Identify yourself," a woman—evidently their leader—said. Her coat was in shades of red and gray, and she wore a few more pins and ornaments on her lapels than the others around her.

Aldwyn didn't try to fake his way through this; why should he? It wasn't as if these people could do anything to him. From the look of their auras, some of them might have some respectable magical power—but nowhere near his level. He remained silent and watched them with a hint of confident amusement.

"Identify yourself," the woman ordered again.

Around her, the others' auras shifted slightly, indicating their nervousness. They'd probably never had to deal with a situation like this before.

"I don't think I will at this time," he said. "I am curious, however, about how you identified me as a threat."

"*Are* you a threat?" Now the woman's aura was shifting too.

Aldwyn wondered if she was even now using some hidden magical means to call in more reinforcements. This was getting tiresome. He hadn't come here to kill anyone, but only to gather information. He hoped they wouldn't force his hand.

"That depends," he said in the same conversational tone. "As long as you do not threaten me, I am not. I would strongly advise you not to do so. Please answer my question. I am genuinely curious."

Her expression hardened. "You obviously think we are fools. Your little trick might have deceived the teleport-pad guards, but we have other systems in place to prevent unauthorized entry to our city."

"Unauthorized? I was under the impression that the magically talented were welcome in your city. Was I mistaken?"

"You are not a citizen of Prensyrrus. You attempted to present yourself as one. That is a violation of the law." She took a single step closer to him. "We do not take kindly to spies. State your name, please."

Aldwyn didn't smile, even though he couldn't miss how nervous she and the others were. In his peripheral vision, he noticed other figures drifting in or appearing out of invisibility spells. They must be truly worried about him.

Good. It was as it should be.

"I do not think I will," he repeated. "My name is irrelevant. You would not know it if I told you."

"What is your purpose for attempting to infiltrate our city?"

He shook his head like a father whose child had just disappointed him. "I had no intention to 'infiltrate' anything. I merely seek information."

The woman snorted. "Information. We are not in the business of providing information, nor anything else, to spies."

Aldwyn remained unaffected. "What do you propose to do with me, then?"

"You are under arrest. You will be detained until such time as we can determine who you are and where your allegiances lie."

"My *allegiances*—" He put stern emphasis on the word "—lie with myself, and myself only."

"We shall see. Please come with us, and do not attempt to escape or make trouble. You won't find our defense systems pleasant should you fail to comply."

She was still nervous. Again, Aldwyn almost smiled, but he didn't. This hadn't been the way he'd planned to get his information about Prensyrrus and the Talented, but it would do as well as any other. He could play along for now, confident these people didn't have a chance to hold him any longer than he permitted it.

"I will comply, for the moment," he said, still projecting his patrician, fatherly mien. "As long as you treat me with the dignity to which I am entitled, and do not attempt to injure me, I am at your service."

Two of the other guards exchanged confused glances. No doubt, this was the strangest and most civilized criminal apprehension they'd ever participated in.

The woman in charge wasn't much better. She looked him up and down suspiciously. "We need to search you."

"For what?" Aldwyn spread his hands. "I've already proven I can deceive the lot of you, so if I were hiding anything on my person, do you honestly expect you will find it?"

He had her thoroughly flummoxed now. "It is protocol," she finally said. "Please come with us."

The group closed ranks around him, none of them getting too close, until they formed a loose ring with the leader next to him where she could keep an eye on him. "This way, please."

Aldwyn allowed them to lead him out of the airy atrium and away from the teleport pads, toward a hallway that had been hidden by an illusion until they approached it. They moved along past what appeared to be blank walls, though Aldwyn's draconic senses revealed several more concealed doors. They didn't stop until they reached the hall's end, where one of the doors shimmered into existence and swung open.

"Inside, please," the leader said.

When Aldwyn passed through the doorway, the tingle of a powerful ward tickled his skin. Making no indication he'd felt it, he continued inside.

The room was small and featureless, with blank walls and no windows. Or at least the walls *appeared* blank, though the telltale glow of another illusionary doorway flickered on the far side. As with the rest of the city that Aldwyn had seen so far, everything looked new and spotless, but unlike the soaring atrium, no effort had been expended here to make the surroundings beautiful. The furniture consisted of an unremarkable table and a few chairs—one on the far side and three more on the near side, facing it. Although the room was well lit, there were no light fixtures or other obvious sources of illumination.

The Talented's version of an interrogation room, apparently.

Several of the guards had peeled off during their trip down the hallway, leaving only two flanking the outside door, and the leader with two others on either side of her near the chairs.

"Remain standing, please," she ordered. "Hold your hands out from your body."

Ah, so this was to be the "search." Aldwyn was willing to go along with the charade as long as they didn't touch him. He stood at attention, arms out, and stared straight ahead.

No one touched him. Two of the others removed elaborate, wand-like devices from within their coats and began waving them around near Aldwyn, starting at his feet and working their way up. Aldwyn had never traveled on a human commercial aircraft, but if he had, he might have likened them to the devices TSA agents used at airline security checkpoints. He smiled slightly to himself and increased the energy to his illusions and mental suggestions. If he *did* possess anything they might consider problematic, they would never find it. Since he didn't, he wasn't concerned. After a moment, the two guards withdrew and put their wands away, shaking their heads at the woman.

"You may sit now," she told Aldwyn, pointing at the single chair.

Aldwyn did as requested. He sat upright, confident, with his hands folded on the table and his glittering, unblinking gaze fixed on the woman. The thought that he was unnerving her amused him. He wondered if she thought the room's wards had effectively neutralized him.

She made a subtle gesture, and glowing words appeared in the air in front of her. She studied them a moment, then swiped them aside and looked at Aldwyn with narrowed eyes.

"The wards should have stripped you of any illusionary disguises."

"What makes you think they did not?" Aldwyn asked serenely. He leaned back, steepling his fingers and regarding her over them. "Has it occurred to you that this might be my true appearance?"

The magical "form" still hung in the air to her right. Her gaze cut sideways to it for a moment, then back to her prisoner. "Remove that coat, then. You are not a citizen of Prensyrrus, and therefore do not have the right to wear it."

"As you wish." Aldwyn slipped out of his illusionary coat and tossed it aside.

The woman nodded to one of her underlings, who picked it up. "What is your name?"

"I prefer not to say at this time. What is yours?"

She looked for a moment as if she wouldn't answer out of spite, but then she sighed. "I am Captain Celindria, of the Prensyrrus Public Sector Defense Corps."

The words weren't precise—Aldwyn's translation spell rendered its best approximation of her title and organization—but it would do. "I am pleased to make your acquaintance, Captain. 'Public' Sector, you say? If that is truly so, then why am I being detained? Am I not part of the 'public'?"

"I don't know *what* you are, and that's what troubles me." She looked him up and down. "What were you doing in Nargul?"

"Visiting."

She frowned. "Visiting. How did you arrive there?"

"You would not believe me if I told you." He pushed his chair back and crossed his ankle over his knee. "Your questioning already grows tiresome, Captain, so I will speed it along a bit. I was in Nargul—and I am here—because I wish to learn. I intended to be discreet about it, but you have made that impossible."

"Learn? About what?"

"Everything. I am new to this area. I had hoped to remain unseen, but since that is no longer possible, I see no reason not to be more obvious about my questions."

"You are not doing the questioning here," she said, her stern frown slipping back into place. "You say you are not from this area. What does that mean? Where *are* you from?"

"Farther away than you can possibly imagine."

The man on her left leaned in to whisper something in her ear.

Aldwyn's sharp ears had no trouble making out the word: "*Resistance?*"

The leader tensed a little, her aura flaring brighter, as if the thought hadn't occurred to her. She considered a moment, then nodded abruptly and stood.

"It is late. Perhaps an evening as our guest will loosen your tongue. Tomorrow morning, we will call in more experienced questioners to continue the conversation." She waved her hand. The glowing, magical form disappeared, and the flickering illusionary doorway Aldwyn had spotted before shimmered into an actual one. It opened, revealing another featureless corridor.

"If you'll come with us, please."

"Where?"

"To your accommodations for the night."

Aldwyn didn't rise from his chair. "Are you planning to imprison me?"

"You will be detained for the night. I assure you, the accommodations are comfortable and your needs will be attended to."

He nodded sagely. "So you *are* planning to imprison me."

"Please follow us."

Humans. They could be amusing sometimes. He wondered how they would react if they had any idea how easily he could destroy them and escape from their so-called 'detention.' Part of him resented allowing them even the illusion of thinking they had any control over him, but despite his impatience, he had learned many things over his centuries on Earth—and especially in the years since he had awakened after his sleep beneath the ancestral Stone home.

Sometimes, you could learn far more when you allowed the small ones to believe they had the better of you.

He could always exact his punishment for daring to treat him so disrespectfully later, if it came to that.

"Very well," he said, injecting just the right amount of boredom into his tone. He stood, made a show of smoothing the lines of his clothes, and clasped his hands behind his back. "Take me to my 'accommodations', then.'"

Something in Captain Celindria's eyes before she turned away from him suggested she might be just a little bit concerned about what he was capable of.

The thought pleased him.

He'd been expecting a prison cell, and was mildly surprised when Celindria and her subordinates led him down another featureless hallway to another teleport pad.

Their destination was a door guarded by a bored-looking man in an unadorned red coat. He straightened his pose as the newcomers approached.

"This man will be detained for the night," Captain Celindria told him crisply. "See to it that he is treated well. He is not a prisoner—yet. For now, he is a guest. Understood?"

"Yes, Captain," the new man said. "This way, please."

On the other side of the door was a large, central square room with several other doors lining three of its walls. Each door had a magically glowing plaque next to it with a notation Aldwyn couldn't read, and a small, currently-opaque panel made of something that looked like glass but probably wasn't, set into the top half.

The man headed straight for the door directly opposite them. He waved his hand over the plaque and the door immediately made a small *click* and swung open. "If you'll step inside, please."

Aldwyn, still amused, did as he was asked. Once again, he felt the faint tingle—a bit stronger this time—of a ward as he crossed the threshold. He turned back to face them, standing just inside the doorway.

"I'm sure you'll be comfortable here for the evening," Captain Celindria said. "If you need anything—anything *reasonable*, in any case—you may press the panel on the inside of the door. Please do not abuse it, or you won't receive a response."

She walked off with her two flunkies, and the guard closed the door. The panel at its top shimmered, going transparent.

Aldwyn didn't think they needed the window to keep an eye on him. He was sure they had magical surveillance devices that would do the job much more efficiently—assuming he allowed them to.

For now, he settled for looking around the room. It was larger than a prison cell and more nicely appointed; it had a bed with a simple but functional comforter, a desk with a chair, another more comfortable upholstered chair, and a soft light panel on the far wall providing gentle illumination. A privacy panel on the far side hid a simple sink and a device that was probably a toilet. The room didn't have a window, but it did have a pleasant, magically glowing landscape on the wall above the bed. Overall, it was the equivalent of a basic-level hotel room.

Aldwyn wondered if the Talented used this room to house prisoners with magic. Were the nonmagical, the "Dim," ever imprisoned here, or were they simply killed when suspected of committing crimes?

Using his draconic senses, he looked around the room. It didn't take him long to spot the surveillance devices: one was high up on the rear wall to give it a clear view of most of the room, while another was directly across from the toilet area. They might want prisoners to *think* they weren't being watched there, but Aldwyn didn't believe it for a moment. If he were incarcerating potentially dangerous people, he certainly wouldn't allow them a place to hide their activities from view.

He walked to the door and looked out the window. The central area around which the cells were spread was empty. Apparently, the guards had some other location—probably a more comfortable one—where they could keep an eye on things. Another look around revealed two more magical surveillance devices out there, and he suspected there were others he couldn't see. Anyone who broke out of the cells would be spotted immediately.

Anyone who wasn't a dragon, anyway.

Aldwyn smiled as he spotted a flash of blue beyond the window on the cell door directly opposite his own. Somebody else was here. He'd considered breaking out of the cell and continuing his fact-finding mission, but this might be a better option.

After all, this whole *city* was split by at least two powerful ley lines. He'd noticed that when he'd arrived, and filed the information away for later.

Clearly, the Talented were strongly focused—perhaps to the exclusion of all else—on magic. So far, Aldwyn had seen no indication of any other mundane weapons or security devices during his time in Prensyrrus. That worked very well when at least one of two things was true: either the people you intended to police had no magical ability, or else they did but it wasn't strong enough to circumvent the security methods.

Too bad for them, but Aldwyn was their worst nightmare.

It took him only a few seconds to simultaneously turn himself invisible and create an illusion of himself trudging over to lie resignedly down on the bed, as if accepting his fate. Another second later and he'd appeared, still invisible, inside the cell where he'd seen the blue aura flash.

Under normal circumstances, wards would prevent ley-line travel—but only if the wards' magic was stronger than the traveler's. Dragons had no trouble passing through most human mages' wards, and even the strongest, such as those built by Aldwyn's troublesome descendant Alastair Stone, could only deter them for a short time. The wards here were adequate, workmanlike, and uninspired—the magical equivalent of a featureless steel door. They proved no hindrance whatsoever.

It truly *was* good to be a dragon.

Aldwyn paused a moment to look around the new cell. The prisoner here was a man, with shaggy brown hair, a lean face, and a resigned expression. He lay on his bed staring up at the ceiling as if unable to go to sleep. Unlike the long coat and other finery of the Talented, he wore a simple but well-made shirt, trousers, and soft boots.

Aldwyn carefully adjusted his illusion, creating a space inside the man's cell where everything would appear as it currently was. Then he sat in the chair opposite the bed and shimmered into visibility.

The man continued to stare at the ceiling, unaware of the new presence in his space.

"Good evening," Aldwyn said.

The prisoner jerked upright, leaping off the bed. When he spotted Aldwyn seated calmly in the chair, his eyes widened. He shot a quick, fearful glance toward the door.

"Do not worry," Aldwyn said. "They cannot observe us. If you remain in this immediate area, my illusions are cloaking us."

The man's aura flared, and his breath quickened. "Who—are you? How did you get in here?"

"How I got in is immaterial, since I am here. I am one of your fellow—'detainees,' I believe they call it, since they seem reluctant to call me a prisoner." Aldwyn indicated the cell with an elegant hand-wave. "Why are you here?"

The man snorted, apparently willing to roll with the status quo for the moment. "They claim I helped one of the Dim."

"Did you?"

He shrugged. "I'm not saying anything. How do I know they didn't send you in here to try to get me to confess to something?"

"Fair enough. I have questions for you, but I care little for your individual circumstances."

The man gave him a look. "You're just full of tact and good manners, aren't you?" He seemed more amused than offended, though.

"I prefer to call it honesty. What is your name?"

He hesitated, but his expression turned resigned. "I guess it doesn't matter if I tell you. *They* already know. My name is Seviath. And you are?"

"A newcomer to your city. I have questions."

"Ah, man of mystery. That's fine. I don't care much about you, either, if we're being *honest* with each other." He put sarcastic emphasis on the word. "Unless you can get me out of here, anyway."

"That would be difficult to do without causing a great deal of trouble, something I don't wish to do at this time."

"So, why should I answer your questions, then?"

"I could force you to answer, if I desired."

"Is that right?"

"I got into your cell without arousing any suspicions, did I not? That speaks to magical ability far beyond what any of these people can match."

Seviath considered. "I guess that's true. And I guess it will depend on the questions. I'm not saying anything about myself or what I did or didn't do."

"I do not care about those things. My questions are of a more…basic nature. As I said, I am new to this place. I was apprehended when I attempted to enter the city from the surface."

"I find that hard to believe." Seviath slid back on the bed until his back was against the wall. "Are you telling me you can get inside a locked cell and create illusions that can fool the security magic in here, but you can't sneak past a few bored guards?"

"I was not aware of the procedure until I had aroused suspicion. Tell me about Prensyrrus."

"Tell you about—" Seviath narrowed his eyes and frowned. "Are you serious?"

"Quite. I am a foreigner, from far away." Aldwyn paused a moment. Even with all his power, it wouldn't be prudent to remain here for long, so he needed to limit his questions. Loriar in Nargul had already told him about the Dim, the surface city, and the Wastes; he could always find out more about those later. "Tell me about Prensyrrus. Are there other such cities, floating above the ground and housing the magical population of this land?"

Seviath snorted. "You're making fun of me, aren't you?"

"I assure you, I am not. And my patience grows short, so please answer my questions." He remembered what he'd told Loriar. "Instruct me as if I were a child."

The man held his gaze for several seconds, then made a scornful noise. "All right. Whatever you say. This is certainly more interesting than counting the spots on my ceiling." He leaned forward, taking on a mocking, almost singsong tone, the sort a teacher might use on a classroom full of preschoolers. "There are five floating cities, along the coasts all over the land. Their names are Prensyrrus, Sholandre, Temolan, Genarra, and Leonessan."

A brief anger touched Aldwyn—he had punished plenty of humans for lesser insults, but for now, it was more important to get the answers to his questions. He could always deal with Seviath later if he chose to. He pointedly ignored the tone, addressing only the words themselves. "And each of these floating cities has a corresponding city on the surface below it, such as Nargul?"

"Right. That's where the Dim live. There are a lot more of them than there are of us."

That didn't surprise Aldwyn. What *did* surprise him were the fluctuations in Seviath's aura, especially when he said 'Dim.' Was he lying—or was he uncomfortable speaking the word, as most humans might be when using a racial slur?

"Let us confine our discussion to the floating cities, then. Are they all similar?"

Seviath shrugged. "I've never visited any others. Most people don't, since it's difficult to get the proper clearance. My allegiance is to Prensyrrus."

There was that word again. "Allegiance. You have sworn such a thing?"

The man clearly couldn't help looking at Aldwyn as if he might be missing a few screws. "Everybody has to—the Talented, anyway. Nobody cares about the Dim. They can't be trusted enough to keep their word, so their allegiance doesn't matter. But every Talented person has to swear loyalty to a house."

"A house."

"House, city, they're basically the same thing."

"I see." Aldwyn thought about that a moment. "How are these cities governed?"

Seviath didn't answer right away. He looked as if he was trying to find any ulterior motives in Aldwyn's deceptively simple questions.

"I assure you, I am not attempting to deceive you. I have no reason to conceal the information I am seeking."

The man studied him, then shrugged and leaned back against the wall. "Fine. I guess this isn't the strangest thing that's ever happened to me, but it's close. The cities are governed by councils. Each city has one, each with its own leader. And then there's a Grand Council, made up of representatives from each of the individual city councils."

Aldwyn stroked his chin. "I see. And how are these council members chosen? Are they elected from among the magical populace, or are the positions hereditary?"

Seviath snorted. "Elected? That's funny. I'm still convinced you're playing with me, though I can't figure out why."

"Answer the question, please."

"It's all about magic, and how much of it you have. The strongest mages have the highest status." He pointed to himself. "Somebody like me—I'm a nobody around here. I have magic so I'm a citizen, but not a lot. That's why I normally live down there." He pointed toward the floor.

"Down there?"

"In Nargul. A lot of the lower-powered mages choose to live there, to supervise the factories and other industries. They don't leave that kind of thing to the Dim."

There it was again—the quick little aura flare that told Aldwyn the man didn't like using the slur. He chose to ignore it for the moment. "The lower-powered mages choose to live on the surface—perhaps because it gives them a chance to feel superior to someone? If one's level of magical power equates with the respect they are accorded, I assume those with less do not enjoy high status in the floating cities."

Seviath nodded, dropping his gaze to his lap. "You got that right. I don't mind, though. That's not why I live down there. I don't mess with the Dim, and they don't mess with me. I just like it better in Nargul. Not so many eyes on me." He lowered his voice and leaned forward. "A lot of the people here are far too full of themselves for my liking, though I'll never say that to their faces, of course. I'm not a fool."

"No…I suspect you are not." Aldwyn considered again. "Let us return to the topic of government. You said the council positions are awarded based on level of magical power. How is that determined?"

"How should I know? There are tests, I'd imagine. They test children, of course, but I think if they suspect someone has a lot of power, they do more tests later."

"What if an individual possesses impressive power, but doesn't wish to serve on the council?"

"No idea. I don't think it's ever happened. I've never met anybody with that much power who didn't want more of it."

Aldwyn steepled his hands. "I see. Based on your experience, what do you think they will do with us?"

Seviath tilted his head at the abrupt change of subject. "That's an interesting question. Me, they'll probably just assign to some job in Nargul that's worse than the one I already had. It's not like I'm accused of anything too terrible. They don't like it when we get too close to the Dim, but they can't prove anything."

"And me?"

"What do they say you did?"

"I attempted to travel from Nargul to Prensyrrus without authorization."

"Huh. So they probably think you're a spy."

"They did use that word, yes."

"Then they'll probably find somebody more powerful to question you, to figure out which other city you're really from."

"And if they determine I am telling the truth—that I do not come from any of the cities here?"

"I don't see how that's possible. Everybody's from somewhere. They might think you're part of the resistance, I guess."

There was that word again. Aldwyn recalled what Loriar had said, that the resistance consisted of mages and nonmagical people who worked together. "Where do the resistance come from?"

"Your guess is as good as mine. They just turn up, and nobody knows where their base is. The Talented are always trying to root them out in the cities."

"I see. And how would my fate differ between these two possibilities?"

Seviath's brow wrinkled. "You're asking a lot of questions I can't answer. I told you—I'm a nobody. They don't tell me these things. But if I had to guess, I'd say if they believe you that you're not from anywhere, they'll probably make you swear allegiance to Prensyrrus and become a citizen."

"And if they determine I am part of the resistance?"

"Death, most likely. Or exile to the Wastes. You do know about the Wastes, right?"

"Yes."

"Well, that's something, I guess. Then you know that, given the choice between those two, death's the better one. At least it's quick. Nobody survives long in the Wastes, but I'd rather die cleanly than get my guts pulled out by an abomination or flayed to pieces by a manastorm."

"Hmm." Aldwyn wondered if a 'manastorm' was the locals' name for the odd, dangerous magical fluctuations he'd encountered while flying in his true form. He didn't waste much time on the thought, however, because he was already forming a plan.

He stood with dignity and straightened his coat. "Thank you. You have provided me with much to think about."

Seviath frowned. "That's it? You're just going to show up here, ask me questions, and then leave?"

"Is there any reason why I should remain?"

"I told you—if you're as good as you say you are, you could help me get out of here."

"As I said, that isn't feasible at this time."

"What if I tell them you were here?"

Aldwyn gave him a sly smile. "Then I suspect they will think you mad, since you have no way to prove your words. As that will likely lead to a less desirable fate than simply being sent back to

Nargul, it is in your best interests to hold your tongue. Do you not agree?"

Seviath glared at him, but then sighed. "Fine. Go. I suspect what's probably in my best interests is to pretend this whole conversation never happened. Good luck with whatever they decide to do with you."

"I do not think I will need luck." Aldwyn faded from view.

CHAPTER EIGHTEEN

WHEN THE LIGHTS CAME UP on a new scene, Stone noticed two things simultaneously.

The first was that the pain in his chest had increased. It still wasn't strong or debilitating in any way, but the throbbing ache was a constant thing now.

The second was that they were standing in what looked like the cluttered living room of a working-class apartment.

Verity stood next to him, no longer holding his hand even though he knew in the real world the connection was still strong—if it wasn't, they wouldn't be seeing this scene now.

Izzy was nowhere in evidence.

Stone looked around, taking in the shabby sofa and chairs, the old tube television, and the threadbare carpet. A couple empty beer cans and the remains of a frozen dinner covered a TV tray in front of the sofa, while the coffee table in front of it was littered with old newspapers and fast-food wrappers. "Where are we?"

"I'm not sure." Verity was looking around too. "This doesn't look at all current, though, does it? Look at the TV. Nobody has those anymore."

Stone walked to the window and pushed the stained drapes aside, hoping the view would give him some clue about where they'd ended up. No such luck, though: outside the window, the only view was hazy, dark fog. It appeared to be nighttime, but no details were visible.

Verity joined him. "That's not surprising," she said in answer to his unasked question. "Whatever this is, the important part is this place, not whatever's out there in the rest of the world."

"That thing's definitely around here somewhere." He rubbed his chest idly. "But why *here*? And where's Izzy?"

"I think we need to find her. Let's look around."

It didn't take long to tour the front part of the apartment. At the rear, a small kitchen had old appliances, a cheap linoleum floor, and a sink full of dirty dishes. More empty beer cans, newspapers, and dishes covered the counters. A small table with three chairs, also buried under clutter, took up the far side.

Idly, Stone picked up one of the newspapers. Because this was Izzy's mental vision, he didn't expect to see anything legible—sort of like the way you couldn't read text in a dream. But to his surprise, one thing stood out among the muddled columns of text and blurry photos.

A date.

"Verity, look at this."

She turned back from where she'd been examining the items stuck to the refrigerator, and glanced at the paper he held up. "That's over twenty years ago."

"Twenty-two, to be exact. So…her vision is set in the past?"

Verity's brow furrowed as her expression grew sober. "I think I might see where this is going."

"Pray, enlighten me. I haven't got a bloody clue. What are we doing in some random tatty flat from twenty-two years ago?"

"I don't think this place is random. Come on—let's go check the back. If I'm right, that's where we're going to find Izzy."

Stone followed her, still confused about what to expect. He'd only ever done this "ride-along" thing with Verity once before, when he'd entered the mind of Daphne Weldon's disturbed son, Jeremy. He'd been unable to interact with the boy at all then, though, so he'd had to stand back and watch while Verity did the heavy lifting.

He'd also done a simpler version with Roy Darner, though—the young man who'd been traumatized when he'd been kidnapped by the Whitworth brothers to participate in their experiments. The two visions had had one thing in common: both relied heavily on metaphor. Darner, represented as a younger version of himself, had led him through a shadowy maze and into his teenage bedroom, while Jeremy had been in a toy store. Both places where the subject had felt safe.

So then, what could this shabby apartment be a metaphor for? Did Izzy feel safe in this pigsty? Was this where she'd grown up?

They moved carefully down a hallway lined with cheap framed prints, peering into a small bathroom before moving on. On the left side, Stone noticed a section of cracked plaster and touched Verity's arm to point it out to her. "Looks like someone punched this."

She nodded, but didn't reply. Her face was set in a concerned, wary expression.

The next open doorway revealed a cluttered bedroom that obviously belonged to at least one adult. Its unmade bed had rumpled sheets, a cheap spread, and a padded headboard, while strewn clothes, both men's and women's, littered the floor and draped the only chair. The room didn't have a separate bath. Verity peeked inside and then moved on.

The only other room was at the end of the hall, behind a closed door. Someone had taped several colorful child's drawings to it. A small white plaque, the kind one might buy from a rack in a dollar store, read *ISABEL'S ROOM*, with a cheerful string of bright flowers surrounding it.

Verity paused in front of it and shot Stone a sober, significant look. Then she gently knocked on the door. "Izzy, are you in there?"

No answer.

She knocked again, a little louder this time but still not sharply. "Izzy? We're your friends. We've come to help you. Can we come in?"

"Wait a minute," Stone said under his breath as the light—or at least part of it—finally dawned. "You're expecting to find a little girl in there, aren't you?"

She nodded, still focused on the door.

Stone did quick math. It was hard to tell from looking at the thin, unconscious figure in the bed, but the photo Ren had shown him of Izzy pegged her at around thirty. If this was twenty-two years ago, she'd be eight now.

But why? If the demon was here, how would reverting to a child help her avoid it? Suddenly tense, he glanced around as if expecting to see the demon charging down the hallway.

That didn't happen, though. The hallway was as quiet as ever, lit by a grimy overhead fixture halfway down. The air smelled of dirty clothes and stale beer.

"You're going to have to open the door. You know that, right?" He kept his voice low, almost a whisper.

"I do. But I want to give her a chance first." Louder, she called, "Izzy? My name's Verity. I'm here with my friend Alastair. You don't know us, but we're friends of Ren Huxley. Can we come in?"

Still no answer.

Stone leaned in to press his ear against the door. No sound came from beyond. "Are you sure she's in there?"

"Yeah. Be ready." She reached for the knob.

Stone didn't bother asking how he could "be ready" when he couldn't affect anything in his bizarre vision. He merely stood back and waited, his gaze fixed on whatever would be revealed.

The door wasn't locked. Verity pushed it open, then stood aside.

The room was pitch-dark. The dim light from the hallway illuminated only a short distance inside, showing the same shabby, tan carpet as the living room.

"Izzy?" Verity drew a deep breath and stepped inside, reaching to her right to flip on the light switch.

Stone followed and closed the door behind her. He checked for a lock, but it didn't have one.

The room was tiny, barely big enough to hold the twin mattress on a cheap metal frame, a nightstand, and a battered dresser that didn't match it. A small window looked out onto more dark fog, and another door opposite it was probably a closet.

"Still no sign of Izzy," he said under his breath. He scanned the room, taking in the toys on the floor and on top of the dresser, the unmade bed, and a few bright but fading posters on the walls. He didn't see any sign of violence or disturbance.

Verity glanced back toward the door, perhaps to make sure it was closed, then indicated the closet door.

Stone nodded, taking a step back and positioning himself between the closet door and the room's door. He had no idea if it would do any good, but his aim was that if Izzy was hiding in the closet, whatever tried to come after her would have to go through him first.

Verity knocked softly on the closet door. "Izzy? Are you in there? It's Verity and Alastair. I promise we won't hurt you. Will you come out?"

If she was in there, she didn't answer. However, a few seconds later Stone distinctly heard something that sounded like hitching breath, or perhaps a low sob.

Verity heard it too. She knocked again, still gentle. "Izzy, come on. We're your friends. We're here to help you. Please come out."

Silence hung in the air, and then a small voice said, barely audibly, "Go away. You can't help."

Verity exchanged grim glances with Stone. "We *can* help you," she said. "That's why we're here. I'm going to open the door now, okay? Please don't be scared."

She waited a moment for a reply. When there was none, she swung the closet door slowly open.

The tiny closet was as dark as the rest of the room had been. A few child's clothes hung on a wooden rod, with more jumbled on the floor next to two pairs of well-worn shoes. From the depths, wide, frightened eyes peered out at them.

The little girl was seated on the floor, her legs drawn up and her back pressed against the rear wall. She was dressed in pink pajamas, her hair in small braids with colorful beads in them. She looked up at them, clearly terrified, and clutched a well-loved brown teddy bear close to her.

"Hi, Izzy," Verity said, crouching. "I'm Verity. It's nice to meet you."

Stone remained where he was. He could hear the smile in her voice, but also sensed her tension. He peered over her to examine Izzy.

He couldn't get a good look in the darkness, but she didn't seem to be injured. That was something, at least. He checked over his shoulder again to verify the bedroom door was still closed, then settled back to watch Verity.

The girl's eyes were fixed on her now. She held the teddy bear tighter and swallowed hard.

"Will you come out of there?" Verity asked, extending a hand to her. "We'd like to talk to you if you'll let us, and it can't be comfortable in there."

Izzy licked her lips, barely blinking. "H-how do you know my name?"

"That's kind of a long story. But I promise, we're your friends. We're here to help you."

The little girl shook her head several times. "You can't."

"Why not?"

Her gaze shifted, looking past Verity, and even past Stone. "Y-you should go."

"Why? Why are you hiding in the closet?"

Another swallow. "He'll…be back soon."

"Who?" Verity looked over her shoulder at Stone.

Izzy said something, but she'd buried her face in the teddy's fur so they couldn't hear it.

"Who, Izzy? Who's coming back?"

Her dark, haunted eyes came up. "Daddy," she whispered.

Out in the front part of the apartment, a door slammed open.

Stone jerked his head up, spinning to face the closed bedroom door. He did it instinctively, gathering energy to protect them from whatever was coming—but then he remembered where he was. "Damn," he murmured. "I can't do anything, can I?"

"No," Verity said. She too had stood. "I'm not even sure *I* can. I think Izzy has to do it herself."

Stone shot a glance back at the terrified little girl, now trying to cower even deeper into the closet. "She doesn't seem prepared to do that, does she?"

"*Girl!*" A deep, thundering voice called from down the hall. "Where are you, you worthless little bitch? Get out here *now!*"

Stone had heard enough angry drunks to be sure the man was heavily intoxicated. "Can we block the door?" he asked, pointing at the bed.

"We could try, but I don't think it's going to do any good." Verity crouched next to the closet door again. "Izzy, listen—you need to trust me, okay? We can't stop this—but *you* can. None of this is real. You're having a bad dream."

Izzy didn't answer.

"All of this, even your Daddy, is a bad dream. You're really a grown-up now. And all it will take for you to make it all go away is to stand up to him and tell him to get out of your head."

Her only reply was a whimper. She clutched her teddy so tightly its furry body folded over at the middle.

Stone didn't blame her. That was a lot to ask a little girl, to stand up to an angry monster of a man more than twice her size.

"*Girl!*" The voice was louder now, though Stone didn't think he'd made it to the hallway yet. Heavy-booted feet stomped, accompanied by the sound of doors slamming and large objects banging around. "Where the *hell* are you? You get your ass out here right now! If I gotta come down there after you, you gonna be sorry!"

Izzy whimpered louder, and tears sprang to the corners of her eyes.

A deep anger began to rise in Stone. His discomfort around children notwithstanding, he hated bullies—especially those who used their physical size and strength to prey on smaller, weaker victims. One look at Verity told him she was feeling the same way.

But this time, all their desire to put themselves between the drunken threat and the little girl was worthless. As Verity had told Izzy, none of this was real. It was nothing more than an illusion, a nightmare placed here by the shred of itself the demon had left inside her head.

"Izzy," Verity said, her tone growing more urgent. "I swear, we're not lying to you. We're your friends, and we've come to help you, but we can't do anything against him. He's not real—but he's real to *you* as long as you believe in him. If you can be brave and tell him to go away, he will."

"I—I *can't.*" She sounded utterly miserable.

Stone wondered briefly how, or if, this agitation was affecting the physical Izzy back in the hospital bed. He tried to pull himself partially out of the vision, to get a brief look at the actual room around him, but he couldn't do it. As long as he was locked into the circle by his grips on Verity's and Izzy's hands, he was along for the ride, and it wouldn't be safe to try breaking the connection even if he could manage it.

"*I warned you!*" the booming voice called from the front room. "*Now you gonna be sorry when I get my hands on you!*"

The walls shook as pounding footsteps thundered down the hall.

"Izzy, *please*," Verity said, rising again to face the door. "You've got to do it. You have to be brave. We'll be right here with you."

"Will he even be able to see us?" Stone asked her under his breath.

"I don't know."

The bedroom door slammed open, revealing a hulking figure standing in the doorway.

Stone's first thought was that this couldn't possibly be Izzy's actual father. The word "monster" fit him with terrifying accuracy. He was at least six and a half feet tall, his broad shoulders and barrel chest almost a caricature of a human being. He wore a white tank top and sweatpants, his bulging muscles rippling under dark-brown skin. His broad face, glowering mouth, and short-cut hair gave him a bullish aspect. To reinforce the impression, a thick gold chain with a horned bull's-head pendant hung around his neck.

His eyes, which should have been dark, instead glowed with red light.

Ignoring Stone and Verity, he stomped into the room and charged over to the closet.

Unable to stop himself, Stone lunged at the man, trying to grab his arm and pull him back. But his hands passed through him as if he weren't there.

"Izzy!" Verity said desperately. "Please—you have to believe us! This can all end if you stand up to him. I promise!"

But small, terrified Izzy didn't seem to have it in her to resist. She whimpered as the massive man grabbed her arm and yanked her out into the room. Her teddy bear tumbled to the floor.

"How many times I gotta tell you!" the man bellowed in her face, shaking her by her arm as she cried out in pain. "You have this place cleaned *up* by the time I get home! It's a fucking *pigsty* out there!"

Verity, eyes blazing, tried to intervene as Stone had, but even she couldn't affect the scene. None of them could.

Except for Izzy. The little girl, face wild with fear, wasn't looking at her nightmarish father.

She was looking at Stone and Verity. Her eyes pled with them to do something. Anything.

"You're in *big trouble,* you worthless little brat!" he was yelling. He flung her down onto the bed, where she rolled into a ball and faced away from him, sobbing. A nearly visible miasma of beer fumes hung around him.

"Izzy!" Verity sounded more desperate now. "I know it's hard. I know it's the bravest thing you'll ever do. But you *have* to do it! We can't help you unless you do!"

On the bed Izzy tensed, almost as if she was considering Verity's words. But then she pulled herself even tighter, her back shaking as the man's massive hands reached for her.

Verity shot Stone an anguished look, and he knew exactly what she was thinking. Had they gone to all the trouble to enter Izzy's mind, putting her body at risk of another seizure, only to be unable to do anything?

A sudden thought occurred to him, and he spoke before he worked it through. "Izzy! Listen to me. This isn't real. This isn't your father. It's a monster. A demon. It's trying to hurt you."

The scar twinged harder, as if someone had dragged the tip of a hot poker down his chest. The hulking man's head jerked around to look behind him, but he didn't appear to see Stone there.

Stone ignored the pain and the demon, focusing on Izzy. "Izzy. You're not a little girl. You're an adult, and an agent. This is nothing but a dream, but this thing in your head is real. It murdered your partner. Do you remember Jack?"

Something in Izzy's body changed when she heard the name. She tensed.

The man grabbed her by the shoulders and spun her around, glaring into her face. He was still yelling, but Stone no longer paid attention to what he was saying.

And now Izzy was looking at Stone.

He fixed his gaze on her eyes and spoke implacably, almost harshly. "*Jack*, Izzy. Do you remember Jack? He was your partner! This thing *killed* him. Ripped him to pieces."

"Alastair—"

Verity's voice barely registered on his consciousness. He waved her off and kept his focus on Izzy. "He killed your *partner*, Izzy. Your *friend*. Are you going to let him do that to you, too? You've got to stand up to him! Tell him to get the hell out of your head! We can't help you. Only you can do this, and if you don't, Jack's death will have been in vain. Come on, Izzy! You're strong. I know you can do it!"

The little girl was still sobbing, tears tracing tracks down her cheeks. Her tiny beaded braids danced as her "father" shook her. She looked at the demon, then at Stone.

"*Do it!*" he ordered.

"Come on, Izzy," Verity urged.

The demon tightened his grip on her, drawing her back as if intending to slam her into the wall. Its eyes burned bright red, trailing flames. Its mouth was open, showing pointed teeth. It barely looked human anymore.

"Izzy!" Stone yelled. "*Do it for Jack!*"

And then, as if a veil had passed over her, something in Izzy's face changed. Her dark eyes hardened, and her small face set into an expression that looked all wrong on her little-girl features.

Resolve. Anger.

Rage.

She flicked her gaze sideways toward Stone and Verity again, then faced her "father."

"You're not *real!*" she screamed into its glowering face. "Go away! Get out of my head!"

The effect on the demon was immediate. It jerked back as if she'd struck it, dropping her back down onto the bed. "You little *bitch!*" it screamed. "I'm going to beat you until you can't see! And then I'm gonna beat your momma for havin' such a rotten little brat!"

He stepped forward again, but Izzy's expression hadn't changed. She'd backed up until she was pressed against the wall, but her eyes had never left the demon. "Go *away!*" she ordered again, in a strong, shaky voice. "Get *out.* I don't want you in my head anymore!"

And then her voice changed, no longer a little girl's but a full-grown woman's powerful, commanding alto. "Get. The *Fuck.* Out of my *head!*"

The words boomed into the demon's face, hitting like bullets. It jerked back again, staggering until it lost its balance and fell over backward, crashing into the opposite wall. It opened its mouth and roared like an angry bull, the sound echoing around the room until Stone wanted to clap his hands over his ears—or over Izzy's.

But he didn't do either, because he saw something else, some-thing that made him flash a wild, triumphant grin at Verity.

The massive figure was coming apart.

It was fading, its overwhelming size and vitality receding. Diminishing. The bellowing roar's volume decreased as if someone had turned a knob.

From the bed, Izzy watched in shaky amazement.

The figure continued to fade until most of its body had all but disappeared, leaving only the gleaming gold bull's head to drop with a solid *thud* to the floor at its feet. The last to go were its burning red eyes, which seemed to be fighting to remain. Before they too vanished, they swiveled around to settle on Stone and Verity.

"I know you," an unsettling, disembodied voice said in the sudden stillness. *"This isn't over. I'll find you. I'll make you beg for death."*

The pain in Stone's chest flared white-hot for a second, and then both it and the red eyes were gone.

Stone barely got a chance to look over at Izzy, still crouched on her bed, when the world went to black.

The familiar hospital room reformed around them.

Slumped across Izzy's bed, gasping for breath, Stone faintly registered the flurry of activity going on around the bed. Strong hands took hold of his shoulders and pulled him back into his chair while voices swirled around him. He fought to stay aware—was the demon here? Was Izzy in danger? Had she seized again, or stroked out?—but his brain clanged with discordant energy and he couldn't fix his attention on anything.

He didn't pass out. He was sure of that, because when the static started to clear he was still sitting in the same chair, shivering as the sweat soaking the back of his shirt dried in the chill of the room. He swallowed hard and dragged his head up, afraid of what he might see.

Most of the crowd of nurses and technicians that had been surrounding the bed were gone now, leaving only Dr. Palmer and one nurse hovering over the unconscious Izzy, and Verity in the chair across from him, looking about like he felt.

"Did…we do it?" he asked.

"Not sure yet." She sounded as tired as he was. "I…think we might have."

Palmer and the nurse ignored them, working over Izzy for several more minutes. There was a definite focus to their actions, but not the same urgency as before. To Stone's untrained eye, it didn't look like a life-or-death situation.

Finally, Palmer swiped a hand across her brow and faced the two of them.

"I don't know what you two did," she said in wonder. "But her vitals are strong, and whatever that weird brain activity was that's been causing the seizures is gone now." She let out a ragged sigh. "It wasn't obvious for a little bit there, toward the end. I was about five seconds away from pulling you out of that. Her BP spiked hard, and the brain activity increased to twice what it had been during the seizures. I'm amazed she didn't do it again."

Verity looked at Stone. "That was a good idea you had, reminding her about Jack. I didn't think so at first, but that's what got her moving."

He nodded wearily. "Sometimes the only thing that can get someone past terror is rage. I took a chance."

"We're going to take Izzy back to her room now," Dr. Palmer said. "I assume you'll want to talk to her when she wakes up?"

"We will," Verity said. "Give us a minute here, would you please?" She looked as if she wasn't in any more hurry than Stone was to get out of the chair.

"Take all the time you need. This room isn't scheduled for anything else until tomorrow."

A pair of orderlies arrived and, together with the nurse, rolled Izzy's bed out of the procedure room. Palmer followed, leaving Stone and Verity alone.

"So…what do we do now?" Verity asked. "We got the demon out of Izzy, which is great, but that doesn't help us find it. And we're going to have to find it. Did you hear what it said? It knows about us now. If we don't go after it, we'll never be able to stop looking over our shoulders."

Stone settled back in his chair, letting his shoulders slump, and gave her a slow, sly smile, like a satisfied cat.

She narrowed her eyes. "What? I always get nervous when you smile like that."

"I'll tell you later. After we talk to Izzy."

CHAPTER NINETEEN

I T WAS ANOTHER HOUR before Izzy awakened, and another after that before Dr. Palmer pronounced her sufficiently strong to have visitors. In the meantime, Stone called Ren to update her, and Verity called Jason and Amber, who promised to remain on standby in case they were needed.

When the doctor finally let Stone and Verity in to see Izzy, they knocked softly on her doorframe. She'd been moved into a private room, and at least as far as Stone could tell, all the monitoring equipment hooked up to her seemed to be beeping away under normal parameters.

She already looked better. Still thin, certainly, but the ashy gray hue had disappeared from her dark skin, and her open eyes showed weariness but also a bright intellect and curiosity.

"Hi, Izzy," Verity said softly from the doorway.

She studied them with no recognition. "Do I...know you?" Her voice didn't have much strength behind it.

"Probably not. I guess you don't remember us. I'm Verity Thayer, and this is Alastair Stone."

"We help out Agent Huxley sometimes," Stone added.

Izzy's eyes narrowed. "Help her...how?"

Stone closed the door and followed Verity into the room. "We're mages. Sort of...independent contractors."

She took that in without comment.

Verity took the seat next to her bed. "What have they told you? What do you remember about what's happened?"

Her confusion turned to suspicion. "I don't know you two. And I only have your word that you're working for Ren."

Of course she'd be wary—she'd have to be, in her line of work. "We understand," Stone said. "But if we're to do anything about the demon who was holding you and your partner prisoner, we've got to know whatever you can tell us."

Her eyes widened. "Demon…" she whispered.

"That's what it was," Verity said. "I know that sounds hard to believe. Sometimes *I* have trouble believing it. But Alastair's dealt with them before, and he's sure of it. Do you remember anything about being held captive?"

"Not…really." Her expression clouded and her gaze shifted to the side, as if she were trying to recall something. When she spoke again, her tone was tentative. "We were…investigating some oddness with a Changeling gang. After that, the only thing I remember was waking up—never for very long—in a room I didn't know." Her eyes locked back on them. "Where's Jack? Is he here somewhere too?"

Verity looked at her lap.

"I'm sorry…" Stone said softly. "I'm afraid Jack is…gone."

"Gone?" Her voice spiked louder and she half-sat up before slumping back to the pillows. "Gone?" she repeated, quieter. "You mean…he's…dead?"

"I'm sorry, Izzy." Dr. Palmer must not have given her the details yet.

"How?"

"Let's not talk about that right now," Verity sounded steady and gentle, like a counselor. "Ren will tell you the details when you're ready. But right now, we need to know what you know about the demon who took you."

"I told you, I don't know *anything* about any demon. I want to talk to Ren."

"She's on her way," Stone said. "But she won't be here for a couple of hours, and we can't wait for her. We've got to get on with this as soon as we can."

"Get on with *what*?" She sat up a little again, more carefully this time. "Who *are* you two? What do you mean, you're 'independent contractors'?"

"Izzy…" Stone walked around behind Verity, gripping the back of her chair. "I'm terribly sorry to be so abrupt with you, but it can't be helped. If we don't track this demon soon, it will slip away again and a lot more people will get hurt. The short answer to your question, at the risk of sounding insufferably conceited, is that we're far stronger mages than anyone in your organization, including you. If anyone's got a chance of taking down this demon before it does more damage, it's us. But only if we act quickly."

When she still didn't answer, other than giving him a hard stare, he pulled his phone from his pocket. "Give me a moment. We haven't got time for this." He tapped Ren's contact, hoping she hadn't yet boarded a plane for Chicago.

To his relief, she answered immediately. "Stone? Is something wrong?"

"Nothing's wrong. We're in Agent Freeman's room right now. She's awake, but she doesn't trust us. Can you please set her right so we can ask her some questions? You know as well as I do that time's of the essence."

"Put her on." She was all business now.

Silently, he handed the phone to Izzy. "Here. Talk to Agent Huxley."

Izzy still looked suspicious, but she took the phone. "Ren? Is that you?" She listened a moment, nodding. "Yeah—I feel like crap, but the doctor says I'll be okay after some rest. Who are these two? Do they—Yeah. Yeah, okay. If you say so. Listen—they said Jack is—" She listened again, then bowed her head with a soft sigh. "Yeah. Talk later."

She handed the phone back to Stone without looking at him. "Okay. Ren says to help you in any way I can. She also said you saved my life. So ask your questions. I'll answer if I can."

Stone exchanged glances with Verity, and then took the lead. "You said you were investigating some 'oddness' with a Changeling gang. Can you be more specific?"

"They weren't acting like they did normally." She settled back against the pillows, obviously more tired than she wanted to admit. "The rumor was that they had a new leader, who was pushing them to do things they'd never done before. But nobody had ever seen this leader. We thought it was—hell, we had no idea. Something supernatural, was all. Maybe a spirit, or a more powerful Change-ling, or even a mage."

Verity nodded. "That was the demon. It must have grabbed you and Jack when you were nosing around. And you never saw it?"

"Nope. All I saw were a couple of the gang members, but I don't remember how often. I never stayed awake for long. I felt like something was…draining me. I never had any strength."

"That's exactly what happened," Stone said. "Demons drain life energy…*soul* energy, if you believe that way. Either way, it has the same result: the victim wastes away to nothing and eventually dies."

Her eyes widened. "Is that…what happened to Jack?"

"Not…exactly," Verity said carefully. "Let's talk about you right now, Izzy. Ren will give you the other details when she gets here."

Izzy looked like she thought they were putting one over on her, but she only bowed her head. "Fine."

"Izzy," Stone said suddenly, "can you tell us about your child-hood?"

"What?" Her head snapped up again, and her expression firmed. "What the hell does that have to do with anything?"

Stone looked at Verity again. Facing away from Izzy, he mouthed, *she doesn't remember.* To the agent, he said, "Please—just bear with us. This does have a point. What was your childhood like?"

"Shitty, when I was little."

"Why?" Verity asked.

"What was your father like?" Stone added.

Her gaze skated away. "I don't want to talk about him. I don't see what this has to do with—"

"When we were helping you," Verity said, "we sort of…touched your mind. Went into the vision that the demon was giving you to keep you unconscious."

She looked surprised. "This…vision…was my *father?*"

"Well, it looked like some kind of representation of your young childhood," Stone said. "You looked like you were around seven or eight years old. Can you tell us about your father?"

Izzy looked as if she wasn't going to answer, then let out a loud, frustrated sigh. "He was shitty too. Drunk most of the time. He'd come home and if everything wasn't exactly the way he thought it ought to be, he took it out on me and my mom. Only thing is, *he* was the reason things weren't the way he wanted them. Mom had to fight constantly to get him to pay for anything, so we never had anything more than basic stuff. She had to work two jobs just to make ends meet because he spent all his money on booze and lottery tickets and shady get-rich-quick schemes."

"I'm sorry," Verity murmured.

Stone envisioned the massive, bull-like man he'd seen in Izzy's head. "Was your father a large man? Physically imposing?"

Izzy's expression sharpened, and she snorted. "Hell, no. He was short and chubby. Shorter than Mom. He always hated that he wasn't big and ripped like his buddies. Thinking back, that was probably part of the reason why he took stuff out on me and Mom, so he could feel like a big man to *somebody*. Why?"

He looked at Verity again. It made sense—the demon would want to present something terrifying, and the man in the vision had certainly been that. Especially to a scared eight-year-old. "Did you live in a small, shabby apartment?"

"Why are you—" Her expression changed, as if something had just dawned on her. "Wait a minute. There was a dream—a nightmare, really. I can't remember much about it, but...I was a little girl. It was in the place we lived when I was little. There was this big, scary dude..."

"Right," Stone said. "That's what we saw. That was the demon. It left a part of itself in your mind, probably while draining your soul energy. That was why you remained unconscious, and kept having seizures. It was mucking with your brain from in there."

"And...you got it out?" She looked at him in wonder.

"Verity did most of the work. But yes, we got it out."

"Oh, God..." Tears sprang to her eyes, and she looked away as she swiped at them. "I guess I owe you two a lot, then."

"You don't owe us anything," Verity said. "But if there's anything at all you can remember about the vision...about where you might have seen the demon, or the leader of the SickBoyz gang..."

Her face scrunched as she obviously tried to recall more details. But then she slumped back into the pillows, frustrated. "I don't *remember*. I want to, but every time I try, it just sort of...drifts away. I'm sorry..."

Stone took a chance. "Izzy, does this look familiar to you?" He summoned an illusion of the bull's-head pendant and thick gold chain her demon-father had been wearing, and moved it so it hovered in the air in front of her.

She gasped. "Where did you see that?"

"The representation of your father in the vision was wearing it."

"I—" She swallowed hard, her face going ashen again. "That— my dad wore that. He thought it made him look tough. I always stared at it when he was screaming at me, so I didn't have to look at his face."

Stone nodded as if he expected something like that. The illusion vanished. "Okay. Thank you, Izzy. I think that's all we need right now. We'll give you our numbers so you can call us if you remember anything else."

She shifted her gaze between him and Verity, then toward the door. "That thing's not going to...come after me again, is it?" Despite her obvious courage, she looked fearful.

"I don't think so. I think it's done with you now—it wants us."

Izzy shuddered. "Shit. I'm sorry about that. I wish I could get out of this damned bed and help you."

Verity patted her arm. "It's all right. We'll take care of it. For now, you need to rest."

"Am I still in Detroit?"

"You're in Chicago," Stone said. "And we're fairly certain the demon can't travel any faster than a normal person. Ren will be here soon, so she can give you the rest of the details. We can talk again after the situation's sorted."

The agent looked skeptical, as if she wasn't convinced it *could* be sorted, but all she did was sigh and close her eyes. "I'm gonna hold you to that, you know."

Outside the room, Verity narrowed her eyes at Stone. "You've got something on your mind. This has to do with that smile you had inside the vision, doesn't it?"

"It does. Come on."

"Where are we going?"

"To the portal. You'll need to go back there and bring Jason and Amber through."

"What will you be doing in the meantime?"

"Calling Ren and arranging transportation back to Detroit. And trying to contact Ian to see if he wants in on the fun."

She grabbed his arm. "Alastair, tell me what's going on. I don't like mysteries in a situation like this."

He stopped and gave her a fair imitation of his smile from the vision. "Did you notice anything unusual when her father—the demon—faded out?"

"Er—" She tilted her head, thinking. "It didn't fade out. It sort of…blew to pieces when Izzy yelled at it."

"Yes, but not *all* of it did."

She appeared momentarily confused, but then recognition dawned. "Wait—that was why you asked her about that bull necklace, isn't it? When he blew apart, it didn't disappear. It fell off and hit the floor."

"Exactly." He set off walking again.

Verity caught up with him. "But I still don't understand. What's the significance of that?"

"The thing we saw—the man that was supposed to be Izzy's father—wasn't actually the demon. It was just a manifestation. I realized that when she told us her real father didn't look like that."

"Okay…"

Stone wasn't concerned that she wasn't following. She didn't have much experience with demons, so it would have been a surprise if she was. "I'm certain the demon pulled that image from somewhere deep in her mind—the part that still houses the scared little girl with traumatic memories of being abused. That pendant was sort of a touchpoint for him to build the whole thing around. It was the center of the whole thing." He swept out through the double doors and into the waiting room, ignoring the nurse at the front desk.

"Alastair—"

He stopped, spinning to face her, still smiling. "I grabbed it before we faded out."

"*What?*" She glared at him, looking down at his hands as if expecting to see him holding it. "How can you *grab* a metaphysical concept?"

He waved her off. "Okay, I didn't exactly *grab* it. But I *did* get a lock on its energy." Rubbing his chest, he added, "It's still twinging. That's how I can tell I've got it."

"But—if you've got a connection with the demon, doesn't that mean *it's* got one with *you,* too?"

"Possibly, but I don't think so. I've been keeping up a sort of mental shield, which hopefully will prevent it from knowing I managed to pull one over on it. It was a bit busy at the time, blowing up and all. But we've got to move fast. I can't hold the shield forever, so eventually it's going to figure things out. Best if we get to it before it does."

"So…are you saying you can *track* it?"

"I hope so. Because if I can't, we may be in worse shape than we were before, because now it knows we're after it."

CHAPTER TWENTY

WHEN CAPTAIN CELINDRIA returned the following morning, she couldn't hide her surprise that Aldwyn was still in the cell where she had left him. When the guard opened the door, she found him standing in the middle of the room, regarding her with a small and knowing smile.

"Good morning, Captain," he said, in the tone of a king bestowing his favor on a lowly subject. "I hope you slept as well as I did."

"Come with me, please."

He stepped readily out into the central space. "Where are we going?"

"As I told you last night, you are to be questioned further."

"There is no need for that."

She glared. "Why do you say so?"

"I wish to speak to those in charge."

"In charge?"

Behind her, her two flunkies exchanged confused glances and tensed a little.

"Yes. I wish to address your council."

Captain Celindria snorted. "That is out of the question. The council is very busy. Why would you possibly believe they would take time from their duties to speak to you?"

"Because I have something they want." Aldwyn remained relaxed, his posture untroubled and his expression challenging.

It couldn't have been more obvious that Celindria, who was probably some middle-tier law enforcement officer more accustomed to dealing with much more straightforward crimes, was out of her element here. Still, she tried gamely to press on. "Oh? And what is that? Please don't waste our time."

"Magical power, and quite a lot of it. I have been doing some thinking, and I have decided I wish to swear my allegiance to Prensyrrus."

This time, her aura flared bright red. Behind her, one of the flunkies couldn't suppress a shocked gasp.

Captain Celindria stared hard at Aldwyn. "You—wish to...*what*?"

"As I have told you, I do not have a home here. I come from far away, from a place to which I do not wish to return, for many reasons that are none of your concern. If I plan to settle somewhere, it is my understanding that certain assurances are required."

She continued staring at him for a while longer, while the wheels turned in her head. Aldwyn could almost read her thoughts: *He's probably toying with us, trying to delay his fate...but what if he isn't? Do I dare take the chance?*

Finally, she drew herself up to her full height, took a deep breath, and said, "Please return to your room. I am not authorized to make such decisions. I will return shortly."

Aldwyn, smile still firmly in place, withdrew into his cell, allowing the flunkies to close the door. He continued watching them through the now-transparent panel in the door.

The flunkies didn't watch him back. It was clear he made them uncomfortable. Instead, they turned their backs, assumed at-attention postures, and stood shoulder to shoulder facing away from the door.

It was nearly an hour before Captain Celindria returned, accompanied by two other people. Aldwyn, who'd begun to debate with himself whether she intended to stand him up, examined them as they approached.

Clearly, these two were of much higher status than the captain. One had the unmistakable look of high-level law enforcement or military with his ramrod posture, simple but well-made high-collared longcoat of deep red, and numerous pins and other adornments on his lapels.

The other was just as obviously some kind of official or politician. Everything about her elegant clothes, her elaborately styled hair, and her demeanor spoke of someone who was used to being obeyed, and accustomed to her creature comforts. She had even more pins and decorations on her lapels than her companion.

She stepped forward as the leader of the group, while Celindria and the new man immediately took up positions at her left and right sides. She eyed Aldwyn up and down, as much as she could through the window in his cell door. "Open the door, please," she said to nobody in particular. Her voice was deep for a woman's, full of authority.

Captain Celindria stepped forward and pressed her hand against the plaque, then returned to her spot as the door swung open.

Aldwyn didn't move. He remained where he was, hands loosely behind his back, and met the new woman's gaze with the same slight, confident smile he'd been maintaining since Celindria first arrived this morning.

The new woman completed her once-over of Aldwyn. "My name is Zavarra. I understand you wish to speak to the council."

"That is correct."

"You were apprehended attempting to enter Prensyrrus without authorization. I assume you are aware that is a crime."

"A crime of ignorance, I assure you," Aldwyn said smoothly. "I am not familiar with your society here. As I mentioned to Captain Celindria, I am new to this area."

"This...area." Zavarra tilted her head. "Your words make no sense. What do you mean by 'this area'?"

"The place I come from is far away from here. But I am here now, and I do not wish to return to my home. I understand that every person with magical ability must swear allegiance to one of your cities. Therefore, that is what I wish to do."

Zavarra looked at him as if she thought she was addressing a madman. "The scan performed on you last night reveals that you are not currently affiliated with any of the houses. I don't know how that can be possible, but you cannot simply appear in Prensyrrus with no indication of where you came from and claim citizenship."

Aldwyn let his smile fade, replacing it with his more customary sternness. "Are you authorized to speak for the council, Zavarra? Because I do not wish to waste my time repeating my requests to increasingly higher levels of underlings. I am also led to believe that your people value magical ability more highly than anything else. Is that true?"

"Of course." Zavarra tried not to look flustered, but didn't entirely succeed.

"Excellent. I am sure your council will find my abili-ties...desirable. If that is the case, I am prepared to swear allegiance to Prensyrrus. If not, then I will be forced to seek more accommo-dating allies elsewhere." He fixed a penetrating stare on her without moving the rest of his body. "Are you willing to take the chance of losing me to another city because you failed to act?"

She held his gaze for an admirably long time before dropping her own. "You have not yet even told us your name."

Aldwyn considered. "A fair point. You may call me Edmund." He used the more common of the two middle names he had chosen to identify himself in his human guise.

Immediately, all three of his watchers' faces flashed disgust.

"Is there a problem?"

Zavarra's lip curled in distaste. "You claim to possess the Talent, yet your name identifies you as one of the Dim."

Aldwyn didn't allow his confusion to show. "In what way? I remind you that the place from which I come obviously has different customs."

The three exchanged glances, and then Zavarra faced him again. "I do not wish to waste my time instructing the ignorant. Celindria, do with him as you will, and do not bother me again." She turned on her heel and prepared to leave.

Aldwyn's anger rose again. How dare these petty bureaucrats treat him with such disrespect? Without even a gesture to indicate his plan, he used magic to pick Zavarra up and turn her back around, then tightened bands of magical energy around her chest until she gasped, unable to get a breath.

Celindria and the other man leaped into action immediately, bright magic flowering around their raised hands. They flung it at Aldwyn, their eyes widening in shock as it merely fizzled against him with no effect.

"Put her down!" the man barked. "I will not tell you again!"

Zavarra couldn't even get a word out. Her face went dead pale as the bands continued tightening around her.

"You will speak to me with respect," Aldwyn said with deadly calm. "If you do not, or if you attempt to attack me again, I will kill her, and then I will kill both of you. Am I clear?"

Celindria and the man continued to glare at him. They summoned more energy around their hands, but this time held it cautiously in reserve. Zavarra continued to struggle, her legs pumping and her face reddening as she fought to get a breath.

"Yes!" Celindria sputtered. "Yes! Put her down, please."

Aldwyn looked at the man, as if waiting. He hadn't changed expression in the slightest.

The man obviously didn't want to back down, but he just as obviously didn't want to watch his superior killed in front of his eyes. "Yes, fine," he snapped. "Agreed."

Aldwyn dropped the spell. Zavarra fell to the ground, her knees buckling under her, and sat with her breath heaving.

"Next time," Aldwyn said, "I will not stop. It was not my intent to cause harm, but I do expect to be treated with the respect due someone of my ability. Now—as I said, I wish to speak to your council and become a citizen of your city. Please arrange that immediately."

Celindria and the man helped Zavarra to her feet. She was still gasping, clutching her middle as if Aldwyn might have cracked her ribs. She glared daggers at him but said nothing.

"I suggest," Aldwyn said conversationally, "that you do not attempt any other attacks on me. I assure you, no matter what you might try, it will not work. You have two choices: accept me as an ally, or declare me an enemy. I promise, the latter choice would not be a wise one." He nodded to the man. "Arrange the meeting. These two will remain here with me. I do not believe Zavarra is capable of walking at the moment."

All three of them remained where they were for a moment, but they were obviously prudent enough not to risk angering Aldwyn again. The man handed Zavarra off to Celindria, who helped her to a chair one of the flunkies had dragged in from an empty cell. Then he hurried off.

"Better," Aldwyn said as if nothing had happened. He addressed Celindria, since Zavarra still didn't look like she was ready to talk yet. "Explain, please, what Zavarra meant when she stated my name 'identifies me as one of the Dim'."

Celindria looked as if she was about to snap off a reply, but took a deep breath, got herself under control, and spoke in an even, inflectionless tone. "You claim to be unfamiliar with our culture. Here, the Talented possess names of three or more syllables. The Dim are permitted only one or two."

Aldwyn examined her aura, momentarily unable to believe she was telling him the truth. But then he recalled the names of everyone with magical ability he had spoken with since arriving here: Loriar, Illindra, Seviath, Celindria, Zavarra, while the nonmagical had simpler names: Mord, Kala, Tular. The pattern certainly held. "That is absurd."

"It is our way. If your customs are different and you wish to be accepted here, it would be best if you adopted a name worthy of your station. Clearly you possess the Talent in abundance."

He could tell by the way her aura fluctuated that she was trying to play to his ego, but he didn't mind that. It was a prudent decision on her part. He considered a moment. "I have many names, in many situations. If Edmund will not do, then you may refer to me as Aristide."

She tilted her head, trying out the unfamiliar name. "I have never heard such a name, but at least it marks you as Talented."

Aldwyn looked past her, to the cell where Seviath had been held. The window on it was opaque now, so he had no idea if the man was still in there. He wondered if the Talented intended to try testing him again, or if his little demonstration with Zavarra had been sufficient to convince them he meant business. He had little patience for waiting around any longer, so he hoped the latter would prove to be true. His plans would be better served by continued subtlety, but he would not give these people infinite chances.

This time, it was only ten more minutes before the man returned, accompanied by a small flock of men and women who projected the same law-enforcement air as he did.

By this time, Zavarra had recovered herself sufficiently to speak. She rose from the chair, trying to hide a wince, and addressed the group. "Did you contact the Council?"

"Yes, ma'am."

"And?"

"A few of them are available and are willing to hear what the newcomer has to say, but they have declined a face-to-face meeting, at least initially." He shifted his gaze to Aldwyn, then back to Zavarra. "He will be permitted to state his case using the meeting-glass."

Aldwyn wondered if a 'meeting-glass' was some sort of magical videoconferencing system. The offer didn't surprise him—the Council members would be fools to agree to an in-person meeting with a man who might turn out to be a dangerously deranged individual with enough power to destroy them all. "And if they find my 'case' acceptable?"

"Then a more formal meeting will be arranged to evaluate your request. If the Council deems it valid, you will be permitted to swear loyalty to Prensyrrus and will be accepted as one of us."

Aldwyn inclined his head, once again the patrician gentleman. "Splendid. Let us be off, then. I tire of these surroundings." He glanced at Zavarra, who still appeared to be in pain. He probably *had* broken at least a couple of her ribs when he'd crushed her—he hadn't made any effort to be gentle. "And, as a good-faith gesture, I will repair the damage I have done. Zavarra, please approach me."

She glared warily at him, but more than any of the rest, she was aware of his capabilities. She allowed Celindria to support her and stood in front of Aldwyn, her aura billowing with trepidation.

Aldwyn raised a hand and concentrated. Healing humans wasn't something he'd spent a lot of time on—his magical interactions with them usually involved either injury or deception—but compared to dragons, their biology was almost laughably simple. It took him only a few seconds to identify the ribs he'd cracked (there were actually three) and summon a magical field around them to speed their healing.

"There," he said, stepping back in satisfaction. "Is that better?"

Zavarra's glare turned to a wide-eyed stare of astonishment. Tentatively, she drew herself up straight, then patted her sides as if she expected the pain to flare up again. When it didn't, she let her breath out, straightened her clothes with dignity, and regarded him.

"Thank you," she said formally. "If you'll come with us, we will take you to speak with the Council."

Aldwyn didn't reply with a smug smile, but he probably didn't need to.

The room they took him to was considerably more luxuriously appointed than the cell block. Aldwyn was already getting the impression that the Talented valued appearances highly, and went out of their way to make their spaces beautiful—except, apparently, where the Dim were involved.

The room consisted of three tiers of seats facing a blank wall. Plush, spotless carpeting covered the floor. The tables were made of polished wood, with comfortable chairs floating magically behind them. On either side, elaborate abstract murals in shades of red embellished with precious metals and stones glowed with dancing magical light. The overall effect was attractive but overdone, as if someone had tried to combine a meeting room with an art gallery. Aldwyn was already growing tired of these pretentious people— especially since, by his reckoning, they had little to be pretentious *about.*

Zavarra, who already seemed to have put her ordeal in the cell block behind her, took one of the two seats in the center of the front row. "Please sit," she said, indicating the one next to her.

Aldwyn took the offered chair, using magic to adjust it to his liking. The others didn't sit, but arrayed themselves along the back wall. The tension in the room would have been palpable even without magical senses.

A few moments passed, and then the blank wall at the front of the room shimmered to life to reveal a similar room, even more luxuriously appointed. This one didn't have three tiers of desks, but only a single one with a long table of pale wood. Three people, two men and a woman, sat near the table's center, each in high-backed, deep red chairs with fancy golden embroidery. Instead of the high-collared red coats Aldwyn had seen on other Prensyrrus citizens, the Council members wore red robes featuring even more intricate designs.

The three newcomers studied Aldwyn while he studied them. They looked younger than one might have expected of a city's leaders, beautiful of face and form in a way that didn't quite seem real. That didn't surprise Aldwyn, though, since illusion seemed to be important among the Talented. He remembered Loriar and Illindra, whose appearances had changed significantly after he'd stripped them of their fancy disguises.

One of the men, seated between the other man and the woman, spoke. His expression and his tone were both even and severe, like a judge. "My name is Bellistrius." He indicated the woman first, then the other man. "This is Darnasia, and this is Krataniath. We are members of the Council of Prensyrrus. We understand you have been apprehended while attempting to enter our city unlawfully."

"I am called Aristide, and it was a misunderstanding," Aldwyn said easily. "Nothing more. As a newcomer to your city, I am unfamiliar with your laws and customs. I wish to remedy that."

"We are told that you desire to declare loyalty to the House of Prensyrrus and become a citizen of our city."

"I do."

Bellistrius's expression grew even more severe. "You are aware that such a declaration involves a magical oath?"

Aldwyn wasn't, but it made sense. "That is acceptable."

"Further, in a case such as yours, such an oath would require additional components not expected of more common citizens."

"Indeed?" He raised an eyebrow. "What sort of components?"

"If you are truly unfamiliar with our ways," Darnasia said, "perhaps you are not aware that a class of people exists who have chosen to undermine our way of life. They do this by infiltrating our society and attempting to sabotage it from within."

"These would be the so-called 'resistance'?"

"Yes," Krataniath said. Neither he nor the other two seemed surprised Aldwyn already knew of them. "We must be ever mindful of their vile influence, root them out using any means necessary, and punish them in the most severe manner."

"Therefore," Bellistrius said, "the oath of loyalty expected of you would bear a harsh penalty should you choose to violate it."

Aldwyn didn't change expression, though inwardly he was amused. Dragons could choose to be bound by oaths with lesser beings, of course—he had done so with his upstart scions, Stone and Harrison. But it was just that—a choice. Unless he explicitly gave his word, as he had done with his scions, his magical protections could easily prevent any such oath from taking effect, without giving anything away to the other side. "What sort of penalty?"

"Death," Darnasia said.

"I see." He leaned back in his chair and appeared to consider.

"If you are willing to accept such potential consequences to prove your desire to become a citizen of Prensyrrus," Bellistrius said, "we would be honored to have you. We understand you are possessed of significant magical ability. Such Talent would find a good home among us, and we can offer you much in exchange."

Aldwyn doubted it, but that was all right. Collusion with these conceited buffoons wasn't part of his plan. "Done, then. When can we begin?"

The three exchanged glances, trying not to look surprised at how readily he had agreed. Of course he couldn't see their auras through the magical viewing window, but he had become adept at reading humans' expressions over the many years he had been forced to live on Earth.

"Preparations must be made, of course," Darnasia said, "but I believe we can arrange the ceremony for this evening."

"Excellent. I shall look forward to it." Aldwyn gave them a small, confident smile as he watched them scramble. He knew exactly what was going on here—they were nervous because they thought he might be up to something, but they likewise didn't want to lose their chance at bagging someone with his level of Talent. Because of what had happened with Zavarra, they might not even be sure they could hold him should he decide to be less tractable—which meant they could potentially lose him to a rival city.

He stood, clearly bringing the meeting to an end before the Council members could do so. "I will see you this evening, then." He turned away from them and faced Zavarra. "I understand you cannot allow me to tour your beautiful city until I am properly oathbound, but I trust my accommodations until then will be of higher quality than your cell block."

"Er—yes, of course." Her narrow-eyed expression suggested she hadn't yet forgiven him for what he'd done to her, but her fake smile indicated she didn't have much of a choice.

He had to give them credit—now that it appeared he was to become a citizen of their city, the Prensyrrus officials spared no expense in trying to impress him.

Even though he was clearly still under surveillance until his oath was secured, they did their best to make him forget it. The suite they took him to was as beautiful and opulently overdecorated as he expected; it had a luxurious bedchamber with a window overlooking an attractive courtyard below and a walk-in closet full of fine clothes—all of them in shades of black and gray, he noticed, with no hint of red— and a bath larger than his previous cell complete with magically-operated shower. The front room featured sumptuous, overstuffed furniture and a well-stocked bar. Apparently, liquor was a thing on this world as well, even among the magical.

They'd apparently known he was coming, because someone had laid out a lavish spread of fruits, meats, and other delicacies on the table in the front room, along with more bottles of various liquids.

"If you desire anything else," Zavarra said, indicating two more flunkies, "you have only to ask. The panel inside the door will allow you to communicate. Someone will come for you later this evening to escort you to the Council chamber."

"Thank you." He inclined his head gravely to her. "I regret that we got off on the wrong foot, as it were. I hope I can remedy that in the future, when we become colleagues."

"I...am sure we can," she said, with all the sincerity of a con man about to fleece a flock of sheep. She made herself scarce as fast as she could politely manage, leaving the two flunkies on either side of the door outside.

When he was alone, Aldwyn made a show of examining the room, projecting curiosity but no tension as he walked around checking for any magical traps or surveillance. He scanned the food and drink for poisons but didn't find any; apparently if the Talented were planning anything, it wasn't in that direction. He did find more magical surveillance devices, even more subtle than the ones in the cell, but this time he chose not to do anything with them. He didn't care if they watched him here, since he didn't plan on doing anything they might find objectionable. There was no need. He could afford to let them think he was calmly accepting his gilded prison. In a few more hours, it wouldn't matter.

They came to get him in the early evening. An hour earlier, a pleasant voice over a hidden magical intercom had informed him they would be coming, and suggested he prepare himself in whatever way he saw fit.

When the door chimed and then opened, several people stood outside waiting for him. Zavarra wasn't there, but Captain Celindria, her law-enforcement superior, and several others Aldwyn didn't recognize were. All of them were dressed more formally than before, and all wore various shades of red, mostly toward the darker end of the spectrum.

Aldwyn had chosen his ensemble from the clothes in the closet, attiring himself entirely in black and avoiding extraneous decorations. Everything fit him perfectly, which didn't surprise him—the tailoring spell was one many powerful mages knew, even on Earth. His overall image was severe and elegant without being pretentious. He deliberately didn't use any magic to "augment" the outfit. He had neither need nor desire to show off for these people.

His escorting group looked him up and down, and he didn't miss the slight confusion on their faces. He thought he knew why: because they'd all expected him to make every possible effort to impress them, in order to bolster his claim that allowing him citizenship would benefit them.

He smiled. Subverting their expectations amused him.

"This way, please," Captain Celindria said. She looked a little uncomfortable in her finery, but soldiered on.

Another teleport pad took them to an extravagantly-appointed antechamber with more magically enhanced murals on the walls. A pair of wide, elaborately carved wooden doors were currently closed in front of them. Aldwyn studied them, noting the impressive spellwork on the wards protecting them. He had no doubt he could breach them, but it might actually require a bit of effort to do it. This was almost certainly one of the most well-protected parts of the city.

"You will be addressing the full Council of Prensyrrus," Captain Celindria said quietly from his right side. "I advise you to treat them with respect and deference. The chamber is both fully warded and protected by the Council's elite guardian force."

"Understood," Aldwyn murmured back.

The doors swung open, revealing a wide chamber lined with curved tiers of comfortable chairs, all facing a long table of deep red wood at the front of the room. The table had no visible door behind it. A smaller table in front of it, covered by an embroidered, red velvet cloth, held a shining silver knife, a golden chalice studded with glittering jewels, and a white drape. Many of the chairs were already occupied, and several more formally-attired men and women turned a little to observe the newcomers, obviously curious. The red table stood vacant.

Captain Celindria gave Aldwyn a gentle nudge. "You'll be in the front row, in the chair set apart from the others."

Aldwyn descended the steps with his head held high and his shoulders squared, utterly unruffled by the intense scrutiny. He glanced first to one side and then to the other, bestowing stern, benevolent nods to some of the curious onlookers. When he reached the ground level, he gracefully lowered himself into the offered chair with the casual air of a monarch claiming his throne.

Even though he didn't take his gaze off the table at the front once he was seated, Aldwyn was acutely aware that every eye in the room was on him. Uniformed, red-clad guards lined the walkways on both sides of the room, all standing at attention with their hands clasped in front of them. Magical sight revealed multiple protective spells, including a ward around Aldwyn's chair and a larger one surrounding the Council's table.

They weren't taking any chances here.

Aldwyn smiled, folded his hands in his lap, and waited.

This was going to be fun.

Behind the table, a doorway shimmered into existence, revealing darkness beyond.

A robed man stepped out in front of the table and spoke, his clear voice magically projected so everyone could hear. "All shall rise for the Council of Prensyrrus!"

All around Aldwyn, the seated figures stood. After a moment, he did as well. He stood at attention and faced the new doorway.

Five figures entered, one after the other, and spread out to stand behind the table, facing the assembled audience. Bellistrius, Darnasia, and Kratariath from before were there, as well as another man and woman. Each was even more elaborately dressed than anyone in the audience. Their spotless, blood-red robes bore impossibly intricate embroidery, high, stiff collars, and impressive shoulders. To magical sight, the robes came alive with bright, crackling color—a combination of decoration and more protective spells.

Aldwyn let his gaze travel along the row, lighting on each in turn. All of them appeared to be at the prime of their lives, strong and beautiful, their skin and posture flawless. A dark-haired man had taken the spot in the center of the group, flanked by the two women—Darnasia pale and red-haired, the other dark-skinned with black hair. Bellistrius and Kratariath, both blond, took the final spots on each end. As yet, none of them were looking at Aldwyn, but he could sense their attention on him nonetheless.

More than that, he could sense the tingle of magical energy moving around him, like a stealthy cat trying to find a way into a mousehole. They were scanning him, trying to discern his level of power. He pretended not to notice, adjusting his own magic to give them a false reading. He needed them to respect his power, but not to know the extent of it.

Not yet.

"You may be seated," the dark-haired leader said in a formal tone.

Everyone in the gallery immediately took their seats. Aldwyn waited until he was the last, then sat.

The five Council members remained standing for a few beats, their expressionless gazes moving over the crowd. Then, as if they'd choreographed the movement, Bellistrius and Kratariath took their seats on the outer edges, followed by Darnasia and the other woman, leaving the leader as the only one standing. He stayed where he was for a handful of seconds, then seated himself.

"This is an unusual session," he said, still without looking at Aldwyn. "We are not accustomed to having our busy schedules interrupted for unplanned events, but in this case, after discussion, we have decided to allow it."

He turned slightly to his right, looking at the row of guards along the wall. "Last night, a man was apprehended attempting to enter our city without proper authorization. He was taken into custody. He did not resist, and claimed his crime was one of ignorance rather than malice. He stated that he comes from somewhere outside our society."

The crowd murmured in surprise.

The leader raised a hand. "It is difficult to believe, of course. At first, our guardian force assumed he was a member of the resistance, attempting to infiltrate our city for nefarious ends. He obviously possesses a high degree of Talent, which, if that were the case, would make him dangerous. However, to prove he is not affiliated with the resistance, he has made the unprecedented offer to swear an oath of loyalty and become a citizen of Prensyrrus."

More murmuring, louder this time. Aldwyn didn't turn around to look at them, but he was certain their auras were flaring surprise.

"Further," the man said, "given the special circumstances, he has taken the additional step of agreeing to a more stringent version of our oath than is normally required—one that will result in his death should he attempt to violate it."

This time, a few audience members gasped aloud. Apparently, this was indeed an unprecedented option.

"The Council has been in consultation since earlier today," the leader continued, "and, given our newcomer's demonstrated level of the Talent, we have concluded that, properly oathbound, he will be an asset to our city."

In other words, Aldwyn thought with amusement, *they do not wish to lose me to a rival city.*

"Therefore, we have agreed to accept his oath and welcome him into our city. That will occur tonight, with all of you as witnesses."

For the first time, he settled his gaze on Aldwyn. "Friends, honored citizens, may I present Aristide."

Aldwyn rose with measured calm and dignity. He made a nearly imperceptible bow to the leader, even smaller ones left and right to the four remaining Council members, and then turned to face the audience. He spread his hands, presenting himself to them. "I am pleased to be here, and I thank you for accepting me into your society." He projected sincerity and warmth into his rolling, pleasant baritone—a trusted and benevolent father speaking to his beloved children.

He felt all their eyes on him, examining him for any sign of a flaw or a misstep, but showed no reaction. Their auras suggested confusion and reluctant acceptance, but they seemed unsettled by his all-black ensemble, incongruous and out of place amid the sea of varying shades of red—a foreign substance invading their oddly organic chamber.

"I see no need for further delay," the Council leader said. "If you will come forward, please, we will administer the oath."

They *were* in a hurry. Aldwyn would have expected more pomp and circumstance surrounding the whole thing, since these people seemed incapable of visiting the toilet without the proper ceremony. He kept his smile to himself this time as he descended the final step. If they were so determined to bag their prize, he had no intention of interfering.

All five Council members rose from their chairs. The leader walked around to the front of the table until he stood on one side of the smaller table—the one with the knife. He waited solemnly.

Aldwyn took his place on the other side of the table, facing the man. Up close, the Council leader looked as flawless as ever, with no sign of any dust, errant hairs, or wrinkles marring his immaculate robe. His skin was pale and perfect, his eyes an impossible shade of bright blue, his dark-brown hair precisely in place with just a hint of distinguished gray at his temples. He looked a bit like a living, breathing mannequin.

When they were in position, Darnasia from the Council table took her place in front of the smaller one, between the leader and Aldwyn.

"This is how the oath will be administered," she said formally. "I will make a small slice on each of your fingers, and you will allow a drop of blood to fall into the chalice. Then you will clasp your hands over it. Council Leader Jesperian will state the terms of the oath, and you, Aristide, will repeat them. The magic will bind it, after which you will be a sworn citizen of Prensyrrus, with all the rights, responsibilities, and privileges inherent in that status." She faced Aldwyn. "Do you understand? This is your final chance to change your mind. Once the oath has been sworn, it cannot be rescinded."

Aldwyn didn't ask what would happen if he did back out—he already knew. They would attempt to take him back into custody, until they could figure out who he was and what to do with him. He wasn't concerned about that, but it could cause him more trouble than he wanted to deal with. This way was easier.

"I understand," he said. "And I do not wish to change my mind. To the contrary, I look forward to my new status. I am optimistic about what the future holds."

She either didn't see his tiny, sly smile, or chose to ignore it. "Very well. Let us begin, then. Please extend your hands."

The leader, Jesperian, held up his perfectly-manicured left hand. Aldwyn held up his right.

The woman picked up the knife, cast something over it that Aldwyn was sure was a sterilizing spell, and then took Aldwyn's hand and made a small slice across the pad of his index finger. A gleaming, bright-red bead of blood welled, stark against his pale skin.

Or at least that was what those present thought. Aldwyn had no trouble forming an illusion of what occurred, while preventing the knife's edge from contacting his finger. He allowed Darnasia to turn his hand over, and extended the illusion so they could all see the drop of blood fall into the chalice.

He continued to hold his hand up as Darnasia cleansed the knife and repeated the action with Jesperian. Another drop of blood—real this time—joined the illusionary one in the chalice.

This was the tricky part, because Aldwyn wasn't sure what was supposed to happen at this stage of the ritual. However, he'd seen enough magical oaths sworn on Earth that he had a place to start with his illusion. He formed a small, glowing cloud of red smoke bubbling up over the rim of the chalice, then watched Jesperian's face and his aura to determine the result.

Apparently, blood oaths on this dimension worked similarly enough to those on Earth that no one seemed surprised by the red smoke. Both Jesperian and Darnasia looked solemn and satisfied, ready to continue to the next stage.

"Repeat after me," Darnasia said, as if reciting from memorized text. "I, Aristide, from this moment forward until the end of my days, swear allegiance and loyalty to the House of Prensyrrus."

Aldwyn repeated the words in the same tone.

"I likewise swear, on penalty of instant death should I violate my oath, that I will take no action against Prensyrrus or its interests, including its Council and duly sworn officials."

Again, Aldwyn stated the words. It was hard not to smile, but he remained impassive.

"I swear that I will make my best effort to be a valuable and useful citizen of Prensyrrus, forsaking all other ties and loyalties, and I will use my Talent to benefit our ideals and our way of life."

That seemed to be the end of the oath, so Aldwyn echoed the woman's words. As he did it, he used magic to summon a faint, growing tingle around his hand and Jesperian's, to indicate the magic sealing the oath was taking effect.

Both Darnasia and Jesperian looked satisfied—and more than a little relieved. "You may unclasp your hands," Darnasia said, taking a step back. When they did, she raised her hands to the assembled group and smiled broadly. "Everyone, this is a joyous occasion. Please join me in welcoming our newest citizen, Aristide, to our beautiful city."

They didn't applaud—apparently that wasn't something they did here—but they did cheer, raising their hands to form brilliant, beautiful patterns of magical energy in the air above them.

Aldwyn faced them and made a courtly bow. "Thank you, everyone. Thank you for your gracious welcome." Then he turned to face the Council members, who had returned to their places behind the long table. "Now, then, before we depart—a small bit of other business, if you please."

The Council members exchanged confused glances. "Business?" Jesperian asked. "But this concludes our—"

"It does not," Aldwyn said firmly. "I am now an oathbound citizen of Prensyrrus, am I not?"

"You...are," Darnasia said cautiously.

"Excellent. And am I correct in my understanding that status, both here and in any other similar cities, is determined solely by magical ability?"

The five at the table were starting to look nervous now, and their auras reinforced it. "I don't understand what you're—" Jesperian began.

"Is it, or is it not, so?"

"It is, but—"

Aldwyn nodded once, satisfied. "Good. Then, as my magical ability no doubt exceeds everyone's here, I wish to make a formal challenge."

The gallery erupted with astonished mutterings.

Jesperian, so far, remained calm. He raised his hand to quiet the audience, then looked at Aldwyn. He was trying to hide both his growing fear and his confusion, but his aura didn't lie. It might have if he'd been trying to hide it from anyone else, but Aldwyn saw through it without effort. "A challenge? To what?"

Aldwyn did smile then, fully aware of how unsettling it was. "To you, my friend."

CHAPTER TWENTY-ONE

L ATER THAT EVENING, Stone and his friends gathered in a large conference room to discuss their next steps.

They were back in Detroit. Verity had returned through the Chicago portal earlier in the afternoon with Jason and Amber, and Ian had joined them soon after. Ren had arranged a flight back to Detroit and met them when they arrived.

"First of all," she'd said to Stone and Verity when they'd descended from the plane, "I want you to know we—I—owe you big for what you did for Izzy. I talked to her a little more after you left, and she sounds like she's on her way to being back to her old self. I don't know exactly what you did, but…thank you."

"I'm just glad we could help," Verity said.

"As am I," Stone said. "But we're not even close to done with this whole mess yet."

They'd caught everyone up with the situation, including the fact that Stone had managed to grab a tiny piece of the demon's essence during their time in Izzy's mind. Ren had seemed particularly interested in that.

"Are you saying you can use that to track the demon down, without it knowing you're doing it?" She sounded hopeful. She'd arranged to have take-out brought in, and the table was covered with plates, cups, and food containers. Nobody had eaten much, though.

R. L. KING

"Not sure yet." Stone had been thinking it over on the flight. The scar on his chest was still twinging—in fact, it had grown a bit more painful the closer they got to Detroit—so he knew he was still in contact with the demon. But the more he'd thought it over, the more he'd realized it wasn't going to be as easy as he'd initially hoped it would. "The problem is, what I've got hold of is essentially a concept. It's a very faint connection to the demon, but there's nothing physical in it to use for a tracking ritual. I'm afraid if I try, I'll sever it and then we'll be back to square one. Detroit's a big place. Even if we confine our search to the area around the Sick-Boyz's territory, we can't just go driving around hoping to pick something up."

Verity pondered, and looked troubled. "I hate to say this, but...what about Izzy's blood? That thing was inside her—maybe there's a connection."

"Good thought, but no. When she turfed it out of her head, she essentially destroyed whatever it put in there. Burned it out. The only bit left is the one I grabbed. And before you ask, using *my* blood wouldn't work either. The secondhand connection wouldn't be strong enough to get anything from."

"What about that piece of demon skin your friend gave you before?" Jason asked. "Could you use that to find it?"

"Maybe, but I don't have a lot of confidence in it. It was always kind of a last-resort option. It's so old it likely doesn't have a lot of energy left in it."

"Damn," Ian said. "So we're back to where we started?"

"Not completely. If we can get closer to wherever it's holed up, the combination of the connection and my scar should help." He looked away, not wanting to speak his next words. "And...if we can't come up with anything else, It's possible you and Verity might be able to do a tracking ritual using me and my connection as the tether, with the piece of demon skin for a bit of extra punch. Between them, they'll probably be strong enough to use."

"No way." Ian shook his head firmly. "It's too dangerous."

"It might be the only chance we've got."

But Verity was looking stubborn too. "The only problem is, if we do that and the demon takes you out, you're our strongest weapon—and the only way to trace the thing. Do you honestly think we've got a chance against it without you?"

Stone growled. She was right and he knew it, but they weren't long on options. "I wish Gabriel were here. Ian, any chance of talking him into joining us?"

"I tried. He apologizes, but says he's in the middle of something he can't leave."

"That's what I was afraid of." Stone had told Ian about the dragons' other activities, at least in a general way. He still had no idea exactly what kind of threats they were dealing with, and they weren't talking, but the only important thing right now was that they weren't going to be any help with this.

"If you can figure out where it is," Ren said, "I can send some people with you. They're mundanes, but they've got access to some pretty sophisticated weaponry."

Stone knew she wanted to help—*needed* to help—but in this case it was a bad idea. "Ren," he said gently, "I don't think that's going to be useful in this case."

"Why not?" She glared at him. "We've got firepower that can take out a city block. If we can track him to where he's holed up—"

"If you go after him with mundane artillery, you're going to end up with a lot of dead agents, probably a lot of dead Changelings, and you still probably won't get the demon. I know you don't want to hear that, but it's true."

She wasn't ready to give up. "What about the military? The National Guard—"

"Do you really want to call up the National Guard in the middle of Detroit?" Jason asked. "Even if they can help, there's no way to keep the media from getting hold of it. It would be a publicity nightmare."

"We've got a damn *demon* loose in a major American city!" Ren snapped. "Do you really think publicity is what's on my mind?"

"It should be," Stone said. "Don't forget—this isn't by any means the only demon loose in an American city. There could be as many as ten more of them out there too. And if they start getting word that the mundanes are bringing in that kind of firepower to try to get rid of them, it might stir them up. They're quiet for now. Let's try to make sure they stay that way."

The agent slammed her fist down on the table. "Then what *do* you suggest we do? I am *not* sitting here on my ass waiting for somebody else to turn up in pieces."

"That's not what we're going to do," Verity said gently. Then she looked at Stone, her expression clear: *right?*

Even though he was as frustrated as Ren, he couldn't show it. He wondered with wry amusement sometimes how he'd ended up as the one all these other competent people looked to for leadership. Back in the old days, the only thing he'd ever wanted to lead was classes at the University. When had he become some kind of action hero?

He let out a long, ragged sigh. "No. That's not what we're going to do. We know where the SickBoyz's territory is, and so far, the demon seems most affiliated with them. We should go back there and do a bit of poking around. With any luck, the connection will strengthen if we get closer."

Ian looked dubious. "That's kind of a long shot. But you're right—I don't see any other possibilities. It's the best we've got."

"Maybe we can grab one of the SickBoyz," Jason said. "Normally I'm not in favor of roughing people up for information, but this is kind of a life-or-death situation. Anybody who thinks that demon will be satisfied with the SickBoyz is deluding themselves. This is gonna do nothing but escalate."

"I agree," Verity said. "Especially since several of the SickBoyz died in that fire at Big Gee's. I wouldn't be surprised if it's already making a stronger move to take over another gang."

Stone jerked his head up. "That's what you can do to help, Ren. Put out whatever feelers you've got in the gang communities. Find out if there are any unusual rumblings. If the demon *is* trying to expand its territory faster, knowing where would be a big advantage for us."

Ren looked at him like she was trying to decide whether he was diplomatically attempting to sideline her. "Okay. But if you go after the demon, I want in on the action. That thing killed two agents—one of them a good friend—and did its damnedest to kill another one. I don't let that go."

Stone almost protested, but then caught Jason's subtle head-shake. "Fine," he said. "It's against my better judgment, but as long as you know what you're getting into, I can't stop you."

"No, you can't." She stood. "Come on, people. Let's do our jobs and find this bastard before he kills anybody else."

Stone didn't want to wait until Ren got more information before they took some kind of action. He convinced her to lend them another van, and the group piled in and set off for the SickBoyz's territory under a heavy disregarding spell provided by Verity.

"I'll call you as soon as I've got anything," Ren told Stone before they left. "But this is a recon mission only, right?"

"That depends on what we find. I honestly don't think we're going to locate the demon this fast, but if we do, there's no way I'm letting it get away."

She glared at him. "Well, at least *call* me with the location. You owe me that much."

"We'll do that," Verity assured him. "But Alastair's right—if we find it, we've got to do our best to take it down when we have the chance."

Jason and Amber had loaded up the back of the van with backpacks full of guns, armor, and more stun and flash-bang grenades. Jason drove, with Stone in the shotgun seat attempting to trace the nebulous thread, Verity and Ian in the middle maintaining the disregarding spell and navigating, and Amber in the rear seat with the weapons, ready to leap out through the back doors if necessary.

"Let's do this," Stone said. He hoped they weren't already too late.

The first thing they noticed when they reached the SickBoyz's territory was the lack of Changelings.

It was already dark; as they cruised around in the disguised van, Stone wondered why they were bothering to conceal it at all. The streets were deserted.

"That's weird," Amber said, peering out the window and scanning both sides of the street. "This time of night, gangs are usually out, being seen and taking care of business. I don't see—or smell—any of them."

"Let's drive around some more before we get too worried," Jason said. "There weren't that many left, so it's possible we just haven't found 'em yet."

Stone had a feeling he was wrong, but didn't say anything about it yet. He sat tensely, watching with magical sight as Jason drove the van up and down the streets comprising the SickBoyz's territory. By the time they'd circled back to where they'd started, none of them had seen any sign of a Changeling, or anyone else. The only signs of life they'd spotted had been a few vehicles driving by, and the occasional pale light burning in an upper-story window.

"Where is everybody?" Verity asked. "I know normal people don't go out much at night around here, but it's odd not to see *anybody*."

"What do you want to do, Al?" Jason glanced at him from the driver's seat, before turning back to the road. "You want to range out a little more and see if we spot anything?"

"If we go out too much further, we'll be in somebody else's territory," Amber said. "Not saying we shouldn't, but be aware. We—wait!" She jerked up in her seat, leaning forward and sniffing the air like a dog who'd just caught a scent.

"What is it?" Ian asked.

"I smelled something. Somebody's nearby."

"Changeling?" Stone shifted back to magical sight, trying to spot any sign of movement.

"No—just a mundane. Scared." She sniffed again and pointed ahead. "I think they're in that alley up there."

The alley in question was narrow and dark, less than half a block up on the same side of the road. "Pull over, Jason," Stone said. "If this is the first person we've encountered and they're scared, maybe they can tell us what they're scared *of*."

Jason parked a couple doors down from the alley entrance and started to open his door.

"Wait," Stone said. "We can't all go."

"Al—"

"He's right," Amber said. "If we show up in a herd, we'll spook them even worse. And somebody's got to stay with the van."

"This should only take a moment," Stone assured him. "Amber, you come with me. You've got the nose, and you're fast enough to catch him if he does a runner." Before the others could protest, he added, "We'll bring him back to the van. Verity and Ian, be ready with disguise illusions."

He could tell Jason, Verity, and Ian weren't pleased about being left behind, but it couldn't be helped. He slipped out of the van, and Amber joined him.

Once they rounded the corner to the alley, it wasn't hard for either of them to spot the hidden figure. The man crouched behind a dumpster, radiating fear so strong it was nearly possible to pick it up without magical sight or Amber's bearish senses. He was looking the other way, though, and didn't notice Stone and Amber approaching until they were in front of him.

"Evening," Stone said pleasantly.

The man made a terrified *eep*. When he saw there was no way to get past the newcomers, he scooted back and pressed his back against the dirty, graffiti-covered brick wall behind him. "D-don't kill me," he pleaded. "I ain't got nothin' you want."

"Nobody's going to hurt you," Amber said. "We just need to talk to you."

"'Bout what?" Fear was pouring off the man in waves. His voice shook so hard it was difficult to tell how old he was in the alley's darkness.

"You've got to come with us," Stone said. He didn't like coercing people, preferring to persuade them, but this guy was scared out of his wits and there was no way he'd go along with them voluntarily. "It's not safe to talk here. I promise, no one's going to hurt you, but we need information."

"You cops?"

"No."

"What kind o' information?"

"About the SickBoyz."

Another bright red plume of fear erupted. "No way, man. I don't know no SickBoyz."

It couldn't have been more obvious he was lying. They didn't have time to stand here and argue with the man, though.

Before Stone could make up his mind what to do, Amber took charge. She bent and took the man's arm, gently but firmly. "Come on," she said in a brisk, no-nonsense tone, hauling him to his feet. "This won't take long, and then we'll let you get back to whatever you were doing."

The man tried to struggle, but his heart clearly wasn't in it—either that, or he was too scared to make much of an effort. "They gonna kill me if I snitch," he muttered.

Amber frog-marched the man out of the alley. "You won't be snitching on them. You might be saving their lives."

He didn't reply to that. When they reached the street, he looked like he might be considering yelling, but Amber gave him a warning shake to indicate that would be a bad idea.

Stone wondered if he was seeing the side of her that used to be a bounty hunter before her children were born. Despite all his magic, he decided he didn't ever want to get on her bad side. He followed as they covered the short distance to the van.

Ian and Verity already had the sliding door open, allowing them to quickly hustle the terrified man inside and close it behind him.

The van's interior light gave Stone a better look at him. A skinny black man in his middle forties, his mismatched clothes and pungent body odor suggested he was probably homeless. When he saw how many people surrounded him, his eyes bugged out and his aura exploded with terror.

"Please don't kill me," he pleaded. "I ain't got nothin'."

Verity shot Stone and Amber a sharp look, but when she spoke, her tone was gentle. "Nobody's going to hurt you. You're safe here, I promise. We just need you to tell us where the SickBoyz are. They should be around here, right?"

"I told those guys, I don't know no SickBoyz."

"Listen," Stone said, trying to sound as calm and nonthreatening as Verity had, "we know you're lying. This is their territory, and they're not here. We need to know why. What's your name, by the way?"

The man tried to glare at him, but almost immediately gave up and slumped. "Dee."

"Pleasure to meet you, Dee."

"Why you wanna know where the SickBoyz are?"

"Because something's going on around here, and we need to find out where."

More fear flared. Dee knew something, Stone was sure of it.

"Come on, Dee. The sooner you tell us what we need to know, the sooner we'll let you go. We'll even give you something for your trouble." Stone hoped it *would* be soon; in the close confines of the van, the man's aroma was eye-watering.

Dee swallowed. His fearful gaze traveled around to each face looking at him, then shot toward the sliding door as if weighing his odds of making a break for it. It didn't take him long to work out it wasn't going to happen. He let out a long, odorous breath. "They took 'em."

"Who took who?" Jason twisted a little more in his seat.

"The SickBoyz. They took a bunch o' people."

Stone exchanged startled glances with the others. That wasn't what any of them had expected. "What people? When?"

Dee shrugged. "Reg'lar people, off the street. Men, women, old folks—didn't matter. Earlier tonight. It was real fast. Just drove by and grabbed 'em. Almost got me, but I know howta hide. I been hidin' from cops for a long time." A little pride touched his tone.

"Do you know why?" Ian asked.

"Nah, man. No idea."

"Do you know *where*?"

He shook his head.

"How many people are we talking about?" Verity asked.

"No idea. I was hidin'. Didn't want 'em grabbin' me. Weird shit goin' down with the SickBoyz lately. They ain't like they used to be."

That was no secret to anybody. Stone pondered. He didn't think Dee was lying about not knowing where the gang had taken the people they'd rounded up. "Are you sure you didn't hear any rumors about why this happened tonight?"

"I don't know nothin', honest." He swallowed. "But…"

"But?"

He looked down at his lap, and once again his aura flared bright. "There's some new dude runnin' the SickBoyz. Ain't never seen him. Nobody has. Word is he's more pissed than usual, though. Somethin' happened to piss 'im off."

That would be us, Stone thought with some satisfaction, but the idea that the demon had escalated against innocent people because of their actions didn't sit well with him. This had to end.

"Okay, Dee," he said, fixing a hard gaze on the man. "Are you absolutely sure you don't know where they might have taken these people?"

But to his dismay, Dee shook his head again, and this time his aura didn't flare. "Nah, man, that's the God's honest truth. If I knew I'd tell ya."

Stone looked at Amber, who gave him a subtle nod. She didn't think he was lying either. He pulled three twenties from his pocket, pressed them into Dee's hand, and motioned for Ian to open the door. "All right, you can go now. I'd advise you to stay hidden tonight, as much as you can. If you're smart, take that money and catch a bus or a cab or something to some other part of town."

Dee made a noncommittal grunt. As soon as the way was clear, he scrambled out of the van and took off running back toward the alley. He disappeared into the darkness, even his aura fading as he must have rounded a corner.

Ian closed the van and settled back in his seat. "Well, shit. That's not good—especially since we don't have a clue where they took these people."

Stone climbed back into the shotgun seat and slumped against the window as Jason pulled away from the curb. "I know you lot aren't going to like it, but unless Ren has turned up anything through her information network, I think we're going to need to try the tracking ritual using me as a tether." He pulled out his phone and tapped her contact.

It wasn't to be, though. As soon as he reached her and told her about what they'd found, she said, "Well, damn. I've got nothing yet. Best intel I've got so far is same as you: the SickBoyz have disappeared from their turf. I didn't even get the part about them picking up people off the street yet, so you've got more than I do."

"Damn. I was afraid of that. Well, keep trying, and call us right away if you get anything else."

"What are you going to do?"

"Try something potentially dangerous to see if we can find the SickBoyz before that demon kills anyone."

"Dangerous? To who?" She sounded suspicious.

"To me, mostly. I'll tell you more after we do it."

"Stone—"

"Talk later, Ren. Keep looking." He hung up before she could reply. To his friends, he said, "Let's find a good spot for the ritual. We—"

"This is a bad idea, Dad," Ian said. "I know it won't kill you, but if that demon takes you out, or worse yet, manages to get a stronger hold on you—"

"I know, Ian. I don't like it either. But we haven't got any other—"

His phone rang again. He was still holding it, so reflexively he glanced at the screen, expecting to see it was Ren calling back.

It wasn't, though. The number was unfamiliar. He flicked a quick look at his friends, then tapped the button. "Yes?"

"This the dude that helped my brother? The one that was at Big Gee's?" The voice was raspy and sounded young—late teens or early twenties at most. It also sounded scared.

"Who is this?" Stone tightened his hand around the phone and ignored the others' questioning looks.

"This Fish. Are you the dude or not?" More urgency now.

Stone stiffened. "Fish? From the SickBoyz?"

"Yeah, man."

"Yes. It's me. I thought I told you to find your brother and get the hell out of town."

"Yeah. We did that. But somethin's goin' down." A pause, and Stone could almost picture him looking around for threats. "Somethin' big. You helped me an' my bro, so I figured I'd return the favor."

CHAPTER TWENTY-TWO

STONE NARROWED HIS EYES, and held up a hand when it looked like Ian might ask a question. "Okay, Fish. We appreciate that. Where are you now?"

"Ain't gonna tell you that. But we ain't in Detroit anymore. Got on a bus and got the hell outta town, jus' like you said."

"So you don't want us to meet you somewhere."

"Nah. Just gonna tell you what I heard. You can do whatever you want with it. Then we're done."

That was fair enough. Stone couldn't blame Fish for not wanting to pull himself and his younger brother into this mess any more than necessary. "Okay. What did you hear?"

There was a long pause, with a muffled conversation. Then Fish came back on the line. "I barely got outta Big Gee's before it got torched."

"Who torched it?" Stone interrupted. He stared out the van's front window. Jason was driving aimlessly around, making turns seemingly on whim. "Do you know?"

"I didn't see. Like I said, I ran. Antwon stuck around—he was the only other one who was awake after you guys laid everybody out and took the chick. He called me a chickenshit for runnin', but I didn't give a fuck. Those guys aren't the SickBoyz anymore. They're just, you know, pawns for some big bad mofo."

Stone noticed something in his voice—despite his gang bluster, it was clear he wasn't nearly as blasé about the situation as he was trying to project. "They're your friends, though, aren't they?"

"They're all dead now, the ones at Big Gee's. Nothin' I can do about it, so I'm gonna take care o' my little bro. You wanna hear this or not? I ain't gonna talk all night."

"Yes, all right. Tell us what you heard."

Another brief, muffled conversation, and then his voice came back more hushed. "It was earlier tonight. Got a call from Nails. He's one o' the SickBoyz—a gobber. He wasn't at Big Gee's."

"What did he tell you?"

"He was scared, man. Scared shitless. I didn't tell anybody I bugged out with my bro, so he thought I was still in the area. He said he was gonna run, and I should too. He said Truck—our old boss, who delivers his messages—called everybody in and told 'em to round up as many people from our turf as they could."

"You keep calling him 'the big bad'. You don't even have a name for him?"

A loud, frustrated sigh came through the line. "You don't *get* it, man! We ain't got a name for him. Ain't none of us ever even *seen* him. Rumor was goin' around if you ever did see him, it was 'cuz he was gonna kill you. Only thing anybody ever seen and told about it was this big weird-lookin' shadow. All we learned was to do what he said or he'd rip us apart. You know, like, for real. He did that."

"Okay," Stone said. "Okay, Fish. It's all right. So your goblin friend decided to defy his order?"

"Yeah, he got the fuck outta there. Dunno if he made it."

"Did he tell you why the big bad wanted these people? Or where they were supposed to take them?"

"He didn't say why he wanted 'em. He never told nobody why he did anything he did, not even Truck. We didn't even know what he wanted with the chick we was guardin' at Big Gee's, except we heard she might've been some kind o' cop."

"But he did say where?"

Another pause, longer this time. "Yeah. We were supposed to grab whoever we could grab—didn't matter if it was dudes, chicks, kids, whatever, just grab 'em. And take 'em to Abbott."

Stone frowned. "What's Abbott?"

"It's this creepy old abandoned hospital, up north of Twelve Mile Road. It ain't in anybody's turf."

"Why not? Seems like a place like that would be prime territory for someone."

Fish dropped his voice. "Yeah. But it ain't. People go there, they disappear. Place is fuckin' *haunted,* man. Everybody stays away, even the cops."

"I...see. And you don't have any speculation about why you were supposed to take these people there?"

"No idea. And I don't wanna know. I am *outta* this whole thing, okay? Only reason I called you is cuz you helped Reggie, and I pay my debts. But we're done now, okay? My advice is to get your ass outta there like we're doin'. You don't mess with this motherfucker. Okay?"

"Thank you for that, Fish. And thank you for calling. You made the right decision. You and Reggie look out for yourselves. You might have just made it possible for us to deal with this situation once and for all."

"You crazy, man. You wanna get yourself ripped up, you go ahead. I'm out."

Before Stone could reply, Fish broke the connection and the line went dead.

Jason immediately pulled the van off the road and parked. "Where we going?"

Ian was already tapping at his phone. "I see an Abbott Mental Hospital. It's been abandoned for years. Is that what you're talking about?"

Stone hadn't put the call on speaker, so he quickly filled the others in on what Fish had said. "I can't imagine 'Abbott' could be anything else. He said it was 'up north of Twelve Mile Road'. Is that the place?

Ian fiddled with the map. "Yeah, looks like it."

"Does it say anything about it being haunted?" Verity asked.

Amber was looking it up as well. "Yeah, lots of rumors about something bad in there, but nobody knows what. A ghost-hunting group disappeared in there a few years back. The cops went in looking for them and there's no record about what happened. Doesn't look like anybody's been back since, at least not officially."

"Brilliant," Stone muttered.

"So, we're going there?" Jason sounded more curious than nervous.

"Doesn't seem we've got a choice—but we've got a little time for some preparation. Jason, call Gina and ask her to dig a little deeper. See if she can get anything about what's really in there. I'll do the same with Ren. Best if we know what we're in for."

"If you call Ren," Verity said, "you know as soon as she finds out where things are happening, she's going to want to bring in her people."

"That's not an altogether bad idea—but not before we've had a chance to go in first. I don't fancy getting a whole lot of people killed."

It didn't take long for Gina to get back to them. They'd only been driving around for about twenty minutes after calling her before Stone's phone buzzed with a video call. He propped the phone on the dashboard and put it on speaker. "What have you got, Gina? I hope it's something good."

"Depends on your definition of 'good.'" It looked like she was sitting in her cluttered office at her apartment, and her expression was dubious.

"What's that mean?" Jason asked.

"I couldn't get anything official about what's going on at Abbott. You're right—it was a mental hospital, dating back to the middle part of the last century. Real shithole of a place, pardon my French. They really didn't treat mental patients very well back in the day, and this was the kind of place where the worst of them basically got warehoused so all the regular people didn't have to deal with them." Her scowl made her opinion about that clear.

"Okay…" Stone wanted to get to the more modern stuff, but he knew better than to cut her off. She wouldn't tell him anything if it wasn't important, or at least relevant. "So are we talking about the ghosts of the former residents?"

"That's what most people think. The place was shut down in the mid-Eighties, partially because that was around the time a lot of mental patients were getting put back on the streets, and partially because it had such a terrible reputation that nobody could sweep it under the rug anymore. Some of their patients were moved to other facilities, others were released to their families, and some were just let go. As far as ghosts—there've been a lot of so-called sightings over the years. You know, the standard stuff: screams, things moving around, shadowy figures, blood running down the walls, etcetera."

"Is that why nobody goes there anymore?" Verity asked from the back seat. "Because the ghosts—the echoes—of the former residents hassle them until they leave?"

"That'd be nice," Gina said, "but no cigar. As far as I can tell, both on the internet and by talking with a few Changelings from the Detroit area, the ghosts could well really be there, but they're not killing anyone. Just scaring them."

"What, then?" Stone was getting impatient. The longer they waited to go in, the more time the demon would have to finish whatever it was planning to do with the people the SickBoyz had grabbed. "We've got to get going, Gina."

"Yeah, I know. But keep your pants on, Doc, 'cuz this is where it gets interesting—and scary. It's not the ghosts you have to worry about. It's the ghouls."

Stone jerked back in his seat. "Bloody hell."

"Ghouls?" Jason demanded. "*That's* what's holed up at Abbott?"

"Yeah, that's the pretty solid rumor from a couple people my friends trust. It's not common knowledge, but it's a pretty good explanation for why nobody ever goes in, and nobody ever comes out." She switched to a deeper voice, probably mimicking a line from some movie Stone didn't recognize.

He let his breath out. That complicated matters significantly. Ghouls were supernatural creatures who sustained themselves by eating human flesh. They were fairly rare and most were highly reclusive, usually surviving by digging up remote graves, but he'd heard stories of small colonies living deep within large cities. They were resistant to magic, very tough, and, like demons, regenerated damage. To kill them, you had to either cut their heads off or inflict catastrophic damage in a short time. He'd once seen one killed by putting it through a wood chipper.

"Wait," Ian said. "The demon's working with the ghouls?"

"I guess that's one way to get rid of the people it kills." Jason rubbed his chin.

Stone stared at his hands.

"Alastair?" Verity looked at him in concern.

He didn't want to say it, but he didn't have a choice. "If there *are* ghouls in there, it makes things a lot more dangerous."

"Damn," Ian said. "Yeah. If a ghoul bites somebody, they turn into one of them."

Everybody fell silent, and Stone knew why. They all still wanted to take down the demon, but the thought of being turned into a ravening cannibal if anything went wrong was enough to terrify any rational person.

"What if," Amber mused, speaking slowly as if thinking it through as she went, "we called Ren and had her mobilize some of the military stuff she claims to have access to. Maybe we can burn them out."

"But what about the innocents?" Verity asked. "If the SickBoyz really did grab a bunch of civilians off the street and are holding them at Abbott, we can't just kill them."

Stone shook his head. "It's not just that. It doesn't solve the problem. In fact, it's more likely to create a worse one. Anything the military or the police can do won't touch the demon. Even if it *is* working with the ghouls, it'll just sit in there, fat and happy, and wait for everything to settle down. Short of dropping the building on it, it won't work. Plus, if we do manage to drive the ghouls out, that puts gods know how many dangerous cannibals out on the street. I know this is going to sound callous, but at least if they're trying to keep a low profile, they're probably killing the minimum number of people they need to survive. If we change that, all bets are off."

"Too bad dropping the building on them isn't an option," Jason said. "Sounds like nobody really wants it around anyway." Before anyone could say anything, though, he waved it off. "I know. We can't kill the innocents."

"What if we could get them out of there?" Ian asked.

"Wouldn't work." Jason fired up the van again and pulled back out into the sparse traffic. "Taking out a building that big, especially fast, requires more explosives and knowledge than we've got. Doing it the mundane way would take days or weeks of planning and logistics, and I don't think it's something you can do with magic, right, Al?"

Once again, Stone wished they had Gabriel, or any of the other dragons. With them, it might be possible. "No, you're right. We need a new plan. Anything else, Gina?"

"Isn't that enough?" she asked with a snort. "You guys be careful, okay? Come home in one piece. I like this job."

After she hung up, Stone slumped back against the window. "I think we're going to have to call Ren."

"You're going to send mundanes in there after ghouls?" Verity asked, surprised.

"No. But we need body armor, more weapons, and somebody to keep lookie-loos away from the operation." He retrieved his phone and tapped Ren's number. "Head toward Abbott, but stop well away. We need to do some recon before we go in."

Ren wasn't happy about Stone's plan, but when he told her about the ghouls, she sobered. "If I send my people in there, they're dead, aren't they?"

"Quite likely. Or worse than dead. I don't know if anyone from your agency has ever dealt with ghouls, but they're not something to take lightly."

"Not directly, though we've done enough research to know you're right." A frustrated sigh came through the connection. "What do you need?"

"As many people under your command as you can get in a short time. We're heading to Abbott now and we need to go in soon if we don't want to find all those people dead. More short-term, we need some body armor, weapons, and—"

"—can she get us a floorplan of the place?" Ian asked from the back. "I can't find a good one online."

"Did you hear that?" Stone asked Ren.

"Yeah. I think I can get that stuff. Can't get any heavy weapons on short notice, though. I'll have to coordinate with local law enforcement, and…" An even louder sigh. "You know this is going to be a clusterfuck, right? I'm not going to have a prayer of keeping the media away from this. Not with that kind of presence outside the place."

"Do what you can. I know it's not ideal, but we'll work with what we've got. Where shall we meet you, and when? Remember, time is of the essence."

There was a long pause, probably while she consulted her sources. "I think I can send the floorplan in a few minutes. The rest of it—best I can do is an hour, and that's pushing it. I can't scare up that kind of gear in five minutes, and I still have to get it to you."

Stone growled. "That's not going to work. We'll have to go with what we've got. I don't like it, but we can't wait on this. Jason, how far are we from Abbott?"

"About twenty minutes, assuming the traffic holds."

"Stone—" Ren began.

"I know. I don't like it either. But if we wait that long, I guarantee at least one of two things will happen. Either the demon will kill all those people, or it will escape again. Possibly both. I don't want to let either of those things happen, do you?"

Her growl was louder than his. "Of course I don't. None of this is ever easy, is it?"

"If it was easy, anybody could do it." He glanced out the front window, watching the blighted scenery roll by. He didn't know if they were still in the SickBoyz's territory now, or if they'd crossed into someone else's. "Call me when your people get to Abbott. If we can, we'll come out and see what you've brought us."

It took them closer to half an hour to get to the hospital. It was on the north side of town, on the outskirts between Detroit itself and a couple smaller suburbs. Jason cruised the area, looking around dubiously. "This looks even worse than where the SickBoyz were."

He wasn't wrong. The buildings here, mostly blasted-out husks of former businesses and apartment buildings, looked almost completely unoccupied. Abbott Hospital itself, an ugly, several-story building of what looked like stained gray concrete, squatted in the middle of a weed-choked, cleared-out space that had probably been the hospital's grounds when it was still in operation. Now, a stout, eight-foot-high fence with razor wire at the top surrounded what Stone could see of its perimeter. No lights illuminated either the building itself or the area surrounding it. When Jason drove past the front gates, they could all see the heavy chain and massive lock holding them closed. Several signs warning people away on pain of arrest, prosecution, and heavy fines made it clear that anyone who knew what was good for them should move along.

"Not that anybody would *want* to go in there," Verity said, frowning. "The whole place gives me the creeps."

"Yeah," Ian agreed. "There's a…feeling about it. I can't explain it, but it's like the *air* is warning us off."

"I'm not getting any of the magic you two are," Amber said, "but the area is making me want to get the hell out of here. If I had fur, it would be standing on end."

Stone knew exactly what they meant, and he didn't think much of it had to do with the demon. It was common for places like this, full of human misery, pain, and despair, to develop a sort of astral miasma. Depending on the extent of the emotional resonance, the energy could be temporary or permanent. For example, the site of a single violent murder might remain tainted for a few months or even a year or two, while a concentration camp, a place where a mass murder had occurred, or even a maximum-security prison could never be truly free of the negative energy. He suspected

Abbott Hospital, based on what Gina had told them about how the patients had been treated, probably qualified as one of the more longstanding sites.

"The Evil would have loved this place," Verity muttered under her breath, shifting in her seat.

She wasn't wrong. Stone wasn't as sensitive to it as she was, but the growing sense of unease was hard to ignore. And it would get nothing but worse the closer they got. He had no idea if there actually *were* echoes of dead patients in there, but it was entirely possible that anyone—even mundanes—who tried sneaking inside would experience a subliminal sense of profound wrongness that would eventually drive them away.

And that was before anybody even brought up the ghouls, who had probably found themselves a sweet base from which to pick off unfortunate homeless people or drifters for their meals.

Ren was right: none of this was ever easy.

Jason drove further down the street, turned a corner, and made a U-turn so he could park facing Abbott. "What do you want to do? I don't see any of Ren's people, do you?"

Stone was already back on the phone to the agent. "We're outside. Have you got anything else for us?" She'd already sent them the floorplan, and Verity, Amber, and Ian had been busy studying it as they drove.

Ren made a frustrated sound in the back of her throat. "Not yet. We don't have a lot of agents in the area, and even the ones nearby can't get here that fast. And local law enforcement is dragging their feet. Do you know how much it sucks that I can't tell them exactly what's going on? If I tell them they're facing a demon and a bunch of supernatural cannibals, they'll call me a crank and file my request somewhere lower than cleaning out the gangs. And if I tell them it's a mundane threat—assuming they even want to get involved with Abbott at all—they'll want to take over and we'll end up with a bunch of dead cops and my ass in a sling."

Stone was afraid of that. "So they're not coming at all?"

"I'm still working on it."

He was about to reply when a loud, strident horn blast broke the night's silence. A moment later, the dark form of a massive freight train thundered past along the east side of the Abbott compound. He waited for it to pass before speaking. "We can't wait, Ren. You know that, right?"

"Yeah, I know." Something slammed on her end—probably her hand on her desk. "Damn it, I don't want you all getting killed over this because I can't get you enough backup. I feel like I'm not holding up my end. You got Izzy back for us, and now I can't even help you."

"It's fine. Really. This is why you called us in to start with. Let us do our jobs."

"Do I have a choice?"

"Honestly—no." He chuckled. "That's the downside of calling us in on something like this—we're rubbish at following orders, the lot of us. Probably a good thing you aren't paying us."

She didn't take the bait. "Watch yourself. All of you. I want to see you all back safe and well. Don't take chances."

"We'll be home by curfew, Mum. And we promise not to wreck the car."

"Stone—"

"Text me if your people actually show up. Must go now." He tapped the button before she could reply and twisted in his seat to face the others, who all looked grim.

"We're on our own, aren't we?" Ian was already unhooking his seatbelt.

"Looks that way, at least for now."

"What's the plan?" Jason, too, was unbuckling.

"Hang about for a few minutes. I'm going to do a little recon."

"What kind of recon?" Verity asked suspiciously.

"Levitating around the area to see if I can pick up the demon's presence." He patted his chest where the scar was.

"Are you getting anything at all from here?" Amber was kneeling on her seat, pulling up the various packs they'd stowed in the back.

"Not yet, but we're not that close. I'm guessing the demon is probably underground, rather than on one of the upper floors."

"I'm betting you're right." Ian was studying his phone, presumably looking at the floorplan. "According to this, there are two underground floors—one for parking and one for various labs and storage. There are also a couple of big operating theaters down there. Somebody's added some notes—the place was originally ten stories, but the top five have pretty much collapsed over the years. The whole building's been condemned, but those upper floors are…super-extra condemned, I guess. It probably wouldn't be possible for any of the mundanes to get up there without a lot of effort."

"Well, that's good. Narrows down our area of search." He opened his door. "Give me about ten minutes to look around."

"You want me to come with you?" Ian asked.

"No, there's no point. You lot get suited up. We can use magical shields to keep the ghouls off us, but I don't want to count on them. The more armor between you and their teeth and claws, the better. Back soon." He pulled a heavy disregarding spell over himself and lifted off the ground before anyone could try to stop him.

He stayed up high, level with the building's intact fifth story, floating around with magical sight up and his attention fixed on the ground below him and the busted-out windows.

It didn't take him long to verify that no living beings were visible—not on the grounds, not inside the building, and not on the broken upper floors as lookouts. He didn't even see the faint green auras of small animals, which didn't surprise him. The place's magical "stench" was faintly nauseating him; any animals would give the place a wide berth because their instincts would tell them anything they found to eat here would be harmful.

Reluctantly, he dropped lower. Despite his flippant responses to his friends, he didn't fancy the demon, the SickBoyz, or the ghouls catching him out alone. But it had to be done—if Fish had given them inaccurate or deliberately wrong information and the demon *wasn't* here, there was no point in taking his friends into danger.

It took until he'd reached the level of the second floor before the twinge began. It wasn't pain, not exactly—more like a bone-deep, unpleasant itch that was impossible to scratch. It crawled along the scar like a line of ants patrolling back and forth.

He rubbed it absently, turning in place in an attempt to get a direction, but that wasn't the way the scar worked. It warned him of the *presence* of demonic energy, but didn't help him to locate it.

But the demon was here, and that was what he needed to know. With a quick glance around to make sure no one had noticed him, he drifted back across the grounds and over the fence to the van.

His friends hadn't been idle while he was gone. All of them had donned Kevlar vests, heavy jackets, and gloves, and Ian was maintaining a disregarding spell while Jason and Amber pulled out guns, ammo, and headset radios and offered them around. As Stone landed next to them, he noticed Verity and Ian waving off the mundane firepower, but they did take radios. Jason and Amber loaded up with flash-bang grenades, two handguns each, and shotguns slung over their shoulders on straps.

Verity was mostly focused on pulling things from her bag and stuffing them into the pockets of her vest. As Stone drew closer, he saw that they were large vials. "Alchemical goodies?"

She flashed him a tight smile. "Yeah. Picked them up from the shop before we left. Nothing deadly, but if the SickBoyz get in the way, some of this stuff could cause some trouble with them. If you see me chucking these, try to stay away from where they land."

"Brilliant. I suspect we'll need all the help we can get."

Jason handed him a radio, a vest, and a pair of heavy gloves. "See anything?"

"See? No." He shrugged out of his coat and allowed his friend to help him into the vest, then checked to make sure the demon knife was still in easy reach in its sheath on his belt. "Feel? Yes. It's in there. The scar isn't directional, but I'd bet a lot that they're in one of those underground areas Ian mentioned."

"No lookouts?" Amber asked, looking dubious.

"Not that I noticed. They could have been hiding further inside the building, obscuring their auras. But I'm not worried about the SickBoyz. We can take them out if we need to." He glanced at Jason, who was eyeing him with a frown. "What?"

His friend didn't look like he wanted to say it. "Do you even *have* a plan, Al? I mean for the demon. I'm not worried about gangbangers—even Changeling ones—either. The ghouls are more concerning, but at least we know how to take them out. You said this demon is tough, nearly immune to magic, and we've got to kill it in one shot or it'll just pop right back up. Have you got a way to do that?"

Stone shifted his gaze to the others. They were all looking troubled; he suspected they'd all been thinking the same thing but didn't want to speak it aloud either. He didn't blame them. All of them trusted him to know what he was doing in magical situations, and he didn't doubt they'd follow him into that building without hesitation even if he *didn't* have an immediate plan. But it wasn't fair to expect them to—at least not without telling them everything he knew.

"Possibly." He paced back and forth along the side of the van, with occasional glances toward the dark form of Abbott to make sure no auras had popped up. "I've got the knife, which any of us can use to hurt it—though I doubt it will be enough to kill it. And remember what I told you before, that when demons first appear here, they haven't got a lot of power? They're counting on a reservoir from their home plane until they can drain enough humans' life energy to allow them their full strength on this one?"

"Yeah…" Ian said. "And you also said these probably didn't have as much of that energy as other ones might, because they were summoned here to be sacrificed."

"Right. Which could be good for us, or it could be bad."

"How?" Verity finished doing up her vest and shifted her shoulders. She obviously wasn't comfortable in it.

"It could be good because the demon could be running low on energy. That might be why it's instructed its gang minions to round up a load of civilians. But demons can't just suck down life energy like they're chugging cups of coffee. It takes time. Less if they don't care about killing the donor, of course."

"So you think it's been okay with not having a lot of energy up until now, because it had plenty to keep itself hidden and keep the SickBoyz in line?" Ian asked. "But now that we're in the picture, it needs a top-off?"

"That's one theory. If that *is* true, it's still got its connection to its home plane, *and* that connection is in this building somewhere, we might be able to sever it." He looked at Verity. "That's how your friends Bron and Nicholas Happenstance took Razakal down in Los Angeles, remember?"

"Yeah." She nodded soberly. "Bron told me about that. It was nasty. A lot of people almost died."

"You said *if*," Jason said. "What if that's *not* true?"

Stone sighed. "Then things get more problematic. If it's already gathered enough energy to sever its connection to its home plane, that means it's already fully here."

"Can you banish it or something?" Amber asked.

"Not without a hell of a lot more preparation than we've got time for, unfortunately. And even then, banishing demons isn't my speciality."

"So that means—what?" Ian leaned against the van's side and stared at Abbott. "We go in there and beat it up, and hope one of us can get close enough with that tiny little knife to cut its throat?"

"If it even *has* a throat," Jason muttered.

"While fighting off the SickBoyz and the ghouls, and trying to keep all of them from massacring any innocents who might still be alive in there," Amber added.

Stone looked down. "Listen," he said, "I don't like any of this. I don't like asking you lot to risk your lives on this—and don't think for a moment that isn't what you're going to be doing."

"Is this where you give us the 'now's the time to back out' line?" Jason glared at him.

"No—because I know it won't work." He paused as another horn blared and another train thundered by. He idly watched the dark form until it disappeared, then sighed. "Let's do this. Unless Ren's people show up with heavy firepower in the next five minutes, we're on our own."

"So what else is new?" Ian asked dryly.

It was a good bet that the SickBoyz and their prisoners had taken advantage of a hole in the fence somewhere to get through, but neither Stone nor any of his group wanted to prowl around the sizable, darkened perimeter of Abbott's fence line to try to find it. Instead, they levitated quickly over while under an invisibility spell. Ian had always been better at the spell than Stone or Verity, so he extended his to cover Jason and Amber while the other mages took care of their own.

By the time they reached the edge of the building, Stone and Verity were both puffing with the exertion of maintaining the spell. The group hid behind an old dumpster, out of visibility of anyone inside Abbott who might be watching, and caught their breath.

"You want to go straight in the front door?" Jason had his phone out and was scrolling around the floorplan. "Looks like there's a reception area, with two wings going off to one side and one toward the back. I don't see the stairway, though."

"It's behind the reception area," Ian said. "There's a door near the elevators."

"Ugh," Verity said, shifting again.

"Vest giving you trouble?" Jason looked her over in concern. "Need it adjusted?"

"It's not the vest. Don't you *feel* that?"

Stone did feel it. Now that they were closer, the area's oppressive sensation of *wrongness* had grown worse. The scar twinged harder; it still didn't hurt, exactly, but now it felt like the ants prowling up and down it were wearing hard-soled army boots. "Do the best you can to shield it. I doubt it's going to get any better when we get inside."

"I smell something," Amber said. She sniffed the air, turning her head back and forth. "Death. Decay."

"Fresh?" Ian wrinkled his nose, but he obviously hadn't picked it up.

"Hard to tell. It's kind of a mix. Some of it's old, but the newer stuff doesn't smell exactly like normal blood."

"What's *that* mean?" Jason frowned. "It's *ab*normal blood?"

Amber's brow furrowed for a moment, as if she were trying to remember something. She jerked her head up. "Wait. I know what it smells like. Remember when we were at the mall in Atlanta, with Tani and Maisie?"

"Ghouls," Stone said grimly. "So that part's confirmed, at least."

"Yeah..." She still sounded like she had something on her mind.

"What is it?"

"Not sure. Let's get inside. I can probably tell you more when we're closer." She pointed. "Not the front door, though. They'll probably be watching that. Let's go in through one of those broken windows on the ground floor."

"Let me go first," Ian said. "I can do a little recon and see if anybody's waiting to ambush us. I'll call on the radio if it's clear."

Given that he hadn't even been breathing hard from maintaining the invisibility spell over himself, Jason, and Amber as they'd crossed the wide yard beyond the fence, he was the best choice. Stone didn't bother telling him to be careful, but just waved him forward and switched on his radio. The others did the same.

The seconds crawled by. Stone peered around the corner of the dumpster, trying to spot his son's aura, but Ian's invisibility spell was even better now than it had been before. Gabriel had no doubt been teaching him some tricks. A few moments later, the radio squawked softly and his voice came through the earbuds: *All clear here. I'm in some kind of conference room, I think. It smells terrible in here. Come on in.*

The others hurried to join him. The window he'd gone through was almost completely clear of glass, with only a couple jagged points sticking up from the bottom of the frame.

Ian had probably been correct that this had once been a conference room, but the only way to tell was the size. All the furniture except for two broken chairs was gone, the floor littered with trash and bits of old wood. The stained walls had once been painted institutional green. The door had been pulled off its hinges long ago; bits of it lay on the floor in the hallway.

"Bloody hell," Stone said. "You weren't kidding about this place smelling terrible." The stench, an overpowering mix of decay, urine, feces, and something he could only describe as 'the distilled essence of wet dog' hung in the air, so strong he felt as if it should be visible to the naked eye.

"No kidding." Amber sounded strangled, her face scrunched in disgust.

"You gonna be okay?" Jason asked her. "You gotta be getting the worst of it by far."

"I'll be fine. I just hope I can pick something out of this. Right now, it's just…ugh."

Verity peeked out through the open door into the hallway. "I don't see anybody moving, to mundane or magical sight."

"Where *is* everybody?" Ian joined her. "You'd think they'd have lookouts."

"Maybe not," Stone said. "If nobody saw them coming in, they probably don't think anyone's coming. I doubt anyone expected Fish's mate to get the bollocks to call him."

"What about the ghouls, though?" Jason asked.

"They're probably underground too—either hiding from the demon and its group, or trying to pick up snacks."

"Wait," Verity said. "I think I see something up there. Can I risk a flashlight?"

"Not like anything that's likely to be in here can't see us without light," Ian said.

"Good point." She dug her flashlight from her vest pocket and directed its beam down the hall toward the central part of the building.

"That looks like a body," Jason said grimly.

Amber sniffed toward it. "Hard to pick out individual smells in here, but I think that's part of the weird blood smell I noticed before."

The group crept forward, keeping their eyes out for anything that might be approaching or waiting to attack.

Stone crouched next to the huddled form, studying it in the beam of Verity's flashlight. It was male and unhealthily skinny, its scarecrow arms and legs twisted and splayed. He couldn't see its face because it didn't have one—or a head. It lay in a puddle of dark-red blood, its neck a ruin of ragged flesh.

Behind him, Verity gasped softly. "Is that one of the ghouls?"

"Something pulled his head off," Amber said, her tone dispassionate and clinical. She crouched next to Stone for a closer look.

"Here it is." Ian touched Stone's shoulder and pointed further down the hall. The unfortunate man's head, its straw-blond hair sticking out in all directions, lay next to a pile of old fast-food wrappers, its wide, yellowed eyes staring sightlessly up at the ceiling.

"Pulled his head off..." Stone echoed softly. "Bloody hell. Maybe we won't have to deal with the ghouls after all." His scar gave a warning twinge.

"Wait..." Jason said. "You think...the *demon* did this?"

"I'm almost certain of it."

"So am I." Amber leaned closer to sniff the body's neck. "I mean, it's *possible* some of the SickBoyz could have been strong enough to rip this guy's head clean off, but I don't think they *would*. This wasn't cut. This was pulled. And not long ago, either. It would take a lot of strength and a lot of rage for a human—even a Changeling—to do this."

"But a demon wouldn't have second thoughts about it," Stone said. "Probably didn't want the ghouls interfering with whatever it had planned."

"Makes sense," Ian said. "Though let's not assume the demon got *all* the ghouls. They're pretty good at hiding. We—"

"Wait!" Amber hissed.

Immediately, everybody shut up and looked at her. "What?" Jason whispered.

"I saw something moving down there, just for a second." She pointed further down the same hallway where they'd found the ghoul.

"Another ghoul?" Stone shifted to magical sight, trying to pick out any movement in the smelly darkness, but he didn't see anything.

"Don't think so. It's gone now. Maybe a lookout?"

"We need to move," Jason said. "If they know we're here, we can't give them time to prepare."

"Let's go," Stone said grimly. He drew the knife from his belt and gripped it. "Ian, Verity, keep your demon-resistant shields up. Verity, you cover Amber, and I'll get Jason. We'll have to stay closer together than I like, but there's no helping it."

Jason and Amber were already drawing their weapons. Amber had a handgun on a lanyard in one hand, and a flash-bang grenade in the other. Jason had unslung his shotgun.

"Let me go first," Stone said. Before anybody could protest, he moved off past the ghoul's headless corpse and down the hall toward the central part of the building. He shifted between magical and mundane sight, constantly scanning ahead of him and confident his friends were doing the same thing.

Nothing popped out at them before they reached the end of the hallway. They moved slowly but steadily, pausing only briefly to peer into the rooms on either side. Few of them had doors, and vandals and thieves had stolen or destroyed all the furniture, so it only took a second to determine nobody was lurking inside.

"At least we don't have to worry about magic," Verity muttered.

"Well, except for the demon," Ian said.

"I don't think this demon is a mage," Stone said. "If I'm right and this one is the weakest of the twelve, it will be strong, nearly impervious to magic, and almost impossible to kill, but it won't be throwing spells at us. Don't assume it doesn't have other innate abilities, though. I think we've cornered it in its lair. It—"

His phone buzzed with a text, and he risked a quick glance at it.

Ren's name appeared at the top, above a terse message: "*My people are still a good 20 minutes out. Trying to be discreet so we don't attract too much attention.*"

He shoved the phone back in his pocket without answering the message, and continued as if he hadn't paused: "—it's likely going to fight even dirtier than usual."

They reached the end of the hallway, which opened out onto the hospital's central reception and lobby area. Stone got only few seconds to look around, taking in the broken reception desk, several shattered chairs, and a lot of dirt and debris, when Amber touched his arm.

"Look," she said, pointing.

He hadn't seen them at first because the wrecked desk had partially obscured them, but two still figures lay on the floor past it.

"Careful..." Jason muttered, looking around even though he was the only one of the group who didn't have special senses. He held his shotgun at the ready as he stayed close to Stone.

When they got closer, Verity made a little gagging sound in the back of her throat. "My God..." she murmured.

One of the figures had probably been a SickBoy. Changelings didn't appear in their true form to magical sight once they were dead, so it was impossible to know for sure since the gang didn't wear colors. A dark-skinned young man no older than his late teens, his face was twisted into a rictus of terror above a throat that had been torn out. Dark blood soaked the front of his shirt and pooled beneath his body.

The other figure was another ghoul. This one was a woman; her head was still where it belonged, her mouth still bloody and flecked with bits of flesh from the unfortunate SickBoy, but this time something had pulled both her arms free of her torso. Her blood mixed with the ganger's to form a sticky sludge on the dirty floor.

"She attacked him," Ian said numbly. "Something got her, but not before she was able to kill him."

"Here's one of her arms." Amber had moved a short distance away and was crouching next to something unseen on the floor near the far wall.

"Here's the other one," Jason said. He was on the opposite side. "Holy shit, there's a whole trail of blood from her to the arm."

Stone shivered a little, picturing the brutish demon pulling the ghoul apart like a wishbone and flinging her arms to both sides. What was he dragging his friends—and himself—into?

"Stay close," he ordered. "And keep those shields up. We've got to find the stairway down."

"It's over there," Ian said, pointing toward the back. "Somebody took the sign, but that's it."

"Let's do this, then." Stone augmented his shield around himself and Jason, and started toward the door.

"Any plan yet?" Jason asked. "Or do we just wing it?"

"I think there's got to be a certain amount of winging it, since we don't know what we're going to find. The priority's the demon, but take the SickBoyz down if you get the chance."

"Maybe not," Amber said thoughtfully as they reached the stairway door.

"What do you mean?"

"Everything Ren's told us suggests they don't want to be following this thing—that they're only doing it because they're scared."

"You think they might turn on the demon if they think we have a shot at taking it down?" Jason asked, looking dubious.

"Hard to say. But if we can give them a chance to do it, it might be worth it."

"Not much of a chance," Stone said, shaking his head. "We've got enough variables in this fight without leaving more enemies up and mobile. Play it by ear—it's all we can do. Ren's people are at least twenty minutes out, she said, so they won't be any help. We can't afford to wait. Not if the demon knows we're here."

They all exchanged glances, pausing a moment to prepare themselves. Jason checked to make sure everyone was ready, then gripped the featureless metal door's handle and pulled.

The door swung open on a darkened space. Instantly, the ripe smell of decay rolled up, joining the stench from the lobby. Amber took a staggering step back, and Jason gripped her arm.

Grimly, Stone raised a light spell and sent it into the stairwell. He almost wished he hadn't.

The walls, the stairs, even the railings were slicked with blood and gore. An arm, clearly ripped free of an unseen body, lay on one of the steps halfway down the first flight. It looked as if some demented artist had pulled it free and then spun around, spattering blood everywhere.

Stone swallowed hard. Normally, gore didn't affect him that much, but the combination of the sight, the stench, and worst of all the overwhelming feeling of demonic energy all around them was making it hard for him to keep his dinner in place. The ants marching up and down his scar were now wearing football cleats.

Around him, the others had all gone pale. "Holy *shit*," Jason breathed.

"I'd say *un*holy shit at this point," Amber said. "Come on—we have to move fast. If they're waiting for us, we're sitting ducks in this stairwell."

"Look." Ian pointed down. "Footprints."

Stone hadn't noticed them before because he was looking at the walls, but his son was right. The impressions from several different shoes indicated that a lot of people had walked through the blood on the way down. Quite a few of them were smudged, as if multiple people had moved through them.

"The SickBoyz?" Verity asked. "Or the prisoners?"

"Probably both," Jason said. "At least now we have a pretty good idea that they're down here."

Amber had paused to examine the arm. "This looks like a woman's—but not dirty and skinny like the ghoul's."

Stone didn't answer, but that didn't bode well. There didn't seem to be that many female SickBoyz, which meant the arm had probably come from one of the prisoners. If the demon was already killing them, they might be descending the stairs into an abattoir—and he might be leading his friends into a killing zone.

"Let's go," he said grimly. "Be careful—the blood's still wet."

"Where are we going?" Ian asked. "The parking garage or the operating theaters?"

Stone realized he wasn't sure. "Let's just get started. The feeling's getting stronger—maybe between my scar and Amber's nose, something will give us an idea."

It wasn't a great idea—none of them wanted to descend into the hellish depths without some idea where they were going—but the alternative was to go back upstairs and wait for Ren's people to show up. Stone was fairly sure if they did that, they'd find nothing but ripped-up bodies downstairs by the time they arrived. He couldn't take the chance that the demon had another way out, since it would be a fool not to.

He augmented his shield again, gripped the railing, and started down. He was glad he was wearing gloves, and tried not to think about the slippery surfaces under his hands and feet. "Ian, which is lower—the parking garage or the surgery floor?"

"Surgery and admin. Seems a little weird, since I'd expect the parking to be at the lowest point, but that's what the plans say."

"I bet I know why," Verity said.

"Why?" The steps were wide enough for two of them to walk next to each other, so Jason was side-by-side with Amber and behind Verity.

"I was reading up on this place on the way over, while Ian was digging into the floorplans. It was pretty notorious for some of the experiments they did in the Sixties, back when attitudes about mental illness weren't as enlightened as they are now. They were trying to 'cure' some of the patients with some fairly unethical techniques, most of which failed miserably and left the patients worse off than they started—to the point where the ones who died were probably the lucky ones. That's a big part of why the place eventually got shut down, though it took almost another twenty years before anything really happened."

"That tracks," Ian said. "There are more surgical suites up-stairs—probably for doing the kinds of surgeries nobody had a problem with."

"Brilliant," Stone muttered. "So we're heading down to the mad scientists' lair. That's fitting."

"Let's hope the demon thinks so, too." Jason glanced nervously behind him, as if expecting something to erupt out of the door they'd passed.

They reached the landing of the first-level basement floor. The door was heavy metal, sprayed with blood, and locked. Like the one upstairs, it didn't have a sign indicating its purpose. Stone hesitated a moment, tempted to open it and look inside. The cleat-clad ants strolling up and down his chest hadn't gotten any more enthusiastic and the demonic miasma seemed to be holding steady so far, so it was impossible to pick out a direction. The bloody footsteps continued downward, however.

Ian gripped his arm. "Look," he whispered urgently, pointing down toward the lower floor.

For a second, Stone didn't see what he was pointing at. He was about to switch to magical sight when a wispy form floated across his field of vision, halfway down the stairs.

"What's there?" Jason demanded. "I don't see anything."

"I don't smell anything, either," Amber added, eyes narrowed.

Stone wasn't surprised. "Bloody hell, you wouldn't," he murmured in wonder. He pulled the light ball back, lowering the illumination below them to a faint glow.

The wispy figure took a slightly more coherent form. It was hard to make out features, but it was clearly a young woman clad in a flowing gown. Her bare feet stuck out from beneath it, hovering a foot or so above the bloody steps.

"Is that...an echo?" Verity whispered. "One of the patients?"

"I think so." Stone focused on the spirit. She looked like barely more than a girl, maybe a teenager, with long, stringy hair obscuring half her face. The other side of her head looked shaved, and sported a silvery opening in her skull. Her sad eyes, sunken into hollows, met Stone's for only a second, and then she drifted downward and disappeared through the door at the foot of the stairs.

"I think that's our cue," Hoping he wasn't making a mistake, Stone continued downward.

They paused once again when they reached the door, which was also smeared with blood. The bloody footprints milled on the floor as if a large group of people had been standing there waiting for something, and the door handle was streaked with tacky red.

Stone looked back at his friends. "It's bothering me that nothing's come after us."

"Why?" Verity asked.

"It could be nothing—they could be so focused on whatever they're doing that they've got no idea we're here. It could be that they're confident enough that nobody in their right mind *would* come after them."

"Or they could all be in there letting us freak out while they wait to jump us," Ian said.

Stone didn't answer.

"Let's do this," Jason said. "The suspense is worse than whatever's past that door."

Stone doubted that. "Keep those shields strong," he ordered, gripping the little knife tighter. Then, with no other reason to stall, he took hold of the door handle with magic and swung the door open.

Beyond it, stretching out to their left, was a wide, dark hallway.

Stone directed his overhead light ball further down the hall before moving inside quickly and stepping to the side so his friends could come through. They all took up positions along the walls, focused on trying to spot any movement. The elevator, wider than a standard one—probably to accommodate patient gurneys on their way to surgery—stood open at the hall's end to their right. Another filthy, scarecrow-thin ghoul body, this one ripped limb from limb, had been tossed into the space.

Jason had his shotgun out, sweeping the barrel back and forth like a cop trying to clear a scene. "Anything?"

"They're down here somewhere." Verity sounded ill. "Not in the hallway, though."

Stone knew exactly how she was feeling, and he was sure it didn't have much to do with the dead ghoul. The psychic-sewer sensation he'd come to associate with demonic energy was stronger than ever down here. He suspected if he, Verity, and Ian didn't have their shields up, they wouldn't be able to function down here.

"Look!" Ian pointed at the floor. Several doors lined the hallway on both sides, but the herd of bloody footprints led to its end, where a pair of wide, swinging double doors stood at the opposite end from their current location. Small windows on each door were bright red with smeared blood. "That's the biggest operating theater. I remember it from the floorplan."

Jason pulled a flash-bang grenade from his pocket, and Amber did likewise. The group crept down the long hall, keeping to the walls and trying doors as they went. All of them were either locked or gone; three rooms with missing doors appeared to have been either offices, supply rooms, or small conference rooms. The floor was dirty, cracked tile, and the walls were painted a fading institutional green, most of it covered with old graffiti. Above them, the receptacles that had once held long-broken fluorescent lights yawned open. The stench was nearly overpowering.

They reached the last of the three offices with missing doors. Stone, taking point, shot a quick glance inside, expecting to see the same empty, debris-filled space as he'd found in the others.

Instead, two blood-soaked bodies lay one on top of the other, as if they'd been tossed there.

Tensing, he held up a hand and directed his ball of light into the room. "Watch the hallway," he muttered over the comm, and entered the room.

Like the others, these bodies had been ripped apart, but this time whatever had done it had tossed all the limbs together in one big pile. At first, all Stone could tell was that neither of them was a ghoul. They were both male, one small and thin, the other taller and bulkier. His shoulders slumped as he got a look at the bigger one's bloody head, and realized he'd seen his face before.

"Gods, it's Fish." The young man looked human now in death, with no sign of the Changeling features that had given him his name. His arm and one of his legs had been ripped free, and something had slashed open his abdomen.

"What's he doing here?" Jason asked. "I thought you said he took off with his brother."

"Obviously he lied."

"Oh, no…" Verity murmured. "If that's him, then the small one—it isn't—?"

Stone didn't want to take a closer look, afraid she was right. If Fish had come back here to help his fellow SickBoyz, maybe he'd brought his young brother along—or his brother had followed. He bent closer, trying to make out the other face's features. He hadn't seen Fish's brother directly, but at least he might be able to identify the age.

He let his breath out in relief. The other figure was white and older than Fish, with scraggly hair tied back in a ponytail and sharp, pointy features. "It's not him. Might be the goblin—Nails."

"Come on," Ian urged. "We can't stop now."

The blood covering the observation windows obscured the view completely, so there was no chance of peering through at whatever was going on beyond them. "Do you hear anything?" Stone whispered to Amber. Her bearish ears weren't as acute as her nose, but still better than human range.

Amber had remained in the hall, and was watching the closed double doors. "Something's definitely in there," she said. "I hear things moving around. It's hard to smell anything in the middle of all this, though. It's overpowering." She tightened her hand on her gun.

They were right: there was no more time for stalling. If they were going after the demon, this would be where they'd have to do it. Stone rose from his crouch and returned to the hallway. He let his gaze trail over his friends, wondering if all of them would come out of this alive.

Jason met his eyes and nodded once, looking grim. He knew what was at stake here. They all did. He pointed his shotgun at the door and waited.

Stone used magic to push the door. He half-expected it to either be locked or blocked from the other side, but it opened easily. The space beyond it was pitch-dark. He sent the magical ball of light in ahead of them, but it might as well have been a mundane basketball for all the good it did.

The cleated ants on his scar went from marching to clog-dancing. "It's—" he began.

From behind them, a powerful force shoved them all into the room, sending them sprawling into the blackness.

The doors slammed shut.

CHAPTER TWENTY-THREE

THE CHAMBER WENT SILENT.

All five Council members were now staring at Aldwyn. Their expressions held a combination of confusion and dawning terror.

Aldwyn merely smiled his fatherly smile and waited for them to catch up. Ever since he had been forced to begin interacting with humans on Earth all those many centuries ago, he'd quickly discovered it was almost always laughably simple to manipulate them by taking advantage of their baser emotions, with fear and greed at the forefront. These people—not human, *per se*, but certainly human-*like* in all the ways that mattered—had been in such a hurry to lock down this powerful newcomer, to secure him (and his power) as one of their own, that they hadn't considered the possibility he might be concealing things from them.

He couldn't even realistically say it pleased him when his plans worked as intended, because it had been a rare situation indeed when they *hadn't*.

Humans, by and large, were just that predictable.

Jesperian found his voice, though it did shake a bit. "What...sort of challenge are you proposing?"

Aldwyn widened his smile. "A contest of magic, of course. If status here is determined by level of magical Talent, then I propose to prove that my own should place me at high status indeed. In fact, I am reasonably certain it will place me at the *highest* status." He stroked his chin. "Which, if the information I was given is correct, means I will be well positioned to take my place among you."

"Among...us?" The dark-haired female Council member swallowed hard. "You mean...as part of the Council?"

"Was I given incorrect information?" Aldwyn asked politely, in the tone of a man genuinely seeking answers. Only the gleam in his eye, which he did nothing to disguise, gave him away. "If magical power confers status, surely those with the highest Talent should lead, should they not?"

Jesperian narrowed his eyes, looking less confused now and more angry. "You...did this on purpose."

"Of course I did."

The Councilman looked as if he couldn't believe what he was hearing. "You swore an oath...bound yourself on pain of death, to support Prensyrrus."

"And support it I will." Aldwyn paced back and forth in front of the long Council table, ignoring the wide-eyed audience and the guards lining the walls. In the periphery of his vision, both magical and mundane, he could sense the guards' tension as they looked to the Council members for a clue about what they should do. They dared not challenge this potentially dangerous interloper without direction, but they clearly weren't comfortable with remaining inactive in the face of a potential threat.

"What gave you the impression that I do not intend to support Prensyrrus?" Aldwyn continued. "I am pleased you have accepted me among you—but I can already see your society has grown complacent. Comfortable with its power and its status. With the way things have always been done. I don't consider stagnation a wise course of action. So, now that I am a properly oathbound member of the House of Prensyrrus, I intend to use your own lawful processes to...shake things up a bit, as it were."

He had everyone's full attention. He could feel the press of their tense auras—not just the Council itself, but the guards and the audience—against him, almost like a palpable force. He spread his hands. "I fear you must assist me, though, since I do not know the means by which challenge is offered. Is it a true battle, pitting my magic against yours in personal combat?"

Jesperian's expression cycled between sudden fear and contempt. "Of course not. We are not barbarians, fighting like the common Dim in the arenas."

Aldwyn inclined his head gravely. "That does not surprise me, since it does not seem to me that any of you would be fit for combat. You are all soft, and that is part of the problem. How can you prevail against your enemies when you have allowed yourself to grow weak?"

"We are not *weak*," Bellistrius protested.

"I don't believe you." Aldwyn continued pacing. "You use your power to assert your will over the nonmagical—which is as it should be, of course—but you have allowed it to go to your heads. I have seen it with my own eyes, in Nargul. Your people don't merely claim the status you are due, but many of you have devolved into petty bullies." He shrugged. "That is of no consequence to me. You do as you will. But I do not consider any of you competent to govern me."

"Now, see here—" Jesperian sputtered. "Guards—"

Aldwyn raised a hand. "Guards, hold, unless you wish to lose your lives. I don't say this lightly, and I would regret having to take the action, so please do not force me to do so." He fixed a hard stare on Jesperian, then swept it across the other Council members. "These are your laws, are they not? I am within my rights as a citizen to make this challenge?"

The guards didn't move, though their tension did grow.

The five Council members exchanged increasingly nervous glances, while trying to hide their escalating fear.

Finally, Darnasia spoke with weary authority. "It is your right. You may give challenge, based solely on the strength of your Talent."

Aldwyn nodded politely to her. "Thank you. And the specifics of the challenge? Forgive me—again, I am new here, and have not received complete information."

None of the rest of the Council members seemed inclined to speak, so Darnasia continued in the same dull, *this-has-to-be-a-bad-dream* tone as before: "According to the law, the Talent and only the Talent confers status. Normally, one's level of Talent, and therefore their status, is determined by testing when the citizen comes of age. But any citizen has a right to give formal challenge to any other citizen."

"What occurs if such a challenge is successful?"

"The victor can claim the status of the defeated."

"Including a place on the Council?"

She looked away briefly, then back up. "Even so, yes. The Council, by definition, is composed of those with the strongest Talent among the population."

"And if the challenge is *not* successful," Jesperian spoke up coldly, at last finding his voice, "the challenged may decide the fate of the challenger. At the highest levels, that includes punishments up to and including death, or exile to the Wastes."

Aldwyn stroked his chin again, as if considering. It made sense—if such a rule were not in place, citizens would be constantly challenging each other, which would result in chaos. If one wanted to make such a challenge, they had best be fairly certain they could prevail in it.

That wasn't a problem for him, of course.

He studied them a moment longer, meeting each of their gazes in turn and holding them for a few seconds. He was making them nervous, which was exactly his aim.

"Done," he said firmly. "I therefore, as is my right as a sworn citizen of Prensyrrus, give formal challenge to Jesperian, the leader of the Prensyrrus Council, to be carried out at the earliest possible opportunity."

The audience, which had been silent up until this point, began murmuring and muttering among themselves again. The guards along both walls stood straighter, at attention, waiting for orders.

Aldwyn didn't look at any of them. His attention remained focused solely on the five Council members. Four of them—Darnasia, the dark-haired woman, Bellistrius, and Kratariath—seemed nervous, a little fearful, but mostly resigned, as if they'd already accepted that this was happening and there was nothing they could do about it.

Jesperian, however, was glaring at him. He had good aura control—for a non-dragon, anyway—but he couldn't completely disguise the red flashes of anger sparking around his normal golden yellow. The mere fact that they showed at all told Aldwyn the man was struggling to control his rage.

This would truly be interesting.

"Please prepare the challenge," he said with a dismissive wave toward the Council members. "I care not about the details, as long as it is a fair test of magical ability." He turned back to Captain Celindria, who had remained stoically in her chair since all of this began. "Captain, please show me to my quarters. And thank you all once again for accepting me as one of your own. I have great plans for elevating Prensyrrus's status among its fellow cities, and I look forward to sharing them with you after the formalities have been resolved."

He followed the stunned Celindria out past the stiff guards and the silent, dumbfounded audience without looking behind him. He didn't need to, though—Jesperian was no longer making any effort to conceal his rage. It wafted over Aldwyn's powerful shields like a warm, pleasant wind.

As was almost always the case when a group of more than one person is trying to keep something a secret, rumors of Aldwyn's challenge to Jesperian began to circulate almost immediately. Aldwyn didn't hear them, of course, since he chose to remain in his quarters until the appointed time, but the sheer size of the crowd gathered in the hall where it was to take place told him everything he needed to know.

This time, he chose his clothing with care. Instead of the severe black, he selected an ensemble in complementary shades of Prensyrrus red, spotless and perfect, topped with the customary sweeping, high-collared longcoat the color of blood and piped with black. Every thread he wore was selected to make a statement loud and clear: he was no longer an outsider. He was a citizen of this place, he intended to claim every right and privilege that status entitled him to, and woe betide anyone who got in his way.

Captain Celindria, who had apparently been assigned as his personal aide for the time being, had paused to look him up and down when she came to collect him. She said nothing, but merely nodded respectfully. "I am here to deliver you to the hall where the challenge is to take place."

"Thank you." Aldwyn stood framed in the doorway long enough for her to get a good look, then followed her out. He hadn't chosen to change his physical appearance at all, wanting no part of the faux youth and beauty most of the Talented apparently favored. Among dragons, youth was not a thing to take pride in—age and experience were what they valued, and they didn't judge their peers based on physical appearance. Aldwyn might look slightly out of place here in his usual human guise of a handsome man in the prime of middle age, but he didn't care what they thought of him.

To care would require him to respect them.

They took a teleport pad to a small antechamber, empty except for a couple of comfortable-looking sofas and several paintings and sculptures in shades of red. A pair of windows afforded an expansive view of the city below and of a large, dimly lit hall lined with rows of tiered seats. As far as Aldwyn could see, none of them were empty. Soft, unfamiliar music played, but no other sounds from the crowd made it through from the outside.

"What is this place?" Aldwyn asked Celindria. He didn't trust her completely, but so far neither her aura nor her demeanor had led him to believe she planned to betray him. She was exactly what she appeared to be: a loyal law-enforcement officer who took pride in her duty—no matter how many strange paths it led her down.

"A quiet room." She stationed herself near the door, facing him. "A place for you to prepare yourself for the challenge. As you can see, it is…well attended."

"Indeed, so it appears." He wondered if some enterprising soul had sold tickets.

She shrugged. "It is every citizen's right to be present for a challenge of this level. They chose the largest possible venue, and still had to turn many away."

"I suppose I should feel flattered. When was the last such challenge?"

She gave him an odd look. "There has never been another."

He raised an eyebrow. "Never? No one has ever discovered they possessed enough of the Talent to seek a position among your Council?"

"If they have, they never followed through. The risk is high, as are the consequences for failing. Not many would take such a chance."

Of course not. He supposed he shouldn't have been surprised. "Do you know the form the contest will take, if not direct magical combat?"

"It will be quite straightforward. There will be tests to measure magical strength, sensitivity, and fine manipulation. They will be administered by impartial judges to ensure no favoritism is shown."

Aldwyn had wondered about that. A society that valued the status quo as much as these people did couldn't be entirely trusted not to put a metaphorical thumb on the scale to ensure it wasn't disrupted. He wasn't worried, though. This whole thing was nothing but a formality.

A soft, pleasant tone sounded.

"That is the signal," Celindria said. "Come—it is time."

As Aldwyn followed her outside, he noticed she didn't wish him luck.

From the wings, still hidden from the audience, he could see that the hall was even larger than he'd expected. Not all of it had been visible from his vantage point in the quiet room, but from here he estimated the attendance to be at least several thousand people. He wondered what the total population of the city was. The crowd's individual and collective auras were alight with tension, anticipation, and excitement, their bodies forming a solid, unbroken mass of red like a storm-tossed sea of blood.

This was probably the most interesting thing that had occurred in most of their lifetimes.

On the wide stage at the front of the hall, separated from the crowd by an open area and a line of uniform-clad guards, the mood was considerably less excited.

Instead of the long table from the previous meeting, Council members sat in carved wooden chairs upholstered in a red, velvet-like fabric. All five chairs floated two feet above the stage at the same level. The one in in the center had the highest back, towering nearly six feet above the seat. The two next to it were a foot lower, and those on either end a foot lower than that.

Four of the five Council members were already seated in their respective chairs, leaving Jesperian's in the middle empty. Each wore even more elaborately embroidered robes than before, and magical energy fairly crackled around their bodies and their chairs. All four of them looked straight ahead, staring into the middle distance without acknowledging anyone in the crowd or Aldwyn. Powerful shields, invisible to normal sight but obvious to magical vision, shimmered around them.

Aldwyn couldn't resist a slight smirk. These people were all about the trappings of their status and position. He wondered if they could back up all their hype. It would be amusing to watch them try.

He glanced across the stage to the other side. He couldn't see Jesperian—not even traces of his powerful golden-yellow aura. Perhaps the Council leader had decided he wanted to make an entrance at the last possible moment—or perhaps he was having second thoughts about accepting the challenge. That would be even more amusing. Aldwyn wondered what the crowd would do if their leader declined the challenge and simply handed his position over to the upstart newcomer.

He almost wished it would happen. This group could use a little chaos in their lives.

The dark-skinned Councilwoman floated serenely down from her chair and took her place at center stage. "Welcome, all," she said, her voice magically magnified to easily carry to the back rows. "Thank you for coming tonight to witness this unprecedented event. For those of you who are unaware of the details leading up to it, let me provide some information."

Aldwyn didn't bother listening to the rundown of the last two days' events. He didn't care what kind of spin the Council put on it—he merely wanted to get on with it. He glanced at Captain

Celindria next to him; she continued to appear tense and uneasy, and his obvious boredom was doing nothing but making it worse. He ignored her and waited with growing impatience for the long-winded woman to finish her spiel.

Finally, after several more minutes, she wound down. Every eye in the audience was on her, the crowd's collective aura flaring with astonishment as the details came to light. Celindria was obviously correct: none of them had ever seen anything even remotely like this in their lives. What surprised Aldwyn was that, when he spent a moment giving the ambient aura a deeper scan, he discovered excitement among the trepidation, and he didn't think it was entirely aimed at watching their beloved leader give an upstart newcomer a well-deserved trouncing.

Did some of Prensyrrus's citizens *want* to shake up the status quo?

Interesting.

The Councilwoman was talking again. "The contest will be judged by five of our most esteemed citizens, who have sworn oaths to ensure impartiality."

From somewhere behind the thronelike chairs, five figures strode out and took their places in a straight line. There were three women and two men this time, their robes simpler and more severe than the Council members', but no less brimming with magic. Their faces and bodies still showed the same beauty as the others, but they appeared a little older and more solemn, as befitted their positions. All five stood with their hands clasped in front of them and looked straight ahead, out into the audience.

The Councilwoman allowed a moment for the crowd to look over the judges, then stepped back to center stage. "To begin our challenge, please welcome the head of the House of Prensyrrus and leader of our Council, Jesperian Ansiliath."

Once again there was no applause, but the auras danced with bright, bouncing colors. A few audience members cheered.

Jesperian, clearly a master at making an entrance, allowed the adulation to swell for several seconds before striding out onto the stage, raising his hands to accept his due.

Aldwyn wasn't the type to roll his eyes, but if he was, he'd have done it at that point. The Council leader wore robes at least half again as elaborate as his four fellows, the red fabric and metallic embroidery so bright it nearly glowed against the stage, the multi-colored magical energy crackling around him visible even to mundane sight. Even more than before, everything about him was perfect, with no hair out of place, no wrinkles in his robe, no lines or flaws on his face.

While studying the advances in technology after awakening from his long sleep beneath Alastair Stone's home, Aldwyn had encountered the term "uncanny valley," to indicate something, usually a human figure, that was perfectly formed but somehow *off* in an unsettling way because computers weren't yet advanced enough to render a completely accurate human being. Jesperian had that look now. None of the Talented seemed to notice or care, but Aldwyn didn't miss it.

He remained standing patiently next to Celindria, watching the puffed-up peacock strut around. He was in no hurry to move things along at this point; it amused him that Jesperian seemed to think the crowd's admiration would do anything to change his fate.

Let him have his delusion.

Eventually the crowd settled, the cheers died down, and the ambient aura returned to its previous level of anticipatory excitement. Jesperian withdrew to the far side of the stage, where he stood straight, tall, and confident. Even his aura appeared so— except to Aldwyn's deeper scrutiny, where the cracks showed.

Aldwyn also noticed Jesperian had not assumed what he no doubt still believed to be his rightful spot in the tallest center chair. Was that because of pride, or because his claim to it was no longer secure until after the challenge?

The announcer was speaking again. "Our challenger is a new-comer to Prensyrrus. He claims to come from somewhere 'far away' and has not revealed his history to us, but he has sworn an oath on penalty of death to support and defend Prensyrrus, and therefore has been given the honor of membership in the House of Prensyrrus. As is his right, he has challenged Jesperian to a contest of the Talent. Please, everyone, welcome our newest citizen, Aristide."

This time, the cheers and the bright, bouncing auras were more subdued than for Jesperian, but the level of anticipation rose. Many of the people present were eager to see if Aldwyn could back up his challenge.

Aldwyn strode out where he could be seen, but did none of the strutting or arm-raising Jesperian had. He merely took his place opposite his opponent, crossed his arms over his chest, and waited.

The cheers settled again, and the hall went quiet.

"As you all know," the Councilwoman said from center stage, "It is one of the fundamental tenets of our society that the Talent is what makes us civilized beings. The gods have bestowed it upon those they deem worthy, while denying it to the unworthy Dim. Because of that, it has always been our way that the strongest Talent conveys the highest status. Our newest citizen claims his Talent is strong enough to take his place at the top of our hierarchy. Tonight, we will find out if he is correct."

She took a few steps back, until she stood in front of the empty, floating center chair. "The contest will consist of three parts: raw power, magical sensitivity, and fine manipulation. Our judges and all of you will bear witness, to assure that the contests are fair and without bias." She turned first to Jesperian, then to Aldwyn. "We will begin with the contest of raw power. If you will step out here and face each other in front of the judges, please."

When they did, Jesperian glaring and Aldwyn with what some of his less reverent Earth associates might call a "shit-eating grin," the Councilwoman raised her hand and a glowing ball the size of an Earth basketball rose from somewhere at the rear of the stage and floated to hover in the air between the two of them, with around ten feet of space between each of them and the ball.

Aldwyn studied it. It seemed solid, not merely an orb of magical energy, but with a crackling golden aura around it.

"This contest is simple," the woman said. "When I give the word, you will exert your Talent upon the ball, attempting to push it away from you until it touches your opponent. The first of you to do that will be declared the victor. Do you both understand?"

Aldwyn didn't shake his head in amusement, even though it was tempting. He merely nodded and waited.

The announcer watched them both a moment to make sure they were both in position and ready, then called, "Begin!"

Aldwyn let Jesperian think he might have a chance, playing with him as a cat plays with a mouse. He allowed the other man to push the ball nearly a foot toward him, all the while maintaining an impassive, faintly interested expression as he watched it move.

The Councilman's magic was strong, there was no doubt about it. For sheer power, it might even have rivaled Alastair Stone's back on Earth. But dragons, even in human form, were simply on another level. Aldwyn pressed back against the orb, not allowing it to move any closer but not pushing it toward Jesperian, letting the Councilman tire himself. The bright, crackling aura around it brightened.

Finally, after putting on what he considered to be a sufficient show to entertain the crowd, Aldwyn brought his true power to bear, taking hold of the ball and pushing it slowly and steadily back toward Jesperian. He could have simply flung it at the man, but where was the fun in that when he could give the crowd the show they'd come here to see?

Jesperian's expression changed from faint triumph to narrow-eyed, tight-jawed concentration. His body shook as he reached deep within himself to access more power, but it wasn't enough. Enhancing the uncanny-valley eeriness of his appearance, his face remained pale and flawless, and no cords stood out on his neck beneath the high, red collar of his robe.

The ball moved steadily, passing the midpoint and approaching Jesperian as the man tried harder—but with no success—to push it away. It hovered five feet from him, then four, then three, then two. Jesperian's body shook harder, a growl escaping his perfect lips.

Aldwyn let it hang there, a foot away from Jesperian, for a while longer as the crowd's aura swelled and cheers and catcalls rose from the onlookers. Then, with an almost dismissive gesture, he flung it into the Councilman's chest, hard enough to drive the man back a step. The crackling light around it flared bright red.

The crowd went wild.

Jesperian, for his part, didn't even try to catch it. He looked stunned, his eyes wide and his mouth slightly open, as if unable to comprehend that he had lost the contest. The red light around the ball winked out, and it dropped to the floor with a *thud* in front of him.

The Councilwoman doing the announcing appeared almost as stunned as he was. She flicked her gaze at the ball, now inert and dull gray, on the stage floor, visibly got herself under control, and looked at the judges.

All five of them had turned silently to face Aldwyn.

She swallowed hard. "T-the winner of the first contest is the challenger, Aristide!"

More cheers and catcalls. The audience smelled blood now, even though this was only the first of the three challenges.

Aldwyn merely remained where he was, looking only a little bit smug.

The Councilwoman turned to Jesperian. "By the rules of the challenge, I am formally required to offer you the chance to concede the contest without further action. Jesperian, do you choose to concede?"

Apparently, people here—or at least high-ranking members of the governing body—didn't say things like "*Hell,* no!" Jesperian only shook his head and said in a firm, steady voice, "I do not so choose." But his true meaning was there in his aura, for those skilled enough to see it.

The woman didn't look surprised. "Then, the second contest will commence immediately. The Talent is not merely power—it is also sensitivity, the ability to notice and identify small changes in the ambient magical energy in an area. In this test, we have hidden a tiny magical construct somewhere in this hall before anyone arrived. To prevent any unfair knowledge of the construct's location, it has been moving in an aimless manner around the hall beneath the onlookers' seats since they arrived. The construct emits only a small amount of magical energy, which the audiences' collective auras will effectively conceal. Jesperian and Aristide, in a moment we will dim the lights in the hall. The first of you to identify the location of the construct by casting a marker over it will be the winner. Do you understand?"

Jesperian, grim-faced, nodded. "I do."

"Yes," Aldwyn said. He had already identified the construct's location, and was currently tracking its erratic movements beneath the seats. The growing swell of the audience's auras *was* making it hard to spot, but once he'd identified it, it had been easy to devote a tiny corner of his focus to keeping tabs on it. For a brief moment, he thought about keeping the knowledge to himself, allowing Jesperian the chance to even the contest again.

But that wasn't the way Aldwyn did things. These people believed magical power conferred superiority—and so did he.

"Very well. Then we will—"

Wordlessly, Aldwyn nodded toward the audience, summoning a small ball of glowing blue flame above the tiny construct's current location and directing it to follow its progress. The lights hadn't even gone down yet.

This time, the audience's gasps were even louder, and they made no effort to quiet their astonished babble.

Aldwyn glanced sideways. The Councilwoman's eyes were wide, her mouth open as she followed the blue flame tracing its way around among the seats.

Jesperian stood still and silent, his face a mask of disbelief.

Aldwyn shifted his perception just a bit to get a deeper look at his opponent. Jesperian's disguise dropped away, revealing a jowly, thickset man who appeared to be in his middle fifties, with thinning salt-and-pepper hair, a gut that suggested he enjoyed good food and drink, and pale, blotchy skin. His bulging eyes were still fixed on the hall, but he didn't appear to be looking at anything in particular. His teeth were gritted, a vein twitching along the side of his forehead.

He looked like a man who couldn't decide whether to pitch a massive tantrum or run off the stage, but either way, it was utterly clear he couldn't believe this contest was going so catastrophically against him.

Aldwyn let his perception slip back to normal, where he could still see through Jesperian's disguise but not at the same level of clarity. It was more amusing to watch the beautiful mannequin struggle to maintain his dignity.

The Councilwoman seemed for a moment not to know how to deal with the situation. She took several deep breaths, turned to look at the other three Council members who had remained seated in their floating thrones, then at the judges, who had turned back toward Aldwyn.

She faced the audience. "The winner of the second contest is— once again—the challenger, Aristide."

The applause this time was more hesitant. The crowd's sense of adventure had obviously been energized by the idea of an unknown newcomer besting the most powerful mage in the city, but now that he was actually *doing* it—and not only doing it, but doing it without breaking a sweat—it seemed the more intelligent and perceptive among them were starting to think about what that might imply for their future.

Aldwyn made a courtly bow, first to the audience and then to the Councilwoman. "Am I to understand, then, that the contest is done? I have won two out of the three challenges, leaving my esteemed opponent little chance to prevail."

"No!" The voice, harsh and abrupt, came from Jesperian. The Council leader whirled to face Aldwyn, fists clenched, glaring. "I do not concede! All three contests must be completed. In order to win the challenge, you must win all three."

Aldwyn pondered. "Is this true?" he asked the Councilwoman.

"It is." She offered him a faint, brittle smile. "We do not make it easy, especially at this level, for anyone to challenge our existing structure. If you fail to win any of the three contests, the challenge is unsuccessful."

More pretension. Aldwyn was growing tired of these people and their ways. "Fair enough. Then let us begin the third contest."

Jesperian looked as if he might say something, but all he did was let out a long, loud breath and subside back to his side of the stage. His aura, despite his attempts to control it, was in turmoil.

The Councilwoman looked back and forth between him, the judges, and Aldwyn, then drew herself up. "The third challenge," she said, sounding considerably less calm than before, "is the most difficult of the three. Raw power is the easiest to employ, and sensitivity merely requires one to embrace their connection to the Talent."

She raised her hands, and two objects floated out from the same place the gray ball had come from. "Fine manipulation, however, demands the utmost control. This is not a contest of brute force, but one of concentration."

Aldwyn examined the two objects with interest. Both of them were roughly round and approximately the same size as the gray ball—but instead of featureless metal, they appeared to be composed of overlapping coils of multicolored rope. As with the gray ball, the objects crackled with magical energy.

"These items," the Councilwoman was saying, "are each made up of five strands of rope—one for each member of our Council. Your task is to, using only magic, untangle the knots in which they have been tied together. You cannot touch the ropes, nor break or otherwise damage them in any way. If you do, an alarm will sound and you will immediately forfeit the contest."

A ripple went through the audience, and Aldwyn could see why. As the Councilwoman had pointed out, this task wouldn't allow him to skate by on his vastly superior magical prowess. It would require simple concentration as well—keeping mental track of five different constantly changing variables.

It wasn't something the dragons liked to admit—and none of them did, at least not out loud where any of the humans could hear it—but intellectually speaking, they weren't nearly as superior to humans as they were magically. Their sheer level of experience, the centuries they had existed on Earth, and the structure of their brains as near-immortal beings made up for much of that, and set them well above the majority of humans. Their ability to examine potential problems many steps out made them dangerous opponents. But in a one-on-one contest against a properly motivated, genius-level human—someone like one of Aldwyn's pair of upstart ex-scions—the outcome was nowhere near as certain as it would be in a test of pure magic.

Aldwyn didn't like contests that weren't certain. He'd taken Jesperian's measure magically and found him lacking, but he had no idea where the man stood intellectually.

Ultimately, though, it didn't matter. It wasn't as if he was actually bound by the oath the fools thought he'd sworn. It would be easier for his plans to have these people's cooperation, but if it came down to it, he didn't need it.

"Let us begin, then," he said with a sly glance at Jesperian.

The Council leader smiled. "Yes. Let us begin."

The announcer stepped back. "The judges have examined both constructs and declared them identical. As the challenged party, Jesperian is allowed first choice."

Jesperian nodded gravely to the judges, the audience, the announcer, and finally to Aldwyn. Then he strode forward, examined both floating balls of cords for several moments, then took his place behind one of them. "I choose this one."

"Let it be so noted," the Councilwoman said. "Aristide, please take your place behind the other."

When he'd done as requested, she continued: "There is no time limit to this contest. A silence spell has been employed over the audience to prevent any distractions. You will begin when I give the word. Judges?"

For the first time, the judges deviated from their straight line. They arranged themselves in a circle around the two opponents, watching from all sides.

"Begin!"

Aldwyn immediately settled into a hyper-focused state, where nothing existed other than himself and the tangled ball in front of him. The world dropped away, enveloping him and the ball in a cocoon allowing no outside distractions in. Aside from his shield, which he always kept active at a basic level, it was as if he were alone in a room.

The ball was an interesting puzzle. Each of the five colored cords was the diameter of a man's little finger, all of them entwined over and under each other to create what should have been an impossible mishmash.

Impossible, unless one realized that each cord had been imbued with magic, and each of them resonated on a subtly different magical "frequency." This allowed them to be manipulated independently of each other, and allowed someone, assuming they could employ the proper focus, to visualize the pattern in which they had been arranged.

It still wouldn't be an easy problem, not even for Aldwyn.

But it was a solvable problem.

He didn't worry about what Jesperian was up to, or how far the Council leader had progressed compared to himself. He didn't care. If he, Aldwyn, won the contest, that would be the best possible outcome. But if he didn't—well, that could have its own pleasures associated with it as well.

Either way, it was a win-win situation, and that went a long way toward helping Aldwyn maintain the relaxed state that allowed his mind to operate at peak efficiency.

He quickly lost track of time. He had no idea if a few minutes or an hour had passed, but he was making good progress with the ball. The trick, he'd realized early on, was that all of the knots and twists had to be undone at once, which required visualizing all of them in his mind and manipulating them mentally rather than physically. Once he had them all properly arranged, it would be a simple matter of pulling on two specific ends, which would unravel the whole thing. The difficulty was that if he pulled on the *wrong* ends, it could snarl the whole thing into a hopeless muddle that might be impossible to recover from.

Patience wasn't one of Aldwyn's strongest virtues—but that was only by dragon standards. By human standards, he could keep this up all day.

He turned the ball over in his mind's eye, exploding the visualization to give himself more space to work with. He almost had it. Just a few more angles to be sure, and—

From somewhere at the periphery of his perception, a loud, strident sound rang out.

He stiffened, a portion of his concentration dropping away and the visualization beginning to fall apart. Had he done something wrong? Had Jesperian, against all possible odds, managed to unravel the ball before he did?

He risked letting his focus fail completely to shoot a quick sideways glance, allowing part of his cocoon to fade so he could see what was going on.

Then he smiled, letting the rest of it go when he realized he wouldn't need it any longer.

Jesperian stood on the other side of the stage, his posture rigid, his teeth gritted, his fists clenched so hard they shook. His ball of cords lay at his feet—not carefully disentangled with each color laid neatly out in line, but in pieces, the shredded remnants covering the floor in front of him.

The audience, the judges, and the Council members were all staring at him in stunned disbelief.

What had happened?

Aldwyn didn't say anything. He could afford to wait.

After a moment, the Councilwoman who'd been doing the announcing found her voice. She cleared her throat, shot another shocked glance at Jesperian, then swallowed. "The—er—the challenge is at an end, due to a disqualification." She turned toward Aldwyn, her illusion-perfect face showing uncharacteristic confusion. "By—by our law, the challenger, Aristide, is declared the winner."

The audience members, even though the silence spell had been lifted, were all rigid in their chairs, staring wide-eyed at the stage as if they couldn't comprehend what they had just viewed.

The judges withdrew to the back of the stage, and the five floating thrones descended to the floor.

Aldwyn aimed his magnanimous, patrician smile at no one in particular. "Thank you," he intoned. "I had almost succeeded in completing the challenge when the disqualification occurred. If you wish me to—"

"No," the Councilwoman said. She still looked shell-shocked, but at least she was making an effort. "No, that...will not be necessary."

"As you say," he said politely. "What is the next step, then?"

Jesperian had not moved. He still stood rigidly where he'd been, his jaw working and his gaze fixed down upon the pile of broken cords at his feet.

The Councilwoman glanced at him, then back at Aldwyn. It couldn't have been clearer to him that neither she nor her four fellow Council members had expected to reach this point. He wondered if they even *knew* what the next steps were.

"We—" she began, hesitated, then took a deep breath and squared her shoulders. "As the victor in the challenge, by our laws you are entitled to assume the position formerly held by the one you have defeated."

"Then I am to take my place at the head of your Council?" Aldwyn continued to keep his tone polite and solicitous, but didn't make any attempt to hide the amused glitter in his eyes.

Jesperian wheeled on him, his eyes blazing, his perfect face darkening with growing rage.

Aldwyn remained silent, waiting to see what he would do.

It didn't seem as if the former Council leader knew, either. He continued to glare at Aldwyn, drawing deep breaths. Several times, it looked as if he was preparing to say something, but each time, he let the breath go and didn't speak.

Finally, after several more tense seconds in which the audience, the Council members, and the judges continued to watch without comment, he spun on his heels and stalked off the stage. "You will all regret this!" he snapped before he exited. "He will betray us all!"

And then he was gone, leaving the Council members to watch after him in horror.

"Er," said the Councilwoman. She swallowed again and smoothed her robes. "Yes. You will take your place at the head of the Council. We must—I hope you understand, but this is an unprecedented situation, and we must consult the law to determine the specific next course of action."

"Of course. But I do not wish to be kept waiting long before I can assume my duties."

Somebody from the guard contingent must have gotten an order, because two of the higher-ranking members, including Captain Celindria, stepped onto the stage and faced the audience. "The challenge is over," she said, her voice ringing out. "Everyone will now make their exit in an orderly fashion."

There was a bit of grumbling, but surprisingly not as much as Aldwyn expected. The audience members stood and, moving in brisk, orderly rows, reached the aisles and walked out of the auditorium. Several of them glanced back over their shoulders at the stage, but in only a few minutes the place was vacant save for the guards, the Council members, the judges, and Aldwyn.

The other Council members rose from their chairs. The announcer woman turned back to Aldwyn. "We will see to the details immediately, of course. Until then, you are technically welcome to do as you please. As the new Head of the Council, nothing in the city is off-limits to you. However, if you will accept a bit of advice—"

"Of course."

"I strongly advise you to remain out of the public eye until you have officially accepted your position. We must arrange for security details, access to restricted areas, and other similar needs."

"I understand," Aldwyn said. "I do not wish to cause trouble for you, since you are obviously not accustomed to this new reality. I will do as you ask—but only for a short time. So please see to it that the process moves with appropriate haste."

The woman and the other Council members looked relieved. "Of course. You will be escorted to new quarters befitting your new position. If you desire anything, you have only to ask and it will be provided." She turned to the other high-ranking guardsman. "Borrandar, please arrange a detail and escort our friend to the penthouse apartment in Larinda Tower."

Before the man could reply, Aldwyn gently cleared his throat. "A moment, if you please."

"Yes, sir?"

"I have become acquainted with Captain Celindria during my brief time here. I wish for her to lead my escort detail."

Everyone exchanged glances again. The Councilwoman cleared her throat. "Er—sir, with all due respect, Captain Celindria is assigned to the Public Sector. Providing security for high-ranking dignitaries is not among her—"

Aldwyn held up a hand, still polite. "Councilwoman, with all due respect to *you*, I don't necessary plan to follow your existing protocols, especially given that I do not technically *require* a security detail. When I formally assume my position, I intend to ask the appropriate parties to look into a suitable promotion for the good Captain."

Captain Celindria tried not to look shocked. Her face managed it, but her aura didn't. She shot a quick, furtive look at the Council members and waited.

Borrondar, on the other hand, didn't look pleased. "This is—"

"Unprecedented," Aldwyn said smoothly. "I suggest you all become acquainted with that word, as it won't be the last time you will have occasion to use it. Captain Celindria, if you please—"

With one last, quick glance at the Council, who didn't seem inclined to argue, Celindria gathered a detail of nearby guards with a gesture. "Sir, if you'll follow us—"

Aldwyn smiled. He didn't miss the darkening of Borrondar's aura as he swept past.

They didn't go outside to leave the building. Instead, Celindria led Aldwyn and the guard detail to a hidden teleport pad, this one large enough to accommodate all of them. They reappeared in an alcove in an empty courtyard garden full of lush plants in shades of green, gold, and red, with magical lights twinkling and dancing around them. Surrounding the courtyard were four soaring buildings made of the same pale stone as the others Aldwyn had seen. The architecture featured intricate, beautiful scrollwork and carvings, but Aldwyn found it both fussy and sterile, as if it had been carved by a machine instead of a living being.

"We will need to walk a short distance from here," Celindria told Aldwyn. "The teleport pads inside the building are not yet keyed to you. We will take care of that immediately, of course."

"Of course." He paused a moment to take in the courtyard. "This place to which you are taking me—am I displacing anyone?" *Jesperian, perhaps?* he thought with amusement. That would be the ultimate gesture of disrespect—to not only take his position, but also his home.

But Celindria shook her head. "No, sir. The Council maintains residences throughout the city, to be occupied by visiting Council members from other cities. You will need to add your personal touches to make this place your own, but of course you will have all the help you desire."

"I see. Thank you."

She looked around, her aura tense and alert. "Let's get you inside. I'll feel more comfortable when the building's wards and security magic are properly tuned to you." She offered him a thin smile. "I hope you understand—all of this has happened much faster than anyone expected."

"I assume things do not often occur quickly here in Prensyrrus."

R. L. KING

That actually got a laugh. "Nothing ever happens quickly here, sir."

"Perhaps that is something else that should be examined." He waved her off. "No matter. Shall we?"

She and the other guards led him down a short, meandering path lined with more magical lights and into one of the buildings, which featured a two-story, open atrium with soft music, a small, multicolored waterfall, and tasteful groupings of furniture on several levels. In the rear was an alcove, similar to a bank of elevators on Earth, with two teleport pads. Captain Celindria stepped onto one of them with one of the guards, and motioned Aldwyn to join her. The other three guards took the other one.

The faint wrenching sensation Aldwyn recognized from the teleporter he'd taken from Nargul enveloped him, and a moment later he reappeared in an antechamber carpeted in deep red.

He instantly knew something was wrong when the guards from the other pad didn't appear next to them. He moved fast, but not fast enough. A blinding white light went off, followed by a massive psychic *boom* and a thundering pressure that staggered him back into a wall.

Near him, someone screamed.

Unfortunately for whoever had apparently intended to assassinate him, Aldwyn never lowered his shields unless he was certain he was safe.

Even more unfortunately for them, his shields were more than sufficient to block the explosion. It must have been a big one, because it actually managed to get a small bit of psychic feedback through to him.

He pushed off the wall, taking in the scene as his vision cleared. He noticed several things simultaneously.

First, Captain Celindria and the guard who'd been on their platform both lay on the thick, red carpet, their bodies twisted. Neither had an aura.

Second, the bomb had clearly been of a magical nature, not a physical one, since no part of the building itself had been damaged.

Third, a trio of furtive, black-clad figures stood on the far side of the antechamber, doing their best to hide themselves under an invisibility spell. When they saw that their bomb hadn't even injured Aldwyn, let alone killed him, their auras flared fear and shock so bright it eclipsed the carpet. They spun in place and immediately attempted to run.

"Hold!" Aldwyn thundered. He raised his hand, and all three of them lifted off the ground, shimmering back to full visibility.

"You don't belong here!" one of them snapped, his face a mask of rage.

"If we don't destroy you, someone else will!" another yelled.

Aldwyn glanced down at Celindria's body. He hadn't *liked* her, exactly—as a rule, he didn't consider humans worthy of his friendship—but she had been competent, efficient, and had treated him with respect. Her death was a waste, and he despised waste.

He turned his attention to the floating assassins, allowing a portion of his own rage to show through. "For whom do you work?" he demanded. "You will tell me. *Now.*"

One of them tried to summon a spell, and another attempted to spit at him. Both were approximately as effective—which was to say, not at all.

Aldwyn settled a crushing magical grip on them and began to squeeze. "I care nothing for your miserable lives. You have attempted to murder me—an unwise move, as you now see too late. If you tell me who sent you, I will give you a quick and merciful death."

One of the assassins, the only woman among the group, bit off what sounded like an obscenity, but Aldwyn's translator didn't render it properly.

Aldwyn favored them with a slow, sly smile. "You had your chance. And in any case, I believe I know the answer. It was the unfortunate Jesperian, was it not?"

They tried to hide it. They truly did. Their aura control was superb; they had probably been trained extensively in it, to carry out covert missions for the Council—or for one Council member, at least—or even been under magical oaths. If they'd been trying to fool another human, even a powerful one, it probably would have worked.

But Aldwyn was no human, and he didn't even have to work very hard to spot the sharp spikes of red that erupted from all three of their auras at the mention of the former Council leader's name.

"I see," he said, back to his former calm. There was no more need for rage now—he had his answer, which gave him his course of action.

Without warning or gesture, he contracted the magical field around the three assassins until they screamed, and continued until their bones snapped and their bodies writhed. He didn't do it quickly. He'd promised them a merciful death if they answered his question, but they'd chosen not to do that.

Choices had consequences.

He watched dispassionately as blood ran from every hole in their heads and their screams died first to faint moans and then to silence. Only then did he release the hold and drop them, and only after their tortured auras dissipated did he take his attention from them. He had crushed them so tightly together that their black-clad forms looked like some kind of broken, multi-limbed creature.

He paused a moment, looking down at Captain Celindria. Her eyes were closed, her mouth partially open. Almost as an afterthought, he used magic—uncommonly gentle magic for him—to untwist her body and lay her out on her back.

Then he narrowed his eyes.

He had things to do now, and none of the people of this accursed city—or even all of them together—were going to stop him.

CHAPTER TWENTY-FOUR

THE LIGHTS CAME UP on a scene straight out of Hell.

Stone couldn't waste much time to take it in—partly because something was shooting at them—but his fast glance around as he and his friends spread out on either side of the doors picked up several details.

The whole room seemed to be painted in blood. The walls, the floor, even parts of the crumbling ceiling were smeared with it, adding a gruesome red tinge to the light. Ian had been right: it obviously had been a large surgical theater at some time, spreading out at least fifty feet on either side and thirty to the back wall. Above, a shadowy balcony indicated a gallery where doctors and other visitors could observe the surgical procedures from a bird's-eye view. The floor was littered with broken furniture, gurneys, and the twisted forms of long-destroyed equipment. The smell of decay—and if it was possible, something worse—threatened to overpower them.

Even more concerning were the figures, though. Magical sight revealed several auras—probably the SickBoyz—crouched behind pieces of ruined furniture, and the room erupted with the sharp, echoing sound of gunfire as at least a couple of the gangers fired at them.

Jason and Amber moved with frightening speed. They ducked to either side and, with yells of "*SHADE!*", their agreed-upon code word for the flash-bangs, tossed the small grenades high in the air.

They went off with sharp, thundering cracks and bathed the room in blinding light. Several of the gangers staggered back, flinching and jerking their arms up to cover their eyes.

"Stay with your shielder!" Stone ordered, moving the same way as Jason. He darted his gaze around, looking for the others. Verity, Ian, and Amber had gone left, the mages already flinging spells and Amber firing her gun.

"Fire from above!" Amber had already raised her gun and was shooting at more SickBoyz barely visible in the elevated gallery.

Where was the demon? Stone risked another quick glance around, and this time it rewarded him with a new scene: the collection of prone forms with weak, flickering auras in the shadows of the room's rear left corner.

Everything was happening too fast to dwell on anything for long, though. Stone shifted his magical gaze around, still looking for the demon, but it was nowhere to be seen. The new perspective gave him a fast inventory of most of what they were dealing with, though, Changeling-wise. He caught sight of a gator-looking man diving toward Amber, a pair of wolves still hiding behind cover on the ground floor, a massive ogre and a furry, bearish man, equally massive, behind a large surgical table turned on its side. He thought he caught a glimpse of a small, froggish figure in the shadows in the room's rear, but he couldn't get a good enough look to be sure. As for the ones in the gallery, they'd ducked down again and he couldn't see them—not even how many of them there were. Stone suspected they were looking at the last gasp of the SickBoyz, and hoped they hadn't stashed more gangers around the hospital to hit them with a rear assault.

With a roar, Amber moved to meet the gator-man, but Stone had more problems on his hands. The ogre and the bear, muscles bulging, had hefted the surgical table and, with deep, full-throated roars, were now bulling their way across the floor.

He prepared a spell, but Jason was faster. His angry, triumphant roar rivaling theirs, he surged forward and landed a solid kick in the middle of the table's flat metal surface.

The kick caught the bear and the ogre, neither expecting one of their non-Changeling prey to possess that kind of strength, by surprise. They staggered backward, nearly tripping over their huge feet.

"Mages! Drive them back!" Stone snapped over the comm. As if they'd trained for this, he, Verity, and Ian all summoned powerful, wide-spectrum concussion spells. The invisible walls of energy hit all the gangers on the floor, shoving them back into the rear wall like a hurricane-force wind. The spell wasn't designed to injure them (though that certainly would have been a happy side effect) but merely to knock them off their feet.

It worked for almost all of them. The only ones who remained firmly planted were the bear and the ogre, but the spells' force did succeed in blowing them back several feet into the shadowy area beneath the gallery.

"Truck!" somebody yelled. "They got too much magic!"

"Keep fightin'!" the ogre thundered back, with a quick glance over his left shoulder.

Truck. Stone remembered the overview Gina had given them about the SickBoyz—Truck was the ogre, the gang's leader before the demon had shown up. He was the one who interfaced between the demon and the rest of the gang.

"Focus on the ogre," he said over the comm. Maybe if they could take Truck out, the others would back down.

The problem was, only the mages could easily keep track of which one the ogre *was,* and the fight was moving far too fast to stop and regroup.

"Holy *shit!*" came Amber's voice from the right side of the room.

Stone jerked his attention away from Truck. Amber seemed to be holding her own with the gator, who was trying to snap at her with his powerful jaws and rake her with sharp claws. So why had she sounded scared?

And then he saw it. "Bloody hell..." he breathed.

From the preternaturally dark right rear corner of the room, deep beneath the gallery balcony, *things* were rolling out. Stone couldn't get a good look at them, not even with magical sight, because his brain didn't seem to want to let him settle on them. His best guess was that they were some kind of horrific, writhing grub-like things—but grubs that moved as fast as a carpet of cockroaches. If it was even possible, their presence added to the room's unworldly stench. They were heading straight for Amber and the gator-man.

One way or another, the demon had entered the fight.

"Look out!" Stone yelled. "Back up!" He thought it was going to be a problem—that the gator would try to hold Amber still, or even fling her toward the disgusting wave of grubs.

Instead, the man's protruding eyes widened and his big, toothy mouth dropped open. "*Fuck!*" he yelled. He sounded like he was barely more than a kid.

From the shadows beneath the gallery, a high, keening scream of agony rose.

Stone didn't want to look away from Amber, but he couldn't help it—the scream sounded like someone being pulled limb from limb.

That was almost right. To his horror, the crouching, froggy-looking figure he thought he'd seen before wasn't crouching anymore. The guy had risen up and was now flailing his arms and legs in a desperate attempt to fling off the demon-grubs that had covered him. Apparently the things had teeth, too, and formidable ones, because little gouts of blood had sprouted from multiple points on the frog-man's body. As he staggered out into the light, still screaming, the grubs had already dug deep into his skin and were wriggling happily, chomping away at him. It took only a few seconds before he stopped moving and collapsed into a heap of shining red muscle and guts, as the grubs chewed on.

At least some of them did. The things were small and the fresh prey had slowed them down, but they were relentless, blindly seeking more food.

And—*oh, gods*—were they *growing?*

"Those fucking things ate Mitch!" one of the wolves shrieked, dancing away from the onrushing carpet.

Stone risked a glance toward his friends. Jason seemed completely focused on Truck and the bear, who'd picked the table back up again and were trying to overpower him with it. Verity had her hands full with another of the wolves. "Ian!" he snapped. "Let's take those things out!"

Hoping the voracious grub-things weren't as magic-resistant as the demon itself, Stone pointed his hands at them, summoning a sheet of magical fire. To his left, Ian did the same thing. Nothing in the room was flammable as far as he could tell (other than the other combatants, but they'd chosen their fate), and he couldn't think of a faster way to get rid of that many creatures in one shot.

The creatures weren't magic-resistant, thank the gods. They didn't scream when the fire hit them—apparently their mouths were more suited for eating than vocalizing—but they did sizzle and pop, twisting on the stained concrete floor like thousands of strips of the world's stinkiest bacon. The heat only made the stench worse, and Stone could hear Ian retching behind him. The gator screamed too, but the frog was far too gone at that point to notice more pain. In a few seconds, the flames had reduced the grubs to a greasy black slick on the floor.

Meanwhile, the SickBoyz in the gallery were still firing down on them. Their shots rang out loud and echoing against the hard tile walls. They weren't very good shots, so most of their rounds didn't hit their marks, but a few bounced off Stone's and his friends' shields.

"Somebody take out the ones in the gallery!" Stone snapped.

"On it," came Ian's immediate reply. He shimmered into invisibility.

From the darkened space beneath the gallery came a sudden, rolling laugh, impossibly deep like the rumbling of tectonic plates within the bowels of the Earth.

"Fools." The voice was almost too deep to be intelligible, full of a gargling rasp that suggested the speaker wasn't used to communicating aloud. Immediately following the single word came a wet ripping sound and a sharp shriek, abruptly cut off. A second later, something—two somethings—came flying out of the shadows and landed with a pair of damp squelches on the floor.

"Oh, God..." Verity moaned over the comm.

Stone didn't blame her. The missiles the demon had thrown were two parts of an elderly man, ripped in half at the middle. They had landed a few feet apart, and Stone inexplicably noticed that the old man had been wearing a gray cardigan and checked brown pants. Both contrasted grotesquely with the shiny red ruin that hung out of him.

Suddenly, Stone's rage rose. He yelled before he thought it through, addressing the SickBoyz. "Why are you people doing this? Why are you *following* this thing? It doesn't care about you! Look what it did to one of your own! It's a *demon*!"

From the back part of the room, some of the other SickBoyz were getting up—but not as fast as before. Their auras sparked bright with fresh fear that hadn't been there before.

Stone tightened his hand around the knife. The demon was back there, hiding in the shadows, letting its minions fight its battle for it. But they couldn't let it stay there forever.

"We've got to take these guys down!" Jason said over the comm. He was still wrestling with Truck and the bear-man, all of them struggling to gain the upper hand with the twisted surgical table, which had to weigh several hundred pounds. The second wolf was moving in from the side.

"Fire in the hole!" Verity called.

Stone's quick glance to the side was in time for him to see her pull something from her pocket and fling it toward the group. It hit the ground and shattered, releasing a billowing cloud of purple gas that expanded to fill a space surrounding Jason, the bear, and the wolf.

Jason knew what to expect. The SickBoyz didn't. Several deep roars and pained screams rose from the cloud, as Jason let go of the table and flung his arms around Truck, who had managed to throw himself out of the worst of the cloud. His intent was clear: to knock the SickBoyz's leader back into the choking purple smoke.

Truck had other ideas, though. Bigger and more muscular than Jason in his Changeling form, he wrapped his massive arms around his opponent and spun him around, trying to do the same thing to Jason. Both of them lost their footing and fell into the cloud.

"Fuck!" the other wolf yelled. "Guys, we gotta get outta here!"

The rumbling, nearly subsonic voice filled the room again. "Run, and I'll find each one of you and pull your limbs from your bodies!"

Stone's scar burned. He didn't have a chance to react to the demon's words, though, or to see whether the SickBoyz decided its threat was compelling enough to stop them from running, because at that moment Verity screamed.

He spun around. Another SickBoy, this one with a green face and a long tail, had dropped on top of Verity from where it had apparently been sticking unseen to the ceiling high above. It had knocked her down, its sticky fingers probing at her shield, trying to get through.

Stone quickly saw that Verity's scream had been more of surprise than fear, though. He flashed her a fierce grin as she took telekinetic hold of the lizard-man and flung him, flailing and yelling, into the still-billowing cloud of purple smoke.

It was about that point that Stone realized the room had gone slightly quieter. It took him a moment to figure out why: whoever had been upstairs was no longer shooting at them. "Ian?"

"Got 'em!" came Ian's breathless but triumphant reply. "Two of 'em, anyway—a goblin and a cat. Dad—there's a big hole up here!"

Stone couldn't take much time to listen to Ian. He checked to make sure Verity was all right and then moved closer to Amber's side of the room, still trying to pick the demon out of the darkness. "Hole?"

"In the ceiling. Straight up to the ground floor, I think." Ian spoke fast, between breaths. "The other goblin booked it out of here."

That was potentially useful information—and it might be the demon's escape route if they didn't take it down. "We've got to focus on the demon," he said. "I'll try to keep it busy while the rest of you take out the others."

"How are you going to—" Verity began.

Stone wasn't sure himself—but then his gaze fell on the twisted, metal table Jason and the two gangers had been fighting over. It lay on the floor near the cloud, which was finally beginning to dissipate.

Again without thinking, he reached out with his power and snatched the table. These days, two hundred pounds didn't take much magical effort to fling around. Hoping his aim was good against his unseen opponent, he spun it around and drove it back into the darkened corner where he was sure the demon was lurking.

This was a stupid idea. It had to be. The demon would never stand still and let him—

An enraged grunt, followed by a rumbling sound almost like a sharp intake of breath, issued from the corner. Immediately, something began resisting Stone's magical effort. He couldn't see what it looked like, not exactly—its figure seemed to writhe and shudder in and out of focus. All he could see was that it was only the faintest approximation of a morbidly obese humanoid, covered in lumps and tumors and bits of misshapen, hanging flesh. Its eyes—at least he *thought* they were eyes, since there were at least five of them—burned bright, sickly red with rage, all of them fixed on him.

What he couldn't see, though, was any sign of a tether—the conduit to the demon's home dimension that would mean part of its essence was still there. This close, if it was there he should be able to see it, which meant the demon had almost certainly already completed the process of siphoning enough energy to bring it fully over.

And that made it much more dangerous.

Already, it was beginning to push back against him. Its strength was incredible. Stone didn't think he'd ever fought anything this terrifyingly, physically *potent* before. The demon might not be strong in magic, but magic wasn't everything. This thing was strong in a much more primal way—one Stone would have a much harder time dealing with.

He couldn't hold it. He didn't have enough power to counter it. Slowly but inexorably, it was pushing the table away, shoving itself out of the corner. Stone bolstered his shield, knowing if it broke free, it would be coming after him first. If his shield didn't hold—

Wait.

Wait.

His shield! The one that was as effective against demons as his normal shield was against magical or physical energy.

A mad plan formed at lightning speed as a long-ago memory surfaced in his mind. A memory of a time when he'd been nothing more than a terrified teenager, a barely-trained apprentice facing another deadly being that had been very much like a demon.

He shot the demon a fierce, cocky grin, hoping desperately this would work or the tide of this battle would turn fast—and not in their favor. With a flick of his mind, he reconfigured his demon-resistant shield, encasing not his own body but the demon's, engulfing both the struggling figure and the surgical table.

The demon roared as its steady progress halted. It rumbled and thrashed—but the shield held, driving it back and pressing it against the wall behind it.

For now, at least.

They'd have to move fast. Stone risked a quick glance around the room, identifying what he had to work with. Jason had staggered out of the cloud, streaked with blood but still mobile. Though it appeared he could see now, he was still coughing and recovering his bearings, still struggling with Truck.

Amber, closer to him, had flung the bear-man away and was about to go after him.

"Amber!" Stone rasped over the comm, reaching down to draw the knife from his belt.

He couldn't hold the demon in place for long. Already it was struggling against him, and its strength was mind-boggling. He redirected a tiny portion of his mental energy to fling the small knife, hilt-first, toward Amber. "Use it on the demon! Fast!"

Amber snatched the blade from the air like a grim-faced football receiver, and was instantly in motion. She vaulted away from the bear-man, who oddly made no more than a token effort to swipe at her as she rushed past. With a roar of rage and not a speck of fear in her aura, she leaped toward the demon and made a mighty slashing motion above the level of the table.

It shouldn't have worked. If Stone had been a betting man, he would have put the odds at at least ten to one against. But perhaps there *was* something in the Universe that wanted Good to triumph over Evil—and there was no ambiguity about who was on which side this time. Even the beings they'd called "the Evil" previously were mostly just alien creatures doing what they must to survive. These demons were capital-E Evil with a big old rotten cherry on top.

Amber's strike hit home, ignoring the demon-resistant shield and slashing sideways across the space between the demon's short, lumpy head and its body. The little knife wasn't long enough to come even close to slicing straight through—that would have been too much to ask for. But it found its mark, trailing a stream of black, reeking liquid behind it. Amber dived nimbly out of the way, a split-second ahead of one of the demon's reaching appendages trying to take her apart, and rolled over and over.

A low, rumbling scream bubbled up from the demon, roaring through the room, penetrating Stone's group and the SickBoyz alike. Stone staggered back, his full concentration on keeping the demon pressed back into the wall. They'd wounded it, and if Thalassa Nera had been speaking truth, its demonic regeneration ability wouldn't heal that wound. But if they didn't do something about it soon, it wouldn't matter.

He couldn't hold it long. The slash had wounded it, but it was so huge even that gaping gash wouldn't incapacitate it. If they didn't do something fast, none of this would matter.

But what could they do? Magic wouldn't work. They couldn't risk another attack with the knife. Stone couldn't hold the shield forever, even against the weakened demon. He felt briefly like a dog who'd managed to catch the bus it had been chasing—but hadn't the faintest idea what to do with it now that it had it.

No, no, no—it couldn't end like this! He hadn't led his friends down here into this hellish slaughterhouse to come this far, only to die because he hadn't thought his plan through! They—

From off to his left side came a sudden war-whoop.

Stone risked a quick glance to the side and his eyes widened.

What the hell—?

Jason wasn't fighting with Truck anymore. The two of them exchanged fast, meaningful glances—a pair of combatants coming to an understanding that the mutual threat they faced was bigger than their personal grievances. Moving with speed borne of his new magical abilities, Jason unslung the shotgun and vaulted across the room, across Stone's line of sight.

It was only then that Stone figured out what he planned to do.

"*Jason!*" he yelled, but he wasn't sure whether he was urging his friend on or trying desperately to stop him from doing it.

Either way, it didn't matter. With the smooth, confident movement of someone who'd done this a thousand times before, Jason leaped up, jammed the barrel of the shotgun into the demon's gaping, reeking wound, and pulled the trigger.

The *boom* echoed through the room, muffled slightly by the demon's flesh. Jason screamed and staggered back, letting the shotgun drop and clapping his hands to his ears as Verity caught him with magic before he fell.

"Fucking *do* something, Al!" he screamed.

Stone recovered his bearings fast, all things considered. To his astonishment, the shot *had* hurt the demon. It lay slumped back against the wall, twitching and stunned. Perhaps once its thick skin was breached, its inner bits were more vulnerable.

But the shotgun blast hadn't been magical (a quick thought flitted through and was gone: *could we make magical bullets? Must ask Harrison*), which meant they had only a short time before the demon recovered itself again.

He couldn't risk looking around to see what the others were doing. If he was going to end this, he'd need an idea fast. A way to take the demon out in one shot, with a massive enough injury to disrupt it. It didn't have a tether, which meant it had fully committed itself to this dimension. If they could hit it hard enough, they could destroy it permanently.

But how? What kind of damage could they—

The building rumbled again, not as strong as before but still noticeable, sending a faint ripple through the floor.

Oh, gods, are there more of them?

But then, from somewhere above, came the far-off sound of a distant horn blast.

The idea solidified in an instant.

He gathered energy and bolstered the shield around the demon, wrapping it around to cocoon it instead of pressing it against the wall. The surgical table dropped away with a loud *thud* but he barely noticed it. "Ian! Where's the hole? Light it up!"

"Dad? What—?" Ian was still in the gallery, leaning over now.

"Just *do* it!" Stone was already levitating himself and the demon off the ground.

"What are you doing?" Verity's voice demanded from somewhere.

Stone didn't know where she, or any of the rest of them, were anymore, including the SickBoyz. "Handle this!" he snapped. Already his strength was beginning to flag, and he couldn't let that happen. "Ian, with me! Through the hole!"

Ian didn't argue, which was good because Stone didn't have the cycles to deal with it if he did. He lifted the demon up over the railing to the gallery and looked around for the hole.

Ian had obeyed Stone's command. A bright ball of light hung in the air near the ceiling, illuminating a rough-edged, eight-foot-diameter hole in the ceiling with a big pile of rubble beneath it. From here, Stone could see straight up through their current floor to another similar hole in the ceiling of the parking garage above them.

He didn't slow. He couldn't. His final, mad plan depended on as much speed as he could muster. If Ian hadn't followed him, he might not be able to do this. The demon was already shaking off the stun. He guessed he had less than a minute.

If he'd been wrong about what he expected to see—

But as he popped out of the upper hole and through the broken window onto the grounds, he saw with triumph that he hadn't been wrong.

Still far in the distance but approaching fast, another of the freight trains was barreling toward them, horn blaring and lights blazing.

He didn't know if Ian was there, and couldn't look, so he tightened his hold on the cocooned demon and yelled into the night. "Ian! Wind! Toward the train!"

It was a good thing Ian had inherited his father's quick mind, because he didn't hesitate. The problem with levitation was that it wasn't flight, which meant, on his own, Stone could have moved at the speed of a lazy, drifting balloon—in other words, not even close to fast enough to get him where he needed to be before that train reached them. But with Ian's blast of wind, Stone and his prisoner streaked through the night like they'd been fired from a slingshot.

The train drew closer, its dark form resolving into a multi-car freight special. Its massive black engine, wheels churning and headlight blazing, rushed toward them like a hungry animal sensing prey. The horn blared even louder, filling Stone's senses.

He'd only have one shot at this.

As they reached the spot above the tracks, Ian released the wind spell. Teeth gritted and head pounding, Stone held the struggling demon in place. He couldn't let it go too early, or it would scramble away and disappear into the night to lick its wounds until it could come after them again.

Wait…Just one more moment…

The engineer must have seen something, because the horn formed a solid wall of sound now. The train was too big, and moving too fast, to stop at this point—which was what Stone was counting on.

The demon had caught on to what was happening. It added its rumbling, rage-filled roar to the train horn's cacophonous blare, struggling even harder to break free of Stone's hold.

And then the train was there, huge and inexorable and frighteningly fast.

Now!

He held the shield around the demon but released his hold, dropping the disgusting package straight down onto the tracks.

For a second, he thought it would break free—but then Ian's shield was there too, holding it in place.

The demon screamed.

The train horn bellowed into the night.

The mammoth engine, all hundreds of tons of fast-moving weight, its light as bright as the sun, hit the demon.

It didn't even get time to scream again as the impact blasted it to pieces—and then it was gone as if it had never been there at all.

Stone, floating above and to the side as the train thundered by, thought he got a quick glimpse of the white-faced, goggle-eyed engineer gaping out through the front window before the psychic feedback overwhelmed him—but that was probably just wishful thinking.

CHAPTER TWENTY-FIVE

"**I** STILL CAN'T BELIEVE you dropped a *demon* in front of a *train*," Ren Huxley said. "Stone, you have got brass ones the size of bowling balls. I'm amazed your pants fit."

"Yes, well, let's leave my pants out of this, shall we? There wasn't much of a plan there. A lot of it sort of just... *happened.*"

"Well, it's a damn good thing it did."

They were sitting around a conference table at one of the Agency's shadowy offices in Chicago, the day after what Ren's people were calling the "Abbott Event." She'd brought in food—several boxes of thick Chicago-style pizza—and listened while they debriefed her about what had occurred deep in the basement of the abandoned hospital.

She'd had some information to share with them as well. Her people, along with a squad of local law enforcement officers and, unfortunately, a couple of reporters who'd gotten wind of the op— had shown up a few minutes after the train incident. By that point the fighting was over, though. By the time Stone had sufficiently shaken off the psychic feedback from having his shield obliterated and he and Ian had limped back to the building, the surviving SickBoyz had all made themselves scarce. Only Jason, Amber, and Verity remained, bruised and bleeding but not seriously hurt, to report on what had happened after Stone and Ian had left. Stone didn't care what the SickBoyz had done; he was sure now that the demon was gone, they'd go back to whatever they were doing before, which was none of his concern. The authorities could deal with getting the terrified civilians out of the basement on their own time.

It was a shame about Fish, though, and his friend the goblin who'd tipped him off. Without those two, they wouldn't have reached the scene with enough time to deal with it.

"What about Reggie, Fish's brother?" Stone asked after everyone had told their stories. He still wasn't very hungry, but had accepted one slice of the thick, pie-like pizza, which he was slowly working his way through with a plastic knife and fork. "Did you find him? Did he tell you what happened with them?"

"Yeah," Ren said grimly. "He said Fish lied to you guys—they'd never left town. They were holed up with some friends of Fish's on the other side of Detroit, but he couldn't leave the SickBoyz to deal with that situation on their own. He snuck out when Reggie was asleep."

"What's going to happen to Reggie?" Amber asked. "He's just a kid, and he's not a Changeling so he won't fit in with the SickBoyz. Does he have anyone who can look after him?"

"We're working on it. He's pretty broken up about his brother, obviously, but he said he wants out of the gang life. Don't worry about him. We've got some options."

Stone was only half-listening. Ever since the demon had been destroyed, he'd felt a combination of satisfaction and unease. He'd barely slept the night before, his dreams haunted by images of the misshapen monstrosity, the grubs devouring the screaming frog-Changeling, and torn-apart old man.

It was over—for now. That particular demon wouldn't menace them anymore, but as many as ten more of them were still out in the world, like ticking time bombs that could go off at any moment. He had no idea where they were or when they'd make their moves, but as long as they existed, they'd always be in the back of his mind.

"Al?" Jason's voice cut into his uncomfortable thoughts. "You okay?"

He jerked his head up, and couldn't hold back an amused smile. Unlike him, his friend had taken to the deep-dish pizza like a starving man, and had already devoured several slices. "Sorry. Was just...preoccupied."

At least they didn't have to worry about the story of what had happened getting out—at least not in its correct form. When Stone had come to along the side of the railroad tracks a couple of minutes later, after the worst of the psychic feedback had dissipated, Ian had been right there next to him, shielding them both with a disregarding spell. There had been no sign of the train or the demon. His son had told him that the train had rolled by without incident, allaying his worst fear: that the impact with the demon had somehow managed to damage it, or even derail it. There really hadn't been any other way to take the creature out, but that didn't mean he wanted any innocent people getting hurt while it happened.

Any *more* innocent people, anyway. Again, the old man's wide-eyed face appeared in his mind, and again he drove the vision down. He hadn't asked if any of the people from the SickBoyz's neighborhood had died; he wasn't sure he wanted to know, since he couldn't do anything to change the situation.

"So, now what?" Amber asked. "Anything else you need us to do before we head home? Now that this mess is over, I want to get back to my kids."

Ren shook her head. "No. Probably best if all of you stay away from Detroit for a while—a couple of the less reputable and more overzealous news outfits are still sniffing around, convinced there's more to the story than some big, bad, but one hundred percent mundane dude taking over a small-time gang and causing a lot of trouble. Some of the other gangs and even the Mob think so, too, but they're mostly happy to let it go as long as everything settles back down and returns to business as usual. As I'm sure all of you know better than I do, most of the mundane general public will do just about any kind of mental gymnastics to convince themselves they didn't see anything supernatural." She sighed. "As for me, I've got a funeral to attend."

Stone tilted his head, still thinking of the old man. "Which one?"

"Heidi Royer. Jack's not having one—it was in his will, that he didn't want a bunch of people crying over him. His body's getting sent home for burial. But Heidi…" She shook her head and didn't meet Stone's gaze. "I'm not looking forward to that."

"May I attend?" he asked softly. "I know her death wasn't my fault, but I still feel at least partially responsible. I'd like to pay my respects if I can."

"I don't see why not. It's tomorrow—I'll send you the details."

"We'll all go, if that's okay," Verity said. "The rest of us didn't meet her, but we're still involved with your agency now, even if it's not as much as Alastair is. It's the least we can do."

Ren didn't say anything, but none of them missed the grateful look she shot them.

Heidi Royer's funeral was held at a small church in a middle-class Chicago neighborhood. It was sparsely attended, making it easier for Stone and his group to tell the difference between Heidi's civilian friends, a small group of women in their thirties and forties who looked sad and vaguely bewildered about what had become of their companion; a few distant relatives who'd turned up, mostly older and more formally dressed; and the people from the Agency, who all wore nearly-identical grim expressions and sat in the back of the church. Izzy Freeman, Stone noticed, wasn't present; she was probably still recovering from her injuries.

When the group drove out to the cemetery for the graveside service, Stone was surprised to see one attendee who hadn't been at the church: a large German Shepherd dog. He wore a studded brown leather collar and a leash held by one of Heidi's friends, and had clearly caught on that something was wrong. He stood with his head bowed, occasionally making little whining noises in the back of his throat. Once, he padded forward and sniffed at the casket as if he knew who was inside.

"Aww, that poor dog," Verity whispered to Ren. "Was he Heidi's?"

Ren nodded without looking away from the casket. "Yeah. His name's Bugsy. I don't know what's going to happen to him. None of Heidi's friends or relatives can take him, and neither can any of the agents. I even asked Izzy, but she's allergic. One of Heidi's friends is looking after him for now, but she said if she can't find him a home, she's going to have to take him to a shelter. It's a shame. He's the sweetest dog, and he loved Heidi. She raised him from a pup."

Stone, who once again had only been half-listening to the conversation, noticed movement in the corner of his eye. When he turned toward it, he caught Jason and Amber looking at each other, but didn't think much of it. The two of them often seemed to be carrying on unspoken communications between them.

The service concluded, and the mourners drifted away in pairs or small groups toward their cars.

"Okay," Ren said, "I guess that's it. Thanks again for helping out with this—or, more accurately, for handling it pretty much on your own. Izzy owes you her life, and so do all those Changelings who made it through this mess. You should feel good about that."

"I suppose I do," Stone said. "Don't hesitate to call if something else turns up. Can't promise I'll be free to help, but at least give me the chance."

"I really should put you on the payroll, you know."

He snorted. "Save your money. It's not like I need it. Take what you would have paid me and put it into a fund to help Fish's brother. That's a better use for it."

"Yeah, I'll do that. Take care, Stone." She nodded farewell and walked off, along a row of headstones back to where she'd left her car.

Stone drifted back over to his friends. He'd lost track of them for a few minutes while he'd been chatting with a couple of the other agents. Verity and Ian were talking softly to each other on the other side of the gravesite, but he didn't see Jason and Amber right away. When he looked around, though, he spotted them returning from where several of the other mourners' cars had been parked. As they drew closer, it didn't take magical sight to tell they had something on their minds.

"All right, you two—out with it," Stone said as he, Verity, and Ian caught up with them and they all changed direction back toward their own rented vehicle. "You're up to something."

Jason and Amber exchanged glances, and both of them wore tiny smiles.

"We've done our good deed for the day," Jason said. "Except it's really better for us, so I guess we had ulterior motives."

"What are you talking about?"

Amber's smile widened a little more. "We've been talking to Heidi's friend. Jase and I talked it over a little, and...well...we *have* been talking about getting a dog for the kids."

Stone stared at them. "Wait—you're going to take Bugsy?"

"Yep." Jason slipped an arm around Amber's shoulders. "He's well trained, and only about three years old. We were gonna get a puppy, but it might be better to have somebody who's a little calmer. Like you said before, we already *have* a puppy."

Amber chuckled. "We were just spending a little time with him. He seems to like us—he's a smart dog. I'm sure he realizes by now that his person isn't coming back. I can't stand the thought of him ending up in a shelter. Heidi's friend says she'll look after him for a few days until we get everything ready, so if one of you magical types will help us get him home through the portal, it looks like we're going to be dog owners."

Stone couldn't help smiling, even in the midst of everything that had happened. "I'd be delighted to help. And I can't think of a better place for Bugsy to end up, all things considered. We can—"

He paused as another movement caught his eye. He glanced past Jason and tensed.

Beyond a black hearse parked along the road for another funeral, a tall, severe-looking woman stood looking at him.

A woman who looked like a prim but sexy librarian.

"Al?" Jason glanced over his shoulder in the same direction. "What are you looking at?"

"Er—nothing. Listen, you lot—I need to take care of something. Go on and take the car to the portal. I'll find my own way home."

Ian's eyes narrowed. "Is something wrong?"

He shot his son a significant glance. "No, nothing's wrong. Just—somebody I need to talk to." The librarian was still looking at him. He couldn't tell from where he stood, but she didn't appear to be blinking. He made a shooing motion. "Go on, off with you all. I'll be back soon."

It was clear they were all suspicious, but equally clear they knew by now there wasn't any point in arguing with him. With final long looks at him, they all headed off.

Stone waited until their car had disappeared around a bend before walking with a slow, measured pace to where the librarian still stood.

"Don't tell me—she wants to see me again. Bit soon, isn't it? It's only been a few days since last time."

In reply, the woman silently held out a familiar rolled scroll tied with a green ribbon.

"Not much of a talker, are you?" He glanced around again to see if anyone was paying any attention to him, since he no doubt appeared to the rest of the world as if he was carrying on a conversation with nobody, but aside from a group gathered around another gravesite a short distance away, the area was deserted.

"Fine, then." He took the scroll, and as he expected, the hench-librarian immediately disappeared.

"Thalassa, you have *got* to find a new way to contact me," he muttered, and opened the scroll.

I no longer wish to wait.

Your business with the demon is concluded.

The ritual will occur tonight.

Formal dress is requested.

All will be explained when you arrive.

Following the words, written in the same neat, calligraphic hand, were a set of unfamiliar ley-line coordinates, and a time: *Eight p.m., EST.*

Stone let his breath out slowly, letting his hand fall to his side, crumpling the scroll in his fist.

So much for their series of getting-to-know-you dates.

Well, he told himself, *it wasn't as if you didn't know it was going to happen.* Also, he couldn't deny the little thrill of anticipation that had taken hold of him as he read her stark words. What else did they really have to wait for, at this point?

He slipped the scroll into his pocket and began forming the pattern that would take him home to Encantada.

He only had a few hours—he needed to prepare.

CHAPTER TWENTY-SIX

Calanar

FOR TREVOR HARRISON, the most satisfying stage of any mechanomagical project was also the most dangerous.

He had been working on this one—a massive engine designed to power an airship large enough to carry twenty people—off and on for nearly six months. Sometimes he had help, usually from Errin or Kira Talon, but the last few weeks he'd been mostly on his own. Errin was busy with her own projects, most of which were of higher priority for the smooth running of New Argana, and Kira had been taking a bigger hand in dealing with the administrative necessities the city required as it grew.

That, and it didn't make sense for them to help him with this stage, since he was the only one of them who truly understood it. Despite her unmatched genius with nonmagical mechanical devices and her growing expertise with electronics, Errin didn't have the innate ability to manipulate the complicated magical structures necessary to power the engine's most delicate workings. And Kira, while both an accomplished mage and a master mechanic, wasn't at Harrison's level and probably would never be.

That was fine, though—Harrison didn't admit it to either of them, but sometimes he preferred to work on these kinds of projects alone. He found the ordered, mathematical precision of the designs, both magical and mundane, satisfying, and the challenge of solving problems at this level of complexity invigorating.

He was in the main work area now, the only one large enough to contain the engine. Most of it had been assembled, but pieces of the mechanomagical core—the part that would draw energy from Calanar's magical field and translate it into motive power—lay neatly spread on tarps all around the engine's main structure.

Harrison himself floated inside it, examining the points at which he'd be attaching the other components. It was a tricky bit of both magic and mechanics—he'd need to infuse them all with magic, then bring them all up here, seat them into their final locations, and connect them together without letting the magical fields around them slip. If he lost concentration or made a mistake in the couplings, the best thing that could happen was that it simply wouldn't work, and he'd have to re-infuse the components and start over. The worst—admittedly not likely, but always possible—was that he could blow up some or all of the engine and potentially cause himself serious injury. It was why he'd ordered everyone else out of the work area for the last couple of days.

He took a few deep, centering breaths, then spun slowly in place six feet above the ground, taking in the engine's interior and the points where he'd need to connect the new pieces. Then he redirected his attention toward the floor. With precise focus, he reached out to the first component, gathering and weaving magic around it until it glowed.

He kept his concentration steady as he repeated the process with eight more of the pieces. They ranged in size from a man's hand to a large microwave oven, and the smaller ones were always harder because they required the most precision.

So far, everything was going exactly as he expected it to, but the most difficult part was still to come. Once he had them all infused, he'd need to hold them in perfect balance as he brought them up here and installed them in their housings.

He reached out to the tenth and final piece, his body and his thoughts tense as he devoted part of his focus to maintaining the magical fields around the existing ones while bringing this new one into the matrix.

Just a few more seconds, and—

"Trevor?"

The woman's voice came from down below, out of his line of sight. It was only the one word, but at this critical stage it was enough to disrupt even his legendary concentration. One by one, the potent glows dropped away from each component in reverse order, until all ten of them sat, inert and mocking, on the tarps.

Most people in this situation might have succumbed to anger. Harrison had asked his associates to stay out of the work area while he performed this delicate bit of mechanomagical surgery, and yet someone had defied him. But he knew his people well enough to know if they *had* chosen to defy his order, something even more important must require his immediate attention.

He floated down, swiping his hair off his forehead and drying his hands on the sides of his heavy, multi-pocketed work pants. He hadn't heard the voice clearly enough to know who it had been, but there were only three reasonable possibilities among the women of New Argana: Kira, Errin, or the healer Illona.

It was Kira. She stood patiently waiting for him to descend, her expression grim. "I'm sorry to interrupt you—" she began, studying his face for any sign of anger or frustration.

"Do not be. I assume if you are here, you have a good reason." He used magic to bring a rag to him from a nearby tool cart and used it to wipe the last remnants of grease from his hands.

"Unfortunately I do. Seviath has returned, and he has some troubling news."

Harrison searched his memory. New Argana had grown large enough in the past couple of years that he wasn't as familiar with all its citizens as he'd been in the early days. That, and he'd always been better at keeping track of concepts, mathematical structures, and physical objects than people. "One of our magical agents in Nargul." He set off at a brisk stride toward the work area's exit.

"Yes. He's told me a little of what he has to say, but he wants to talk to you right away."

"Tell me what you know, and take him to the small conference room. I will join you after I have made myself presentable."

Kira smiled a little, taking in his grease-streaked work clothes, but quickly sobered. "He was arrested by the Talented, and briefly imprisoned in Prensyrrus."

"Did they suspect him of any involvement with us?" Harrison swept through the open door, which slid closed behind them. The details were coming back to him now: Seviath had a cover identity as one of the low-level Talented, assigned as a foreman for a fish-packing plant in Nargul. His job while there was to identify potential new prospects, both magical and nonmagical, to bring to New Argana.

Kira had to pick up her pace to keep up with his long stride. "No. They accused him of being too lenient with his workers. They kept him for a couple days, then reassigned him to a garbage-processing plant as a punishment."

"Why has he returned, then?" Harrison reached the teleport pad at the end of the hall and stopped.

"He met someone while he was imprisoned. He says he was suspicious enough at the beginning, but that wasn't what made him return. Trevor—whoever this man is, he's apparently challenged Prensyrrus's council leader. And won."

Harrison didn't show any reaction. He never did. But this was truly shocking enough news to justify the interruption of his work. "Take him to the conference room," was all he said.

When Harrison arrived at the small conference room ten minutes later, impeccably dressed and showing no signs he had been buried in the guts of an engine only a few minutes previously, he found Kira there with a man he faintly recognized.

Seviath was one of the newer recruits to New Argana, identified during a recent campaign to locate more prospects in the sprawling, forested town of Nargul. Tall and lean, he had unkempt brown hair and an expression of cynical good humor. Right now, though, his troubled aura belied the expression.

When Harrison entered, he leaped from his chair. "Thank you for coming so fast," he said. "You're going to want to hear this, if you haven't already."

"Please—sit," Harrison said, indicating the chair Seviath had vacated. "Tell me what has happened."

Seviath looked across the room at Kira, who was standing near the window. He tried meeting Harrison's intense gaze, but couldn't do it so he fixed his own at some point on the wall beyond him. "I got myself arrested. My own fault—I let one of the workers get away with taking time off to care for his sick mother, and of course one of the toadies reported it back to the Talented."

Harrison waited.

The other man seemed unsettled in his presence, which wasn't uncommon, but he soldiered on with his story. "They took me back to Prensyrrus to question me overnight before they decided to punish me by moving me from the fish plant to one that processes garbage. But the night I was there, a man came into my cell. I don't mean one of the Talented guards. I mean he just—appeared there, in my cell."

Harrison raised an eyebrow, but still didn't speak.

Now, Seviath did look at him. "You did hear me, right? He *appeared*. In my *cell*. Out of nowhere."

"That is unusual," Harrison said calmly. "But not outside possibility. They could have employed illusions."

"They could—and he did. He used an illusion to make sure nobody could see him in there, or that we were talking. I was sure even then that he had significant magical power."

From the side of the room, Kira smiled, and Harrison knew why. It wasn't uncommon for people in his presence to unconsciously slip into a more formal pattern of speech, and Seviath was no exception.

"Continue," he said.

"What did the man look like?" Kira asked.

"Not like one of the typical Talented. I'd have thought at his obvious power level and ability with illusions, he'd have looked perfect and artificial, like all of them do. But he didn't. He looked a little older than the usual Talented. Attractive, but not beautiful. Medium brown hair, tall, broad shoulders." He shrugged, and frowned. "He had a definite look of intelligence, which didn't fit with the questions he asked me."

"What did he ask you?" Harrison leaned forward a bit, fully intent now.

"He asked about things everyone should know. He wanted to know about Prensyrrus, and the other floating cities, including how they were governed. He claimed to be a 'foreigner,' from somewhere far away. He said he was arrested when he tried to travel from Nargul to Prensyrrus without authorization."

Harrison exchanged brief glances with Kira, who looked confused. He didn't show it, of course, but he was as well. There were no "foreigners" on Calanar. It simply wasn't possible. The chaotic magic in the Wastes was deadly to everyone except the Travelers, who had a distinctive appearance and didn't interact with the Talented. They rarely even approached the ground cities. Everyone else either lived in one of the five floating cities or in one of the ground settlements below them.

"What did you tell him?" Kira asked.

Seviath shrugged. "I answered his questions, but only in a general sense. He didn't stay long. I didn't quite know what to make of him—I'm fairly sure part of why the Talented took me back to Prensyrrus was because they suspected I was part of the resistance. I thought they might have sent one of them into my cell in disguise, to try to get me to talk."

He shifted in his chair. "I thought it was odd, but I didn't think of it again until after the Talented finished questioning me. They decided I wasn't part of the resistance after all, so they sent me back to Nargul. The next day, I started hearing rumors from the some of the other overseers who still lived in Prensyrrus."

"Rumors?" Harrison rose from his chair and walked to the window, looking out over the rocky green hillside.

"That a newcomer had showed up, sworn allegiance to Prensyrrus and became a citizen, and then immediately challenged Jesperian to a contest of magical talent."

Harrison turned back around. "Kira informs me that his challenge was successful."

"Yes. That's what I hear. They're trying to keep it quiet until they figure out how to deal with it, but word gets around. It was hard to hide it when the challenge took place in front of a whole hall full of people." Seviath swung his chair around to face Harrison. "And from what I've heard, it wasn't even a contest. This newcomer nobody had ever seen or heard of outclassed Jesperian so thoroughly that he stormed out of the hall after he lost. And that isn't all."

"Go on."

Seviath looked troubled. "This truly is just a rumor. They're keeping this one under tight lockdown and I wasn't able to verify it, but I figured I'd better tell you about it in case it does turn out to be true. They're saying Jesperian sent his people against the newcomer after he lost the contest, and the newcomer not only killed the assassins, but traced them back to Jesperian...and killed him as well."

Harrison tensed. This was chilling news indeed. He had no love for the Talented, and in fact refused to set foot inside any of the floating cities except in cases of extreme need. But for the most part, the Councils kept order and enforced their laws, maintaining a society that abhorred deviations from the status quo. They might look the other way when some of their more sadistic citizens caused trouble among the nonmagical in the ground cities, but for the most part they were normally as predictable as clockwork.

If a newcomer from somewhere no one knew had entered the scene with enough magical power to defeat the man who was, by the Talented's laws, the most magically powerful citizen among them, claim his position as head of the city's government, and get away with killing the former leader following a failed assassination attempt, that could lead to chaos. And chaos in Prensyrrus, once the word got out to the other cities, could result in even more chaos. At first glance, a destabilized governmental system among the Talented might be good for New Argana and the resistance—but only on first glance.

Chaos, especially among a volatile group of people wielding powerful magic, wasn't good for anyone. Not the Talented themselves, not the nonmagical people on the ground, and not New Argana. The last time such disorder had reigned, the end result had been the war that had made most of Calanar unlivable.

As Harrison thought the situation through, examining potential implications, Kira spoke into the silence. "Do you know anything else about this man? Anything that might help us figure out who he could be and where he came from?"

Seviath thought about it. "Not...much. As I said, he didn't look like the typical Talented. He was attractive, but not beautiful. He looked older than most of them—I'd say early middle age." He stabbed a finger up, remembering. "Oh, and he spoke oddly."

"Oddly? In what way?" Harrison asked.

He shook his head, frustrated. "I...can't say, exactly. I can't recall it well enough to try to mimic it. He had a precise way of speaking, but his accent wasn't like someone from Prensyrrus, or even Nargul. He was very polite, but...severe. Despite his simple questions, I got the definite feeling he's intelligent."

"What is his name?" Kira leaned forward. "Did he tell you, when he came to your cell?"

"Not at the time. I told him mine, but all he said was that he was 'a newcomer to the city.' I didn't hear his name until a couple days later, after the rumors started getting out." His gaze went fuzzy for a moment as he consulted his memories. "It was an odd name, one no one had ever heard before. Something like... 'Ahr-iss-teed.'" He tripped over the unfamiliar syllables.

Harrison had been about to turn back to the window, but went still at the name.

Kira, of course, noticed immediately. "Trevor?"

Harrison ignored her. "Repeat that, please," he said, fixing his laserlike attention on Seviath.

"Er—I might have gotten it wrong, or misheard it. As I said, there are a lot of rumors. But that was what it sounded like. Ahr-iss-teed." He frowned. "Do you know it?"

Harrison turned away, pressing his hands against the window, his memory returning to a time a few months ago when he and his fellow scion Alastair Stone had faced their "sire"—the dragon from whose line they both descended—in a contest of magical prowess. They had won, but only because they had tricked the dragon into stepping through a portal to a pocket dimension with nearly no magic. With preparation, he and Stone had been able to access Calanar's magic as they did when they were on Earth, but the dragon had had no such preparation.

Stone had introduced the dragon to him at that point; he recalled the words as if hearing them now: "*Harrison, this is Aldwyn*

Aristide Edmund Stone. Our shared ancestor, a millennia-old drag-on, and, if I might be so bold, a right persistent pain in the arse."

Aristide.

Could it possibly be?

Had Aldwyn found a way to Calanar?

Had he, perhaps, managed to figure out how his scions were accessing magic from somewhere else—and traced it back to its source?

"Seviath," he said with measured calm. "When you said he spoke with an odd accent, was it perhaps something similar to this?" For the last part of the sentence, he slipped into a British accent. He was no actor, but he managed a passable imitation of Aldwyn's rich, precise baritone.

Seviath's eyes widened. "Yes—that's very much like how he sounded." Warily, he added, "Do you...know this man? Is he part of the resistance, acting under your orders?"

"He is not part of the resistance." Harrison deliberately didn't answer the other part of the question. He prowled back and forth in front of the window and didn't look at either Seviath or Kira. "One last question," he said, stopping in front of Seviath. He formed a three-dimensional illusion of Aldwyn next to the man and turned it slowly in place. "Did Aristide look like this?"

Seviath studied the image, surprised. "That's him. Not exactly—the man I saw looked younger than this, but that could easily be an illusion. He certainly had the magical talent to fool anyone in Prensyrrus. And he wasn't dressed like that. But I'm sure that was him."

Harrison showed no visible reaction. "Thank you, Seviath. You were correct to come to me with this."

The other man rose as the illusion faded. "What do you want me to do now?"

"Return to Nargul, continue with the job they have assigned you, and see what else you can learn about this new situation in

Prensyrrus. I suspect it will not be long before the news extends to all the cities, if it hasn't already."

Seviath looked relieved to get out of Harrison's intense presence. "Thank you. I'll let you know if I hear anything else."

He departed, leaving Kira alone with Harrison.

She looked troubled. "Is this something we need to be concerned with?"

He didn't answer.

"Trevor?"

It took Harrison a moment to pull himself from his thoughts. He jerked his head up and settled his gaze on Kira as he replayed her words. "Yes."

"Who *is* this man? How do you know him? Is he a threat to us here?"

He considered how to respond to that. "I believe he is…someone I know from my other world. I don't know why he is here, or how he came to be here." Turning away from her, he gazed back out the window. "Is he a threat to us? I don't know."

"Do we need to make any preparations?"

Harrison arrived at a decision. "Not at this time. Contact our other high-level agents in the other cities, including Olystriar in Temolan. Find out what they know, but don't tell them anything else. We must have accurate information, not rumors."

"And what are you going to do while I'm doing that?"

"Nothing, yet. Not until we have more concrete details. But if Aristide is indeed the man I think he is, I must contact an old associate. He will want to know about this new development, and perhaps he will have thoughts on our next steps."

"Is this someone I know?"

"Yes. I will tell you more after I have spoken with him."

Without giving her a chance to answer, he swept from the room. Once again deep in thought, he didn't stop until he reached his penthouse. There, he stood at the window. The view was the same as it had been from the conference room, albeit from a much higher vantage point, but he paid it no attention.

Aldwyn, on Calanar.

If it did turn out to be true, Harrison could not see any way in which it would mean anything good for their world.

CHAPTER TWENTY-SEVEN

S TONE DIDN'T EVEN TRY to anticipate where the unfamiliar ley-line coordinates Thalassa's hench-librarian had delivered would take him. All he knew was that they didn't point at her New York City penthouse. He did wonder why, since that seemed to be where she was most comfortable, but it never paid to think too hard about why dragons did what they did.

When the scene solidified around him, he had to stop and marvel at it. He was glad he hadn't wasted his time with speculation, because he wouldn't have come close to the truth.

He stood on what looked to be a high mountaintop. The air, moving in the faintest of breezes, was warm and pleasant, with a crisp, woodsy scent. Above, a million stars shone against a velvety blanket of pure black.

Definitely not New York City, then.

He paused a moment, looking around with magical sight, but Thalassa was nowhere to be seen. It was obvious which way he was meant to go, though: a path lined with flickering magical lights stretched out before him, leading into a stand of shadowy trees.

He didn't bother to call for her. He didn't want to break the spell of this beautiful place, and there would be time enough for conversation later. Instead, he moved slowly and deliberately up the path toward the trees.

As he drew closer, he realized two things about them: first, they didn't have auras, and second, they were wrong for the location.

Stone wasn't as well-traveled as his adventurous son, but over the course of his life he'd visited many parts of the world either on business or on holiday. He'd always been a city boy, though, preferring metropolitan areas and pastoral countryside to exotic wilderness, so it was entirely possible—likely, even—that he wasn't even close to familiar with every kind of tree that grew on Earth.

Even so, he was fairly certain these lush specimens with their artfully twisted trunks and low-hanging branches didn't occur naturally this high above sea level.

He smiled. Of course—this was Thalassa Nera he was dealing with. Naturally, she'd want to control every variable of their experience here. He wondered if it was part of the ritual, or if she'd just altered the scenery to her liking.

He continued along the path, which rose at a gentle angle. As he entered the forest, the interlocking branches and deep green leaves high above formed a natural tunnel, blocking out the sky. The overall feeling wasn't oppressive or creepy, though; to the contrary, the trees seemed to enfold him in a comforting, reassuring cocoon, inviting him to continue along the path.

Up ahead, the faint sounds of music reached him. It didn't get any louder as he continued, though, but remained at a level barely above subliminal—present, but not intrusive.

The trees thinned and then parted to reveal a clearing. Stone paused before stepping into it, taking in the scene.

Once again, he didn't know what he'd expected—perhaps an intricate circle with a carved wooden canopy bed at its center, like something out of one of the old, darker-edged fairy tales. What he *did* see was a simple table with two high-backed wooden chairs in the middle of a flat patch of luxuriant green grass. A bottle and two glasses sat on the table, along with a lit candle and two place settings. Beyond, a narrow brook meandered by, adding its whispering notes to the rustle of the trees and the music.

Thalassa stood behind the table, facing him. Her expression and aura were both unreadable, but something about the way she held herself, like a panther crouching stock-still on a high branch in preparation to pounce on unsuspecting prey, suggested intensity.

"Good evening, Thalassa. Quite a lovely venue you've chosen here." He studied her without appearing obvious about it, well aware that she'd know—and probably expect it—either way. She wore a long gown of the same dark green as the trees' leaves, as body-hugging as the others he'd seen her in but with a high slit up the left side, emphasizing the beauty, power, and confidence in her slim figure. Her hair, which had been done up in an elaborate style last time they'd met, hung loose over her pale shoulders. Her makeup was so perfect it was probably part of her illusion, emphasizing her brilliant green eyes and high cheekbones.

"Alastair." She inclined her head, a regal queen taking her due from a favorite subject. She was checking him out too, and made no effort to hide it.

He was glad he'd taken her "formal dress" request seriously. This time, he'd chosen to return to the full black tuxedo similar to the one he'd worn for their first encounter, taking a chance he might be overdressed for whatever else she had planned. He'd chosen wisely, apparently. "Decided you were done with our little dates, did you?"

She flashed a wry, small smile. "You did say—" Her gaze shifted a moment as if she were recalling something "—'give me a ring when you are ready and you won't keep me away'." Her green eyes settled back on him as she nodded toward the table. "I trust your demon situation went well."

Keeping the same calm, outwardly casual pace as before even though his insides were humming in pleasant anticipation, he walked to the table and pulled her chair out for her. "I'm not sure 'well' is the right word for it—too many people died for that—but the demon's been sorted."

"I heard you dropped it in front of a train. Very innovative." She settled gracefully into the chair, allowing him to push it in for her.

Stone took his place opposite her, wondering how she'd heard that. He supposed dragons had information networks he couldn't begin to comprehend, so he didn't bother asking. "Again, 'innovative' might be giving me too much credit. I didn't have a bloody clue what I was going to do with it when we went in there, but thankfully the opportunity presented itself and I took it." He chuckled. "Your knife was a big help, though—one of my more physical friends managed to get close enough to slice its throat, or at least whatever passed for its throat, and another one shoved a shotgun barrel in the hole and gave it some fresh ventilation. Without that, I wouldn't have had a chance to stun it long enough to get it to the train. So, thank you for that."

"I am pleased it was useful."

He tilted his head at her, trying to decide if she really was or if she was just being polite. Since he'd never experienced her being polite for politeness's sake, he chose to take her words at face value. "Still got at least a few more of them out there, but I'll be honest—I'm not in a hurry to hunt them down. As long as they keep their heads down and don't cause too much trouble, I've got other things I need to be getting on with."

"Indeed." Her eyes narrowed, and her lips quirked in a sexy, predatory smile. "Speaking of other things," she purred, "let us have no more talk of demons this evening, shall we?"

"I'm happy to oblige." He nodded toward the place settings. "Are we having dinner?"

"We are. Only a light meal, but there are—things we must yet discuss before we begin the ritual."

That wasn't a surprise, since she'd never given him the details. He remained silent, waiting to see where she would go with this.

She raised a hand and a soft, pleasant *bong* sounded from somewhere in the forest, as if someone had struck a far-off gong. Seconds later, a figure emerged into the clearing bearing a tray.

Surprisingly, it wasn't one of the ever-present librarians Thalassa seemed to employ for all her menial tasks. Instead, a humanoid creature that appeared to be made of green and gold sparkling air drifted over, placed bowls in front of Thalassa and Stone, then departed. It made no sound the entire time it had been present.

"Did you give the librarians the night off?" Stone asked. The bowls contained a light, steaming lobster bisque that smelled delicious. He picked up the wine bottle, and when Thalassa didn't object, popped the cork and poured them each a glass.

"They did not seem appropriate for this evening." She took a delicate taste of the wine, her gaze still fixed on him.

Stone was about to ask why, but then got it. Given what they were planning tonight, the presence of other women—even women who were probably elementals or illusions—wouldn't fit the mood.

They remained silent as they ate their soup. The music was just barely loud enough to make out the melody, which Stone didn't recognize. It sounded classical, but with an exotic overtone he'd never heard before. He focused on it as he pretended to concentrate on the soup, but in reality kept flicking glances at Thalassa. His anticipation combined with a little unease as he remembered their last encounter. She must be ready now, or she wouldn't have summoned him here—but what had she done to *get* ready? It went against everything he was to share a bed with a reluctant or unwilling woman. He'd slept with plenty of willing partners where both of them had considered it nothing more than a night's trifle, a bit of pleasure that didn't imply any ongoing commitment—but those women had been unequivocally and unquestionably willing. Enthusiastic, even.

"You seem troubled." Thalassa had finished her soup and was now watching him over the top of her crystal-clear wineglass. "You are not having regrets about our arrangement, I hope."

Yes, because that would work out so *well for me,* he thought. "No. Not at all. I thought perhaps…*you* might be, though."

She didn't answer right away, instead choosing to take another sip of wine and continue to watch him for a while first. Finally, she said, "This must be done. This opportunity is far too valuable to let it slip away."

He frowned. "If you'll forgive me, Thalassa, that's not terribly encouraging. I know you don't give a damn about my delicate male ego, but you've got to understand—if you're not on board with this whole thing, I won't go on with it."

Her eyes, almost unnaturally green, narrowed dangerously. "You have given me your oath."

"Yes, and I absolutely intend to see it through. But my impression from our previous encounters was that you were fully in favor of the situation. The *whole* situation."

"I do not follow." Her chilly expression hadn't thawed in the slightest.

He sighed. How could dragons be so intelligent and yet so thick? "Thalassa, let me spell it out for you. It's been a long time since I've been as physically attracted to a woman as I am to you. You're beautiful, you're brilliant, and you're sexy as hell. You still scare me—I'd be an idiot if you didn't—but I'm willing to overlook that because, despite the oath, I *want* to do this. But if it's going to work, *you've* got to want it too. Not just the results. The actual process. Otherwise, you won't get what you want."

Something shifted in her gaze: a hunger joining the chill. "You would deny me?"

Damn. Was it possible she *wasn't* being thick? Did she truly not understand? "Look—I've had a lot of experience with this sort of thing. But the one thing I've never done, never will do—*can't* do—

is do it with a woman who isn't willing. This isn't a 'lie back and think of England' sort of thing. You've got to *want* it, or it won't work. I won't be able to do it if you're hesitant or uncomfortable. Am I making myself clear, or have I got to spell it out for you with a human male anatomy lesson?"

Her steady gaze shifted again. "You are saying you will not be able to perform the act."

Finally. He set his wineglass down and leaned in toward her. "Yes. That's exactly what I'm saying."

"I could arrange certain alchemical mixtures to—"

"*No,* Thalassa. There will be no alchemical mixtures, or mental gymnastics, or anything else unnatural. At least not any that aren't necessary for the ritual. You're asking me to help you produce a *child.* That means a lot to me, but those are my terms. Take them or leave them." His voice was rising, and he quickly dropped it back to a normal level.

She didn't answer, but she was looking at him with more intensity than before. He could almost see the wheels in her head turning as she sorted through possible replies.

"I'm not asking you to have any feelings for me. No emotional commitment. I get that, and I don't want it either. But—"

"I want you," she said, her voice husky. She looked as if she were seriously considering lunging across the table at him. "I do not understand this feeling. I have never experienced it before, and it…troubles me."

He chuckled. "Trust me—I get it. But that's the thing about being human: sometimes we don't get to pick who we're physically attracted to. Do you think I would have chosen to have my hormones curdled by a nasty dragon lady who doesn't like me and has the power to wink me out of existence if I offend her?"

She regarded him a moment, and then her lips twitched up in the slightest of smiles. "From what I know of you…yes."

The growing tension, or at least some of it, ebbed away, leaving Stone amused. "Well, you'd be right. I've always had an unfortunate thing for dangerous women. So you can rest assured, even though I'm still not entirely in favor of fathering a child I might never see, in a physical sense, all systems are go from this end." He leaned in, softening his voice. "I promise, Thalassa—if you'll trust me, I'll show you how much pleasure that human body of yours is capable of. You might be surprised."

She didn't look like she believed it, but her expression grew thoughtful. She nodded once, then glanced off to the edge of the clearing. Immediately, the sparkling green-and-gold humanoid returned again, this time bearing a tray with two covered plates. It placed one in front of each of them, removed the covers, and silently departed.

Stone spared only a brief look at the meal—it was fish of some sort with a few asparagus spears, artfully presented and exquisitely prepared—before returning his attention to her. "Will you trust me?" he asked gently.

She didn't touch her food, but instead met his gaze across the table. "I...will," she said at last.

A small part of him found the whole situation amusing: if anyone had told him a couple of years ago that he would be spending his evening holding the hand of a nervous dragon virgin during a ritual to produce a half-dragon child, he'd have suggested they seriously consider dropping the dosage of whatever recreational pharmaceuticals they were indulging in.

Still, that probably wasn't the strangest thing that had ever happened in his life, and he'd learned to roll with these sorts of things.

Plus, even after everything, his body was still telling him in no uncertain terms that it wanted him to get on with this.

It was a good thing his brain was still fully in charge. He sampled the fish to give Thalassa a bit of space (it was as delicious as it looked, the meal obviously designed to be artistic as opposed to filling), then asked in a more conversational tone, "You said we were eating first because you had some things to tell me about the ritual. Suppose you do that so I know what I'm getting myself into? I've got to admit, this might not be the most romantic thing to say, but as a scholar I'm fascinated, not only to view a dragon ritual but actually participate in one. Though I doubt I'll be getting any papers out of this particular bit of study."

Surprisingly, she looked almost grateful for the change of subject. "The ritual is not complex. Its purpose is twofold: to ensure conception, and to maximize the child's magical potential."

Stone shivered as a memory he'd tried hard to forget surfaced. He tried to quell the reaction before Thalassa noticed.

But of course she noticed, because she never missed anything. She tilted her head. "Is there a problem? I would not have thought either of those purposes would come as a surprise to you."

"They're…not. Pretty much what I expected, actually."

"Your reaction suggests otherwise."

For a moment, he thought about waving her off, telling her it was nothing and moving on. But the way she was watching him— was she truly interested in his answer? The words popped out before he could stop them: "That…sort of happened to me."

He didn't think it was possible to rattle her, but her eyes widened slightly. "Oh?"

"Long story. I've never told anyone else. But I'm told a similar ritual was performed on me before I was born. To maximize my magical potential."

"Indeed." She looked intrigued, but also troubled. "I was not aware human mages participated in such rituals."

He gave a bitter snort. "Most of them don't. My mother and my grandmother were a couple of madwomen. I don't really want to talk about the details, if you don't mind. You just caught me by surprise a bit. Please, go on."

It appeared for a moment that she might press it, but finally she let her breath out and continued. "The ritual for me is somewhat different than it would be for a male dragon, since I will be carrying the child. Because this has never been done before, no research was available. It was necessary for me to modify the ritual on my own."

Stone sipped his wine. "Are you receptive to questions from the class? Because I've already got several."

She waved a thin, graceful hand in a 'go on' gesture.

"You say you'll be carrying the child. Just like a human woman? Nine months, bizarre cravings, the whole bit?"

"Nine months, yes. As for the other more…unpleasant aspects of human pregnancy, I have various means of mitigating them."

"Well, that's handy, I suppose. So, I won't be getting midnight calls from you asking me to fetch garlic ice cream and mint-infused escargot?"

She gave him a look.

He raised his hands in an amused warding gesture. "Okay, okay, sorry. So…this modified ritual. Tell me about it."

She picked at her fish, but it was clear she wasn't any more interested in it than he was. "There is a circle, which I have already prepared. It will be necessary for you to add a few final touches to it, to imbue it with your own essence."

Stone wondered how successful he would be at making alterations to a dragon's circle, but he supposed she wouldn't ask if she didn't think he could do it.

"Both of us must consume an alchemical mixture, designed to enhance our compatibility."

"Enhance our compatibility?" He wasn't sure how he felt about downing unfamiliar alchemical concoctions. From the way she'd described it, she would be the only one to do that.

Her smile was small and predatory, but not chilly. "Yes. To ensure that the conception occurs properly. Despite the fact that, for all intents and purposes, I am indistinguishable from a human in this form, I am not a human. There are differences, and without aid, they will be enough to prevent the child's conception. It is impossible for any dragon, male or female, to produce offspring with a human without intent and magical intervention. You do not wish to do this more than once, do you?"

"That depends." He met her gaze with a challenging one of his own. "The ritual, maybe not. The other bit, though—"

She gave him a 'hush, you' look. "I assure you, the mixture will have no obvious effect on you, mentally or physically, and will clear from your system in a few hours. I could have put it into your wine and you would not have noticed."

He shot a sharp glance at his glass. "But you didn't."

"No, of course not. I gave you my word I would not deceive you in any way."

He still didn't like it, but if he couldn't trust a dragon to know her alchemy, he was in more trouble than this. "Okay. So we drink this mixture to get our physiologies in sync. What else?"

She tilted her head, and a brief shadow passed across her face. "This is the part with which you will likely find discomfort. As will I. But it is a necessary component of this ritual."

"This ritual? This particular one, you mean? As opposed to the one the male dragons use?"

"Just so, yes." When Stone didn't reply, she continued: "In order to ensure the ritual functions correctly, we must join not only physically, but mentally and aurically."

Stone tensed. "And what...does that mean, exactly?"

Thalassa's expression was serious, and she didn't look away from him. "I am no more comfortable with it than you are. The male dragons must perform a version of it as well. It is an interval of intense vulnerability, which is one of the main reasons many more scions do not exist. Even for the males, it is not a simple or altogether pleasant process."

"Wait a minute," Stone said, narrowing his eyes. "You're telling me that *dragons* open themselves—their minds, their auras, their...*essence*...to mere humans? Not even scions, but normal human mages?" He tried to imagine someone like the lofty Aldwyn doing that, and couldn't.

"They do. But they get around it by wiping their human partner's memory of the event after the act is complete. The human woman believes only that she had a pleasurable experience with a powerful stranger, but cannot remember the specifics."

Stone glared at her. "You are *not* going to wipe my memory, Thalassa. If that's what you've got planned, I'm out. I'll take Door Number 2. I'm sure one of the other dragons can help me sort out the pain."

She raised a hand, and actually looked concerned. "No, Alastair. I am not going to wipe your memory. You have my word. That...is why this is so troubling."

His glare turned to an astonished stare as the implications of that sank in. "This is harder for you than it will be for me, isn't it? You're going to open yourself up to me. And you're going to let me remember whatever I discover." He let his breath out. "Bloody hell. You must really want this child."

"More than anything I have ever wanted in this world."

He was fairly sure this was the most earnest thing she'd ever said to him, with no sign of her usually haughty, prickly distance. He looked down at his plate, his thoughts whirling.

Could he do this? Open his mind, his thoughts, his emotions fully to another person—a *dragon*—without any of his normal barriers in place? He'd mostly come to terms with the idea that he'd be fathering a child he might never know, but to allow a dragon that kind of access to his innermost secrets?

He leaned back in his chair. "Thalassa, I—"

"Before you say anything else, keep this in mind: I will be as vulnerable to you as you are to me. You will likely learn things about me I would prefer remain hidden, as I will about you. It is the nature of the ritual: that trust is an integral part of ensuring that the conception occurs."

Stone fought through his careening thoughts. "And you couldn't have told me this *before* I agreed to it?"

"I did not know all of it. As I said, it was only after you agreed that I began my research into the specifics of the ritual. Before that, I had no need. The knowledge, combined with the fact that I would never have the chance to put it to use, would have been…painful."

He stared at her, surprised at himself. Was that a little compassion seeping through his reluctance? Compassion for *Thalassa*? As someone who had never experienced a deep desire for offspring, he couldn't fully understand all the implications of what she was telling him. But he was certainly perceptive enough not to miss the deep sadness, combined with a scrap of hope, in her demeanor. This was definitely uncharted territory.

"So…" he said slowly, "why tell me all of this? You probably could have got by with a lot less detail—and you could have wiped my memory without ever telling me it was an option. Left me the memory of our night together, but taken away the part where we bare our souls to each other. Why didn't you?"

She looked suddenly tired, as if she had been fighting something for a long time and was finally letting it go. "Several reasons. The most important one is that it would not have worked."

"No? Why not?"

"Because you are not a normal human mage. You are a scion. Recall that this union will be the first of its kind since we arrived on this world. Scions carry our blood—strong ones like you and Mr. Harrison more than others."

"Wait a minute," Stone said, catching on. "You *can't*, can you? You can't wipe a scion's memory."

"We can, with great difficulty—although it would violate our agreement never to harm a scion. But in the case of this particular ritual, attempting to do so has a high chance of producing…unexpected consequences."

"Such as?"

She gave a brittle smile. "I do not know—hence the 'unexpected' part. But it could prevent the conception from taking hold properly, it could adversely affect the child, or it could damage you. I do not wish any of those to occur."

He tilted his head. "Any of them? Even hurting me?"

Her expression hardened. "Do not assume any feeling that does not exist, Alastair. But I *am* grateful to you for assisting me in this process. I am well aware that if you had chosen not to accept my alternative to your oath, my chance of producing a child would remain nothing but a vain hope. I see no reason to cause you harm."

Stone didn't bother asking why, if he'd turned her down, she wouldn't simply have approached Harrison. The man was so emotionally closed-off he made Stone look happy and well-adjusted by comparison. There was no way he would ever agree to opening himself up like that, and Stone suspected Thalassa knew it.

So he was the only game in town.

To his surprise, it finally settled in that Thalassa *didn't* hold all the cards here.

She *needed* him. She'd been trying to hide it, but it was true.

To his even greater surprise, that thought, more than anything else, calmed some of his concerns.

Not all of them, though. He stroked his jaw and pondered. "Suppose I do go along with this—agree to give you access to my innermost self, I mean. What are you going to do about it?"

"I do not understand."

"Yes, you do. You don't know what you're going to find in there. Suppose you discover something you can use against me in the future? What's stopping you from doing it?"

A brief, odd look flashed across her face before her mask was back in place. "Nothing except your trust in me. As I have told you before, Alastair—I have no particular interest in your activities beyond those that affect our…arrangement. I would have no need to use anything I learn about you against you, because after our bargain has been completed, we will both go our separate ways and continue our own affairs. How much contact have you had with me in the past?"

She had a point, he supposed. But still—

This time, the brief look was frustration. "If that is not sufficient to convince you—I believe you humans have the concept of something called 'mutually assured destruction.'"

He jerked his head up. "What?"

Thalassa chuckled mirthlessly. "Not actual destruction. But you will no doubt learn things about me that would be valuable bargaining chips if shared with others of my kind. As you must trust me, I must likewise trust you."

That was a good point. Part of him, the pathologically curious part, wondered what he'd learn about her. "So, you're not going to insist on another oath that I don't reveal anything or I'll go up in a column of flame."

"No. Trust is vital to the success of this ritual. I will do nothing to jeopardize it—even if it means leaving you with information you could use against me."

Stone looked down at his plate. He'd barely touched the light meal, but he'd already finished his glass of wine. Instead of pouring another, he rose and began pacing the small clearing. "This is a lot to drop on me, Thalassa. You know that, right?"

"I do." She remained seated, her hands on the table. Her head didn't move, but her eyes followed him as he moved around.

He realized she was waiting for his answer. She'd told him everything she had to share, and now it was up to him whether this evening would continue.

With a word, he could put an end to her dreams of bearing a child.

He wasn't sure he liked having that kind of leverage over a dragon—especially not *this* dragon. It seemed rather like holding the proverbial tiger by the tail, and there were many more ways he could get his head bitten off than he could tame the tiger.

But as he looked into her eyes, he noticed something he'd never seen there before.

Vulnerability.

It wouldn't last, of course—she'd be back to her cold, prickly self before he knew it—but for just this moment, she was already laying herself bare to him, before the ritual even began.

Putting her deepest desire in his hands.

He ran his hand through his hair and turned away from her, looking at the twisted but oddly beautiful trees surrounding the clearing.

This might be the most important decision he ever made in his life. Whichever way he chose, many things would change for him. There was no way to avoid that.

Still, ultimately, it wasn't a decision at all.

Slowly, he turned back around to face her, a slow smile touching his lips.

"Let's do this, Thalassa. Otherwise, I'll have got myself all dressed up for nothing."

Her answering smile was more genuine than any he'd ever seen her give him.

He didn't have long to speculate about where the actual ritual would take place—would she whisk him back to her New York City penthouse, or take him somewhere he'd never been before?—because as soon as he gave his agreement, she rose gracefully and nodded toward the other side of the clearing, behind him. "Let us go then, unless you wish to finish your meal."

"Er—no. I'm sure it's quite delicious, but…not a priority to-night." Damn, but she was sexy. He'd managed to put those impulses aside for a while in favor of discussing aspects of this ritu-al that could have profound effects on him for a long time in the future, but now that they'd sorted the details, his desire for her was making itself known again.

It probably had something to do with the fact that the fleeting vulnerability had vanished, replaced by her usual brilliant, danger-ous intensity. He'd never been a knight in shining armor type, longing to swoop in and rescue the damsel in distress. He much preferred women who could just as easily rescue *him* if need be—not to mention keep up with him intellectually. Throw in the su-preme confidence of a dragon and the beauty that came with it, and it would have been difficult for him *not* to want her.

No more talking.

It didn't surprise him in the slightest that another opening had appeared in the dense forest on the other side of the clearing—one he was certain hadn't been there when he'd arrived. At Thalassa's gesture, he passed through it ahead of her—

—and found himself somewhere else entirely.

He stopped, sweeping his gaze around the scene. "Well," he said softly, "no one can ever say you don't go out of your way to impress a date."

She'd managed to make the place both intimate and spacious at the same time. The room had a high ceiling, rising at least two sto-ries above them and illuminated by faint, dancing lights resembling flickering fireflies. All four walls and the ceiling were glass, reveal-ing a view that was nothing but black sky and stars, as if the room perched on top of a high peak. It reminded Stone a little of Trevor Harrison's Nexus—at least until he lowered his gaze to take in the furnishings.

In pride of place in the center, raised on a platform strewn with soft rugs, was the bed, almost sinfully sensual with a thick, dark-green comforter and pale silk sheets. Surrounding it were a series of candles on tall stands, along with the most intricate magical circle Stone had ever observed. Instead of being drawn, it was carved into the floor, glowing faintly in the soft green-gold light even without magical sight.

"Bloody hell…" Stone murmured. "I hope you don't expect me to add much to that. I don't even *understand* it." It was true. He'd never seen a circle of this type in his life. It had to be of draconic design—the kind of magic they never allowed mere humans to see.

Until now.

"Do not worry." Thalassa's quiet voice came from behind him. "Your contribution will be minimal, but vitally important. I will instruct you when the time comes. Before we continue, though, we must drink the potion."

By now, Stone was all in with this evening. He made no further protest as she led him to a small table outside the perimeter of the circle. A dark, sculpted bottle about the size of a soda bottle stood between two carved, golden chalices. When he looked at it with magical sight, it glowed so brightly he could barely look directly at it.

He remained silent as she picked up the bottle, removed the cork, and poured liquid into the two chalices. It was hard to pick out colors in the room's scant light, but the potion was dark and viscous, bristling with magical energy. The word *potential* came unbidden to his mind as he accepted one of the chalices.

Thalassa raised hers to her lips, and he followed suit. He tipped the chalice back and swallowed the contents without hesitation. It was thick and silky-smooth, like liquid chocolate, and had a sweet, earthy flavor he'd never tasted before. Other than a faint tingle rippling through his body, the potion had no other noticeable effect.

"The mixture will require a few moments to reach full strength." Thalassa's voice was soft and husky now as she took him in with a hungry gaze, and Stone had no doubt she was as eager to move on to the main event as he was. She approached the circle and studied it.

"What have I got to do?" Stone looked over the circle again. Up closer, it was even more impossibly complex than he'd initially thought. Every one of the symbols was made up of smaller symbols, their thin lines drawn with a precision he didn't think any human hand would be capable of duplicating. Even more impressive was how the symbols seemed almost to be three-dimensional, extending to float slightly above the floor. He wondered how long it had taken her to construct the circle—and how long she'd had it waiting. The thought of trying to make any changes to it, to risk smudging it or obliterating some of the beautiful work, filled him with sudden dread.

She seemed to pick up on that, because she moved to stand next to him, brushing her bare arm and shoulder against him. "You have only to add a drop of your blood," she said, producing a tiny silver knife from somewhere. "I have already done so with mine. Together, our life energy will join to empower the circle and prepare it for—what is to occur."

Normally, the thought of anything involving his blood would have given Stone pause, but the electric feeling of her proximity, perhaps combined with the concoction he'd just swallowed, had added an enticing urgency to the proceedings. If he didn't trust her by now, something was wrong.

He took the knife and pricked his finger without hesitation, then crouched and allowed a drop of his blood to drip onto the circle at the indicated place.

Instantly, the drop began to spread, filling the symbols closest to it and picking up speed until it stretched out to encompass the entire large circle. It didn't make sense that one tiny drop of blood could fill so much space, but magic often didn't make sense.

Stone watched, fascinated, as the glowing energy's color changed—everywhere his blood touched a brilliant purple rose, and

432 | R. L. KING

the gold grew brighter as his component joined hers. When the process completed, every tiny, intricate line of the circle now consisted of pulsing lines of green, gold, purple—and, when Stone squinted a little, the tiniest hint of sparkling silver along one edge.

It was without doubt the most beautiful magical construct he had ever seen in his life, and even looking at it filled him with that same sense of *potential* he had felt when the potion suffused his body.

This was a place where something important was going to happen, and the very air seemed to be holding its breath in anticipation.

He glanced at Thalassa. She wasn't looking at the circle.

She was looking at him.

Her green eyes burned and danced with smoldering intensity. Her intent couldn't have been more obvious if she'd been holding up signs.

"Are you ready?" he asked, surprised at how husky his own voice sounded.

Her only reply was to lean in closer, but it was the only one he needed.

They came together as one, almost as a powerful magnet drew them to each other. Stone pulled her into a crushing embrace as she did the same to him, their lips pressing together as if they had both been waiting all their lives for this. The taste of the wine once again joined with the faint taste of blood. This time, when he moved to undo the back of her dress and slip it from her, she made no move to protest. Her hands moved with equal deftness to slide his tuxedo jacket from his shoulders.

His memory of what occurred next wasn't clear, but not in the sense that she had removed any of it from him. It was more as if the sheer intensity had overwhelmed his capacity for analytical thought, so he gave up trying. If asked to recreate the next hour later, he wouldn't have been able to describe how they had shed their clothes, how suddenly they were on the bed in the middle of the circle without conscious memory of crossing the circle, or what, specifically, they had done. What he did remember, though—what would likely remain in a place of honor in his mind for the rest of his days—was the sheer, mind-blowing *wonder* of it all: the feeling of joining not only his body, but his mind, his aura, everything that made him *him,* with another being who understood every implication of what that meant. The pleasure of it, the relief of sharing this act with someone without the need for boundaries or subterfuge or hesitation, raised sensations in him that he didn't think his body was capable of.

All the time, though, he remained mindful that, for all her intensity, her hunger to wring every possible bit of sensation she could manage from this, this was still her first experience as a human. Normally, he had to remain in magical sight to watch his partner's aura for subtle cues, but this time that wasn't necessary. He wasn't sure if it was the potion they'd swallowed, the circle, or merely the fact that she was a dragon, but he had never in his life felt more *joined* with another being. Their bodies were separate, but their *souls* were one.

It wasn't until afterward, when both of them lay back panting, exhausted but unutterably satisfied, staring up at the flickering fireflies high above, that some coherent thoughts began to creep back into Stone's mind. He didn't want them to—the only memory he wanted to hold on to didn't need words—but the images that flashed across his mind's eye refused to be shoved aside.

A vast, verdant landscape with high crags and lush, twisted trees like the ones in the clearing where they had met that evening.

Graceful, winged creatures gliding across a deep purple sky dotted with unfamiliar stars.

A massive golden form with tiny, interlocking scales, its wings folded against its lithe but powerful body, its bright green eyes glittering and whirling as they watched him.

Other forms: one larger, more muscular with bigger, red-purple scales and shrewd, fathomless dark eyes. One smaller, delicate but full of wrath.

A sense of deep anger, along with a profound, life-changing loss borne of a betrayal that occurred before human civilization began.

Stone lay silently, gaze still fixed upward, as the images coalesced in his mind.

Bloody hell...

"Alastair?" Her voice was still husky, soft but not gentle.

"Thalassa..." He turned on his side to face her. She lay on her back; even though she had the silken sheets and deep-green comforter pulled up to conceal her naked body, he could still picture it with utmost clarity in his mind. It was as clear as the visions that swirled in his mind—though much more pleasant. To divert the inevitable conversation to come, he attempted to change the subject. "Did it...work? Do you know?"

Her smile was faraway. "It did. I can already feel her life force kindling within me."

He swallowed hard, his gaze drifting down to her abdomen hidden beneath the covers as the full force of the realization finally hit him.

My daughter.

My half-dragon daughter.

He smiled back at her. "That was...amazing. *You* were...amazing."

She chuckled faintly. "You were a talented teacher."

"Oh, I don't know about that—I think you might have been having me on about that being your first time. I never would have guessed if you hadn't told me." Inwardly, he winced at this inane conversation. He'd certainly had his share of pointless pillow talk with women following sex, but this was...different.

She didn't seem to mind, though. She almost seemed relieved about it. "I did a bit of...research, after our previous encounter."

His eyes widened. "You didn't." He grinned as he pictured her curled up in a comfortable chair next to a fireplace, reading bodice-ripper novels—or more. She didn't seem like the pornography type, but one never knew. The one thing he could be sure about with Thalassa was that it wouldn't do him any good to try to figure her out.

Except he *had* figured her out—at least part of her—and now he felt as if he knew things he had no business knowing.

"I did. Does that surprise you?"

"A little, to be honest. The mental picture is…amusing."

"I am pleased I can amuse you," she said archly.

He rolled onto his back again with a sigh. His mind and his body were sending him mixed signals: he couldn't remember the last time he'd felt more physically relaxed, but no matter how hard he tried, he couldn't push aside what he'd seen.

"You are troubled." Now it was her turn to roll over. She moved closer to him and put her hand on his chest. It was still warmer than a human's—maybe even more so now.

Of course she'd noticed. He looked down at her long, blood-red fingernails. She'd scratched him with them a few times during their passion, but now her hand lay there gently, almost as if she were trying to reassure him—or possibly to claim him. "I guess I am."

"You saw things."

"I did." And now, for the first time, he wondered what *she* had seen.

"I told you it would happen. It is the nature of the ritual."

"I know." He put his hand over hers, but didn't look at her. "What about you? What did you see?"

She shrugged a delicate shoulder. "Do you wish me to tell you? I gave you my word I would not use anything I learned during the ritual against you."

Should he ask? Perhaps it would be best to let it go—to not know. But he'd never been the kind to accept that, and nothing had changed. "I want to know."

Thalassa pondered, moving her fingers gently under his hand. "I learned that, as far as you are aware, it is not possible to kill you. I must admit, that is a fascinating and unexpected bit of information—and one that explains a great deal about you."

Stone tensed briefly, but then forced himself to relax again.

"I learned this occurred on some other plane—I do not know its name, or where it is located, but it highly magical and it is somehow connected with your friend Mr. Harrison."

Still, he didn't reply. What could he say? He couldn't change the fact that she knew these things.

"I learned of your mother, and your grandmother—at least as much as you know of them. And of your twin sister, and your profound guilt at being forced to destroy her. I learned that she lives again, in another body with the aid of a now-dead necromancer, and you are concerned she may return to trouble you or those you care for again."

Stone let his breath out. "I'm not surprised you got all that. You did say this potion of yours would draw out things we'd prefer to keep hidden."

"Does it disturb you that I know these things?"

He realized it didn't. That seemed odd at first glance—as private as he normally was, the thought of anyone learning his deepest secrets should have been unsettling. But he supposed it wasn't. Whether she knew these things or not wouldn't change much, especially since she'd given her word never to reveal them. In a way, it was almost a relief. He'd never been comfortable with sharing the most fundamental part of himself with anyone voluntarily—doing it this way was weirdly cathartic.

He shrugged. "It wouldn't matter if it did. There's no putting that particular genie back in the bottle." He turned his head to face her, and met her gaze straight-on. "You're beautiful, you know—in your human form *and* your dragon one."

She shifted a bit.

"I wish I could see it—your true form. I understand now how dreadful it must be for you all, to be stuck in these puny human bodies when you have the memory of *that*."

"Yes," she said a little wistfully. "You saw something else too, didn't you?"

He nodded, turning his hand over to grip hers. "You and Stefan—you were mates."

Her hand tightened. "Yes."

"That other dragon, the smaller one I saw—she was your daughter, wasn't she? Yours and his?"

Her eyes closed, and for a long time she didn't answer. "Yes."

He wondered if he should go on, but couldn't stop. "I…don't understand all of it. Probably because your lives are so much longer than ours, which meant so much more was flashing by. But I felt—something about a betrayal. An event that still troubles you to this day."

Something in the room's ambient changed. The candles had already gone out following the ritual, but now fireflies high above dimmed as well, casting the space into near-darkness.

Thalassa's voice spoke into it, soft and without emotion. "Dragons do not mate for life. We can be killed—as you well know after the Unspeakable forced Cassius to murder Vic—but barring catastrophic injury or special circumstances, we do not die. As you might guess, the concept of a lifelong mate to an immortal being is…ill-advised. But yes, Stefan and I were mates for a time, back on our home dimension prior to our exile. We produced a daughter together. I will not tell you her name, because I will not speak it."

Stone noticed a change in her voice—a harsh bitterness that hadn't been there before. "Wait—this betrayal. Was it Stefan who betrayed you? Is that why you two don't get on?"

"No." The bitterness faded, replaced by despair. "We were not compatible. Both of us were young, and it took us some time to realize it. When we did, we went our separate ways. It was easy for us to avoid each other. Our home dimension was vast and our kind prefers solitude."

He thought about that, then recalled what else she'd said. "You said you don't speak your daughter's name... *She* was the one who betrayed you, then, wasn't she?"

Another long pause in the darkness. Only her hand tightening on his chest, threatening to dig in but coming just short of it, indicated the depth of her anger. "Yes. You recall, I trust, the story we told you when you were first informed of your status as a scion? About the schism between our kind that resulted in our exile?"

"I do." Stone thought he knew where this was going, but didn't say so. He wanted to hear it in her words.

"Stefan and I, along with several others, sided with those who opposed the status quo. Our daughter...did not. She was young and full of passion, allowing her heart to lead her actions rather than her head. She had met one of the ruling class, who led her astray with promises of power and privilege. He convinced her to feign interest in our cause, and was part of the group who turned against us. It was her testimony at our trial that was pivotal to our conviction."

He stared at her—or at least at her faint outline in the darkness. "Gods...Thalassa...I'm so sorry."

"Do not be. Someday, perhaps, if we ever find a way to return to our home, we will finally meet again and address her actions. Until then..." Her voice turned bitter again. "She argued for exile instead of death—so I suppose I should allow her at least that small bit of gratitude."

Stone couldn't pick out an ounce of gratitude in her voice. As he struggled to find the right thing to say, another thought popped into his head. "Thalassa..."

"Yes?" She pulled her hand away and rolled onto her back again.

"Is...Gabriel—?"

"My son?" She chuckled grimly. "No. Stefan found another mate after we parted. She, too, sided with the ruling class and thus wasn't exiled, but their son did not. Gabriel was very young—barely more than a whelp, the equivalent of a human in his early teens—when we were exiled, but he was highly intelligent and knew his own mind. Stefan was not in favor of his joining us in exile—his youth would have given him amnesty—but he insisted."

Stone pondered that, wondering if part of her animosity toward Kolinsky was based on bitterness that their shared daughter had betrayed them, but Kolinsky's son had not. Still, none of it was truly any of his business, and it wasn't as if he could change any of it now.

"Thank you for telling me. I know that had to be difficult for you. I promise, I won't bring it up again."

"I appreciate that." Her voice took on a bit more animation—perhaps she truly did.

"So..." he ventured. "What happens now?"

"What do you mean?"

The fireflies blazed again, revealing her looking at him. The anger and bitterness were gone, leaving only glittering curiosity and a faint, knowing smile.

"Well..." He spread his hands, encompassing the bed. "We've...completed what we came here for. The proverbial bun's in the oven, so I've discharged my oath. Do I just gather up my clothes and do the walk of shame?"

"The walk of...?" She tilted her head, confused.

He chuckled. "Never mind. It's a human thing. And I couldn't do it anyway, given I haven't got a bloody clue where we are. What I mean is...well...I enjoyed our evening together. Very much."

"I…did as well." She was still looking at him as if trying to work out where he was going with this.

He shifted his gaze away, then back to her. "You know, I never did get to plan one of our evenings. You sort of cut things short before I got a chance."

"That is…true." Her gaze grew contemplative, and a little of the old hunger smoldered in her eyes. Then they narrowed. "Do not presume that any of this implies any sort of ongoing romantic relationship."

"I wouldn't dream of it. It would never work, anyway. The truth is, I like you a little more than I used to, but I still think we'd end up killing each other—or whatever passes for that between a couple of mostly-immortal types—if we tried to be more than…frenemies with benefits."

She cocked her head. "Frenemies?"

"Another human term. The meaning should be obvious."

"Indeed. And…I agree."

"But…" he ventured, with a sly, sidelong glance, "that doesn't mean we can't get together now and then for… pleasurable evenings, when you're available. You know—a nice dinner, perhaps a show, and…whatever else might happen after?"

She licked her lips in a slow, sensual motion, and looked once again as if she might gobble him up in one exquisitely delicious bite. "No. It…does not."

Her sly smile sent a satisfying flutter through his body.

He got home, somehow.

He was fairly sure she was responsible for it, and he never did find out where they'd been. For all he knew, she could have taken him to the other side of the Earth, another dimension, or yet one more of her masterfully crafted illusionary scenes.

It didn't matter, since he didn't care.

The only important thing was that when he stepped out the other side of the doorway she had created for him, he found himself standing in front of his Encantada house. From the look of the dark sky and the moon high above, it was after midnight.

Raider greeted him with enthusiasm when he entered, rubbing against his legs and purring much louder than his smaller, non-Changeling form could have managed. Stone bent to stroke his head, still smiling. "Hello, Raider. I've had quite an amazing evening. If you come to bed with me, I might even tell you about it. I never promised Thalassa I wouldn't kiss and tell my cat, after all. But first, I suppose I should be a good boy and check my messages, shouldn't I?"

He'd left his phone at home, partly because he didn't think it would work wherever they might go, but also so he wouldn't be tempted to check his texts. With the demon situation handled, nothing important enough to be worth offending a dragon over should be happening tonight. Whatever it was, it could wait.

He did have a couple of texts—one from Verity and one from the University—but neither was urgent. He was about to toss the phone back on the nightstand and head off to take a shower when he noticed he also had a voicemail from an unknown number.

By this time, he'd learned not to assume unknown numbers were telemarketers, even though they usually were. He sat on the edge of the bed, turned up the speaker, and tapped the button as Raider settled in next to him.

"Dr. Stone."

Stone tensed—not just because the voice was Trevor Harrison's, but also because the man had actually left him a voicemail. He *never* did that.

"Please return my call at your earliest convenience." There was an ever-so-slight emphasis on the word *earliest* in Harrison's normally inflectionless tone. Then the connection broke.

Stone sighed. Leave it to Harrison to call and leave the first voicemail he'd ever left, but not give him any details on what it was *about*. The man could be frustrating sometimes.

Still, as much as Stone would have liked to get into a hot shower and a warm bed, it wouldn't be wise to wait until tomorrow. It wasn't as if Harrison wouldn't be awake. Stone wasn't sure he ever *slept*.

He tapped the button to return the call, trying not to speculate about what the problem was. He hoped it wasn't another demon. He'd had quite enough demons for the foreseeable future.

Harrison answered on the first ring. "Dr. Stone."

"Good evening, Mr. Harrison. Here's me returning your call. I do hope it's something important, because frankly I've just come back from a most extraordinary evening and I'm looking forward to a hot shower and a nice, warm bed."

"I believe Aldwyn has located Calanar."

Stone jerked his head up. His whole body went stiff. "What?"

Harrison didn't answer.

Stone took a few deep breaths and swallowed, his evening's pleasant buzz departing like a fading wind. "How? How do you know? How did you find out?"

"I will explain what I know. There is no need to meet immediately. Are you available tomorrow?"

"Er—yes. I'll make myself available."

"Tomorrow, then. Contact Mr. Nakamura when you arrive. Good evening, Dr. Stone."

It took Stone a moment to realize Harrison had hung up on him. He chuckled wryly. Some things never changed.

But bloody hell, what *next*?

He reached out to stroke Raider, and noticed his hand was shaking.

If Harrison was correct—and when was he ever *not* correct?—and Aldwyn *had* managed to find Calanar, that would change a lot of things in a lot of ways he hadn't even begun to comprehend yet.

He let himself slump backward onto the bed, the phone slipping from his hand. Immediately, Raider climbed on top of his chest and perched there, peering down at him.

He'd begun to suspect something long ago, but these days he was fairly certain of it.

The Universe had definitely decreed that dull moments were for *other* people.

Alastair Stone Will Return in
POISONED VINES
Alastair Stone Chronicles
Book Thirty-Four

Look for it in August 2023

WE LOVE REVIEWS!

If you enjoyed this book, please consider leaving a review at Amazon, Goodreads, or your favorite book retailer. Reviews mean a lot to independent authors, and help us stay visible so we can keep bringing you more stories. Thanks!

If you'd like to get more information about upcoming Stone Chronicles books, contests, and other goodies, you can join the Alastair Stone mailing list at **alastairstonechronicles.com**. You'll get two free e-novellas, *Turn to Stone* and *Shadows and Stone!*

WHO IS THIS R. L. KING, ANYWAY?

R. L. King lives the kind of exotic, jet-set life most authors only dream of. Splitting her time between rescuing orphaned ocelots, tracking down the world's most baffling cheese-related paranormal mysteries, and playing high-stakes pinochle with albino squirrels, it's a wonder she finds any time to write at all.

Or, you know, she lives in San Jose with her inordinately patient spouse, four demanding cats, and a crested gecko. Which, as far as she's concerned, is way better.

Except for the ocelots. That part would have been cool.

You can find her at *rlkingwriting.com*, and on Facebook at www.facebook.com/AlastairStoneChronicles.

Printed in Great Britain
by Amazon

24333414R00253